The Fifth Horseman

Bilingual Press/Editorial Bilingüe

Address
Bilingual Press
Office of the Graduate School
SUNY–Binghamton
Binghamton, New York 13901

The Fifth Horseman

Clásicos Chicanos/
Chicano Classics 1

JOSÉ ANTONIO VILLARREAL

Bilingual Press/Editorial Bilingüe
BINGHAMTON, NEW YORK

Text © 1974 by José Antonio Villarreal
Introduction and Bibliography © 1984 by Bilingual Press/
   Editorial Bilingüe

Second edition. First edition published by Doubleday &
   Company, Inc., Garden City, New York, 1974

ISBN: 0-916950-49-2

Library of Congress Catalog Card Number: 83-72426

PRINTED IN THE UNITED STATES OF AMERICA

Cover design by Christopher J. Bidlack

Back cover photo by Gerald Whitaker

About Clásicos Chicanos/Chicano Classics

IT IS WITH GREAT PLEASURE that the Bilingual Press initiates its Clásicos Chicanos/Chicano Classics series with the publication of José Antonio Villarreal's *The Fifth Horseman*. This novel was originally issued in 1974 by a commercial publisher with no apparent commitment to significant works of Chicano literature apart from their sales potential, much less to providing an opportunity for Chicano cultural development and affirmation. *The Fifth Horseman*, like so many other works of high literature, Chicano or otherwise, that have been marketed as if they were so many cans of produce, was not permitted to find its readership and was off the shelves and remaindered within an absurdly short time of its publication. Neither our author nor La Raza was well-served.

The Clásicos Chicanos/Chicano Classics series is intended to ensure the accessibility over the long term of deserving works of Chicano literature and culture that have become unavailable over the years or that are in imminent danger of becoming inaccessible. Each of the republished volumes in the series will carry with it a scholarly apparatus that includes an extended introduction contextualizing the work within Chicano literature and a bibliography of the existent works by and about the author. The series is designed to be a vehicle that will help in the recuperation of Raza literary history, maintain the instruments of our culture in our own hands, and permit the continued experience and enjoyment of our literature by present and future generations of readers and scholars.

We are pleased to exemplify through publication of *The Fifth Horseman* a literary criterion for inclusion in the Clásicos Chicanos/Chicano Classics series that is open, inclusive, and broadly defined. It is one that encourages all deserving works by Chicano authors, including those that reach out and embrace established genres and literary cycles. This is the case specifically with Villarreal's work, which contains elements of both the novel of the Mexican Revolution and the American historical novel.

G. D. K.

Contents

Introduction

Luis Leal

The Fifth Horseman and Its Literary Antecedents

THE FIFTH HORSEMAN, the second novel by José Antonio Villarreal, the author of *Pocho* (1959), was first published by Doubleday & Company in 1974. The dustcover blurb states that the novel is set during the Mexican Revolution. In a much more explicit statement, Juan Bruce-Novoa in *Chicano Authors* declares that the novel "can only be categorized within the subgenre of novel recognized as the most typically Mexican: the novel of the Revolution" (p. 38).

To a critic acquainted with the subgenre, *The Fifth Horseman* is much more than that, since it can also be classified as a historical novel. The significance of Villarreal's work lies precisely there. It is a link between the literature of Mexico and the literature of the United States, for it has the characteristics of both narrative traditions—the novel of the Mexican Revolution and the American historical novel. It could also be considered as an American Western novel and even as a product of borderland literature, a distinctive literature that has representatives on both sides of the border, the American Southwest and northern Mexico. It could be said that Villarreal's represents both sides.

Since *The Fifth Horseman* falls between the novel of the Mexican Revolution and the American historical novel, it is necessary to examine these two subgenres. As of today, comparatists have given little attention to the relationship between the literature of Mexico and that of the Southwest, notwithstanding the proximity of the territories, the parallel historical development, and the cultural similarities. It is true, however, that attention has recently been focused on the literature of the borderlands, a geographical area whose culture presents distinctive characteristics.

Critics who have written about the novel of the Mexican Revolution are not in agreement as to its categorization. Some consider it period literature, while others consider it a subgenre. The first group has in mind the fiction about the Revolution written in Mexico by Mexicans and published between 1910, the year the conflict began under the leadership of Francisco I. Madero, and 1940, when Lázaro Cárdenas ended his term as President. The peak was reached during the 1930s; after 1940 fiction writing in Mexico moved away from the realistic representation of social problems toward a treatment of cosmopolitan subjects and the use of new literary techniques.

The other definition considers the novel of the Revolution as a subgenre. According to this view, novels of the Revolution are those that treat events that occurred between 1910 and 1920 (the year Obregón assumed power and the nation attained certain political stability), regardless of the year the novel was published. Since *The Fifth Horseman* appeared in 1974, it would not be considered a novel of the Revolution under the definition of period literature, but it would be if the subgenre definition is accepted as the most appropriate. However, *The Fifth Horseman* is written in English and was published in the United States by a novelist of Mexican descent born in Los Angeles, California, which may disqualify it under both definitions, although the author is now a Mexican citizen.

Regarding the relationship of Chicano literature to Mexican literature, Villarreal has said, "Mexican literature is not that different from American literature, excepting for the idiom, because in the development of literature in the western world, Spain contributed to the development of the English novel" (*Chicano Authors,* p. 43). On the other hand, he has also said that he is an American writer and that Chicano literature is "a part of American literature, as the southern writers, as the western writers, and as any regional writers are a part of American literature" (p. 42).

In order to resolve the problem of classification, it would be much more satisfactory to call *The Fifth Horseman* not a novel of the Mexican Revolution but an American historical novel whose subject matter is Mexico, a subgenre that has a long and prestigious history. Indeed, as early as 1976 Francisco Lomelí and Donaldo Urioste called *The Fifth Horseman,* "an historical novel that marks another first for Chicano literature: expands its literary space and thematics beyond the realm of Aztlán" (*Chicano Perspectives,* p. 49).

There is no question, however, as to the similarities between *The Fifth Horseman* and the novels of the Revolution, not only in the treatment of subject matter but also in the presence of certain themes, such as machismo, the role of women, racial clashes, hatred of Spaniards, the rise of the peon in the revolutionary armies, and the attitude toward the so-called betrayal of the principles of the true Revolution.

There are similarities between *The Fifth Horseman* and certain novels of the Revolution, such as, for example, the use of language. Villarreal uses English with Spanish syntax, in addition to phrases, idioms, and vocabulary typical of the people who formed the armies of Villa and other revolutionaries. Then, there are several scenes and references that bring to mind novels by Azuela, Guzmán, Yáñez, Rulfo, and others. Perhaps the most important reference, which occurs twice, is when General Rodolfo Fierro executes a group of federal soldiers. This is a well-known episode found in Guzmán's *El águila y la serpiente* under the title "La fiesta de las balas," a piece often anthologized. Details related to the life and deeds of General Villa bring to mind Guzmán's *Memorias de Pancho Villa,* a four-volume work first published in 1951. The train scene in which Heraclio is running away from the *obregonistas* is reminiscent of the many train scenes found in the novels of Azuela. The taking of Zacatecas is similar to that described by Azuela in *Los de abajo*. Similarities between Villarreal's novel and Rulfo's *Pedro Páramo* are found in the characterization of David Contreras, the illegitimate son of the *patrón* don Aurelio; like Abundio in Rulfo's novel, David hates his father. Another similarity is that don Aurelio's and Pedro Páramo's haciendas are not touched by the revolutionaries, since they are protected by one of their men— Heraclio in *The Fifth Horseman* and El Tilcuate in *Pedro Páramo*. The scene where Carmen returns from the capital to the hacienda is similar to one found in the opening chapters of *Al filo de agua*. Because of these similiarities it is first necessary to examine the nature of the novel of the Revolution.

The two definitions mentioned above, and others that offer some variants, are based on the content of the novels. To be included a novel must treat the Revolution of 1910-1920. More recent definitions amplify the nature of the novel of the Revolution and include such works as José Revueltas' *El luto humano* (1943), Agustín Yáñez' *Al filo de agua* (1947), and more recent novels such as Juan Rulfo's *Pedro Páramo* (1955) and Carlos Fuentes' *La muerte de Artemio Cruz* (1963).

In order for the novel of the Revolution to be considered a subgenre and not merely a period piece, it is necessary to define it not according to the date when it was published or written, but to take into consideration its internal characteristics, such as the absence of a central dominating figure, the presence of the common people as the true hero, the episodic nature of the plot, the use of a popular style in the dialogues and a journalistic style in the exposition, the depiction of violent war scenes, and the predominance of a descriptive technique. No less important is the criticism made of social institutions prior to 1910, and even of the Revolution itself.

Not all novels of the Revolution, of course, present all the characteristics enumerated. Nevertheless, most of them have the basic ones, which are: (1) the world they create is the Mexico of the revolutionary years; (2) the subject matter is the Revolution of 1910-1920; and (3) the techniques by means of which the events are related is that of the eyewitness reporter writing a story for a newspaper. Typical novels of the Revolution are *Los de abajo* (1915-1916) by Mariano Azuela, *El águila y la serpiente* (1928) by Martín Luis Guzmán, *Campamento* (1931) by Gregorio López y

Fuentes, and *Se llevaron el cañón para Bachimba* (1941) by Rafael Muñoz. The first two appeared as serials in newspapers, *Los de abajo* in *El Paso del Norte,* a Spanish language newspaper published in El Paso, Texas, by the Mexican revolutionary Fernando Gamiochipi, and *El águila y la serpiente* in Mexico City in 1927.

Even though *El luto humano* (1943) has a Mexican rural background and a social theme, Revueltas uses a technique that is quite different from that of the novel of the Revolution. With it, a new trend of fiction writing was introduced in Mexico, a trend attributed to the influence of William Faulkner, although Revueltas denied that he had read the North American novelist before writing *El luto humano.* Whether he did or not, the structure of his novel, which is much more complex than that of the novels of the Revolution, reflects similarities with some of Faulkner's works.

When we study the criticism written about the novels of the Mexican Revolution we discover a strange contradiction. Critics generally consider these novels to be of poor literary quality, more in the nature of historical documents than works of art. Yet, they dedicate long and elaborate studies to them. The novel of the Mexican Revolution is the aspect of Mexican literature that has received the most attention, both within and outside of Mexico.

Ernest Moore, as early as 1941, published the first *Bibliografía de novelas de la Revolución Mexicana,* a painstaking work in which more than 280 titles are documented. In the introduction he observes that more novels have been written about that historical event than any other, a fact that "demonstrates the importance of this literary movement" (p. 8). Yet, in the same introduction he says that, "Having come *after* the struggle, it was not a theoretical novel, but realistic; more historical and brutal than fantastic and delicate ... it was like life itself during those days, that is, chaotic, without plot, without composition, without balance, without beauty" (p. 10; my translation, as are those that follow).

Moore was an American and it could be said that perhaps he was not able to appreciate the nature of this kind of novel. Let us see then what a Mexican, one who more than anyone else has provided a penetrating analysis of the psychology of the Mexican people, says

about the same novel. In July of 1943, Octavio Paz published a
review of the novel *El luto humano* by José Revueltas in the
periodical *Sur* of Buenos Aires. There he rejects in absolute terms
the novel of the Mexican Revolution and realist fiction in general.
He says,

> The novelists of the Revolution, and among them the great
> nearsighted talent of Azuela, blinded by the furor of the gunpowder
> or by the diamonds of the generals, have reduced the subject matter
> to this: many deaths, many crimes, many lies.... In that manner
> they have mutilated novelistic reality, the only one that counts for
> the true novelists.... All the 'Novels of the Revolution'are nothing
> but reports and chronicles... without excluding those of Mariano
> Azuela (Larbaud used to say that Azuela reminded him of Tacitus:
> strange praise for a novelist!). (p. 92)

As late as 1962 Paz maintained the same attitude toward the
novel of the Revolution. In an interview published that year in
Hispanoamérica en su nueva literatura, the interviewer, Claude
Couffon, asked him this question: "In your judgment, what is the
importance of the novelists of the Revolution? I am thinking,
concretely, about Martín Luis Guzmán, Mariano Azuela, and,
younger, Rafael Felipe Muñoz." Paz answered:

> I do not deny the historical importance, so to speak, of those
> novelists; but, in substance, they do not interest me. Martín Luis
> Guzmán, Azuela, and Muñoz are naturalist novelists who de-
> scribed, as witnesses, with great mastery, Mexican society face to
> face with the Revolution. As documents, their works have capital
> importance. But for the writers of my generation, for me, they do
> not open any new perspectives. (p. 75)

Paz's opinion is not an isolated one. A few years before, in 1938,
Rafael Solana had characterized the novelists of the Revolution,
and also the Contemporáneos who wrote novels, with these
sarcastic words, which are pertinent in light of Villarreal's novel:

> But neither Torres Bodet, who fights alone, nor the two thousand
> novelists of the Revolution..."the Botas stable," breathe any
> longer a pure and healthful air. The one... is not preoccupied with
> filling his pages with truly emotional, human values.... The others
> are unable to deviate an inch from that "Rancho Grande" of the

novels for which, unfortunately, [the model] came to be *Los de abajo.* (*El Popular,* June 12, 1938, p. 5)

This dislike for the novels of the Revolution, or for certain of their aspects, among critics and intellectuals (but not among the people, who keep reading them) has lasted until our own day. In 1951, in his *Trayectoria de la novela mexicana,* Manuel Pedro González, an admirer of Azuela and the other novelists of the Revolution, nonetheless had this to say:

> All the so-called novels of the Revolution are fragmentary, episodic, and frequently appear to be reports or chronicles. Each one of them focuses on only one aspect or sector, on only one personality or one variant of the terrible hurricane. Not even the three greatest works inspired by the Revolution—*Los de abajo, El águila y la serpiente,* and *Ulises criollo*—are all inclusive. In them we only perceive certain aspects or profiles of the Revolution, generally negative and pessimistic. (p. 92)

In her book *Novelistas y cuentistas de la Revolución* (1960), Julia Hernández enumerates the *defectos* and *cualidades* of these novels. Among the defects she lists the following: one does not know where the novel ends and history begins, the judgments are those of the newspapermen, the dramatic element is excessive, they are limited by *costumbrismo,* they frequently lack esthetic depth. Six years later (1966), John Brushwood in his book *Mexico and its Novel* said that the novels of the Revolution are

> lineal accounts, episodic, with sketchily drawn characters. In general, everything—structure, style, characterization, even ideology—is subordinated to each author's need to tell what it was like. *Vámonos con Pancho Villa,* the first novel of Rafael Muñoz, is a fine example of a highly readable account which, on analysis, appears to be artistically defective in every conceivable way. It would be a waste of time to specify the book's faults, which it has in common with so many others. The essential question is why it is a good book if it has so many counts against it. (pp. 206-207)

The above examples are sufficient to show the trend in literary criticism against the novel of the Revolution. However, that trend began to change in the late sixties. A re-evaluation of the novel of the Revolution was initiated by Carlos Fuentes, who, in his book *La nueva novela hispanoamericana* (1969), admits, although begrudgingly, that

> the marching people of Azuela, Guzmán and Muñoz, perhaps in spite of their authors, break with the romantic popular tradition in fiction, with the fatality of nature, which is impenetrable, and the archetypal banana Republic dictator, to expose them as static and transitory realities. *Los de abajo, La sombra del caudillo,* and *Si me han de matar mañana,* in spite of their possible technical defects, introduce an original note in the Hispanic American novel: they introduce ambiguity. Because of their revolutionary dynamics the heroes can be villains, and the villains can be heroes. (p. 15)

However, Fuentes had to add:

> Nevertheless, there is a compelling lack of perspective in the Mexican novel of the Revolution. The themes at the tip of their fingers about which the authors were itching to write forced them to use a testimonial technique which, to a large extent, did not allow them time to penetrate deeply into their own findings. It was necessary to wait until 1947, when Agustín Yáñez produced the first modern vision of Mexico's immediate past in *Al filo del agua,* and until Juan Rulfo, in *Pedro Páramo* in 1955, was able to proceed with the mythification of the situations, the characters, and the speech of the Mexican countryside, closing forever, with a golden key, the documental technique of the [novel of the] Revolution. Rulfo converted Azuela's and Guzmán's seeds into a dry and bare tree from which hang somber fruits. (pp. 15-16)

One year before Fuentes wrote the above words, Paz had expressed the same idea about the ambiguity of the novel of the Revolution. The question, Where do we see the subversive nature of the Mexican novel? was answered by Paz in the following manner:

> The Mexican novel was born with a subversive writer, Mariano Azuela. Although he was not a great writer, at the moment that the Revolution triumphed he denounced it and exposed its secret, shadowy parts. Another contemporary of Azuela, Martín Luis Guzmán [created], in his novels, central characters that are old revolutionaries who are not heroes. Guzmán does not present to us a world of good and bad characters, in black and white. He is not Manichaean. He reveals the essential ambiguity of man and society. (*Insula,* July-August 1968, p. 12)

As recently as 1973, Paz again made reference to the novel of the Revolution. He said to Julián Ríos: "The corruption of the Revolution is one of the thematic constants of Mexican literature. It was born with the novels of Mariano Azuela and Martín Luis Guzmán. The curious thing is that now Martín Luis Guzmán is one of the great defenders of the present pseudo-revolutionary regime" (*Solo a dos voces,* 1973, p. 7).

Paz and Fuentes, of course, do not write with fervor about the novel of the Revolution. Neither do other contemporary critics. However, we do have several very well documented studies, most of them done outside of Mexico. In 1967, Adalbert Dessau published in East Germany his thorough study *Der mexicanische Revolutionroman,* translated into Spanish and published in Mexico City by the Fondo de Cultura Económica in 1972 under the title *La novela de la Revolución Mexicana.* In England in 1971, John Rutherford published his study, *Mexican Society during the Revolution,* and in 1972 his *Annotated Bibliography of the Novels of the Mexican Revolution of 1910-1917.* These and other studies provide us with the materials necessary to carry out a re-evaluation of these novels. Some individual works, such as *Ulises criollo* by Vasconcelos, have already been vindicated as important, with a value that exceeds that of the simple historical document, report, or chronicle. Today, even the *talentos miopes,* to use the metaphor that Paz applied to Azuela, can see that *Los de abajo* offers the reader not only an eyewitness account of the fighting, but also a rich vernacular style and a world inhabited by real human beings.

The influence of the novel of the Revolution upon the Chicano novelist, if we are to believe what they say, is not as widespread as is usually believed. Tomás Rivera acknowledged reading the novels of Gregorio López y Fuentes and Ron Arias those of Martín Luis Guzmán. Much more important has been the influence of Agustín Yáñez, Juan Rulfo, and Carlos Fuentes. Until Villarreal published *The Fifth Horseman,* no Chicano novel had as its central subject the Mexican Revolution. It is true, as Guillermo Rojas has shown, that some Chicano novels, all of them written in Spanish *(. . . y no se lo tragó la tierra, Estampas del Valle, Peregrinos de Aztlán),* resemble in technique, style, and structure the novels of the Revolution. But they cannot be considered as belonging to the subgenre, since their subject matter is not the Revolution, their heroes are not former revolutionaries (as in the case of *Pocho*) and they are set in the Southwest and not in Mexico.

On the other hand, *The Fifth Horseman* deals with the Mexican Revolution, the characters are revolutionaries, it is set in northern Mexico, and the conflict is the struggle for power between Villa and Huerta. As in most novels of the Revolution, the action is seen from the perspective of the *villistas,* since the authors, with the exception of Romero, who was an *obregonista,* were devoted followers of Villa, as is Villarreal. *Los de abajo, El águila y la serpiente,* and *The Fifth Horseman* end with the defeat of Villa by Obregón at Celaya. Villa's army withdrew to the north and a large number of *villistas* came to the United States, where their sons became Mexican Americans and their grandsons Chicanos. As Bruce-Novoa has said,

> The novel creates a mythological, heroic ancestor of the modern Chicano. It is highly significant that, at the end of the novel, its protagonist, an authentic hero of the Revolution, must choose between betraying the revolutionary ideals or becoming an outlaw in the eyes of the victors; he must choose, that is, to remain in the army and reap the benefits plundered from the people, or to remain on the side of the Mexican people and break with the military. He is true to the ideals of the people's revolution, and so must flee Mexico, becoming one of the thousands of refugees who sought temporary refuge in the United States, and who eventually stayed on to become the grandparents of the Chicanos of today. (*Chicano Authors,* pp. 37-38)

It must be stated, however, that the victors, the *constitucionalistas,* led first by Carranza and then by Obregón and Calles, also had a large popular following.

The historical frame of reference of *Pocho* begins when the armed conflict phase of the Revolution ends, while *The Fifth Horseman* extends the time frame to include the last five years of the Díaz dictatorship. After a prologue about the battle for Zacatecas on June 24, 1914, which serves as a narrative-historical frame of reference and also to introduce the young hero Heraclio Inés and his lover Xóchitl, the author goes back in time to the year 1905 to describe life at the Hacienda de la Flor in Zacatecas and the education of the hero, born there in 1893. Of the novelists of the Revolution, the only one who recreated hacienda life was Mariano Azuela, whose firsthand knowledge enabled him to write such realistic novels as *Mala yerba* and *Esa sangre,* both of which, like the first part of *The Fifth Horseman,* are set in a hacienda in central Mexico.

Both authors rely extensively on *costumbrismo.* Villarreal describes the rodeo, the ride of death, the taming of a wild horse, the training of a *jinete,* and relations between the *peones* and the *patrón.* But also, like Azuela, he criticizes the hacienda system; *la tienda de raya,* by means of which peons were kept in virtual slavery; the *rurales,* the famous *porfirista* mounted police who imposed law and order by indiscriminate hangings; the paternalistic system imposed upon the peons by *caciques;* the sharp class distinctions based on race (Spanish vs. Mexican); and the prejudice against the Indians. Of interest in the first part of the novel is the detailed description of the honor system followed by the *jinetes,* represented by the five brothers of the Inés family—or rather, the four brothers, since the youngest, Heraclio (the fifth horseman) represents the revolt against the system. "'The others do not fight, do not talk back,' said Heraclio. 'I am the only one. It seems to be my way of life.'"

The action unfolds chronologically to the year 1915, when Villa is defeated and Heraclio decides to come to Los Angeles rather than join the *constitucionalistas* and betray the people who fought under Villa and Felipe Angeles, the representatives of what he thinks is the real Revolution. The development of the plot, however, is not episodic, but well integrated by means of a central character and the use of transitional motives to give unity to the narrative sequence. In this sense it is more like Guzmán's *La sombra del caudillo,* but the ending of the novel and the fate of the hero are similar to Guzmán's *El águila y la serpiente.* Both works end with the protagonists, who are followers of Villa, on their way to the United States. In this respect, these novels are similar to the Western, which usually ends with the hero disappearing into the distance. Heraclio leaves Torreón after killing General Celestino Gámez, who has abandoned Villa and joined Carranza and his *constitucionalistas*. He disappears into the mountains and heads for Los Angeles. *The Fifth Horseman* ends where *Pocho* begins. Juan Rubio, Richard's father, says, "It is impossible for me to be a soldier for Obregón." Besides, he is, like Heraclio, a *jinete* and would rather run cattle than work as a farmhand. Juan Rubio thus became "a part of the great exodus that came of the Mexican Revolution. By the hundreds they crossed the Rio Grande, and then by the thousands." (*Pocho,* 1970, p. 15).

Two elements found in *The Fifth Horseman* separate it from the novel of the Revolution: the romantic subplots—the love affairs of Heraclio, first with Carmen, the *patrón's* daughter, and then with the Maya girl Xóchitl—and, more important, the fact that historical events are observed from a distance in time, a technique associated with the historical novel but not with novels of the Revolution, whose authors were eyewitnesses writing about what they had observed. The narrators are often actors in their own stories. Because of the time element we are inclined to classify *The Fifth Horseman* as historical rather than a novel of the Revolution. Here it is pertinent to mention a novel of the Revolution written and published in the United States by Alberto Rembao, whose *Lupita; A Story of Mexico in Revolution* (1935) deals with three Mexicans in the Revolution. Can this be considered the first Chicano novel about the Mexican Revolution? Perhaps, if we keep in mind that Rembao, although born in Mexico, was educated in the United States, where he remained the rest of his life. In New York for many years he published the widely read review *La Nueva Democracia.*

In American literature, the novel with a Mexican background has a long tradition. It was first introduced in 1826 by Timothy Flint, the author of *Francis Berrian; or, The Mexican Patriot,* whose central theme is the romance between Berrian and Martha, the daughter of don Pedro Alvaro, the Governor of Durango. The protagonist participates in the war for independence from Spain, under Morelos.

In spite of the great difference in style, technique, characterization, attitude toward reality, and the time element, there are certain similarities between *Francis Berrian* and *The Fifth Horseman*. Don Pedro Alvaro is not very different from don Aurelio. Both Berrian and Heraclio are outsiders who fall in love with the daughters of their socially superior masters. Both families object and strongly oppose the relationships, although for different motives: don Alvaro because of religious reasons and don Aurelio because of class distinctions. Both Berrian and Heraclio join revolutionary forces, Berrian those of Morelos and Heraclio those of Villa. When the insurgents capture the Alvaro family, Berrian saves their lives; when the revolutionaries try to kill the new *patrón* of Hacienda la Flor, Heraclio defends him and his Spanish friends. In the end, both don Pedro and Carmen's Spanish husband, who has inherited don Aurelio's hacienda, are killed by the revolutionaries. In both novels, the fictitious protagonists serve under historical characters.

Flint's novel is not, of course, historical. The first writer of historical novels about Mexico was Robert Montgomery Bird, the author of *Calavar; or, The Knight of the Conquest* (1834) and *The Infidel; or, The Fall of Mexico* (1835), both about the conquest of Mexico by Cortés. The main source of information for the reconstruction of the events was Bernal Díaz de Castillo's *True History*, although other historians (Solís, Clavijero, Robertson) are also mentioned. Bernal Díaz himself is a character in *The Infidel*, where he appears as a historian, an obvious anachronism.

After the publication of William H. Prescott's *History of the Conquest of Mexico* in 1843, a number of authors used the information provided to write historical novels. Among the most important were Joseph Holt Ingraham, who in 1845 published *Montezuma the Serf; or, The Revolt of the Mexititi: A Tale of the Last Days of the Aztec Dynasty*, and Edward Maturin, author of *Montezuma, the Last of the Aztecs*, also published in 1845. These books indicate the interest in Mexico just before the war of 1848, an interest that did not subside, for the Mexican American War gave novelists new themes to explore. Interest in the Spanish Conquest also did not disappear; as late as 1873 Lew Wallace published his successful *The Fair God; or The Last of the 'Tzins,* dealing with Cuauhtémocs's rise to power and *la noche triste.* As in *The Fifth Horseman*, all of these historical novels contain interwoven amorous subplots.

Beginning in 1850, the Irishman Mayne Reid, who was in Mexico during the Mexican American War, wrote several very successful novels with a Mexican background addressed to a teenage audience. In Mexico, however, his novels were severely criticized, especially by the leading critic of the period, Ignacio Manuel Altamirano, who said of Reid: "Así pues, descartaremos también de las novelas de costumbres algunas del americano Mayne Reid, que tiene pretensiones de imitar a Cooper, y que ha pintado a los mexicanos de un modo que ni ellos mismos se conocen" (*La literatura nacional*, I, p. 35).

In the 20th century the Revolution has attracted the attention of a large number of novelists, stimulated first by the war reports of correspondents such as John Reed and then by accounts of the conflict by Anita Brenner, with her very popular book of photographs of the Revolution, *The Wind that Swept Mexico.* As early as 1935 an account of the novel of the Revolution was published in the United States. Berta Gamboa de Camino's "The Novel of the Mexican Revolution," an essay included in the book *Renascent Mexico,* edited by Hubert Herring and Herbert Weinstock, is perhaps the first study of the subgenre.

The first novels written by Americans with the Revolution as a background were those of Edwin Milton Royle and George Agnew Chamberlain. In 1916, the year that *Los de abajo* came out in book form in El Paso, Texas, Royle, in New York, published *Not All the King's Horses,* about two American mining engineers who are killed during the Revolution. Some years later, in *Temescal* (1925), Henry H. Knibbs wrote about adventures in Mexico during the early years of the Revolution, and Malcolm Wheeler-Nicholson, in *The Corral of Death* (1929), described adventures along the border during the same period.

In *The 42nd Parallel* (1930), a novel by John Dos Passos, who had visited Mexico in 1926, there is a chapter ("The Camera Eyes

[25], Newsreel XVII") dedicated to revolutionary Mexico. Mac, a Wobbly, participates in the Revolution from the assassination of Madero to the year when Obregón comes to power. Among other novels with the Revolution as background or theme we find George B. Rodney, *Riders of the Chaparral* (1935), about a Mexican studying in the United States who is called back to participate in the Revolution; Carleton Beals, *The Stones Awake: A Novel of Mexico* (1936), which emphasizes the participation of women in the Revolution; Dane Coolidge, *Wolf's Candle* (1936), dealing with the adventures of an American; Heath Bowman and Stirling Dickinson, *Death Is Incidental* (1937), which describes the effects of the Revolution on the lives of the people in San Miguel de Allende; Gregory Mason and Richard Carroll, *Mexican Gallop* (1937), in which a New Yorker goes to Mexico and briefly participates in the conflict.

In the United States, as in Mexico, novels with scenes about the Revolution diminished in number after 1940 but did not disappear. Such novels include Helen Virginia Botsford, *Ashes of Gold* (1942); John Houghton Allen, *Southwest* (1953), in which there is a tale about Rodolfo Fierro; Robert Ramsey, *Fiesta* (1955); Glendon F. Swarthout, *They Came to Cordura* (1958), about Pershing's punitive expedition against Villa; and Paul Bartlett, *When the Owl Cries* (1960), among many others, Bartlett's novel is similar in certain aspects to *The Fifth Horseman*, since it describes the effects of the Revolution upon a family of the hacienda class.

In other novels about the period, reference is made to the Revolution without using it as a background or theme. Typical of this type of novel is Josephine Niggli's *Step Down, Elder Brother* (1947). Set in Monterrey, it deals with the life of the members of a proud upper class family and the prevailing class struggles typical of Mexican society during the years of transition from a dictatorial government to a more democratic one. This narrative trend has been continued by Christopher Davis, whose *Suicide Note* (1977) tells of a journalist who goes to Mexico to write a story about the widows of Francisco Villa.

The Mexican Revolution will continue to attract the attention of future novelists, both here and in Mexico. *The Fifth Horseman* derives its meaning by placing the Revolution on central stage and not by making it a simple *telón de fondo*. The lives of the characters cannot be fully explained without taking into consideration the events that took place in Mexico between 1910 and 1915. At the same time, *The Fifth Horseman* is an excellent contribution to the American historical novel, like those of Beals or Davis. As a Chicano novel, its merit lies in having gone beyond the perimeter of the Southwest with a theme that does not deal directly with the lives of Chicanos, but which explains their origins and gives them a historical sense of belonging, as well as pride in the deeds of their ancestors.

UNIVERSITY OF CALIFORNIA
SANTA BARBARA

The Fifth Horseman

Este libro es para mi querida esposa,
Bárbara Gentles de Villarreal.

THIS IS A BOOK OF FICTION. It is not my intention to set down a scholarly history of the Mexican Revolution of 1910. I have deliberately presented events in a way they might best enhance the pattern of my tale, and am therefore at the mercy of the learned reader who will meticulously dissect my narrative for flaws in chronology, etc. And, yet, the essence of the novel is true.

There was no Heraclio Inés, as there were tens of thousands of Heraclio Ineses who died for a right they believed was theirs.

There *was* a Madero; there *was* a Porfirio Díaz and a Victoriano Huerta, and there *was* a Villa. Men such as these are real; other characters are imaginary.

And the peon is real. This is of men. This is of the peon, who exists yet today. This is of the slave anywhere, any time.

Cañitas de Felipe Pescador
Summer 1972

. . . How could we dare
spill the blood that unites
us? Where is the joy in
the killing of kinsmen?

Bhagavad–Gita

The Prologue

Zacatecas, June 24, 1914

FROM THE SUMMIT, the searchlight spread upon the Constitutionalists as they sought shelter among the rocks on the extended promontory. They called it a mesa, but it was not really that, for, although it was above the besieged city, it was below the plain which is the Central Plateau. To the left towered the Bufa, the highest point on the hunchbacked range which overlooked the city. And the Bufa must be taken, or the capital could not be held.

The promontory was two hundred yards wide and a thousand yards long. It was grassy, rocky, and exposed. Below was the city, still in Federal hands, and above, at the base of the mountain, Federal troops were entrenched with machine guns at ready, capable of stopping any assault. Forward by a hundred yards were Federal fusiliers, dug in shallow trenches behind rocky barricades. In the darkness, the Constitutionalists surged to take the land from the enemy, but the searchlight was trained upon them and the machine guns cut them down. They ran back, leaving their dead and wounded, and there were cries from the maimed and the dying on the mesa.

During the daylight hours, the Rebels lay back, out of range, while the Federal troops reshaped their bulwarks, and the moans were fainter now from those expiring in the sun.

That night there was a quietness, broken only by an occasional cry, and suddenly the Rebels charged again, were repulsed,

1

charged once more, fell back, yet attacked again and died in the light of the merciless beam from above them. The searchlight was to them now a supernatural eye before the dawn, and the second day was like the first day as the second night was like the first night. And now, on the third night of the attack, the Man arrived.

He had been kept away by his superior, Carranza, because a victory here would make him too big a man in the eyes of the masses, but after six days of siege and two days of futile attack, he disobeyed his orders, and brought with him twenty thousand warriors from the north, among them his elite corps of cavalry, the Golden Ones. While his military trains were still arriving, he left a caboose which was his headquarters, and went to see for himself that which they had told him was happening to his boys, for those surrounding the city were also his armies, although under separate command for this action.

His huge red stallion stepped gingerly among the rocks, and he sat him seemingly impassive, in the full glare of the light as his men retreated from the first assault. He watched them run past him and he did not speak. He made no attempt to stop them, but remained there while the stragglers crawled to safety, then waved once and an adjutant came to him.

"Bring me the General Angeles," he said calmly to the wide-eyed adjutant who was fighting to keep his horse from bolting. He remained there, and after a while wheeled his horse and walked him slowly back and into the safety of the shadows.

"Heraclio!" he called.

"At your orders, my General," said a young major. They were in a shelter behind a solid wall of rock, and here and there fires were being lighted. The major sat his horse, almost casually. He was a figure in bronze, from his low brown boots, the tacos on his calves, to the narrow-brimmed hat. His horse also was golden colored and only his spurs clashed with the uniform. The General looked at him and did not speak. The major remained by his side.

They were joined by an angular tall man, with long yet thin mustaches. "My General," said the newcomer, and saluted smartly. The general waved a hand indifferently in return.

"General Angeles," he said, "at approximately three o'clock in

2

the morning, like in the song, you will destroy for me that God-damn searchlight which is giving me much anxiety. You will do it in this way. The boy here will take himself fifty jinetes and follow the attack by those on foot by three minutes. He will either go over or through the first lines of defense, it is up to him how he does it, and harass those people over there with those automatic weapons that are killing us in quantity long enough for you to set up one of your apparatuses. You will go as far as the first line of defense only. That is near enough, no? And you will have your people ready because it is only a few shots that you will get. Get for me that searchlight and we will eat in a restaurant this coming day."

"What is the terrain like on that promontory?" asked Felipe Angeles. His face was alert, his mind already on the problem, and his military bearing was in all of him, even in his voice.

"There are rocks, and there is grass where there are not rocks, but where there is neither grass nor rocks, there is mud, for it has been raining here for some time and no one felt it was important enough to tell me." He looked up and the sky was darkening with clouds again, and they looked low enough to obscure the Bufa with its floodlight, but he knew better. "And there are bodies all over the area, and some yet with life. You had better send small details out to throw some of those poor unfortunates over the cliff. The quick you will bring here, but the others you must get out of there for they will be in your way later. Bring back only those you are certain are alive. We do not have the time to make sure; and do not send the men too far, else we will have to send others for them."

"Very well, my General," said Angeles. He did not have all the information he wished, but he knew he would not get more. "It will be as you have ordered." He saluted once again, always the officer, and left to give his own orders and to put a cannon in position for the maneuver.

"And you, why do you wait?" asked the General of Heraclio even though he had not spoken directly to him.

"For your orders, my General. What do you wish me to do once I destroy the second line of defense?" said the major.

"Want you to do? Why, climb that cunt of a mountain, that's what . . . and see what is on the other side. Go over the top, then

3

climb back around down into the city. That is what I want you to do."

Heraclio knew he was dismissed, but his question had been but partially answered and he hesitated.

"All right," said the General. "What else do you want to know?"

"It is then to be an all out attack. We are not merely to take the mesa and wait until daylight?"

The General was impatient with him. "Is it that you have been here as long as I have and yet do not know what is going on? It is impossible to keep that mesa unless we take the mountain also, and we cannot take the city until we take the mountain, for they have artillery up there. And we could never climb the mountain in the daylight. Is it to be an all out attack?" he said sarcastically. "Do you think I would send fifty horsemen on foot to take that Goddamn mountain? Besides, there will not be more than a handful of you left by then." Then he spoke quietly, his anger dissipated with the realization of what he had just said. "To take that mountain is the key to the whole thing, boy. They have everything there, and when we go past that, they have more down below, but by then we will have our momentum and it will not matter greatly. We must close with those people on top of the Bufa by six o'clock at the latest. No, boy, we will not stop. When we move, in a short while, we will not stop until we are in the city."

Heraclio saluted and rode away. He picked his fifty men and told them to be ready when he called, then rode away from the troops to a lone fire. Xóchitl waited, looking very small against the background of the flames. She took the reins and led the horse away. They did not speak and Heraclio threw himself full length on a petate near the fire. In forty-five minutes he got up and she gave him a plate of beans and some tortillas.

"You unsaddled the horse?" he asked.

"Yes, he is comfortable," she said.

He looked up at her, a scoopful of beans part way to his mouth. "What is wrong with you?" he asked.

"Nothing." She laughed suddenly. "It is that sometimes I feel you like that horse more than you do me."

"It is only natural that you should sometimes feel that, because I do," he said. He was chewing now, looking very stern, and then he looked up to her face and they both laughed. She moved be-

4

hind him as he sat on his haunches eating, and threw her arms around his neck almost upsetting him. "I do not mind, really, you know," she said, "about the horse. I do not mind about your wife, either, because she is back there somewhere and I am with you wherever you go. And when the other women soldiers ask me, do I not want to have a child by you because they can see that I am yours because I love and not because I like this of being with the army, I tell them, no, because to have a child I would have to give it some of my life and my time and I cannot do that because all my love, all my life is for you." He did not know what to say, and she continued, "And if I should act like a woman now and again, it is because I am Spanish and because of that, I am a sensitive one."

He laughed, for she had adroitly taken him from the mood she very nearly created, by referring to their mutual joke. Because she was a true mestiza, half Spanish and half Indian, she was right when she called herself a Spaniard, and he was right when, as he often did, he called her Indian.

He said in jest, "Do you know you can be shot around here if you insist on calling yourself a Spaniard?"

"Bah!" she exclaimed. "Who will dare harm me when you are my protector? Tell me." She leaned forward and his hat fell, almost into the hot coals of the fire.

"Stop it!" he said. "Someone will see us and go tell that I am a child and a dolt."

"Tell me that, now," she said. She pulled a handful of hair fiercely. "Tell me who will dare say that Heraclio Inés is not a man? Tell me that!"

And it was true, he thought, that they only acted like children sometimes. Odd that it should be like this for them. How since she came to him six months ago, they were more like companions than lovers. And it came to him that they were indeed but children. He had been at this business almost four years and was but twenty-one years old and she barely sixteen. Every woman he had ever been with had been older than he, except his wife, of course, and that was a different life. This was the first time in his life he was able to enjoy the pleasures of youth. Now he set his plate down and leaned back, looking at the fire but talking to her.

"Xóchitl," he said, wondering what perverseness had compelled

5

her mother to give her an Indian name in a Christian world, "when this is all over, I will take you to my land. And I will build for you a little house and take care of you until one of us dies."

She believed him and knew that this was his way of saying that he could not do without her, and did not think about his wife because that was something else and was not an obstacle.

And now that he had said it, he was not embarrassed, and he lay back on the petate and pulled her down onto his chest. "I do not want you to go into this one, Xóchitl. Leave the fighting to the men and to those who are more men than women."

"It will be bad, then," she said.

"It will be very bad."

"Worse than Torreón?"

"It will not last as long as Torreón, but if anything can be worse, it will be here."

She placed her face in his throat. "And for you?" she asked quietly. "Will it be very bad for you?"

He was going to say that it was always bad, but because he always told her the truth about these things, he said, "He does not think I will live through the night."

"That man!" she exclaimed, and made as if to get to her feet. "What is this brute who would send you to do something he knows will mean your death! Has he no feelings at all—is he an animal?"

Heraclio held her strongly. "Do not talk like that!" he said, just as harshly. "He knows what he does."

His hands bit into her biceps but she stared into his face impassively. "You say he has affection for you and yet he can send you to die? Why?"

"That is because he is a man," he said simply. "But I will not die tonight, India." He released her arms and she fell atop him again. He spoke lightly. "Tomorrow night we will lay together as we have. And do not join the attack because I want you rested when I come to you."

She kissed him passionately and his hand went down her back and under the waistband of her skirt. She pushed herself away from him. "Come, we must fix some shelter," she said.

"It will not be necessary," he said. "We will go in a few minutes."

6

Immediately she became the soldier's consort. "Give me your gun," she said.

"It is clean—the rifle also," he said. "Take care of your own arms, but do not move with the others. Be prepared only if they come here."

They were on their feet now and he put his arms around her. "I know why you join the attack, Xóchitl, and I am pleased. But not this time."

"When do you go?" she asked, still standing against him.

"When the rains come."

"Is that what he said?"

"No," said Heraclio. "He said three o'clock, but I am beginning to think like him, and I feel he will give the word when the rains begin in earnest."

She put on a weskit over her shirt and adjusted a cartridge belt over her right shoulder and across her chest. She buckled a light gun belt around her slim waist. Her gun was small, a .32 revolver. She took her carbine in one hand and walked to where he was preparing himself for battle. He had filled his bandoleers and now fastened them across his chest while she saddled his horse. He checked his sidearm once more, then tested the cinch before he mounted. There was a light drizzle and he knew there was not much time. He leaned down from the saddle and kissed her ear.

"Tonight," he said.

The mustache made her shudder for an instant.

"Tonight," she answered, and smiled.

At one-thirty in the morning, the General sent another assault wave to the base of the Bufa. "To keep the Federals alert," he said. He lay on a field cot and slept, protected by a sarape from the light rain and early morning chill. He slept but a few minutes, waking when the machine-gun fire ceased. It was as if the silence had disturbed his sleep.

"They are returned, then," he said. "It is unfortunate that the boys should die merely to make the enemy think I am stupid. But today I can spare a few men." Members of his staff sat around him and he stood up, walked away from the fire to the edge of the group, and talked over his shoulder to them as he urinated. "It is good for fighting and climbing mountains that it is cold,"

7

he said. "I do not care for the rain but it will serve us well this day." He returned to the fire and sat on his haunches, holding his hands before him for warmth.

From below them, beyond the firelight among the rocks, they heard strains of guitars and raucous voices singing:

> Moya se fué por delante
> mirando por las laderas
> se llevó cincuenta gallos
> pero de los más panteras

This was the ballad of the fearless old man, José Luis Moya, who with fifty men had taken the Bufa and the city back in 1910.

"We will eat now, sirs," said the General, "and then let us see what they are made of on the other side." He called for an adjutant. "Go to Maclovio Herrera and tell him that his people will attack at three o'clock or when the deluge begins, whichever is earlier." He dismissed the adjutant without halting his speech. "Pánfilo," he said to General Natera. "You will take your troops on that little plain as soon as Felipe gets me that little light. Go right up and over the Bufa, and if you reach the city before I do, I do not want to see one Spaniard alive. I will come in on horseback under the viaduct, for although I am of the mountains, I am not a mountain goat that I should climb rocky crags, and besides, this is your state and it is only proper that your troops should have the most illustrious part of the battle, and they should be the first in its capital.

"Very well, my General," said Pánfilo Natera. He had commanded the troops which had laid the siege nine days ago and had failed to move into the city. This was a strange relationship, for Natera, although he walked in the shadow of his commanding general, had a deep respect for him and was not a bit resentful of his glory. And yet, he was his own man, not a blind follower, extremely capable, and agreeable to anything which would help rid his native state of the hated Federal troops. He was in turn respected by the other.

Silent, they ate, and then the General called for his horse. "It is nearly time," he said. The sky was now a mass of clouds, and the boom of thunder suddenly fell over them, but they did not see the lightning. And the rain fell heavily.

8

The assault wave crept silently on foot, bent over instinctively, unnecessarily, in the blackness of the night. Then the men straightened up but yet walked stealthily. It was quiet except for the pounding rain on the plain, and of a sudden, from Heraclio harshly, the word, *"Cuaco!"* that word for horse which also means *move!* And fifty horsemen exploded forward and the still night was blasted by their thunder. Behind them, but not at full gallop, came the mules, dragging the fieldpiece, the gunners running at breakneck speed alongside, stumbling, recovering, but always moving forward even on hands and knees, and General Felipe Ángeles, astride a small mare, trotted calmly beside them, now in the full glare of the searchlight. The foot soldiers were at the first breastwork, fighting hand-to-hand, when the horsemen of Heraclio went over them. Some fell, but not many, and now the machine gunners could not make up their minds to fire because their own soldiers were somewhere before them. The light had come from above just when their commander decided the first line was expendable, but it was too late, for Heraclio's men overran them. The cavalry cut at the enemy with sabers or leaned over to fire point blank as they went by. The few gunners able to fire were crushed by the horses they slew. The horsemen spun around and now they roped the enemy as it ran, dragging the soldiers over rocks, smashing their bodies.

Intense fire came from above, around the unperturbed Ángeles, who from the saddle patiently gave his gun crew corrections and at the third salvo destroyed the searchlight and brought darkness again on the promontory. The night was filled with yells and screeches as the first part of Natera's eight thousand men ran in the direction of the Bufa.

Heraclio climbed the mountain with his men, ignoring age-old paths, and behind him the cliffs were covered with ascending men. Some lost their hold and so fell and were destroyed, but others took their place, and below them, the promontory, too, was filled with men. There was an intense barrage on the plain from above, but the horde came on, shouting, screaming, stepping on their own dead, and it was dawn when the fighting on the mountain began in earnest, and hundreds died near the summit, but Natera's waves came on, so that eventually the attackers broke through by sheer weight and began the downhill fight circling

9

toward the city. Halfway down the mountain, where the first houses were found, they were stopped by sharpshooters and well-placed automatic weapons, but the unending mass of men behind them pushed them forward, and now for the first time since the attack began, their officers whipped them into order, their firing became deliberate, heavy, and yet they were thrown back. Their backs were to the mountain and their men were still pouring down upon them, so that a sudden disorganized flight became an attack because they could not retreat. Suddenly from their left, the General appeared on his big red horse and threw two thousand of his horse at the flank, so the men on foot went into the cobblestone streets, and Natera gave the order once again, and every one of those first defenders was killed.

By three o'clock in the afternoon, all the armies were in the city, but there was firing on the outskirts, where machine guns were trained on every avenue south, and all who attempted to escape were slaughtered. In a canyon, where a few hundred people were able to get away before the city fell, among them General Barrón, who had commanded the stronghold, a thousand camp followers, women, and children were slain before there could be a restoration of order.

In the main plaza, the General gathered his staff. Prisoners were herded into the square. "Those that are of the military," said the General, "strip them of their arms and ammunition, then give them a choice. Or they are with us, or they walk out of the city. We cannot feed them. They may walk away and not be bothered. All animals remain—we may yet have to eat them. Political prisoners will be shot immediately. I do not wish to be bothered with any of that. There will be no favors, no considerations. The Spaniard also execute."

He was finished with that, but the Spanish blood was diffused in the people, and many fair, blue-eyed Mexicans were dragged from their homes and shot, so, in every street, every alley, blood ran in rivulets. And this continued until darkness fell. The Rebels, who were drunk with glory, then drunk by the sadistic pleasure of killing enemies of the people at will, were now physically drunk and committed a multitude of atrocities, and the General Staff went to the General and said:

"The people of the town have come to beg your mercy, General.

The men are violating the city. We have controlled those under our command, but they ask that you do something before your men destroy the capital completely with their looting and raping."

"Let my people be," said the General. "They have fought valiantly and they deserve their reward."

"But, General. They are breaking every law of decency. There is a man outside, on his knees, crying. His daughter was raped before his eyes. His wife escaped, but another daughter, a child of twelve years, is missing. This is against the laws of God and of men, my General."

"I do not know that of the laws of God," said the General, and not in arrogance. "He has not been in México for many generations, or we would not be here today. As for the laws of man, here, there is only one law—and I make it. These people have been in the city and lived in peace with the enemy. They have traded with him, and are, in fact, sympathetic toward him. We display our patriotism by dying for them. Cannot they do a little? An army *must* have women. That is clear, is it not?"

By now, only the Golden Ones, the elite corps of the General, foraged at will, until a medical officer came to him and said, "I will not speak to you of moral issues. It is only that you must do something with these dead, else there will be sickness and disease in your ranks."

And the order was given that the dead should be burned, for they could not be buried. In the center of the plaza, wagonloads of bodies were dumped to form a huge pile, and gasoline and other combustibles were poured, then torches were put to it. Eerily, in the city, lighted by burning houses and the ghoulish bonfire, drunken soldiers gathered bodies of men, women, children, and animals and made new stacks, until the entire city was lighted as if by sunlight by the gruesome pyres.

And in the bonfires, the dead seemed as if alive. Their tendons, severed or expanded by the heat, moved their limbs, and indeed some of them smiled grotesquely or frowned, or grimaced, so that the soldiers were sobered by the thought that some might yet have life.

On the Bufa, men with torches dumped bodies into now useless mine shafts. And in the canyon where the few escaped, children suckled from the cold breasts of their lifeless mothers.

11

The First Book

Hacienda de la Flor

DEATH HAD BEEN AROUND Heraclio Inés from the beginning of his time, for his mother died almost at the exact moment she delivered him. And it seemed destined that he would live in violence and become a part of the great rebellion which swept down across his native state of Zacatecas, devastating even his birthplace, the Hacienda de la Flor.

La Flor was small, as haciendas go, comprising a mere hundred twenty-five thousand acres when Heraclio was born, sometime in the year 1893. It was the time of castration, and all the cowhands were gathered at Peñuelas, which was the station on the hacienda where this work was carried out, and Juan Inés, who was high in favor with the landowner, don Aurelio Becerra, was directing the operation of making steers of two thousand calves at the precise moment his wife was struggling desperately to rid her body of this huge child. In the end she was able to do this but did not live to see the thing which killed her. And so it was that on the following day, Juan Inés rode slowly the twenty kilometers to la Flor, the center of the hacienda, to make funeral arrangements for his wife and to have a look at his last-born.

He rode slowly, for there was no hurry now, and he allowed his horse to stray from the road, off into the brush, and realized suddenly, now that he was alone, that he was sad. He thought of Marcelina, his wife, now lying dead in the house his own father had

13

built back in 1850, when he, Juan, was born. He had played with her when they were children, and had married her because his father had said he should marry her, and his father had been right, for she had been a good wife and had given him many sons. And they were good sons, devoted to the service of the patrón with the same zeal he possessed. He felt a sudden lightness, a faint sense of freedom, despite his sadness, and was disturbed, for it was almost as if he were pleased that his wife was no more. A sudden searing pain at the pit of his stomach horrified him, for there was no denying that he felt the beginnings of passion, and he knew that this was not a feeling for his wife, but for something unknown.

He had known but three women in his life, and knew none but his wife until he was thirty-five years old. Then suddenly within a month, he had joined his friends in revel and had been with a prostitute. Marcelina had been enough for him, why this? Her very docility had been a stimulus, and even a week ago, before he had gone to Peñuelas for the castration, they had cohabited.

The feeling passed, he was almost home, and he could think clearly of why his life had always been so orderly and he knew that it would remain so. And without realizing it, his thoughts returned to the sensual as he looked across the prairie. He was alongside the neighboring hacienda called Tetillas, and he looked at the two hillocks that gave the hacienda its name. How like a woman's breasts they really were! The entire plateau was a woman, supine, and the two hills touched the sky, tantalizingly, one slightly larger than the other. Even that. He had been told, for he did not know, because he had not really seen a woman's body in his life, that it was also that way with women.

He thought without guilt. Curious, perhaps wonderingly. He came to the walls of the hacienda and went through the main gate, sitting erect, though mourning, allowing the horse to find its way to the house at its own pace. He did not dismount, but leaned back as the horse walked into the house, through the kitchen and out another door to the corral in the rear. Then he dismounted, unsaddled the beast, watched it for a moment as it rolled over on its back, kicking and snorting as it scratched itself, then he walked into the house. Inside, he dropped the saddle and mochila on the ground and walked into his bedroom. He knelt

14

before the makeshift frame, used as a bier, cried for a time, then prayed. When he was finished, he rose and left the room. Now he must see the newborn. There was death in his house, but there was also new life, and here, too, was a ritual.

No one had spoken to him, but now his daughters came and threw their arms around him, wailing in the manner of women, and his sister came to him also and told him to be comforted. With his sons, he exchanged a simple embrace. And now the child was brought to him and he took the bundle, hefted it, and smiled.

"It is a big boy Marcelina has given me. A big boy!" He moved to the doorway so he could better see the dark, ugly blob of a face. The thing in his arms made no sound, made no movement. And he said once more, "A big boy to serve the patrón. He must be at least six kilos!"

"The patrón is outside," said Teodoro, the eldest son.

Juan walked out into the sun, still holding the child in his arms. "May God give you a good day, don Aurelio," he said to the landowner.

"And a good day to you, Juan." Don Aurelio sat astride a black stallion. He leaned down and placed a hand on Juan's shoulder. "I came to tell you that I accompany you in your grief, Juan. And tonight there will be a priest here for Marcelina's wake."

"Thank you for your trouble, don Aurelio," said Juan.

"It is no trouble, man. You know it was my own father's wish that I do everything possible for the Inés family." He paused, and when Juan did not speak, he asked, "And what have we here?"

Juan raised the infant up in his hands. "In all humility, don Aurelio," he said, as if the act was not humble in itself, "I present to you another to serve the family of Becerra. As a favor to God, will you give him your blessing?"

"But of course!" Don Aurelio moved his hand with crossed thumb and forefinger, very much like a priest, and said, "I bless you, in the name of the Father, and of the Son, and of the Holy Ghost, Amen." Then he turned once again to Juan Inés and asked, "Since the priest will be here tonight, will you baptize him then?"

"Yes, if it will not be too much trouble," said Juan.

"And what will you name him?"

15

"If it pleases you, patrón, I will name him Aurelio, for he is my last, and I have not passed your name on to any of my boys."

"It pleases me," said don Aurelio. "And I would like very much to be the godfather."

"Thank you, thank you," said Juan. "It shall be as you say, and he will serve you well, I will see to that." He almost began to say something else, stopped, then seemed to make up his mind to speak after all and said, "I would like your permission to make his middle name Heraclio, patrón. It was his mother's wish."

Don Aurelio frowned. "In honor of the bandit? I did not know that you concerned yourself with tales of those outside the law, Juan."

"You know I do not, don Aurelio," said Juan. "It is because of my woman. A romantic notion because of the ballads and stories of Heraclio Bernal. It is because she is dead, patrón. It is only for that reason."

"Very well," said don Aurelio. "But I prefer to think that it is in honor of the first Heraclio, a great hero of ancient Greece. You do not hear ballads about him, but he was a strong man and performed great deeds."

And a neighbor, a slight girl of sixteen years but already showing evidence of the child that was in her belly, came up and took the infant from Juan. She was considered a strange one, and it was said that she was well on the way toward becoming a witch.

Timotea, Juan's sister, snatched the child away and said, "Away with you, María! Keep away from the child!"

María smiled and her eyes seemed distracted. "Never mind," she said. "I have had a good look and I know."

At this, the women of the house were frightened and the men were made uncomfortable. "You know what, girl?" demanded don Aurelio. "Speak up!"

"I know that he will have your name but he will never be known as Aurelio. And that he will not serve you as the others have done, for he will be different. He will be a violent one and will die violently." She spoke to the patrón with an arrogance and familiarity which amazed the others, and he grew red around the face, then stern and said, "Away with you, crazy! Soon I will be believing those who say you have occult powers and drive you from my lands."

16

María laughed. "You will never drive me from your land, Aurelio." And she sauntered off, toward the jacal where she lived alone.

Don Aurelio watched her and said, "She is certainly a crazy one. I told poor Pascual Contreras I would care for her, and now, seeing her in her condition, I grieve that I have neglected a good servant and friend's daughter. Do you, Juan, have any idea where she picked up that bundle she is carrying within her?" He looked directly at Juan Inés.

Juan returned his look, his face inscrutable. "I do not know, patrón. There has never been any talk about a man visiting her, but it is not difficult to see how it happened, for she lives alone. And she confides in no one."

"If I knew that, I could do something to help her," said don Aurelio. "Of the things she said, never fear. She is a little off, you know, and that of prophecies and witches is not true anyway."

"I know," said Juan. But he did not know. And as for his womenfolk, they believed María, and feared greatly, and although they knew don Aurelio was the father of the unborn child, they gathered in the kitchen to pray for Heraclio, then placed him in his crib near the body of his mother.

That Juan was bothered by María Contreras' words was evident in that he gave orders in his house that henceforth his new son would be called Aurelio at all times. The name Heraclio was to be reserved for his Confirmation, which would be in his twelfth year, and by then, Juan thought, there would be no problem. But as happens in these things, people called him and thought of him as Heraclio, and so before he was a year old his own family began to call him that.

That Heraclio had received a prophecy at his birth was not unusual, but these things were usually of the wishful variety—the wish for a long life, the wish for a happy and fruitful life. But Juan knew that there was evil in María's prophecy, and did not stop to think that the evil lay really in regard to don Aurelio, and that she had simply done this because don Aurelio had offered the child his patronage and protection as a godfather. Juan did not think of this because that between his patrón and the orphan

17

girl was not his affair. Concubinage on the part of the landowners was an accepted thing.

And so he thought of the incident as an omen, and he spent most of his free time with the child, took the baby with him while it was yet too young to walk, on his rounds and visits in the immediate area. One day, when the boy was five years old, he said to him:

"You will be going to school this year. For one year only you will attend school, to learn to add and subtract and divide. Then you will tend sheep. Your godfather has willed it that you will one day be in charge of every sheep and every sheepherder on the hacienda."

"Yes, Father. But what of that of Ineses and horses?" asked the boy.

"Well, you will always ride horses," answered Juan, but he felt regret that here would be an Inés who would not be a horseman.

Disappointment was in the boy's face and voice. "But to be a sheepman all my life, would that not bring discredit to you?"

Juan Inés was patient with his young son. "You will not be a sheepman all your life, Heraclio," for he too had now succumbed to the habit of calling him this; "you will someday be a 'counter' and then later, when you can read and write, you will be a clerk, right here in the Big House, and if God favors you, you may even be an administrator someday. It is for bigger things that your padrino has taken an interest in you."

"Then I wish I had never been his godson," said Heraclio perversely, "for even a clerk is less than a horseman."

"How can a five-peso-a-day clerk be less than a fifty-centavo-a-day jinete? Will you tell me that?" Juan was now losing his patience.

"You know very well why," said the boy.

Perhaps because Heraclio was his last-born, perhaps because his wife had died so that he should have one more son, Juan was gentle again and tried to explain what a gift this was, what an honor it would be for the family of Inés.

He placed his hands on Heraclio's shoulders and pulled him toward him. "All this," he said, scarcely knowing where to begin, "is because of something that happened a long time ago. My father, Crispín Inés—your grandfather—once saved the life of the

18

father of don Aurelio. It was during the French occupation, you did not know about that, but the French once had all of México and sent a prince to be our ruler. I remember this well, as I was twelve years old at the time. I do not know why, but don José Becerra chose to oppose the new government and he was captured. The soldiers went to Río Grande, but they detailed three men to take don José to Fresnillo, where they would hang him. My father followed without being seen, and that first night, while two of the soldiers slept, he crept up to the sentry and with a knife took his life, then carried don José a league into the mountains. The soldiers, not knowing the way of the land, could not find them, and my father untied the patrón and gave him his horse so he could flee. Then he came on foot all the way to the hacienda.

"After Maximiliano was disposed of, don José returned from the north where he had been hiding, and his reward to my father for having saved his life was eternal protection for the family of Inés from the landowners. He gave us the plot of farmland we own so we could raise our food, allowed us to possess our own animals, and since that day there is nothing against our names on the books at the hacienda store, because by their kindness the Becerras have made us self-sufficient. And when my father died, he left me with the responsibility of serving the patrón faithfully for life, and of passing the tradition to my sons. Therefore when you have sons, you too will pass this on, for our stature comes not from being great horsemen, which we are, but from our service to our patrón. Don Aurelio, your godfather, is kind to you. We cannot insult him by refusing, even if it were possible to deny his wish. He will make you more than a mere peon—we cannot begin to imagine what he will do for your children.

"And that is why, Heraclio. And you must be of good cheer, because you have been blessed."

"Yes, Papá," said the boy, sagely knowing he should not object further, but he was far from satisfied. His wishes meant nothing in this matter.

Heraclio did not have time to think too much about the plans for his future, because that afternoon, his father took him to Toribio, another station, about five miles distant from the main buildings. Thirty mares were being broken for shipment to the capital, and it was almost in the form of compensation that he would never be a part of this life that Heraclio was given an opportunity to see this at such an early age.

The settlement at Toribio consisted of a group of buildings set in a semicircle, surrounding an intricate system of stone corrals, the largest of which was separated from the others by a passageway about thirty yards in length and four feet wide. A gate at the far end of this enclosure opened to a fenced pasture of some ten hectares. Here, animals ridden once were broken gradually by being saddled every day and ridden at intervals, until the time when they would be driven to Peñuelas for shipment south.

Singly, the animals were sent up the passageway. Once in the large corral, the beast was immediately dropped by ropers, and just as quickly a jinete was on its back, grabbing a handful of mane with the left hand, waving a sombrero wildly in the right, with rowels digging deeply into the animal's tender belly. Today, the mares were young, less than three years old, and bucked very little or not at all, so that the only excitement for Heraclio, who had seen cowboys on the hacienda riding half-broken horses which showed more spirit than these, came from being present. He was in the company of men who were doing man's work.

"You are enjoying yourself?" asked Juan Inés of his son.

"Yes, Father." It was a bright sunny day and they sat on the stands overlooking the corral, built there so the landowner and his guests could watch rodeos in days of fiestas.

The work in the corral went fast, and a cowboy came to Juan Inés and said, "With your permission, don Juan, we will send two or three larger animals into the corral so the boy, here, can see some real riding."

"Good, Pancho, good," said Juan. He turned to Heraclio and on impulse asked, "How would you like to see your father dominate a horse?"

"I would like that," answered the boy.

They walked down to the stone wall and Juan left his son there. He borrowed spurs, for they had come from la Flor in a surrey. There was a little fear in his chest and he wondered why he had suddenly decided to do this, but he was a horseman, and he shook

20

off the fear and walked to where the passageway opened into the corral.

"We have a few stallions that came in the roundup," said Pancho. "Do you want us to ride two or three before we give you one?"

Juan smiled. "You think I have lost my nerve because it has been years since I last did this?" The man started to protest, but Juan cut him off. "Since we do not lie about these things, it is not necessary to be polite. A minute ago I was about to change my mind, but I am quite all right now. Get me a horse, I wish to perform the ride of death for the boy."

The men gathered around then. This was something for a special occasion, when young cowboys were trying to outdo one another, and although they all welcomed such a feat of horsemanship, it was not done in the regular routine of work. In fact, not many jinetes could do it, and it was not considered dishonorable if one refused to try it.

Pancho said, "It is not necessary, don Juan. As you say, it has been many years, and perhaps the conventional ride will be enough to please your boy."

"No," said Juan. "This will be the last time I do this. In a year or two I will surely lose my courage for it and I want my son to see me. Lend me your spurs."

"Very well," said Pancho.

Juan Inés adjusted the spurs.

Concepción Inés, youngest of Heraclio's four brothers, came in from the range and went to the wall to talk to his little brother. He was sweaty and dusty so he took his hat off, hanging it on the pommel, and ran his hands through dark, thickly curled hair. His eyes were blue, as were all the Ineses with the exception of Heraclio's, and he was a handsome figure as he leaned over to chat with the boy. He put his hat back on and pushed the wide brim back, away from his eyes.

"Are they getting a bronco ready for you, little one?" he asked. Laughing, he took Heraclio under the armpits and put him on his horse's neck.

"You know they are not," answered Heraclio. "It is for my father that they are preparing a horse."

A group of cowboys came to them, and one of them said to

Concepción, "It is good that you are here, Concho. Your father would perform the ride of death. Will you help us dissuade him?"

Immediately, Concepción became serious. He seemed much older than his sixteen years, but, then, he had already been on the range two years. He was almost haughty. "Do you suggest that he cannot do it?" he asked.

"No, no," said the man, silently damning the stupidity of the Inés pride. "It is only that he has not practiced this for some time!"

Concepción said, "I cannot dare offer advice to my father. I should not have to tell you that. If he chooses, he will do it. And if he cannot do it, I will do it—and if I fail also, the baby here will ride your Goddamned beast!"

"All right, Concho, all right," said the man, and walked off.

"Why do you become angry?" asked Heraclio. This was his first contact with family honor.

Concepción placed him back on the wall. "People will sometimes forget what we are," he said. Then he joked once again and teased in a low voice. "You know that we have horse blood in our veins, do you not? And that there has never been, nor will there be, a horse that will not kneel to us?" He rode over near his father before Heraclio could reply.

The wild stallion came out of the passageway snorting and pawing very much in the manner of a fighting bull. Two riders worked it toward the far wall, darting back and forth to cut it off. Juan Inés followed slowly, gradually moving away from them so that when they had the bronco near the wall, he was forty yards beyond, still along the fence. The riders made the stallion trot between them and the stone fence, then they were cantering, so that by the time they reached Juan, whose horse was already moving, they were at a strong gallop. The riders veered away, and now Juan Inés sped side by side with the wild horse, following every contour of the wall. Slowly, he raised his feet to his saddle and then crouched upon his horse as he came ever closer to the other horse, then suddenly leaped upon the stallion's back. But he miscalculated slightly and the hand that reached for the mane struck the side of the horse's neck with fingers extended, and he groped wildly with his good hand for a grip as he went over, and his legs tightened instinctively but by now there was no horse between them, and he saw the underside of the beast just before his body struck the stone fence and his neck snapped.

Almost before his father struck the ground, Concepción, who had been following at a slower pace, uttered the cry, "*Cuaco!*" and dug his spurs deep into his horse, climbing to all fours even before intercepting the bronco, jumping as they came together for a moment. He had his hold, his legs were tight around the body, his spurs bloodied the animal's sides. The stallion began a series of bucks without slowing down, writhing and twisting, off balance, nearly falling, but then stopped its wild run and bucked straight, and when that did not remove the foreign weight from its back, ran toward the fence as if to destroy itself, only to cut sharply just in time, bucking once again, and suddenly settled down, and Concepción placed his hat over the animal's right eye, never relaxing his hold on the mane or the grip of his legs; warily watching it, he made him walk in a circle to his left, then placed the hat over the left eye and made it walk around to the right. When he was satisfied, when the stallion stood with legs spread apart, its body trembling, its withers shaking, he raised one leg over its back, sat sidesaddle for a moment, then allowed himself to slide to the ground.

There were no cheers, though everyone watched and admired. Concepción went to where his father lay. Heraclio ran to him, crying, "He is dead! My father has died!" And Concepción pushed him aside and went to his father's body and kissed the face. Then he put his arms around Heraclio as he knelt there, and said the words Juan Inés would have said. "This is but a part of the life we have, Heraclio. Every time we mount a beast, this can happen to us. My father knew it; he taught it to us but he never told you because this is not to be your life. It is but our destiny." His soft voice became stern again. "Now you can stop your crying. When an Inés cries, only his own can be present."

Heraclio nodded. Concepción had somehow included him as one of their breed. He knew he would be a part of this, and, somehow, that he *would* never lose this tie with his family.

The cowhands moved close to offer their sympathies.

"Leave us with our dead," said Concepción coldly. To Heraclio he said, "Remain here with him. I will get a wagon and we will take him home."

23

The boy stood there by the wall and looked at what remained of Juan Inés.

II

IN THE YEAR 1905, when Heraclio Inés was twelve years old, the Hacienda de la Flor was at its height of prosperity. It was an incorporated municipality with public administrators appointed by don Aurelio Becerra, the landowner. It had a population of 1500, nearly a thousand of these in the main settlement and five hundred scattered among the five estancias, or stations, within the boundaries of the estate. Each estancia had a caporal as its head, and under him were two or three lesser foremen, depending upon the number of workers there were.

There were clerks and storekeepers, hired in the city, to assist the administrator, but at this time there was no priest on the hacienda. The entire hacienda was surrounded by a stone fence, three hundred years old, and at its widest point, from east to west, it would take a horseman several days to traverse it.

The Casa Grande, ancestral home of the landowner, was situated in the main part of the settlement. Its doors and windows were heavily barred, and a high thick wall surrounded the main house and secondary buildings. These were the arsenal, workshops, a forge, warehouses and granaries, the store, the jail, and stables. Near the thick oaken door at the wall was the chapel. Within the walls were patios, many trees, in an otherwise treeless terrain, extensive flower gardens, and outside, yet nearby, was a private orchard with an infinite variety of fruit trees, so don Aurelio Becerra and his family could enjoy fruit in season at all times.

Don Aurelio ruled over his domain in a patriarchal manner. Like all landowners, who comprised the highest social class in México, he took pride in the fact that he took good care of and protected his peones. As was the custom, he allowed every family an adobe hut rent free. If there was none available, the peon was allowed to build one. He also let them have a milpa, and on occasion someone would have his own cow. He rarely paid wages in money. Those who were not in debt received time checks to be cashed at the hacienda store, which supplied them with every physical necessity of life. As for the spiritual, he had a priest visit twice a year—during Lent and during the Christmas season. All other visits by the clergy were of a social nature or for the Becerra's personal guidance. While on these visits, the priest might hear confession for a few penitents, but for the most part, the peones and their families had don Aurelio to turn to when they needed God.

Don Aurelio possessed a large residence in Mexico City, a house in the country in France, had family connections in Spain, was surrounded by luxury, and enjoyed life while on the hacienda with rustic simplicity. He controlled his workers throughout his estate with solicitous, paternal discipline, except when there was a serious offense, and he arbitrarily decided when a serious offense was committed. Because it was almost entirely self-sufficient, it was necessary that the estate be so large. Although la Flor was not agricultural, it was imperative that there be a good-sized acreage of tillable soil. This was located south and west of the main buildings. Directly south, the Tecolote Mountains, the entire range completely within the hacienda proper yielded stone, lime, and other minerals for the small open hearth. From the north, beyond the grazing lands which immediately surrounded the main part of the hacienda, clay for adobe, wild herbs, and salt abounded! Eastward, in the foothills barely visible, were small forests which supplied timber, and beyond that was rocky wasteland, mountain land where the hacienda's seventy-five thousand sheep grazed.

It was in this area one night that Heraclio Inés and David Contreras, illegitimate son of María Contreras and don Aurelio Becerra, prepared to bed their flock for the night. They moved up a small valley—so small it could be called a gully. David was at the rear of the flock, carrying a lamb in his arms and shouting to the few stubborn sheep that wanted to go in their own direction. Heraclio was now a full-fledged pastor. He walked near the lead sheep, staff in hand. The camp for the night was a triangular slope, with the boys' camp at its apex. Heraclio stationed his dogs from one side of the apex in circular fashion around to the other side. Each would remain in its place during the night, protecting the flock from predatory animals.

When Heraclio returned to the sleeping site, David was milking the last of three goats which were allotted to every flock. "Come, Daví," he called, "we had better eat now, for we should sleep early tonight. Tomorrow we must be up before the sun."

"Yes, and tomorrow night you will be back at the hacienda while I must remain here another fifteen days," replied David dejectedly.

This was their fifth year at this work, and they had been together for over a year. They had become closer than if they had been brothers. Although David was a few months younger than Heraclio, and as colero was more of an assistant, the boys complemented each other in their work. They lived in the hills the year round. Once every two months they returned to the hacienda for three days of rest, then on the fourth day they rejoined their flock. There were boys like themselves all over these eastern hills, but those, for the most part, were in the company of their fathers or older brothers. For they were sons of shepherds who were sons of shepherds. On the hacienda, the progeny of artisans became artisans, that of land or agricultural peones became field laborers, those of horsemen became horsemen. And so Heraclio's and David's five-year stay in the hills was not justified even traditionally, for the pattern rarely changed.

"It will not be like this much longer," said Heraclio. "I promise you, Daví, that I will persuade my brother Teodoro to take you from this occupation. Then we will be out on the range together as always."

"No, Heraclio," said David. "I will be tending sheep until I die as my father did before me." He lived the lie his mother and his neighbors had told him—that his father had been a shepherd who died in the hills. "And besides," he added, "you know what a dog your brother is. He will do no one a favor, least of all you. I am surprised that he is taking you from this life—that I cannot understand."

"That is simple," said Heraclio. "He cannot stand the thought of any Inés working with sheep, even if it will lead to being an administrator. Also, I think he can buy more tequila when I earn fifty centavos a day than he can now with the twenty-three I receive. Since he is now a caporal, and since the Becerras look favorably upon an Inés, he was able to convince don Aurelio that he could do more for me as a cowhand than as a sheep-herder."

"That son of a bitch!" said David suddenly harshly.

Heraclio was suddenly alert, suddenly fierce. He said, "Watch your tongue! Do you speak of my brother?"

David looked at him, hurt at having been misunderstood, fearing that he might insult Heraclio in either case.

"Your godfather. Our patrón, the great landowner, don Aurelio Becerra. He is the one I call the son of a bitch. Make of it what you will!" He added this without bravado. He added it because he wished to show that he was not physically afraid, that his only fear was that he might offend Heraclio, whom he loved. But because from this day their relationship would surely change, Heraclio was suddenly one of the others, and he, David, was alone again. He was on his feet with his knife in his hand.

Heraclio laughed. He, too, felt awkward and attempted to make things right once more. "Sit down, Daví. I make nothing of that," he said. "But we *are* supposed to feel nothing but gratitude for my godfather, and are to speak always in a favorable manner about him."

"Are we?" David was not prepared to forget so soon.

"Come, Daví," said Heraclio. "I thought you spoke of my brother. His mother was my mother, so if you call him that, what does it make me?" As David remained sullen, Heraclio continued. "And as for the fact that I am leaving, it is not my fault that don Aurelio is my godfather."

"It is not my doing either," said David, "that he is my father!"

"Oh, Daví," exclaimed Heraclio, and almost threw his arms around his friend. "I could give my life that you should have never discovered that!"

"But I do know it," said David, and cynically, "Would you give your life to undo it?"

"You know I would."

David sat down and gave him a push and everything was fine between them again. "That was good, Heraclio, what we did to the lion," he said. They had been away from the hacienda for three weeks, and the major part of this time had been spent in tracking a mountain lion which had been harassing their flock. They had finally cornered it in a box canyon and stunned it with their slings, so that their dogs could finish it off. The experience had given David a sense of completeness he had never known.

"Yes," said Heraclio, "and do you remember how yellow his eyes were before you hit the side of his head with the first stone?"

"That was something," said David. "That certainly was something!" They ate their hardtack and jerky and were quiet for a time. Then David said, "You know, Heraclio, this business of being a bastard is not really much different from being an orphan, except for the mothers, I think. I think the mothers have it much harder. If people think bad things, one never knows them, but the mothers know. And you know, if my father had really been a pastor I would not feel bad about being a sheepman."

"I suppose the idea is in having a father," said Heraclio. "I do not really know. That of the mother is true, because I feel good that my mother is with the angels, and I truly feel sorry for yours."

"I just feel that I do not belong out here," said David.

"We do not, either of us. It is my godfather's doing that I am out here in the first place, and it is his doing that I am to leave—I suppose it is his doing that you are here too."

They could not follow through with an idea, their area of experience being limited, but they could speak of what they knew. "It is bad for my mother, living alone. It is bad that we live in la Flor, where everyone knows her disgrace. The least your godfather could do is to clear her name on the books at the tienda de raya. Then, perhaps someday we could have enough to leave here. I would work hard in the city and we could be happy. It is bad that she practices the mysterious arts—she can really do some strange things, you know. She can put you to sleep, she can keep you awake for long periods, she can remove a stomach-ache as easily as she can give you one."

"I have heard."

"She can almost make you crazy and she can frighten one half to death, but I do love her."

"That is natural, for she is your mother." They lighted cigarettes. "I suppose nothing is half bad if one's mother does not suffer. But I tell you again, Daví, I will not rest until I take you from this work, even if I have to take my brother's job from him."

Since the last was child's talk, David did not answer. He moved

28

to another subject. "What do you figure the count to be tomorrow?" he asked.

"We have twenty missing that we know of this month. That brings the six months' total to one hundred and thirty-one. You know the administrator will be pleased, for some of the men will be missing two and three hundred this time. This is always a bad time of year for sheep. It is as if all the wolves in México come to Zacatecas," said Heraclio.

"And the Goddamned cat," said David. He took his bedroll and withdrew a few paces away. "Buenas noches," he called.

"Buenas noches, Daví."

"You know, Heraclio," called David across the darkness, "sometimes we are almost like grownups."

"I think we always are, because we are men."

"We have three thousand sheep," said David with pride.

Heraclio was brought out of a deep sleep by the barks and howls of his dogs. He reached for his coat with one hand as the other searched under the bedclothes for his knife. Dawn was breaking and he realized that the disturbance was caused by the arrival of the men from the hacienda who were to count the sheep before he could be relieved. David was already milking the goats with the idea of having a fast breakfast before the work began.

"Thank you, Daví," he said, "for letting me sleep." They had got into the habit along the way that when one was up before the other, he did not disturb the sleeper for a few minutes. They always thanked each other for such small favors. In doing this now, Heraclio made it seem that this morning was not different from any other. He was beginning to feel sad at the prospect of leaving his friend.

Again they ate the hardtack and beef jerky, drinking hurriedly from the gourd, which was the only utensil they were allowed to carry. "We should have slaughtered an animal yesterday," said David. "I am sick of this fare, and we have one to kill yet this month."

"Yes, but the month is young and the dogs are finding game. It is better that you have that in reserve," said Heraclio. While David put the food away, he rolled and tied his bedding. He handed his pouch of stones to David and said, "Here, Daví. Take

29

my stones. Then you will not have to always be looking for stones as you walk along. Take my sling also, for the new boy."

"Thank you, Heraclio. I will give him the sling but he will find many stones before he learns to use it, so I will keep yours." They were on the subject now, so they dropped their unspoken pretense.

"I would like to have a cigarette, but they are close now and it would be my fortune to have one of my brothers show up. I would not like it if they caught me smoking."

David had his cigarette lighted and offered his friend a few puffs. They could hear the riders now, and David said, "I will say good-by now, Heraclio. Give me an embrace."

They clasped each other lightly. The riders soon appeared from behind a clump of mesquite. There were six men and a small boy in the group. The contador, his four assistants, and Heraclio's brother, Concepción. The boy who would take David's place as colero, now that David would be made pastor, brought up the rear, riding a donkey.

As they rode up, Heraclio was, as always, struck by the prettiness of his brother's face and figure. Concepción came up to him, leading a horse. He threw the reata to Heraclio and with the free hand he pushed his hat away from his face. He looked down at Heraclio and said, "Well, little brother, are you ready to begin the count?"

Heraclio was suddenly reminded of that day when his father died. Concepción had looked just like this, even to the point of pushing his hat back, and he had looked down from his horse exactly in this manner and spoke to him. He would have joked with him, but he suddenly remembered also how Concepción had protected the family name after his father had fallen, by riding and conquering the wild animal. He said very seriously, "Yes, Concho. I have been ready for this count a very long time."

"Unsaddle your horse before you do anything," said Concepción. "He has been wearing that thing most of the night." He dismounted and began to take the saddle off his own horse.

Heraclio walked to David. "If you are ready, we will start now, but first, while I take the saddle off, will you bring me the remains of the missing sheep so the contador will give me credit for them."

David shook his head toward Concepción and said, "What is

the matter with the pretty one? He is very nice to you today."

"Concho is good to me," replied Heraclio. "I suppose it is because we are the youngest of the lot. But hurry so we can begin."

When David returned with a large canvas bag, Heraclio had the saddle off and was talking to the contador. He was a stout man, called Juan Vásquez, who because of his lack of horsemanship, and because of his ability with figures, had the job of moving from flock to flock, making his count and carrying the responsibility of producing in good health as many sheep as possible for shearing time, or when there was to be a shipment to the slaughterhouses in Mexico City. Occasionally he would relieve a herder during his three-day holiday, but ordinarily his assistants would do that job. It was his habit now to return to the hacienda every day, if possible, and some days did not even go into the hills. He was working toward the administratorship of the entire sheep operation on the hacienda and he could help his cause better if he worked around his superiors.

Heraclio said to Juan Vásquez, who had dismounted, "May God give you a good day, señor. How did the morning find you?" He spoke respectfully, in a manner of addressing his elders.

"Very well, and yourself?" answered Juan Vásquez; then impatiently and with importance, he added, "We have to work fast, for I am to see the patrón on important business this afternoon."

Heraclio opened the bag and took from it seven pieces of sheepskin, two jawbones, and one hoof. The contador produced a piece of paper from somewhere inside his hat and a pencil from his shirt pocket. Then he painstakingly listed the items, his facial expression undergoing many changes, as his tongue moved from one side of his face to the other. When he was finished, pencil and paper disappeared in their hiding places. He pulled a piece of string from his pocket and once again importantly called his men. "Let us get to work," he said.

Meanwhile, Concepción had taken Heraclio's belongings down to the bottom of the gully where he had tethered the riderless horse. The three boys walked behind him and, on reaching the bottom, waited for the sheep to start moving down. The contador stationed himself beside them, string in hand, while his men seemingly lost themselves in the milling flock. Their job was to send the sheep down in twos and threes to facilitate the counting.

Concepción now stood next to the contador, where one of the helpers would ordinarily be, to separate the lame, old, or those with lamb from the rest of the flock. Men would be sent later to take them to herders who were in charge of only these animals.

The sheep started down the hill, and as the first two passed the contador, he began to count aloud, "Two, four, seven . . ." Upon reaching one hundred, he tied an overhand knot on his string and began the count again. He had twenty-nine knots on it when he noticed that the remaining animals would number less than one hundred. At the fifty mark he tied a square knot, and the remaining fourteen he put down on his paper.

He mounted his horse and rode to a point where David and Heraclio were talking. The new boy was already taking charge of the misfits. The fat man said, "The flock numbers twenty-nine hundred and sixty-four, plus the ten you lost, which makes it twenty-nine seventy-four. You have one hundred and thirty-six missing from the flock you had five months ago. You lost only five this month that you could not account for, but do not worry, you did very well. I only hope David does as well."

"I am certain he will do better," said Heraclio. The man Vásquez's manner suddenly irritated him and he added, "and I am not worried. The administrator and the patrón will be satisfied with my work."

Concepción rode up to hear the last part of the speech and said to Heraclio, "Is it that my little brother is finally showing his true blood?"

"You should teach him to show better manners toward his elders," said Juan Vásquez.

"And you would do well to not let a child get the better of you," replied Concepción. "And besides, you need not fear that he will take your position, for he is going where he belongs, and the only time he will ever handle a sheep now will be on our kitchen table."

"I do not know of what you speak!" said Vásquez angrily.

Concepción stared at him and then wordlessly turned his horse and said, "Let us go, Heraclio. Leave the fat one to his kind."

"You had better take the donkey with you," said Vásquez.

"You take it," called Concepción. "You are the one who insisted the new boy should not ride the spare horse."

"Sheepherders always ride burros, you know that. You should not have brought the horse for your brother."

Concepción was angry and moved toward the contador once again. "How would you like it if I lassoed you and dragged you a little way? Out here with the sheepmen you are boss—to me you are that." He snapped his fingers. "Provoke me one more time and I will surely break you. You have been here a long time, you were born here. You know us, so take care!"

Vásquez was afraid and said placatingly, "I but tried to do what is right, Conchito. It is my responsibility to respect tradition in my area of work."

"There is another tradition you should know and never forget," said Concepción. "An Inés never rides an ass!" He turned away again.

Heraclio called to David, "I will come to see you next week. And I will keep my promise."

David waved. As Heraclio disappeared down the gully, his eyes filled with tears.

III

HERACLIO JUMPED FROM HIS MAT, straightened his blankets upon it, then rolled and set it against a wall of the room. To his right was a marble basin upon a small stand, and set within the basin was an earthen jar filled with water. This and the bed mat were the only furnishings in the room. The floor was of clay, hardened by decades of use, evened by innumerable wet sweepings.

Still sleepy, he poured water into the basin and splashed it on his face. It had been some time since he had been called to breakfast, so he hurriedly tied his huaraches and ran his fingers through his hair as he entered the kitchen.

Concepción was seated at the table with Juan, who was two years his senior. Juan was of medium stature and somewhat dark in contrast with his brother. He had a small black mustache which in a curious way added a shade of handsomeness to a face otherwise devoid of beauty. It was a cold face, cold eyes, cold mouth— a face that could never show emotion. But if his face was not attractive, his body was. He seemed larger than he was. At twenty-

33

six, he had more than a decade of range work behind him. His legs were slightly bowed, his waist small, and his arms and shoulders were powerful. And his muscles, although defined, were long, athletic.

Both men wore tight-fitting trousers which buttoned from thigh to ankle. Their blouses were buttoned down the front, and at the bottom the ends were tied neatly in a square knot. Over the shirt they wore a short jacket. Their spurs were turned up so they might not strike the ground when they walked. They kept their large, wide-brimmed hats on while they ate.

Behind them, their wives were busy around the small fire. The aunt, Timotea, kept the food warm and personally tended to the table. Across the kitchen, Rosa, Teodoro's wife, was on her knees over a metate, grinding corn to be used during the day. At another table, Manuela, Elías's wife, made chile in a molcajete. And alongside Timotea, Juan's wife, Nacha, patted corn into tortillas and cooked them on a sheet of tin which was over the fire.

Heraclio said good morning to the women, purely from habit, for they did not really interest him. They were women and rarely spoke when their men were present. They communicated with each other in low voices and even in whispers, sometimes, but they did not speak aloud unless they were addressed. Any questions, demands, or requests they might make of their husbands they did so in the privacy of their room or on their marriage bed.

Rosa he remembered well, although he had not been around her the last few years, for he had many times felt her sharp tongue and heavy hand. It had been her responsibility when Teodoro or the aunt Timotea was not present to take care of the running of the house. And she controlled Heraclio and his sisters-in-law with an iron will. Until recently, she had been the only being on earth Teodoro loved and this despite the fact that she had borne him a daughter with regularity almost every year until now they had seven of the nine she had delivered, and finally a few months ago she had given light to a boy which would usurp her place, for Teodoro could love but one person at a time.

Nacha was Juan's wife, and she, because she had never been able to conceive, loved her husband with the zeal of a mother. She was unobtrusive, content only to have ready anything her

Juan might desire, seemed dull, but only because she had her own sadness and because of her sadness she had once tried to please her man and in the end contributed to a greater tragedy, although she was confused about this. In her efforts to make up for that which she could not give and fearing that he should discard her for a woman who was complete in every way, she committed the great wrong of attempting to please him sexually, which was altogether a wrong thing for a woman to do, and then as a complete surprise in the end she pleased herself, committing the greater sin of achieving a climax one night while satisfying her husband and it was now Juan's turn to be confused, for he had never seen this happen, but he was confused for only a short while because, being a man, he was a sophisticate and had been with whores who had told him about this, and he knew that only whores and men had orgasms, so while poor Nacha lay in his arms, relaxed and spent, a faint smile on her plain face, he suddenly leaped out of bed and, pulling her to her feet, slapped her silly, calling her a bad woman. And henceforth, Nacha took her position on her back rigidly and thereby pleased her man, but he had made her touch heaven, and as she had no children to occupy her thoughts, her mind was constantly on her husband's body, and as she padded around the house on her flat feet, saying very little, keeping out of the way, or holding a niece or nephew warmly against her fat bosom, she began to think of any man's body and she remembered that she had once had a feeling she would never have again, and in time she could not recall just what the feeling was, yet it was something to remember. And all the prayers she offered to the Blessed Virgin did not help her.

Manuela was the wife of Elías and she spent her time agreeing in everything Rosa said and imitating everything Rosa did even to the point of having a houseful of daughters. All her children had survived and she now had six. Seven years earlier, when she had first come to this house, she discovered that it was no contest between her and Rosa, so she made an adjustment and was content to be first in Rosa's favor and second in command of the womenfolk. And she punished the five-year-old Heraclio then to keep in practice, so to speak, for she was aware that no one reigns forever except in heaven.

The only sister-in-law who did interest Heraclio was Concho's wife, Otilia, and this was partly because she was the wife of his favorite brother, and partly because she was really of his generation, being but four years older than he was. He had not seen her too many times, as she was from El Fuerte, a neighboring hacienda, and had been married to Concepción less than a year. He had not seen her at all until she was three months married, for Concepción had for the first time in his life gone against the wishes of Teodoro and held the wedding in her home rather than at la Flor, but during his three-day visits from his duties as a shepherd, he grew to like her. Since she was but a child herself, they found things to talk about, and she teased and played with him, while Manuela would tell Rosa, "Look at her, look at her, she thinks she is a little girl, and with that thing already living in her womb, blessed be the Lord!" And Otilia would laugh mischievously and say, "If my man does not mind, then you should not mind either. And I am but a little girl, I have not yet sixteen years—would you were that young, no?" she could not help adding. But Rosa could not afford to allow this shameless thing to get the better of her and talked to her husband, and Teodoro gave an order to Concepción. And now Otilia would say, "Yes, Rosa. Immediately, Rosa." But she did not stop her teasing with Heraclio completely. She did not stop her laughter, and she said to the boy, "I will do everything she says except I will not get dried up and hold my face like this," and she would make a wry, distorted face, and they both laughed. "There is too little mirth in this house, Heraclio. Hurry and grow so you can bring home a wife to keep me company and we will fill this old house with happiness—but do not bring one who looks like this"—she made the face again—"but like this," and she transformed her face into such warmth and beauty that the boy would gasp and thus was guilty that he had somehow betrayed his family by joining this outsider in ridiculing it. He stopped laughing and said, "We *are* happy here, Otilia," and she said, "Well, then, we should look happy," and she said it that way, including herself because she had detected his discomfiture. "My father said that you should always look the way you are and feel or people will not know how to treat you. I suppose that means that when you are happy you should look happy and when you are sad you should look sad, and when you are cruel you should look cruel." "Your father must be the greatest man in Zacatecas," he said, still serious. "No," she answered, "my husband is, but my father used to be." She pleased him then, but he still frowned, so she threw her arms around his neck and squeezed him tightly. "Do not be angry, Heraclio. I am an Inés now too, do you not know?" He laughed and said, "If you were not so pretty you could be a witch." "I am a witch," she answered, and this had to stop because now they were both laughing too loudly.

And she was lovely—as beautiful as Concepción was beautiful. Timotea Inés became a mother to the boys when their own mother died. She went through life with no thought other than she must do her duty to her responsibility. It was this sense of duty which kept her from falling under Rosa's power, and yet she was never fully in control of her house. She loved Heraclio most because he was the baby, but she needed the entire family in lieu of the husband and family she would never have. Once she had had a short intense struggle with Rosa, as silent as it was fierce and brief, and Rosa, who had more guile, fell back, giving the older woman her place, and gradually succeeded in usurping her although Timotea was never really aware of it.

Heraclio sat at the table next to his brothers. His aunt set a plate before him and a small basket with tortillas alongside it. "Good morning, Heraclio," she said, kissing him on the cheek. "Would you like a filet or a piece of udder?"

"Good morning, Tía," he said. "I have not eaten udder in a long time." He did not speak to his brothers.

Otilia came into the kitchen, holding the baby, and took a seat near the fire. She opened her bosom and gave a slight hitch so her left breast plopped sensually out toward the child's face. Half drugged with sleep, its mouth open wide not unlike a young bird's, it made two or three tries until it found the nipple, and relaxed, sucking contentedly, but not before Heraclio had looked at the loveliness of the act and the beauty of the body. The dark, livid aureola was deeply imbedded in his mind.

Juan gazed at him. "So the little man finally decided to get out of bed?" he said.

"It was the mat, Juan," said Heraclio. "I am not accustomed to sleeping in such comfort." His face was red, for he had been at fault.

Juan still looked at him but did not talk to him directly. "Perhaps he would like to tend sheep for another few years or at least until he learns to get out of bed before the half day."

To be admonished was one thing, but now he was being ridiculed and Heraclio was angered. He turned to Juan and said quietly, "If this is the way it will be here, I am certain that my sheep were better company, my brother."

Juan's face was ugly as he stood up. He reached across the small table and hit the boy's face with the back of his hand so that he fell over backwards on the floor. No one said a word, no one moved to help him, the blood trickled out the corner of his mouth and ran down his chin. He took a mouthful of water from a gourd which hung near the door, and when he had washed out his mouth, he picked up his chair and sat at the table once again. He had not uttered a cry; he did not say a word now as he continued to eat.

Gradually his brothers relaxed, and the women resumed their murmuring in the background. "What time will Teodoro return?" asked Heraclio of no one in particular.

"He should be here now," said Concepción, "but do not hurry, you will not be going with us this morning. Go to the cemetery with my aunt and do not eat too much at noon, for Teodoro said you are to break your hymen today." He walked over to his wife to touch her lightly on the cheek, then followed Juan out of the house to the small adobe room built in the rear where their saddles and equipment were stored.

Heraclio ate silently. His aunt came and sat across from him and said sadly, "What has just happened will happen many times before you grow up. You take your punishment well, and I am pleased, but for the sake of your mother that you never had, Heraclio, do not speak to your brothers in that manner. It will be a difficult enough life for you without that."

"Do not worry yourself, Tía," he said. "If that is the worst that it can be, I will be all right."

"But you must mind and respect your brothers at all times," she said, anxious for a promise but refusing to ask for one.

"I will try to remember, Tía," he said. Then, to reassure her further, he added, "Concepción has always treated me very well."

Rosa, who had been listening intently to the conversation, said,

38

"All your brothers treat you well. You must learn that when they punish you it is for your welfare, because they love you."

"Yes," said Timotea, entirely oblivious to the hatred in Rosa's words. "It is not a matter of that. All of them will treat you well, for you are their brother and the baby, but if you do not mind them, it will go bad for you. Teodoro and Elías are much harder than Juan."

He looked across the room to Otilia and she nodded and he knew he had an ally for whatever it might be worth, and he said, "I will not forget," but he knew that was not enough for his aunt and he could not very well add the "Tía" now, so he said once again, "I will not forget, Tía," and she was satisfied.

"They will be here soon," she said, "and I fear greatly that you will be sick tonight. Come, let me get my shawl and we will go to the tienda de raya. You will not have to wear those clothes again after today."

They walked up the street, and where it curved it ended at the gate of the Big House. They had been in the sun but now they walked past the chapel, along the tree-lined alameda which followed the fence line completely around the estate, eventually leading to the orchard a mile away. Beyond the chapel, a short distance, was the front entrance to the house proper. The granary, the arsenal, and maintenance buildings completed the cluster of buildings. A large, barred room had been added to the arsenal to serve as a jail.

Heraclio and his aunt stopped at the store where he was outfitted in chambray trousers, skin tight at the legs, with buttons at the calf. He discarded the loose white breeches, and then the huaraches, for he was to never wear huaraches again. His boots were ready for him, handmade by the local artisan and deposited at the store. He received a hat then, not as wide-brimmed as those the field peones wore, but wider than the simple straw sombrero he had worn as a shepherd. He kept his shirt and his aunt paid for the merchandise with hard money.

They returned to the chapel and walked along the side to where the burial ground was. Heraclio had never been to the graves of his parents since his father died, and he was curiously unaffected as he knelt on the hard ground. Instead of praying, he tried to imagine how it would be for him this afternoon. He gave that up, however, because as he thought back to that day in Toribio when the cowboys were breaking the mares, it had seemed quite easy, but then the thought of what had followed frightened him. He had no idea how it would be for him. He knew that he would be upon a wild horse and beyond that he knew nothing. Out of the corner of his eye, he looked at his aunt in search of a change of expression in her face which would indicate that they were finished here. His knees and back ached, and the sun beat down on his head so he wished he could put his hat back on.

Finally, Timotea crossed herself and stood up. "I am going to light some candles," she said. "If you do not wish to go into the church, you may wait for me."

"I will go with you," he said, although he did not want to do so. They walked to the side entrance of the chapel. They dipped their fingers in the ancient urn, genuflected as they crossed to the other side where the statue of the Virgin of Guadalupe stood high and benign above them. Timotea placed two cents in a small plate at the base of the idol, then lighted two candles. They prayed again.

Outside they walked rapidly back to the house. Voices could be heard from the kitchen as they approached, and Heraclio knew that Teodoro and Elías had arrived.

His oldest brothers were not as tall as Concepción and here again there was a sharp contrast, Teodoro being almost blond with expressionless blue eyes, Elías dark yet blue-eyed also. Teodoro had a small sharp face which gave him a wizened look making him seem older than he was.

The men greeted their aunt respectfully, as was due someone of her station, although they had seen her when they left at dawn. A few moments passed and Teodoro said in a gruff voice, "What is the matter with you, boy? Have the hills made you forget your manners or do you not want to talk to your brothers?"

Heraclio, whose head was full of apprehensions of what was to happen to him within the next few hours, said distractedly, "Good morning, Teodoro, how are you and you too, Elías?"

Elías noticed the slight swelling on the side of Heraclio's mouth and said, "I see someone has begun to teach him manners already. Watch your step, little one, for from now on you are in a man's business and will receive one lesson after another."

Timotea gazed fearfully, frightened at the scene, and Heraclio

40

somehow noticed her and with a magnificent effort controlled himself and did not betray his anger. He laughed lightly and ran his fingers lightly over the soreness around his mouth. "What am I to do this afternoon, Teodoro?"

Elías, who had been waiting for a retort, smiled inwardly. He knew that it was not fear which had made Heraclio change his mind. The boy was canny and it was good, but he also knew that it would not be until this afternoon before they could know what kind of a man he would be. And all the brothers feared that he might reveal himself as mediocre.

Teodoro did not miss this either and was also happy about his little brother, but when he spoke he was serious, and he was rough, for his word was law and he must play the part. "There is a colt which has never been ridden," he said. "Within the hour you will have the honor of being the first to attempt it. And do not think this merely talk—do not for a minute believe that it is not an honor, for the horse is a noble beast, and because of that, we are nobler because we control him. You can do it if you are really our brother. We began at this age, so do not think of it as a great deed, which it would be if you were not an Inés."

Heraclio nodded, his sudden fear making him unable to speak. The traumatic image of his father's broken body alongside the stone fence blotted everything. He had ridden since he could walk, although he had not done much riding in the last four years, but to have to break a pony on his very first day made him weak. And here again was the idea of the family; being an Inés made things different, and although he felt something of what his brothers felt, the responsibility was suddenly too much for him. It was his first clash with an external, intangible force. He waited a moment, and when he was certain his voice would sound right, he said, "If you do not want me for a little while, I will pay my respects to my godfather." He walked out into the hot sun.

But although he went back within the great wall of the estate, he did not stop at the house. He was attempting to make his mind believe that he was capable of the test which was before him. They had all done it at the age of twelve, and they were not braver or better than he. But his reasoning did very little good, and in the end he knew he could not make himself unafraid, but

41

he must force himself to perform the deed without betraying his feelings.

He returned to the house but his brothers had already departed. His aunt brought him a pair of spurs his father had used as a boy. He thanked her dumbly and walked out of the house to the corral.

The site chosen for Heraclio to meet his first horse in what, he believed, could surely be his end was the corral behind the Big House. It was situated within the wall of the estate and in a central position within the boundaries of the most populated section of the hacienda, yet only Heraclio's brothers were present when he arrived.

Heraclio secured the spurs to his new boots, nodding his head as he listened to Concepción's instructions. Nearby, Juan and Elías were on horseback, talking to Teodoro, who sat on the stone wall. Across the corral, a young colt trotted back and forth, showing fear in its movements and bewildered at finding itself suddenly confined after a life of freedom. It was a beautiful spring day, cool—but the sun beating on the white, hard ground of the corral, which was entirely devoid of shade, made the boy feel hot, and as his head bobbed to assure Concepción that he was listening to his advice, his mind was on the coolness of the grassy pastures to the east, where the sheep were now lambing and where David Contreras was enjoying a life which must be much better than this. He straightened up and the colt had not ceased his nervous pacing, and suddenly Heraclio looked at his brother's face, fully, with a wordless plea that he should impart in a moment all his knowledge, all his skill that he, Heraclio, might be saved.

Concepción sensed fear and he said, "It is not easy—no. But it is simple. You hold the mane, usually, but for this one time we will use a hackamore. You must be brutal, for the animal is a brute —you must declare to yourself that you will be brutal. And yet, and here is the strange thing, you must be tender, even kind, for this is your personal beast—you own him and you must care for him. Teodoro has taken pains to make a good selection. The horse has Arab blood and it has English blood, and does not carry a single drop of the puny Spanish line. When he grows he will be fleet and strong and will serve you well. Be careful that you do not injure him too much."

42

"I will be very tender," said Heraclio sarcastically.

Concepción did not hear him. He concentrated on getting his instructions across to the boy. "When you have ridden him two or three times, we will put your saddle on him. Until then, you ride bareback. Now the trick is in your legs—always the trick is in your legs. They are to be tight around the body—do not relax even if he is broken. And your spurs must go deep, not to make him buck, he will surely do that on his own, but to teach the beast that you have the power to hurt him. He cannot throw you off and you can hurt him—it is the first step toward dominating him. In the end, when he knows you are his master, then he will be truly yours and he will follow you."

"You are talking too much!" called Teodoro from the fence.

"Let us begin," said Concepción. "Remember, keep the legs tight and the spurs deep. Good luck."

Juan moved the colt to the center of the corral and Elías came from the side, twirling his reata, and lassoed the forelegs so the colt did a half somersault, landing heavily on its back. It stood up and hobbled forward and Juan roped its hind legs so that it fell, more gently this time, and Concepción was over its back, forcing the hackamore over the resisting jaws.

Heraclio hesitated and in his impatience Concepción was rough. "Get yourself on the cuckold!" he ordered.

Heraclio straddled the animal, although it was on its side, and he grasped the hackamore with both hands.

"When he comes up, straighten yourself on its back," said Concepción, and leaped out of the way.

Juan and Elías flicked their reatas, and it was a moment before the colt realized he was free, and in that moment he brought all his strength to bear in one tremendous effort to regain his feet and then leap into the air, and Heraclio dropped the hackamore and threw his arms around the great neck and, clinging momentarily to the side of the animal, grotesquely, one leg over its back and one leg trailing, did not survive the first jump and was flat on his back, curiously not feeling pain, thinking only that everything had stopped inside his body, and the horse came down near his head. He lay there, rigid, unable to move, his eyes wide, staring at the underbelly of his enemy, and the colt whirled away from him, covering his eyes and face with white dust.

43

He knew that he was breathing then, for the dust made him choke, and he sat up, rubbing his eyes, drawing huge gasps of air. When he could see again, Teodoro was sitting on his haunches next to him.

"Get yourself up," he said, not unkindly. "The horse is ready for you."

He looked then and it was true. The colt was down and his brothers waited for him.

"Not again," he said. "No, Teodoro, not again, please!"

"Get yourself up," said Teodoro. "You must ride the beast because you are who you are. If you fail to ride it today, we come back tomorrow and you try again, but you cannot give up. This is beyond our power, to give up."

They talked there in the sun as if they were discussing a problem at home. "No, Teodoro. I beg of you! Allow me to be mediocre. Many cowboys are not jinetes. There has to be an Inés sometime who cannot break a horse!"

"No. There can be no such monstrosity!"

"I will be content to be a plain cowhand."

"But I will not," said Teodoro. He had his quirt in his hand, and, still squatting, he struck Heraclio full force on the face with it. "You are taking too long, boy," he said.

Tears came from Heraclio's eyes but he did not cry aloud. He was suddenly beyond hurt and in a wrath. And he knew he would not obey Teodoro, no matter what should happen to him. His brother stood up and beat him on the back with the quirt, and he placed his hands behind his head, covering his face with his arms and elbows.

"Get yourself up out of your own foulness, you dumb shit!" said Teodoro. And Heraclio realized that he had urinated while he was on the horse. The dust had turned to mud at the front of his trousers, and this shamed him, so he got to his feet and moved toward the colt.

He managed to right himself on the animal's back before he was thrown this time, but his body hit the ground with a terrible force. He was stripped of all dignity as he regained his footing, and it seemed to him but a moment when he was again on the ground, and as he rose slowly, Teodoro was upon him, beating with the quirt, and kicking him so that he cried aloud in his rage

44

and in his pain. Nine times in all he was thrown and felt Teodoro's wrath that he could not stay on the horse. Teodoro now beat him because he lacked ability and not because he lacked courage. The boy stood panting in the sun, his body now numb so he felt no pain, his tears were exhausted. He was tired in a way that did not seem possible, and his face was a grotesque mask, white dust thick upon it, marred by a line from each eye where the last tears had rolled, and from each nostril where blood had run freely down over his lips and onto his chin. He whimpered from deep within himself, and like a somnambulist, he turned to look for the horse once again.

Elías brought a gourd and he drank a little water, and Juan said to Teodoro, "We should stop and try another day. The horse is taking too many falls and might break a leg."

"Fuck the horse!" said Teodoro. "One of them will be dragged out of here, but we do not stop!"

Concepción talked to Heraclio. "Hurt him! Punish the animal—kill it if you must! It does not matter—there are other horses and this has become more than a lesson in breaking a horse. Dig your spurs into him, and punish his head with the hackamore, that is why we put it on him."

The horse was hardly spent, but he was sore from having been roped so many times and had lost some of his spirit. He lay now, hobbled, again on his side, and Heraclio straddled it once again, and suddenly he felt a resurgence of strength—a strength he did not know he possessed and he could smell the horse smell strongly, and he did a curious thing. Not knowing why, he ran a hand caressingly down the dusty neck of the animal before his brothers released him.

And he felt power in his legs as he pressed them tightly, and his spurs bit into flesh but not underneath where the horse is tender, because Heraclio's legs were still too short, and when the horse could not dislodge him immediately, it began to gyrate, to buck to the side and once when it had all four feet on the ground, Heraclio remembered and pulled on the hackamore with all his strength so the head seemed to come back into the neck and then further back and the forelegs up, high in the air until they crashed over backwards, and now the horse was hurt and took a moment to recover and in that moment, Heraclio, who had fallen clear,

45

was quickly upon it before it regained its feet. The colt bucked twice, then stopped and walked slowly once around the corral, and then a second time, then bucked once more suddenly, but Heraclio had not relaxed, and the horse was his.

He walked home then, without saying a word to his brothers, and no one tried to stop him. Near the corral gate, he took his spurs off and carried them in one hand. Limping, he went past the store, and then the chapel, out the main gate and down the narrow street. His strength left him and there was a soreness between his legs and in his buttocks. His back and arms burned him and now he began to stagger a little. He was dizzy, and he wanted to lie down there, in the middle of the street, lie down forever, but he stumbled on, and the last few yards to the house were the most terrible. When he reached the front door he merely leaned on it and fell into the kitchen. He held the spurs tightly in his left hand.

When he regained consciousness he was on his side on someone's bed. For a long time he lay with his eyes open. Then he turned over on his back and uttered a cry, but he remained in that position until he was able to lie without too much pain. He sensed the presence of someone in the room and finally realized that Otilia hovered over him, staring anxiously at his face. She kissed him beside the mouth.

"You are all right, Heraclio, my brother? Tell me where the pain is worse."

His mouth was dry and he had difficulty speaking. His lips felt very large. "I hurt everywhere, Otilia. There is not one place in my body that I do not hurt." He asked, "Who put me here?"

"Your aunt and I."

He blushed at the knowledge that she had seen his body. "What is wrong with my back?" he asked.

"Welts—such as those made by a whip. He whipped you, Heraclio? He dared?"

"With him it is not a question of daring. Yes, I remember now he whipped me. With that Goddamned quirt of his he whipped me."

"There are welts on your face, too," she said.

He thought, That was the first one. That was the one which made me lose fear. He touched his face and on his left cheek,

46

running from his mouth to the ear, were three ridges. And his hand moved so his fingers touched the ear and he withdrew it quickly, the sudden pain was so sharp.

"The ear is blue," she said, then she began to cry. "Oh Goddamn him! Goddamn him!" she sobbed.

"They will hear you," he said.

"I do not care!" But she stopped. "I must tell them you are awake," she said, "but first I must know something. You broke the horse, we know—but were you broken?"

Her look was so intense that Heraclio was disturbed that this should mean so much to her. "No," he said. "Teodoro did not break me. I know he is my master. But he also taught me I need not fear. For that I should thank him, but he did not break me. So you see, he will never really be my master."

"I am glad," she said. "I am so happy this is the way it is. Because you are different. They are so dominated by him, your brothers—my own man, Concepción, walks in his shadow, and yet with them it is not a matter of being broken like an animal, because it is their way of life and they have always been this way. Since your father died, Teodoro is the father in this family. With you it is different, do not ask me why and do not ask me how I know. I simply know it."

"You are right, I guess," said Heraclio. "Because this afternoon I would have died from Teodoro's whippings—gladly, rather than bow down to him."

"Why did you do it, then?"

He was embarrassed again, then looked into her eyes. "Because the Goddamn horse made me piss in my pants and I became angry."

She laughed then for the first time, then sobered quickly. A sudden thought made her ask in fear, "You said you would have died—why? Is it sometimes so important, do you think, that one should die?"

"I do not know why," he said, "because I do not know, except that today it was important to me that I die."

His body was wet with suet which had been applied to his bruises, and the room seemed filled with the rank odor of the grease. He felt squishy between his legs and he had reason to be embarrassed again in her presence. "Otilia," he said. "I will never

47

be angry again when you criticize my family. I am alone now. I do not have a family."

"You cannot say that," she said.

"Yes, I can say it. That is why I do not hurt inside. All my pain is what you saw on my body, for I left my family in that corral. I am not quite, but almost thirteen years old, and I know this. I remain here only because no one can teach me to ride like the Ineses can. And if I knew how to go about it, I think I would even change my name."

It was the stubbornness of a child, she knew, yet she was frightened. "It is not good that you should talk this way, Heraclio," she said. And she crossed herself, for it was blasphemy. "Do you reject my husband also?"

"Yes, Concho especially. Juan and Elías did not surprise me. But your man did when he allowed Teodoro to do what he did with me. I would not have allowed it to happen to him. I would have sooner killed my oldest brother, who is now my father, then have allowed him to do such a thing. They saw it all. They watched it happen, my brothers did. Why should I love them. And this is the strange thing, I thought it was all because of the Goddamn horse and it was not. It was not because of the horse at all and in the end I loved the horse and I lost all my love for my brothers. And a strange thing happened there in that corral. I saw again my father die. I saw again Concho ride the horse that made us orphans, and I knew that Concho's ride was not important, and that my father died for a very unimportant thing."

She cried silently and refused to listen to more of this. "I must tell them you are awake," she said, and moved to the door.

"Only one thing more, Otilia. I must tell you this."

She stopped at the entrance.

"I do love you, you know."

She ran from the room.

In the evening his brothers came and made him get out of bed. They were almost solicitous about it and he agreed because he must, but also because he understood that if he did not a stiffness would set in which would keep him in bed for days. He was barely able to walk and he could not sit, his buttocks were so sore from the hard back of the animal. He did not talk much to his brothers although they talked to him, and they seemed pleased that he

48

passed a test of courage, and they made jokes about his sore ass. The next day he was given a day of rest, and that day he made a vow that he would never cry again and another that he would become the best horseman in la Flor, which meant that he would be superior to his brothers.

And on the following day he was on his horse again, this time without the hackamore, and he did not believe anything could cause so much pain as the spine of a horse. He held onto the mane with one hand and held his hat in the other, in the manner he had once seen so long ago, and he knew that he could never change his name because again he now remembered his father and he was atop a beast and he could not be thrown and his eyes were full of tears despite his protest.

And this day he put the hackamore back on and he rode his animal home.

And that same day, he went to the saddlemaker to pick out his saddle and he began to braid his quirt that night. He walked home with his saddle on his shoulder and as he walked he knew that people looked at him and suddenly he was an Inés, and he knew that this was preordained and could not fight it, but he could not love his brothers. He was one of them, but he would never love them again.

He was up early every morning and put the saddle on his horse and walked him around the small enclosure, then one day he mounted him with the saddle on, but only walked him a little. Then the bridle, and he had a fight to get it on the first time, but he won out and twice a day, now, he saddled and bridled the animal, and one day he walked it through the house and out the kitchen door in the manner of Inés men, and he rode down the street a little way.

And the next morning at three o'clock, Teodoro called him to go to work.

They went to Toribio and he broke four young mares that day and was thrown only twice. And that night they remained there, in the house of an uncle, and the next day he broke a stallion, his first full-grown horse, and he was enjoying the battle by now, so he took another one before they returned to la Flor.

For a time he worked the range around the hacienda proper. He learned to handle a rope well enough to down his own beast, and

49

soon learned to down one and mount it, all in a moment, get on it somehow before it got up, then straighten up and ride it. Sometimes he was thrown, but more often than not he stayed on, so he was becoming a jinete, the most difficult part of being a horseman.

Coming home in the evening, a few leagues from the house, his brothers showed him things he did not know. They played with each other after the long day's work was done, competing in equestrian skills, frolicking on horseback.

"Throw down your quirt, Heraclio," Elías would call, then threw himself at a full gallop toward him, leaning down from the saddle without slackening speed, and picking the quirt up with his hand.

Or as they passed near a herd of mares, Teodoro would say, "Cut me out a beast, boys," and Juan and Concepción would run a mare away from the others, and Teodoro would gallop behind the frightened animal, and as he neared it reached down low in the saddle until he held the tail in his hand and at the right moment hit his own horse with his spurs to get the last ounce of speed from him, and twisted the tail upward, flicking the mare over and leaving it lying on its back.

Although Heraclio could not do these things, he knew that someday he would and he was pleased and he was happy.

When he was more adept at the art of roping while on foot, and he could bring an animal down and mount it, he was taken far out onto the range, a trip of a day and part of a night. He had a blanket and a pouch with jerky and hardtack, and a rope. They all went with him, since they taught him together, never singly.

"Where are we going?" he asked Concepción.

"To get you another horse," he said. •

"But I have a good horse. I do not need another horse," said Heraclio.

"You never know when you need another horse," said Elías.

Heraclio remained quiet, satisfied that they thought he should have another horse.

They stopped for the evening meal and sat around together, for the night was chilly, but Teodoro spied a stray calf and would have meat, so Juan roped the calf and hog-tied it, and Concepción reached under between its hind legs for the sac and cut it off with one stroke. Heraclio was the only one who watched the steer slink off, lowing, its hind legs wide apart.

Juan had the fire going before Teodoro cut the tough membrane around the glands. They roasted them over the fire on the points of their knives, and Heraclio was given a small portion because he had never eaten them. He thought them delicious, but could not rid himself of the image of the castrated calf.

At midnight, they stopped to sleep, and at dawn they woke him and Teodoro said, "You have your reata, get yourself a horse."

"Are there horses here?" asked Heraclio.

"Certainly there are horses here. Animals in this area are rarely captured. They live and die out here naturally, with dignity."

Heraclio was still ignorant of what was happening. His brothers were all smiling. "We should wait until it gets a little lighter, no?" he asked.

"You wait," said Teodoro. "We are leaving now. Saddle your beast and put a lead rope on him. We shall take him with us."

Heraclio was angry as he realized his situation. "You are leaving me here, twenty, thirty kilometers from home, without a horse? Why did you not tell me? Did you fear I would be afraid? You make me do a man's work and yet you treat me like a child, and the rest of you stand there grinning like idiots. Where is the humor in all this? And what am I to eat?"

"You brought more food than we did," said Teodoro, and he was also angry that Heraclio should speak the way he did. "You will stay out here with your blanket and your rope and you will get yourself a horse or walk all the way to the hacienda. And if you walk, I shall be waiting for you. You will be amazed at what I can do with a full-sized whip!"

Heraclio saddled his horse quickly and considered making an attempt to escape, but his horse was not full grown yet, and he was not the rider they were, so he gave the horse to Juan and curled up in his blanket and was asleep before they left. It was his only way of showing his disdain.

When he woke up, he sat for a long while thinking. If he had known about this, he would have prepared himself somehow for the ordeal. He realized that he did not even have his knife with him, for he had abandoned the habit when he left David Contreras. Now he was frightened that he should encounter a wild animal and he jumped to his feet. He strongly considered making himself a sling, but of course he did not have the necessary materials, and so finally he decided he must find a horse. He had but a vague idea of how he was to go about doing this. The times he had roped a horse and mounted it had always been near the hacienda, and these animals, although they had never been ridden, were not so wild as to run away from a man on foot. They had seen men many times, and since men left them alone, they had no cause for fear.

He had seen droves of outlaw horses when he was a pastor. He remembered standing atop a mesilla, looking down into a small valley and sometimes saw a herd grazing, or else streak across the valley floor, and he knew that he should climb higher to see what was around him. He was not afraid of being unable to find his way home, but he must climb high also, to ascertain exactly where he was.

It took him two hours to reach a point which gave him an unobstructed view north and east, and he knew that they had traveled in a southerly direction at least for a time when they left la Flor. It was a magnificently clear day, almost midday, and there before him stood the neighboring tetillas, seemingly a few hundred yards away, but he knew that he could see for a very long distance, and his knowledge of the mountains told him that it would take him three days to walk to that hacienda. He was not discouraged, but he must be practical because he was alone. He did not have water and not much food. He looked further and found the area where he had tended his flocks in the old days, and decided that a good eight-hour walk would take him there. If he must walk, he would go there first and rest with the shepherds, perhaps he could find David, and get the water he would need. He had no fears about finding water now, but on his way home would be another thing. He climbed a little higher and he was atop a small plateau and went across to the other side and there were similar plateaus all around. Below and to his right was a wide ravine, somewhat greener than the area of sage and cactus he had been in, and he sat down here to wait.

Over the distant mountains to the west and south he knew lay the city of Fresnillo, and for a moment he considered going there instead and continuing on south, but only for a moment, for it was not yet time for him to leave. He must become a peerless cowman first, and he felt it in his heart and suddenly cursed that he should succumb to the family pride. In the city he would wait on tables, or become a stable boy, or in some way be a servant, and to be a house servant was undignified for an Inés, but suddenly he knew that to serve the whims of the capricious rich would be undignified to him whether he was an Inés or not and he was satisfied. Where he received his talent for patience he did not know, and did not care, and did not think about, else he would have been disturbed, for it was precisely because his people had been peasants for centuries, of the serving class although not involved with emptying chamber pots, that they would never be in a hurry. He sat for hours, watching the area below him, and did not move a muscle, and finally in the late afternoon he knew he must go down and find some water.

It was much greener down here than he had thought, and he stumbled across some chards which told him that at one time someone had lived here, but it must have been a very long time ago because there was no other evidence. He found a papaya tree, but it was too far north for it to bear fruit. He found cactus with edible pears, so he ate, and when he was finished, he took a leaf and broke pieces of it, being careful of the needles, and chewed so that he did not have to look for water. It was very cool and he sat and ate a piece of hardtack and rolled himself up in his blanket. He had not seen horse dung.

Sometime in the early morning hours he awoke. It was bitter cold, and he had to walk around, wrapped in his blanket, until the sun came up. When it was warm enough, he lay down again and slept. This time he opened his eyes and did not move a muscle for fully five minutes, for a great stallion stood grazing a few feet away from him. The horse moved away a few paces, turning away from him, and he was on his feet, reata in hand, giving a great cry to startle the animal into quick action, but his rope did not fall true and he had but one foreleg, and the horse stumbled momentarily but regained its balance, and disappeared into the trees of the lower end of the ravine. And Heraclio had lost his rope.

There was but one thing to do, and so he walked in the direction the horse had gone. He did not hurry, for he could never expect to overtake a running horse. In half an hour he found his reata. He tracked the horse a while longer, and it was not difficult, for the grass here was a few inches high and he knew that here he would find water and here also he would find his horse. The manantial was not far, and he went to it and placed his face into the cool, cool spring and drank deeply, then he was suddenly cold. He removed himself from the spring, then moved higher, and sat himself to wait. He dozed and wakened suddenly. He could see nothing, but a foreign sound had disturbed him, so he had his rope ready and sat up on one knee. They came in then, singly at first, and then in twos and threes until he counted twenty in all, and at the end he recognized his horse, and he waited again patiently, although he could have had another, smaller one at any given moment. He did not want a mare, for he was not certain the stallion would attack him if he attempted this, so he waited for twenty minutes, scarcely breathing, until the stallion's suspicious nature was reassured, and it placed itself in a position where it might be captured.

Then again he yelled fiercely and jumped into the center of the herd, and as the animals milled to find room to run, he had his chance and this time did not fail and as the stallion was still in mid-air, upside down, he was moving toward it, and as it slithered its hoofs in the wet grass, trying for a foothold so as to regain its feet, he was upon its back and the reata worked up the legs so the horse was hobbled tighter and it had to move away and it was a minute before it worked itself free, so Heraclio was ready.

Curiously the horse did not buck immediately, but ran in a true line for a time, and when it was in a clearing, and its footing was sure, it bucked still running, then stopped and went high in the air, and began the violent twistings, and it seemed that it would never stop, and Heraclio was exhilarated by the nobility of the animal and he was afraid, for who would help him if he went down and there was no cover here for him. And in a sudden glimpse of his life, he knew he loved his brothers as much as he hated them, for without them there could never be this, and this was the epitome, he knew. This was what made a man and he would be a man when he dominated this animal and he was thirteen years old.

He grasped the mane with the left hand and waved his hat around, and his legs were so tight around the huge sides that his scrotum ached, and when the horse stopped bucking for a moment, he hit him on the side of his great head with the hat and yelled, "Again, horse! Again!" He wanted him to spend himself further. And finally it was over and they walked back and the horse did not buck another time.

Heraclio reached down to pick up his rope, and it was the first time he had ever done this, to reach down from the side of an animal, even though the horse was standing still. And he was extremely wary, but the horse did not move, and then he went over and picked up his blanket and pouch and started for home. After a while he worked his blanket under him and then fashioned a hackamore of sorts out of his reata. It was just a loop around the jaws with an end extending on either side of the head, like reins. They moved almost a mile before he was able to get it on the horse and then the horse bucked again and he was in trouble, for the blanket hindered him, but the horse stopped bucking as suddenly as it had begun, and they went on in a gentle lope and suddenly they were cantering, and then for a while, Heraclio let it gallop.

IV

THAT FIRST YEAR Heraclio did not work on the range every day because he was still very young. Two or three days a week, when there was range work to be done near the hacienda, he went up at sunup and returned at dusk. Sometimes he did not work for a fortnight, and then again he was sometimes taken to Toribio or Peñuelas for a week at a time. His brothers allowed him to learn slowly, now that they were satisfied he would be a horseman. When he did not work, he went out to the range alone, to practice with the reata, and he sometimes worked for hours perfecting an approach and throw.

On the hacienda, he spent his time seeing all there was to be seen. He had never been abroad much, and aside from the little street on which his house stood, he had not investigated the settlement at all. Now he walked through every street which lay spokelike on one side of the Big House, always ending at the main gate. Every street led to the chapel and safety. Every road led to the cemetery.

He was thirteen years old and he had not seen any of this. He did not know anyone near his age, except, of course, the shepherds in the hills. Now he saw boys walking out into the prairie with the milch cows, there to watch them all day, keeping them away from the crops. The fieldworkers he did not see, because they went out with their oxen before daybreak and returned after dark.

He was amazed at what a solitary life he had led. Even as a little boy, he had rarely been allowed to play outdoors. Other children played in the loose dust of the street, or played at the edge of the settlement where the range began. They were dirty and had runny noses, and Heraclio, because he was an Inés, could never be dirty and could never have a runny nose. Somehow, he could not help but feel a pride in all this—that he had been a full-fledged pastor, that he was a jinete, not accomplished, but certainly adequate for the time being, and that he was an Inés. And this was the strange part, that it was a fine feeling to be an Inés. Yet he wondered how he could feel he was different from the people he saw, when they were in fact the same; they all served the patrón. Although he was incapable of thinking this out fully, he sensed that his pride was not from serving don Aurelio. Yet he felt proud, and he felt superior.

He talked to people, usually women, because at this time of day the men were in the field or on the range, and they all knew who he was, and he was taken into houses where cheese and meat and sometimes jocoque were set before him and he ate with hot tortillas as they were made. He found relatives he did not know existed. His mother's cousins who did not count because they were not Ineses. He learned that to the west, about ten miles, at the railroad stop of Cañitas, there were more of his mother's people, who lived there in freedom although the village was on hacienda property. And it was in this way, too, that he discovered that there were other people named Inés and related, some closely, but not of the direct line of his father. These men tilled the soil, were taciturn and unresponsive, proud in their own way, but the women welcomed him with open arms and in the manner of women remembered every connection, every date important to

56

the family, and filled him with tales of the history of the Inés clan.

His mother's people were simple folk, and they were, at least on the hacienda, sheepherders every one. Heraclio knew that they were fierce, though gentle and unpresuming, for he remembered well the man of the hills. They were not armed, whereas his brothers usually carried sidearms, but they had always with them their slings, and here again Heraclio remembered the accuracy of the instrument, and knew, too, that a missile from a sling could be as deadly as a bullet. And his knowledge of the sling became as a common denominator, for he demonstrated his skill, and competed with them, and showed so well that they were pleased.

And it was also in this manner, moving around the hacienda, that he discovered Antonio Rivera. They had known each other years ago, although neither remembered this, for their fathers had been friends. Antonio's father had been a field peon, but Juan Inés had never been a pretentious man, and the two had enjoyed a warm friendship. When the two men visited each other, the two boys played together for a while, and Antonio's father had died a few weeks after Juan Inés was killed. But this had been long ago, and when the boys met again, it was as if they had never seen each other.

It was in the orchard that they met. Heraclio, finding himself near there, decided to get himself an apple, and walked between the rows so that he would be visible to the old warden. Peones had been shot and killed for poaching, and he wanted to be recognized, for the Ineses had the privilege of the orchard. He reached the apple grove and took an apple, then sensed movement and looked up into the tree. Barely three feet away, a brown face stared impassively at him.

"What are you doing here, boy?" he asked, not knowing why he uttered the question in this manner.

The other boy was catlike as he jumped down. He crouched and drew a knife. "Defend yourself!" he said.

"Put the knife away," said Heraclio.

Antonio looked at him warily. "I will not be flogged," he said. "I will die before I will be flogged."

"Who is to flog you, man? Where is my whip? I do not even carry a knife."

"I saw you coming," said Antonio, "and I hid in this tree, but it is my misfortune that you chose to find me. It is your misfortune also."

"You are ranting," said Heraclio. "What is it to me that you steal an apple?"

"You are a don."

And Heraclio realized that alongside Antonio, who wore white breeches and tattered huaraches, he must indeed look like a don. His hat was cocked low over his forehead, and he felt like gentry, so he must appear so.

"No," he said. "We are peones—I am Heraclio Inés."

"You are not a peon. You are horsemen and you are an Inés. They say that is the same as being a don."

"They err," said Heraclio. "When one is in bondage it matters not whether he empties pisspots or works with animals. So put that knife away, please. We are peones. It makes no difference how we serve don Aurelio."

"You are poaching too?"

"Call it that."

"We had better go, then," said Antonio, putting his knife away. "The old man is bound to find us soon and he will shoot." At that moment, there was a yell from the other side of the orchard, and they ran, zigzagging from tree to tree. They came out of the orchard and ran on a dry creek bed. They slowed down and talked as they walked, pausing occasionally to throw stones at a lizard sunning on a rock or at a ground squirrel as it scurried up the bank.

"I bet I could hit one if I had a sling," said Heraclio.

"How would you know about a sling?"

"I was a pastor for almost five years."

"I am a fieldworker," said Antonio, and was impressed that Heraclio had been a shepherd. "What is it like, in the hills?"

"It is not good, when you are there, but once you leave you wonder why you did not like it. Now it is different, for I have found a love for the horse, but when they brought me back, I would have given anything to return to my flock."

"I have always wanted to be a shepherd. I have not thought too much of the other because that is beyond my reach, but I have always felt that tending sheep would be much better than yoking

58

the oxen. Of course, this way I can be home with my mother every day and once a month, like today, I get a day off from my labor. But I have always thought of tending sheep."

Heraclio said, "Shepherds always think they would like to be field peones. Men like to be with their wives at night and boys like you and me like to be near their mothers. I have no mother."

"I have no father," said Antonio.

"I also have no father," said Heraclio. He was silent, then changed the subject, for he had never thought about being an orphan, and he was beginning to feel a slight sadness. "Do you ride?"

"Burros," said Antonio. "We are burro people." But he did not sound envious, nor did he seem bitter.

"I like you," said Heraclio. "I wish to be your friend."

"I like you also," said Antonio, "because you had no fear when I challenged you."

"You are not afraid also," said Heraclio. "What is so strange about courage?"

"I have never known anyone else who had no fear at all, even grown-up people."

"I have known fear very strongly," said Heraclio.

"Then perhaps you are braver than I am because I have never known it."

And it was so. Heraclio discovered as the days went by that Antonio was indeed fearless. He took him riding after a time, and let him use his spare horse, which was the colt, and in the moonlight he showed him how to do some of the things he had been taught. Antonio showed a proficiency for equestrianship, but there was something lacking in his spirit. To revive his interest one day, Heraclio decided to let him break a horse. They had fallen into the habit of riding every evening, and Antonio was content to gallop in the moonlight and perhaps merge with a herd. They were out on such a night when Heraclio said:

"I will down a mare, Antonio, near your feet, and you jump upon its back quickly, before it has an opportunity to stand."

"Very well," said Antonio without hesitation. And Heraclio coached him in everything he should do, then ran an animal near and dropped it as he said he would. Antonio, who was extremely nimble, was atop it in an instant, and the mare regained its feet and in one or two jumps sent Antonio to the ground with such force that the wind was knocked out of him. He sat up groaning and Heraclio sat his horse nearby laughing at his friend. Antonio laughed with him and as he got to his feet, suddenly cursed.

"I believe I landed on fresh horseshit!" he said, wiping particles which still clung to his face. Yet he could not resist laughing along with his friend. "Heraclio," he said, "for our friendship and if that is not enough, for the memory of your mother who is now a saint, please rope me another one."

And once again Antonio was catapulted head over heels from the animal, and it was painful, for there were large rocks here. He sat on the ground with his arms on his knees and his face on his arms, and said seriously yet unquestionably in jest, "I shall return to my oxen, and plow furrow after furrow into the distance. And I shall instruct my children to do the same after me. I shall say, 'I once was a horseman, yes, believe me it is true, and all the glamour you see is but an illusion. Be kind to your burros, my children, and care for your oxen, for this is the good life.' I have finished, Heraclio."

Heraclio laughed again. "Come, my friend. I shall get for you another."

"No more."

"Would you have it said that you gave up?"

"Certainly. It is no disgrace to give up, Heraclio. You may count the stars in heaven and grow tired and give up and not feel one bit ashamed. Or you might try to pick up an animal and hold it above your head, and yet give up, for it is a futile thought. You do not give up, you simply learn that you cannot do it, that is if you are dumb enough to have thought you could do it."

"You are not afraid," said Heraclio, with fear in his heart that this might be so.

"No, Heraclio. You should know I am not afraid. It is only that I prove nothing by breaking my bones on these rocks. I am simply proving that a horse is stronger and can knock me down. Why should he not be, he is so much bigger than I am. And then the accuracy of the beast, Heraclio. Consider that. He left a pile of dung there and then threw me right into it."

Heraclio laughed but was disappointed. He had felt that any-

60

one if given a chance would feel what he felt, what he knew his brothers felt when battling a horse. "I am sorry," he said. "And I am confused because you feel nothing."

"I feel nothing except a soreness from hitting the ground."

"Because I feel. Sometimes believe me, Antonio, I feel as if the blood of the beast comes through my crotch and mixes with my blood. That is how I feel. Maybe my brothers are right about it being in the family. I do not know but I am sorry you do not feel the same way."

"I do not feel too much anyway," said Antonio, "and do not be sad because of it. I feel love for my mother and I feel love for you, so I do feel something."

When he was fourteen years old, Heraclio was on the range every day. He performed the work of a grown man and was paid his fifteen pesos every month for his labors. It had been impossible for him to convince Teodoro, who was now a caporal, that David should be given an opportunity to become a cowhand, yet, oddly, Teodoro had immediately agreed when he spoke up for Antonio.

"But why?" he asked his older brother. "If you denied my wish about David, you so quickly consented about Antonio."

Teodoro had reason and logic for every decision. "His mother is a witch and he is by tradition a shepherd." He refused to even mention David's name.

"But Antonio is by tradition a field peon, what is the difference?" asked Heraclio. He would not accept the witchcraft part of Teodoro's answer.

Teodoro was patient for a moment and said, "Antonio's father was our father's friend. It is for this that I do what I do. And also, because he is not a bastard. We know who his father was."

And Heraclio was angry. "We know who David's father is also."

In a tone of dismissal, Teodoro said, "I do not know whose son he is, except that he is from the promiscuous witch." David had been right, and Heraclio accepted defeat. It was difficult and a disappointment, but David made it less difficult by being bitter and disagreeable every time they met.

V

ONE DAY, DURING HIS FIFTEENTH YEAR, Heraclio and Antonio Rivera rode in to la Flor from Peñuelas. He had a worn saddle cinch and they stopped at the saddlemaker's to have it repaired before going home. They were there for an hour or more, talking to the old artisan as he worked.

"I am sorry to come to you at this hour," said Heraclio politely, "but I must fix this now or fall on my head when I rope a steer."

"Do not be troubled," said the old man. He was in his eighties, extremely dark, a full-blooded Maya from Yucatán who in his youth had succumbed to a wanderlust which curiously left him when he reached this far north. "I was waiting here anyway. For the diligence," he added.

A coach traveled twice a month from the city of Fresnillo to the town of Río Grande, stopping only at the large haciendas.

"You are expecting someone, don Guadalupe?" asked Heraclio. He was not being inquisitive, not even curious, but merely courteous to an older person.

"A great-granddaughter," answered the old man. "She is coming in from a convent in Zacatecas. I have not seen her in over a year and am overjoyed that she will now be here always."

"She was to have been a nun," said Antonio.

"No, no. She is yet but a child. Did I say nunnery? No, a convent it was. An orphan's convent, for she is only now approaching her twelfth year."

"She is an orphan, then," said Heraclio.

"Not in the true sense," said the old man. "She has a father. You know him, Antonio Ortiz, the personal coachman for the Becerras. And she has her poor old great-grandfather, not altogether poor, but not a peon, who may be old and yet not feeble, to look after her, but she will reside in the Big House. The father is a good man, an excellent coachman, but an imbiber of strong drink. He cannot keep her, although he is not a woman's man, I am thankful for that. He does have one woman, in Río Grande, and a young family by her. You can see that it would not be a good life for Marcelina to be with her father." He worked skillfully as he spoke. He rambled on and Heraclio and Antonio must listen. "A great beauty, too, I can tell you, this woman of his in Río Grande. And I should not be surprised, for my granddaughter, the girl's mother, was a lovely woman. It is one woman at a time for Antonio Ortiz, but always the most beautiful one. He has that way, I can say that much for him. You know him, of course?"

"Of course, don Guadalupe," said Heraclio. But in his mind he could not imagine the dandified coachman as a lover. He was a good servant, impeccable, courteous, and he was a drinker, everyone knew that, but as a conqueror of women's hearts, he could not imagine this. For Antonio Ortiz was but a house servant, and although his position as coachman was one of prestige with most people, a male house servant was still the lowest of the low. One must have dignity to be a full man, and, to Heraclio, Antonio Ortiz did not have dignity.

"The diligence should be here soon and here is your cinch," said the old man.

Heraclio saddled his horse and led him by the reins as he walked with the old man to the main gate. Antonio followed them on his horse. The old man continued to talk as they walked.

"She will be in the Big House," still talking about the great-granddaughter, "because don Aurelio has set one wing aside for a convent of sorts for the children of the landless gentry. All Spanish girls, of course, but Marcelina will also be there because her father is esteemed by the patrón. In a way it is an honor, I suppose, but I am not taken in by all this, because to me, and I have lived many years, a patrón is still a patrón. And we are all vassals."

"Yes, sir," said Heraclio.

"There are to be two nuns also. To teach them things, I suppose."

The coach arrived then and Heraclio said good-by to the old man and mounted his animal. He sat his horse next to Antonio and watched the coach come to a stop. A young girl, quite small and seemingly very thin, ran to the old man and embraced him. She looked once at Heraclio, then averted her face quickly. The old man took her bag and then held her arm as he led her away.

Bag after bag and a huge trunk were taken from the top of the

63

coach by peones. They quickly carried the luggage through the gate and into the house. A young man about Heraclio's age helped a young girl out of the vehicle.

Heraclio stood on his stirrups and placed a hand on his friend's shoulder. "Look," he said. "Look at the ankle on the patroncita."

"How good," said Antonio. They watched as she picked her skirts high and placed a foot on the ground. The calf, well formed, as well as the ankle, was visible for a moment. "She has grown," said Antonio. "I remember her well."

"I have never seen either of them in my entire life," said Heraclio. "Although, of course, I know very well who they are."

Carmen Becerra spoke to her brother. "There is yet one more bag inside. See that someone gets it, will you, Crispín—and my papá has not even come to greet us."

"My father is now having his dinner, I am sure, and will not be disturbed. And it is your fault for carrying so much equipment."

"It is not equipment, they are my dresses."

"And for what do you want dresses out in this desert?" But he looked around for someone who would carry the last piece of baggage. There were no house servants nearby and so he looked over to Heraclio and said:

"You, boy! Get off your horse and take a bag inside for the señorita."

"Take the bag yourself, don Crispín," said Heraclio. "You are as big a boy as I am."

"How insolent!" exclaimed Carmen, and looked at Heraclio for the first time.

"What are you called?" asked Crispín, his face red in sudden anger.

"Heraclio Inés, but certainly not to serve you."

"I am ordering you again to dismount and help my sister or . . ."

"Or you will have me flogged?" said Heraclio, and laughed. He touched his horse lightly and walked it past the couple and looked down at her face as he passed by. "Bring yourself," he said to Antonio.

"One does not look at the patrón's daughter like that," said Antonio as they moved down the street. "And why did you refuse

64

to do her a favor, for she is a lovely thing even though it is a mortal sin for peones like us to look at her with that in mind."

"Because she did not ask me," said Heraclio. "And I did not like the fellow's manner." He suddenly felt like showing off and said, "I will race you to the end of the street."

"No," said Antonio. "You always win."

Behind them the coach was gone and a house servant came out for the bag. Inside the house Crispín asked his father, "Who is this boy Heraclio Inés?"

"My godson," answered don Aurelio. "He is the son of a devoted servant who is now dead. Why do you ask?"

"For no reason," said Crispín. "I just met him by the zaguán."

"He cuts a fine figure, no?" asked his father.

"I do not know. I saw him but casually."

"There *is* a reason," said Carmen, "and he is fine-looking, but he is insolent."

Her mother spoke up. "What is this? What is this? The peon was insolent to you, Carmencita?"

"Not to me, to Crispín."

"Keep silent!" said her brother.

"He *was* insolent, and you know it!" she said. "And he called you *don* Crispín with such sarcasm."

"It is better that you have a talk with this boy," the patrona said to her husband. "His brothers are good servants, but you have had reports about him before, Aurelio. A peon should not have an attitude, as my father used to say."

Don Aurelio laughed. "It is not a serious thing, Gertrudes. The boy is Crispín's own age and they will see much of each other all summer, and I will wager they will become good friends."

"Why do you refuse to have a talk with him?" asked his wife.

"Because I do not think it necessary and because I like the boy. And in spite of what your father used to say, I like to see spirit in a peon or two." His tone changed suddenly and he said, "Now you must forget the subject just as you are forgetting your place."

"Yes, Aurelio," she said.

He stepped into the reception salon of the Big House. Don Aurelio came to meet him and led him to the far end of the room.

65

At one side, Carmen talked animatedly about the capital, answering her mother's questions about relations and acquaintances in the city. Across from them, Crispín sat with one leg thrown over the arm of his chair. Heraclio wore spurs and although they were turned up they jingled pleasantly on the thick carpeting as he walked.

"Buenos días, Heraclio," said doña Gertrudes.

"Buenos días, madrina," he answered. She looked sharply at him, angry that he had called her *godmother*. He stood before them, holding his hat in front of him in the manner of a peon waiting for his master's orders. He said to don Aurelio, "You wished to see me, patrón?" in the humble inflection of speech of the peasant. But there was not a trace of humility in his bearing. He was not yet full grown and was already taller than the men around him. He stood, legs slightly apart; his trousers of soft leather, brown, clung to his thighs and buttocks. He was not thin waisted, yet he gave that impression because his hips were small and he was already thick through his shoulders and arms. He was clean shaven and square jawed. His eyes were gray and his hair was black and curled thickly. He had a deep tan, and this was the only thing that seemed Indian about him.

"You are very handsome," said Carmen impudently, with a half smile on her face. "Even though you are rude."

Now it was her turn to receive a sharp look from her mother.

"It is you who are being rude now," said Crispín.

"You remember my children?" said don Aurelio.

"Not really," said Heraclio. "Last night was the first time I have seen them as far as I know. I was in the hills tending sheep for so many years and before that I was quite young, so if I saw them, I would not know."

Carmen spoke again, the smile on her face now full. "You need not impress us with details as to the extent of your servility. We know you are not servile."

"Carmen!" said her father in reproof, yet somehow softly. "Will you have a glass of jerez, Heraclio? I have just this moment decided to give Crispín his first drink, and it is fitting that as your godfather, I should do the same for you."

"Thank you," said Heraclio.

Carmen looked at the two youths and at her father. "You are

66

so naïve, Papá. But then, perhaps Crispín and Heraclio can become compadres over the *first* drink. A christening! A christening!" and she clapped her hands.

Doña Gertrudes smiled. A gentlewoman could always put a peon in his place. She placed a restraining hand on her daughter's arm, however, when don Aurelio, obviously displeased, said:

"If you do not practice more control on your daughter then I shall be forced to do so myself, and I do not have a gentle hand. This is what comes from sending her among the sophisticates in México. In the capital it is nothing but bad manners and lack of respect for elders and guests. Forgive the child, Heraclio."

"It is nothing."

A mozo brought a decanter and glasses. The sherry was cool and pleasing, but both Crispín and Heraclio drank it at one drink, while don Aurelio was savoring his first sip. He frowned. "It is because you do not know how to drink," he said, really explaining to himself.

Heraclio and Crispín laughed silently to each other and at that moment they were friends.

"I asked you here, Heraclio, to ask a favor of you," said don Aurelio.

"You have but to command, sir," said Heraclio.

The landowner misunderstood and was angry. "Stop it! I have been indulgent with you because your attitude amused me. But Carmen was right, although she had no right to say it, you *are* rude."

"Forgive me, but I said that with sincerity."

"If you did that, then you should forgive me, but frankly, Heraclio, it pains me to discover bitterness in you because there is no reason for it." Heraclio sat down.

"I want you," continued don Aurelio, "to teach my children to ride. Crispín will someday own all of what is la Flor. He has never been on a horse as far as I know, and it is time he learned. They will be here for the summer and so you can begin today."

"It will be my pleasure," said Heraclio.

"You can stay around here all the time instead of on the range, and if you wish, we can even fix a room for you here in the Big House."

Carmen felt safe after a moment of silence. "He would rather be with the cattle, Papá—or with his sheep. But I would be very happy to receive lessons from him."

Doña Gertrudes did not need a glance from her husband. To tease and put the boy in his place was one thing, but this was outrageous flirting, and although her husband had missed it, she was shocked by the double-entendre. She took her daughter from the room, for it was time to have a talk with her. She must tell her that arrangements were already being made for her marriage and that she should conduct herself in the manner of one who would soon be betrothed. Time had passed so quickly that they had not realized that Carmen was now almost sixteen.

"Well, then, it is settled," said don Aurelio. "You two have another glass of wine, and then go on about your business. Excuse me, Heraclio, and thank you." He left the two boys in the room.

"Shall we go to the stables?" asked Heraclio.

"No. Let us wait for my sister. She will come down after my mother's lecture, but do not expect her to be crestfallen or weepy. She is not that way. Does she shock you?"

"No," said Heraclio truthfully. "She amuses me because she is such a child."

Crispín laughed as if this was the most humorous thing he had ever heard. "Do not let her hear you say that."

"Well," said Heraclio, "it is true."

And Crispín suddenly realized that it *was* true, and he said, "You are probably, in your own way, much more worldly than we are."

Heraclio smiled, "Well, this is not the first drink I have ever had, and as a matter of fact . . ." He gestured toward the decanter.

"Of course," said Crispín, "what was I thinking of? But this is not drink. This is sweet and perhaps it can knock you silly, but it is not drink. Just a minute."

He returned with a bottle of tequila, and he filled the glasses and took the bottle back to the closet. "Have you ever had this?" he asked.

"Not from a glass," said Heraclio. "Salud."

"I have forgotten that of yesterday," said Crispín.

"It was my fault entirely, I assure you. I should not have made such a great thing of it."

68

"No, it is I who am to blame. I am supposed to have all the graces such as tact and consideration and things like that."

"I forgot," said Heraclio, "you were born with it, were you not?"

They both laughed at this.

It happened that Crispín had some experience with horses. In the capital, his classmates often took him to the stables near Chapultepec or to ranches not far from the city, where they sometimes competed at feats of horsemanship. Some of these youths belonged to the Society of Charros. They met every Sunday to demonstrate their skill and made up for their lack of talent by the quality of their horses. They were dilettantes, but they were adequate horsemen, and it was with these people that Crispín learned to handle a horse as well as his station required of him.

Over the glass of tequila that first day, he told Heraclio, "I can get along on a horse and you need not be troubled with teaching me. Give the lessons to my sister."

And thus it was that Heraclio and Carmen went out to different sections of the hacienda every morning after breakfast. Once, he took Crispín with him to Peñuelas, and Crispín, who had spent most of his life in the city, was amazed, seeing for the first time the work that was done on his hacienda by his people. "It will ruin forever the excitement from the charreadas in the capital for me," he told Heraclio. Then he said, "Heraclio, if I could take you to México for even one afternoon, we would break every dandy at the club. You would perform and I would wager with them, and oh, how they love to wager on their meager skills. We would simply take their money and their property. One afternoon, Heraclio, that is all I ask."

"You are crazy," said Heraclio. "I have no wish to go to México." But he was pleased, and he lied, for every peon wished to see the capital someday.

Most mornings, however, he rode with Carmen, and at first they almost had a falling out because she refused to ride sidesaddle.

He was mocking and said, "It is not merely that you are a woman and it is undignified for a woman to ride astride a horse like a man, but you are a lady, a Spanish lady, and your subjects would surely suffer to see your legs open that way to the back of a gross beast."

She was angry, yet would not admit that he was uttering indecencies. "You will saddle me a horse, Heraclio Inés, right this moment you will saddle me a horse!"

"Your chair is ready, señorita." He made a leg awkwardly.

"Not that one, imbecile! A real saddle!"

Heraclio was enjoying himself and so allowed her the liberty of calling him a name. "I shall ask your father's permission to change saddles," he said, not quite smiling.

She was furious. "I order you to get me a regular saddle!" She almost screamed, and the game was suddenly over for Heraclio, and he said quietly:

"You will learn that I cannot be ordered. And now climb on the horse with or without my help—or go back into the house and practice manners with your mother. She needs some too." He left her in the pasture with the horse and walked away.

And that evening a mozo came from the Big House and said, "The señorita, María del Carmen, wishes that you return tomorrow morning to resume the riding lessons."

Heraclio smiled and told the servant that he would be there.

Two weeks later he said to her, "Carmen," by now he called her by her name when they were alone, "I am going to grant your request. Tomorrow I will let you ride like a man."

"What if my father should discover that I am doing that? It would go badly for you, and that is what you were afraid of, was it not?"

"It would be unpleasant, but not bad," said Heraclio. "No. I am not afraid. I decided to do it the moment you asked me, but I wanted you to learn to ride like a lady because of your station in life. And you will keep riding sidesaddle. It is only on occasion that I will allow you to ride the other way."

The two weeks they had been together had been pleasant. Carmen had listened and learned quickly, was civil, yet she maintained a superior attitude, almost haughty. He was not bothered by this because she did not directly insult him, and he was quietly amused by her behavior.

She continually talked to him about the capital, and the fiestas, and of her fine friends who lived there. "And there is Paquito

70

Paz," she would say. "He is tall and slim, and very handsome. He is such a fine dancer and dresses only in the latest style from Spain. He does everything so well and on Sundays he is a charro."

"I have heard of these Sunday cowboys," he said. "Crispín has told me and I laugh."

"You have no right to laugh," she said, "at people who are superior to you. These are gentlemen I am talking about. They have people like you there just to groom and saddle their animals."

Heraclio was incredulous. "You mean they do not saddle their own horses. They do not break them, train them, groom them?"

"Of course not. That is no task for gentlemen."

"They are not even men," said Heraclio. "What a most pitiful lack of balls."

She colored and said angrily, "And they, at the very least, know how to speak to a lady."

"I have never been around a lady," he said.

The following day she saddled her own horse. Heraclio had long ago dismissed the groom, since he always checked to see that everything was in order before he permitted her to mount anyway.

"You will saddle your horse and soil your hands for once," he said, expecting her to argue. But she surprised him by saying:

"Very well, Heraclio."

From the time he first began to ride with her, he had always touched her, always casually and lightly. He took her arm when helping her mount, put his own arm around her waist for a step or two when she dismounted, held her hand longer than he should, and she was unaware that she was being seduced. Although she did not recognize it, his very nearness gave her pleasure, and she disclosed this fact to him once when she said angrily, attempting to shame him:

"At least in the city, all the boys I knew took a bath once in a while," and Heraclio, knowing that she was conscious of his very own odor, laughed. He did not know women, but he did know animals and was strongly aware of the erotic quality of smell.

Once they left the buildings in the distance, Heraclio took the saddle off her horse and left it on the fork of a tree. He gave her his mount and climbed on her barebacked animal. Now she realized that she could not break him with words and began to tease him in the manner of a woman. When they sat and rested on cool

71

grass beside a water hole, she took her combs from her hair and allowed it to cascade, golden to her waist. Or she might stumble a bit as he helped her, and brush against him for an instant. She wore always a riding skirt, and now she managed to sit so that a portion of her leg was exposed, or patrician-like she would sit straight, profiling, and her bosom would rise, full, and she knew what she had.

Heraclio was not unaffected, but he was not deceived. And she began to tease and play with him again. "It is too bad, Heraclio."

"What is too bad, mistress?"

"Oh, that you are handsome and yet it is your lot to be low-born and uneducated. To think that we might have married if it had been different."

"Yes," he said, seeming to agree with her. "You could have been born a peasant."

"How repugnant!"

He was becoming angry. "At least that way you would have had a bit of color to you. You are much too white to be attractive to a man."

She was content to have made him angry, since that was the most she could ever do to him. Now, to make him jealous, she said, "I suppose I shall make up my mind soon to marry Paquito Paz."

"You should," he said. "Then you could share your underwear with each other."

She controlled her own anger and said, "Are you not going to remove this saddle today?"

"No."

"Why? Is it vindictiveness because I spoke to you the way I did?"

He seemed very serious and said, "No. It is that if you ride too much like a man, you may injure yourself down there, below— you know, and no man will want you. Even Paquito Paz, the ox, will return you and the dowry to don Aurelio, and where would he be with a used daughter and no prospects of marriage. Why he would have to order a peon to save you from being an old maid, and of course a peon could not refuse."

She reddened and knew she should not put up with this, but

72

all she could do was to say that they should go back to the house. She would not ride with him again.

That night he was out until the early morning with Antonio, and when he came in to breakfast, late, she sat in the kitchen talking to the Inés women.

"Carmencita was out for a walk," said Timotea, "and stopped in to chat a little. But she refuses to take nourishment in this poor house."

He stood in the doorway and farted.

"Heraclio!" said Timotea and Rosa in unison.

Otilia laughed aloud. Carmen remained completely composed.

"We have taught you better manners than that," said his aunt. "Carmen is not only a guest, she is a Becerra. She is quality and she is delicate."

"Too delicate to do that herself, I suppose," said Otilia. Carmen looked at her and they stared into each other's face with immediate antipathy in that way peculiar to women.

"Heraclio works at being rude," said Carmen. "He thinks it a virtue to be impolite."

"Perhaps you would rather cure a stomach-ache, señorita," said Otilia.

Heraclio sat down across from Carmen. "You have broken your fast?" he asked. She shook her head. "Eat with me," he said.

They ate sweetbreads roasted over the fire, and the tortillas were hot in their mouths, and the chile was strong on the beans.

"Let us go," he said, and for a moment thought she would say she was not here for him, but she did not say a word and moved away from the table. She thanked the women and said good-by.

"Heraclio," called Otilia, and he turned, his hand on Carmen's arm above the elbow. "Watch out for that one," she told him. "She can be trouble for you."

Outside, Carmen said, "She is not very tactful, your champion."

"Otilia is simply honest," he said.

"I do not like her."

"That is because she is more beautiful than you are."

They walked in silence and Carmen went into the Big House while he got the horses. When she met him outside by the zaguán, her lips were redder than usual and there was a hint of color high up on her cheeks.

73

"What is that you have on your face?" he asked.

"Oh, you noticed?" She sounded too casual. "It is rouge, which most women of quality in México now use. Well, the young ones, at least. I smuggled this home—you will not tell on me?"

"No. I have seen it before—on whores, but they use much more of it than you do."

She seemed about to cry, and not in anger. "Do not speak to me in that way, Heraclio, I beg of you," she said, and for the first time since he had known her sounded like her natural self. He liked her and said:

"All right. I am sorry. This time I truly am sorry. And we will be friends?"

"We will always be friends," she said.

They climbed partly up the slope of a long hill. They looked out over the hacienda and there was nothing there but hills, and mesas, and sage, with an occasional cluster of trees. But she said, "It *is* very beautiful, Heraclio. And I am happy I find it so, because I believe I will always live here. Crispín has no inclination to become master here. I know. I do not know what he wants but I do know it is not this."

"He seems to love it too."

"And he does love it, but that is all, you will see. He will think back to it always, and imagine that he really lived here once, but he will not remain here."

They dismounted and she found herself to be suddenly filled with pleasure. She said, "Thank you for everything, Heraclio, my peon," and threw her arms around him and kissed his cheek.

Deeply conscious of her body, he misunderstood and thought she was toying with him again. Angrily, he threw her to the ground and fell upon her, forcing her mouth open with his own, feeling her teeth as she reluctantly accepted him. He leaned back then and undid the front of her dress and cupped her left breast, then gently pulled it free from the garment.

I must keep my legs closed! she thought. It was the only defense she could think of, to keep her legs closed tightly together. She was afraid, and yet she shuddered violently as Heraclio moved his head and ran his tongue around the nipple gently, then she felt it quicken as if to life as he took it in his mouth for an instant.

"You are heavy," she said softly, and he drew back and helped

74

her to her feet. She fixed her dress and allowed him to help her to her horse. She did not speak until they were near the settlement. "I cannot ride with you tomorrow because it is my father's birthday," she said.

"I know."

She placed a hand on his arm. "Please do not think that it is because of what happened. That will not happen again, of course, but it is not the reason. It is my father's birthday and I shall be busy."

"I know that."

"And thank you again, Heraclio. Now especially, for the kiss. I did not know. I tried to make you think I knew all there was to know and now you see I know very little."

"I am only sorry I frightened you, that is all," he said. "I am not sorry I kissed your breast, only that I frightened you."

She smiled. "I think it would be more horrible to never be frightened like that," she said.

Teodoro Inés had been a lonely man all his life. As the first-born, he had known parental affection and attention, then had seen it dissipate completely when the second son was born. He had been given tasks to do at a very early age, and then, soon, he married at a very early age, and so time found him with a wife and family even before his father died. He was a silent man, generally uncommunicative except, of course, when giving an order or a reprimand.

And yet this same Teodoro was the gayest man on the hacienda when drinking. He lost the inhibitions which kept him from being natural, and he became jocular and very brave. When Heraclio was yet a boy, the four older Inés brothers were the scourge of the central plateau. They would sometimes drink for three and four and five days at a time, and at that time no village or ranch within fifty miles was safe. During these drunken periods, they reached every degree of intoxication. They laughed, they cried, they sulked in self-pity, and then they brawled, and somewhere, sometime, they lost consciousness, singly or collectively.

But this life ended for Teodoro, and thus for his brothers, when his first son was born about the time Heraclio became a jinete. And it was really before that, because a few weeks before his wife's confinement, Teodoro, on impulse, made a vow through the priest during confession, to the Holy Child of Atoche, in which he promised to abstain completely from strong drink. He kept the vow and three weeks later his wife was delivered of a boy, and of course, he knew why. So now, he who had witnessed a miracle made it his mission in life to see that his entire family attended Rosary whenever possible, and that it followed the word of the Lord to the end.

It became worse, as the months went by, and he took to making novenas and then pilgrimages, and on his son's birthday he took his wife and older daughters, all in their bare feet, to the shrine of the Santo Niño de Atoche, which was some twenty kilometers into the mountains. He was loyal to his God as he was loyal to his patrón, and in his mind he somehow associated the two, since between them, they destroyed his every insecurity. And so, now, in the summer of 1909, on the day that don Aurelio completed the fifty-third year of his life, Teodoro gathered the brothers Inés, they who had once disturbed an entire village with their carousing, and declared that they would go to the chapel and give thanks that their patrón had survived another year.

"It is in the nature of a pilgrimage," he said to them, "although the chapel is but a thousand meters away. We shall go from here on our knees, to show the people of la Flor the glory of the patrón and of God!"

He left the room then to see his son, and Heraclio said, "Cannot anyone tell him that this is blasphemy?"

"Quiet," said Juan. "Nothing is blasphemy where the patrón is involved."

"I was there," said Elías, "yesterday, when Teodoro proposed this thing to don Aurelio. The old man said, 'It seems a drastic thing to do, Teodoro, this that you propose, and it is not necessary, I assure you,' but the vanity was exposed and he knew that he was pleased."

"Ah, knees," said Juan, in a rare attempt at humor, "I am sorry for you, the pair of you, but I can do nothing."

"If my father were alive he would kick him to death because of this," said Concepción.

Heraclio said, "Let us all simply refuse." And suddenly, they were all against him, for indeed here was blasphemy.

76

"You will do as we do," said Juan, "and you will keep your mouth tightly closed. You have not the liberty to criticize."

They confused him, these, his brothers, but he followed them down the street to the chapel. Teodoro and Juan were first, then Elías and Concepción, then Heraclio. The five brothers, Ineses all, heads bent low, hands clasped before them with thumbs crossed, in the attitude of penitents, painfully made their way up the narrow street, and the neighborhood was quiet at the spectacle. Along the houses, where men could not hide quickly enough so that they would not be seen seeing this, conversation ceased, and the silent men pawed the ground, embarrassed, and affected a natural pose which was more unnatural because it was a conscious thing. But at the far turn, before the entrance to the zaguán, a group of boys who were Heraclio's age stood and there was a definite murmur before they fell silent, and among them was Antonio Rivera, pained and suffering at his friend's indignity. Heraclio looked up then and saw Antonio's face, and stood up, dusted his trousers, and said:

"Bring yourself."

At the house he took his hat first, and then they saddled the animals. They rode into the sun, through the arable area and into the tall corn. They did not speak, and Antonio followed his friend until they had made a great circle and they were once again at the house.

"There is a spare mat in my room," he said. "You know that my house is yours."

"Thank you," said Heraclio. "I had hoped that you would offer it."

"Another thing—and I hope you do not grow angry that I should suggest it. Would you want me to come inside with you?"

"I understand and I am not angry, for you are thinking of me. I love you, but I could not stand by and see you do harm to one of my brothers—you know that. But I thank you sincerely, Antonio, and one day will repay your loyalty."

He left his horse in the street, dropping the reins so they fell to the ground, and the horse remained there rooted as if tied to a stake. He entered the house, not because he had reason for being there at this hour, but because while on his ride he had realized that he should not procrastinate now that the crisis he had

77

known would come was eminent. He was not nervous, not afraid; neither was he particularly indifferent about how he would stand up to Teodoro and his brothers. It was simply a thing which must be faced, and which he wanted to face, and because of the inevitability of the scene which was about to be enacted, he was not even curious as to the outcome.

Although most of the family was in the kitchen, all was quiet in the house. An air of foreboding lay thick around him, and in a far corner Elías, who strummed incompetently at the guitar, practiced fingering, and the sound of dissonant notes, quiet also, added to the weird feeling in the room. Teodoro was nowhere to be seen, but his presence was very much with them in the form of the horsewhip, neatly coiled, on the dining table.

And Heraclio laughed at the incongruity that Teodoro should now expose a sense for the dramatic.

He came into the room then from the side, his eyes very nearly closed, and with his first words as in a rage, face livid, lips almost curled back over his gums.

"Ungrateful wretch! And where did you take yourself?" he said and asked.

"A stroll, Teodoro." Heraclio's calm served to anger further the older brother.

"Where is your pride? Where is your sense of loyalty and where is your sense of gratification that you are privileged to serve the patrón who is your protector? Tell me that!"

"My pride?" asked Heraclio, and his voice seemed low in contrast to Teodoro's shouts. "Why, my pride is between my legs, and my loyalty is to my pride. And as for the privilege of serving the patrón, I give that to you, take it as well as his protection, for I serve him no longer."

"Serve him no longer! How can you say such a thing? To refuse to serve him whom you owe so much! He without whose grace you would not even exist?" He was in such wrath that he jumped up and down in his agitation.

Heraclio was suddenly also in a rage. "Just who in the hell do you think he is, God? Wake up, for Christ's sake! You are a man, and you work the range—a jinete, an Inés who dominates animals, and you think it is pride that makes you grovel in the dust to that man! You venerate the patrón who is not fit to clean your

78

boots! Our own father would not have gone that far, although it was he who taught you to serve don Aurelio, as his father before him taught him to serve, and as his father before him. We owe him nothing! Nothing, do you hear? Who is he? He sits up there in the Big House, or takes a turn on his blooded horse, or goes to México or to Spain to rest from his labors. Any fool can see it is all wrong.

"I repeat, I will not work for that man again! Our father died in his service. Is that not enough to give for this debt we seem to owe?"

Teodoro stood with his hands at his sides, his face a bloodless mask, and he shook uncontrollably. When he spoke, a spray of spittle gushed forth. "It was you who killed my father! Yes, just as you killed my mother you killed my father. He was showing off, for his little man, impressing a baby, and he died. And before that you committed matricide by the grotesqueness of your delivery! It was you and you would blame don Aurelio!"

Elías did not stop plucking on the guitar, but he looked up, and Concepción and Juan moved forward as if to speak, but tradition and duty were too strong, and they remained silent. But Heraclio would not be denied, and he said:

"You are insane, Teodoro! If I for a moment believed what you say, I would tear my own heart out. So that is the why of all that has passed—that is the reason for the hatred mingled with filial love. And now the atrocity you have perpetrated. You have dared question my father's motives and his judgment. You have dared accuse him of being an exhibitionist!" And he knew he had finally hurt Teodoro for there could be no blasphemy like this. This had been a slur on his father's manhood, and that is why the others would have spoken, had their laws been less strong.

And Teodoro cried in the center of the room and tore at his hair and screamed over and over again, "Forgive me, my father! Forgive me for desecrating your memory! Forgive me!" The last was a gasped out plea. He stopped suddenly, for the fact that his other brothers had not objected, made clear the fact that Heraclio had rebuked him. He was angry, and he was grieving, but now a calmness of purpose moved him to the horsewhip.

"You are not honoring me," he said. Heraclio's lack of loyalty and gratitude for the patrón did not matter now. "You have dared disobey my commands. Move out to the corral."

But as he moved with the whip in his hand, Heraclio stepped close and grasped it with his left hand, then hit his brother on the neck with the side of his fist, knocking him down on his face. He leaned down quickly and took Teodoro's gun, carefully keeping his eyes on the others, not knowing what they would attempt to do. They did not move, and Elías, seemingly unaffected, yet picked at the guitar.

Teodoro sat up, and Heraclio said, "I will say this one time only. You will never whip me again, any of you. From this day when you come to me with that idea in mind, come to kill, for I will surely kill you. I am finished with this life. I shall remain here for a time—as long as I wish because it is my home as well as yours. But from this day I do not work unless I have the urge for activity. You are my brothers and I will be treated like a brother, you are men, and I will be treated like a man; I refuse to remain an animal." He threw the gun on the table and walked out to his horse.

VI

THAT HERACLIO WAS ABLE TO HOLD FAST to his decision to stop working for the hacienda was unusual. It was only because his family was in a unique position with the landowner that he was able to exercise a prerogative which in theory belonged to every landless man in México. Peones were kept on the hacienda because of the debt at the tienda de raya, but they were told, and they knew that if this responsibility did not exist they were free to leave, or to live on the premises as they wished, for the forerunner of the vassal system was the system of the encomienda, created by Spain to keep order and to ensure maximum production in the colony. The encomienda was a protectorate, as the word implied, and a worthy Spaniard—usually one who had performed a service to the king, or a relative, or a bankrupt member of the court—was given an extensive area to protect. They owned the land and lived as lords, but the life and soul of every Indian within their domain was their responsibility. And the idea that this land belonged to the native, that he was not forced to work, was very strong. With the years, however, the peones were in bondage, and it was only through this tie and through loyalties such as the Inés clan had that the hacendado was able to keep his serfs.

In a situation such as the Ineses enjoyed, the bonds of debt were unnecessary, and it was rare when a man would rebel and leave his birthplace. But for Heraclio Inés it was different, and he had every legal right to do as he wished, and he had no moral responsibility in regard to service on the hacienda. Ordinarily also, the head of the family would have taken care that one or another of his sons who had the idea of escaping all this would fall back into line, but the patriarchal authority of Teodoro Inés had collapsed, and there was nothing anyone could do.

And thus it was at the age of sixteen, Heraclio Inés became a man of leisure. The evenings were spent with Antonio Rivera, either riding around the hacienda or at dances in Río Grande. His daylight hours were spent visiting Crispín or riding with Carmen. He did not talk much with his brothers, but then they had never been a very communicative clan—and yet, the family relationship at home was not particularly strained.

With Carmen his hours were very pleasant now that she behaved more naturally with him, and it was only on occasion that she showed signs of her contrary nature. And then one day she had the cooks prepare a lunch basket and they left to spend the day out in the hills. They rode toward the Rancho Grande, through acres of cornfields and came to a water hole in a hollow which had overflowed to form a large pond.

It was near lunchtime when they arrived, and she spread the food on the grassy bank and began to eat. He did not eat much, and lighted a cigarette.

"May I try that?" she asked.

He handed her the cigarette and put it to her mouth. She blew the smoke out slowly and he laughed. "You are supposed to swallow it," he said.

"I know. The women I have seen do this in the capital always try to swallow the smoke." She laughed also, and he was disappointed that she had not answered him angrily. "They choked," she said, still laughing.

"You try so hard to appear worldly," he said. "Why do you not stop trying to impress me with what you know?" She was hurt, knowing that he was disturbed by something, and yet she was determined to be good this day. "I stopped that long ago, Heraclio. You know that—and you will not get me to fight today, because I am enjoying myself too much. The day is so pretty, and the water looks so clear—although I suppose it is dirty, and the grass is so soft and green. Come, eat some more and be pleasant again."

He was almost surly and he realized it suddenly, not knowing why. It was a beautiful day, and the place where they sat was almost a meadow, and behind them, a hundred yards, the cornfields sprang up tall.

"Tell me," he said. "Have you known many men?"

She laughed this time. "No, silly. Are you jealous of a Spaniard?"

"Why should I be jealous?" he answered. "Especially of a gachupín? Do not be crazy."

But she sensed his feeling and did not laugh again. She placed a hand on his arm and said, "Forgive me, Heraclio. I should not tease you—at least not today. No, I have never known a man. A few times I have danced with boys who held me much too close, and believe me I did not enjoy it. I have known no man, and I am not ever again going to give the impression that I have. I realize it can be dangerous."

He sat quietly, almost morosely. She said again, "Eat, Heraclio. Do not allow the day to be wasted by a mood. We are friends— and I can think of no one else I would rather spend time with than you."

He turned to her then. "I am sorry, forgive me. I have allowed a great many things to break into my thoughts and ruin what should be a pleasant time."

She was pleased, and in her happiness threw her arms around him and kissed him beside the mouth. He allowed her weight to topple him over on his back, and when he kissed her she responded. Slowly, he turned over so they lay side by side, his left arm under her head. Her eyes were opened wide and she looked at him, searchingly, questioningly, as if she were seeing him for the first time. She had said that this would never happen again, and she had believed it, otherwise she would not have accompanied him so far alone, but at the moment it was such pleasure just to lie with him, everything around her was so quiet, and she reached with her free hand and touched his face lovingly, then pulled his mouth to hers once again.

They did not say a word and she helped him undress her, and then he, too, was naked, and she shivered although she was not cold. He played with her then, with her breasts, with her nipples, and he kept his bare leg between her own, pressing his thigh against the bony hardness under the softness of her pubis; and instinctively he knew when he must enter her, and they smelled each other strongly. He was atop her body and to her he seemed huge, and she uttered a cry of pain. He thought she objected and would have stopped, but she clasped him to her more strongly and brought her body up to meet his. Again they struggled to come together, and now she was in a frenzy, moving wildly under him, and it was as a task to him to accomplish this act, to do for her. Instinct against tradition told him he must please her, and he seemed detached and feared that he would be incapable, feared it with all his being that he would be unable to satisfy her desire and, therefore, he would be but half a man, but he remained firm and now so great he hurt, and suddenly she gave a loud cry as he entered her body and her scream was of joy despite the pain, and she shook in a spasm and it was all over for her even as he emptied into her.

She lay, breathing faintly, and he thought she was ill, but suddenly she gasped and took deep gulps of air, and turned to him again and held him close.

"Heraclio," she said. "After everything, my own Heraclio."

He kissed her lightly on the throat and felt a contentment he had never known. That he had been her first man had meant so much to him, he knew now. And he had a resurgence of desire, but his own soreness told him how she must feel, and that he must wait.

The seminal smell was strong around them and she said, "I must cleanse myself. And there is blood, also." He came up on one elbow watching her, marveling at how natural she could be, how proudly she walked, nude, with lovely legs, her buttocks rubbing soft, white, as she walked, and he knew she had no need to be comforted. She squatted like an Indian woman and washed herself, then, standing, she bent over, half facing him, to wash her legs, and her breasts fell sensually, elongated and full like fruit ripe from some tree, and the sun on the water reflected upward, striking her golden hair. And he knew this vision was one to be cherished, knew this was a sight few men ever had.

She returned to him, limping slightly. "You have given me a soreness," she said, smiling, teasing.

"I am sorry," he said. He stood up and came against her, and they kissed long standing there in the open meadow before they dressed. He brought the horses while she gathered the food. He tied the basket on her horse, then picked her up and placed her on his, and mounted. Holding her against him and leading the other horse, they turned in the direction of la Flor. They rode for a time, quietly, not speaking, only the occasional grunts of the animals and the hollow sound of hoofs audible. Each was still captive by the beauty of what had transpired, each afraid to destroy the magic, each in tune with the other's thoughts.

After a time, Heraclio was hungry and they stopped on the trail to eat. They kissed again before he set her off the horse, and they grew hot with desire, but they broke apart, and he let her down. They sat cross-legged as they ate, Heraclio ravenously, and they drank from a gourd.

"I thought you were not hungry," she said, and he was not angered by her teasing. "And you are in a much better mood than you were earlier, I wonder why." She was smiling.

He grinned self-consciously. "I suppose I was hungry and did not know it," he said.

She was so happy. Later she must think—later she must face herself about this thing she had just done, for although she seemed frivolous, she was in fact a serious, responsible girl, now a woman, and the act they had committed was not a simple unimportant prank of a schoolgirl. But now, she was happy and, she knew, very much in love with this peon who sat before her who smelled of the earth and of his horse and yet smelled of himself. He seemed almost swarthy near her, and his Indian blood was unmistakable, and yet the Spanish was also so strong in the shape of his head and face, in the curls of his hair, and even in the grayness of his eyes. And suddenly she must say it, she must impart to him the idea of why she had behaved like a bad woman and of why it had not really been an immoral thing.

"I love you, Heraclio." Seriously, looking straight into his eyes

84

giving the most simple explanation, and she knew somehow that this was enough, that she should not say more about it, for he understood.

"I love you also," he said, equally sober, satisfying her, easing her sense of impropriety.

She chewed thoughtfully for a time. "So you see," she said, munching, "I did not know anything after all."

He was pleased and suddenly remembered her movements, her gyrations, her abandonment, and felt a pang, a suspicion that she had been experienced.

"You are scowling again," she said. "I have said something wrong?"

Instantly he felt the truth and was safe. He decided he did not like these feelings.

"That is much better," she said. "You are very handsome when you scowl—but you look thirty years old or more. You also look handsome when you laugh, and I like that better." She spoke matter-of-factly, aware that she embarrassed him, but telling him something, not talking to inflate his ego. "They would eat you up in the capital, my charro. All those sophisticated women, pale and skinny, smoking and using rouge and now some even drink in the better places, of course—conversing with delicate young men who do not really seem too different from them, really, now I see in retrospect. They do not know. They simply do not know, and if I were to take you to México, and they should see a real man, they would swoon, I swear. If I should keep you from bathing for about a month, you would drive them crazy."

He laughed. "You and your brother are both insane. He would take me to México to teach the men a lesson and you would take me to México to teach the women a lesson. Am I some sort of freak, a phenomenon to be exhibited?"

"No, no, my love." She placed a hand on his arm, thinking she had angered him, but he smiled and she was reassured. "I would only let them see you and smell you, they who place so much importance on the ability to converse about the latest balls, and the latest music, and the latest books. Have you ever read a book, Heraclio?"

"Never in my life," he laughed. "Except the primer, of course."

"They are such a bore," she said. "All about the same people who read them. All about people like Paquito Paz and the society in the capital or the society in Spain. Weak young women who faint all over the place, and the highest point of emotion is to have a sweet-smelling boy whisper risqué things which are really not risqué to you or to hold your hand or for one to have a real good cry over another sweet-smelling boy. You know, the way I was when I first arrived this year. They are a funny lot, these people in the capital, they would turn their heads if they saw horseshit in the street, and yet they gain much pleasure in using the word in private."

"These are the people who rule us?" said Heraclio.

"I suppose. But not all the people who rule are like that."

"What do they do, these people like this Paquito Paz?"

"Oh, he has a commission in the army. All the sons of the better families are commissioned in the army. Crispín is a lieutenant, although he refused to accept it. They gave it to him anyway."

"And you will be like that someday—like those women you talk about?"

"Never. I will never return to that. I will go to México to visit some day, of that I am certain. But I shall never live there. This year I must go to the North American United States to a university in the state of Washingtón, who was the Miguel Hidalgo of the gringos. Crispín and I go together, but I go for but one year. After that I shall remain here. I love this earth," and she picked a handful of dirt and moved it through her fingers. "I am really of the land—I know, you think because I am Spanish I do not know of this, but I tell you, Heraclio, not only the Indian knows about the earth. In Spain there are many peones. You would not think so since every Spaniard you have ever seen seems a rich one. But there are almost as many peones in Spain as there are peones in México. I do not know about the other world, for I have only been to Spain and to England, but I assure you that in England, although they do not exist like us on haciendas, there are many poor people, much poorer than any peon on la Flor, and they too are peones. So you see, it is possible for us, the gachupines, to think about the land."

"I suppose so," said Heraclio. "I did not think you could talk so much." He teased her now. "Is this what will happen every time I love you? Will I have to pay for your favors by listening to all this gossip?"

"No, peon. I will pay for your favors by shutting up."

And they both laughed because they were content and because she had called herself a gachupina and had called him peon.

Always in the evening they managed to spend at least a few minutes together, either in the company of Crispín or in the presence of her father and mother. It was understood that Heraclio visited the Big House because don Aurelio was his godfather, and he talked and joked with Carmen because by tradition, as her father's godson, he was a brother to her. There was no suspicion on don Aurelio's part, but doña Gertrudes, with the intuition of a woman, never took her eyes from them when they were together.

She had told her daughter of the coming of Domingo Arguiú, a distant relative from Spain, who was of the best possible background, actually from an off branch of the royal family, but whose family in recent years had the misfortune of losing their wealth. He would come to the New World to again give the name Arguiú meaning by forming an alliance with the house of Becerra. Aurelio, after all, did not really have the proper background, for all his money and land, having descended from a Spanish soldier who after distinguishing himself in the wars against the Indians had been given this vast area of land which was now theirs. This man had not taken an Indian wife, but instead had sent to Spain for a sturdy peasant from Granada, and although through the centuries the bloodline had improved, for it could not become worse, doña Gertrudes' husband definitely did not come from quality. This, of course, explained his vulgar habits such as this one of allowing an arrogant peasant the freedom and liberty of his home. Domingo Arguiú, of course, would change all this, and with Crispín married to a girl of a good family, perhaps even of royal blood, for most of these good families were somehow losing their wealth, her two children would ensure the success of la Flor as one of the leading haciendas in México.

She watched the young boy and the girl, and she had apprehensions, but she shrugged them off, although she remained wary, for Domingo Arguiú would soon come, and when her daughter returned from school in the north, they would marry.

Crispín suspected a romance of sorts, but this amused rather than angered him, for it was a pleasure to see his sister, who had the independence of a man, under someone's dominance. Had he suspected an illicit relationship, there would have been a tragedy, for either he or Heraclio would die.

And it was a natural thing for Carmen and Heraclio to ride out on the range together, and they returned to their little lake time and again. Or they went out to where they had first kissed, although in spite of the fact that they had much more cover there, it was much too close to the settlement for safety. Once, when they were alone in the Big House, he went to her room, but that too was dangerous because the maids and house servants would surely find them out and expose them.

It became Carmen's habit now to try to make something of the future, for although Heraclio seemed content with the relationship as it existed, she was not, and, being honest and being the patrón's daughter and thus of the ruling class, she had the right and the courage to speak, unlike another woman in a similar situation who could not dare question her lover.

"What are you going to do with me, Heraclio Inés?" she asked, as they lay together after making love.

"Do with you?"

"About me—yes. What is going to become of us and our great love which is greater than all of México?"

"You will marry your gachupín," for she had told him of the arrangements being made. "You will marry him, and since Crispín may not return here to stay, you shall be the patrona, and you will rule my own children someday."

"I do not want your children to be my peones," she said. "I want them to be my children."

"That is impossible," he said.

"Why is that impossible? Do you not want me?" And she took his hand. "Here, feel," she put it on her breast, "am I not good enough here? Or here," she placed his hand on her stomach, then moved it around to her hips, "or here? Does it not seem to you that I could give you sturdy children even though I am not a peasant woman? Is it an Indian that you want?"

"Perhaps. I do not know. Certainly to marry a Spaniard is something to be considered."

She was angry. "You say that as if to be Spanish is to be a pig!"

She jumped to her feet, standing over him, looking very patrician. "Look at me," she demanded. "Look at me and tell me what is so different about me. How am I different from the woman of your people except that I may be fairer, and even that is not absolutely true. Some of you people look just like us, like that sister-in-law of yours—the arrogant one—she could be as Spanish as I am."

He said, "Come down here," and she pulled her combs from her hair and let it fall to her hips.

"I say, look at me! How am I different? I have tits, no? And I have an ass, no? And I have a belly to carry children in, and I have this thing down here between my legs that you like so much that you would kiss it if I were to ask you? What is it that you want, Heraclio—what?"

"Do not talk like that!" And now he was angry. "You sound like a woman from the brothels!"

"You peasants make me sick!" she exclaimed. "Perhaps my mother is right after all, although you made me disbelieve her for a time. You are peasants and you are low—lowborn and thus, you live as you should, to serve those who are better. And you, all of you are so senselessly proud. Of what? You cannot marry me because I am Spanish and to do so would be a degradation. Well, then, how can you fuck with me so quickly? Tell me that?"

He took her ankles and dropped her near him. "I have already told you not to talk like that!" He slapped her twice, hard, and she did not cry, was not surprised or shocked, just looked at him fully, and he held her down, a hand on each arm.

"You are so dishonest," she said. "You can do something but you cannot call it by name." The left side of her face was livid, turning bright red, and he was angry and now confused, but the language which had offended him now acted as an aphrodisiac because it had come from her lips, and so he kissed her, hungrily, with his mouth open wide, as if they had not been together a few minutes ago, and she resisted momentarily, and then met him with an aggressiveness equal to his, and when they were one, they hurt each other, and then they were each finished, and they lay, panting, twitching, completely exhausted and each knew that there was nothing in life like this.

"That was something," he said at last.

She turned to him and snuggled close. "Are you going to beat me every time I talk like that? And will it always end like this when I talk like that and you beat me?"

"You are crazy."

"Because if it does," she said, and the impish smile was on her face, "then it will be worth the beating, only this time try the other cheek, for my left one is sore," and she opened her mouth as if to speak and he quickly covered it with his hand. She looked at him and her eyes told him she was still smiling. When he took his hand away, she grew serious.

"Did it ever occur to you, Heraclio, that I am also Mexican? Even though I have no Indian blood, I was born here and am as Mexican as you are?"

"I have never thought about it," he said. "I can honestly say that I have never at all thought about you as being Spanish or Mexican until this afternoon."

"Well, it is true. And I do not want you to ever call me Spanish again, for after all that is but the blood, but this is my heritage, this México, and I have a love for it that is surpassed only by my love for you. And we can marry someday, this I know, if you would want me, for things are changing, and it is not rare for mixed marriages to occur, it never was—it is only that of the peon and the heiress, if you would call me that. Imagine what it could mean if we have the courage to do this—all over México there must be others in our position—another peon somewhere right this minute loving the mistress of the land, another son of a landowner, cohabiting with a maid."

"I told you that is an impossibility. And this man Arguiú, what about him?"

"My father will settle some money on him and send him to the capital, and there he will doubtlessly make his fortune, far from the rough country of the hacienda, which he would not like at any rate."

"And your father—he will agree to this great match of yours? Do not dream, Carmen. This is a big thing and physically impossible."

"You do not want me?" she asked.

"I do not say that," he said. "I but say that this cannot be. That you are wishing for something that the destiny has long ago decided is not for you nor for me."

90

"I do not believe in this of the destiny—because I am not Indian, you will say—but I do believe in love and I believe that I have the right to marry whomever I please, and that I can best fulfill my responsibility to my vassals if I marry the man I want. Things are changing, they must change. We cannot go forever making strangers marry with each other—it is the grossest of violations to our dignity. We can change it, Heraclio, believe me."

"I cannot."

"Then tell me this. I am not a crying, simpering woman—you know that. And although my heart will break, I will not fall to pieces, but I must know this. Is it because you do not want me as a wife? Is it that? Is it that as a mistress I can be with you, but not as the mother of your children?"

He was quiet for a minute because she was beginning to make him angry with all her talk, and he felt pushed against a wall. Finally he spoke and said, "Let us not talk about this thing. Forget all of it and live as we have, and enjoy that which we possess."

She would not be put off. "We must talk. Nothing changes because we should choose to ignore it. Like the possibility that I may have your child one of these times. We do not talk about it but it can happen. With all that seed you put into me, do you think we can always be lucky?"

"I have thought about it," he said, as if with resignation, as if he must tolerate this talk for a time.

"And what have you thought?" she asked quietly, deliberately, not in anger. "Flight, my love? The coward's way? My man, Heraclio Inés, choosing the way of the coward?"

"You are correct," he said. "That is exactly what I have thought, but not out of cowardice. There is simply nothing else I could do. Should I kill your father and your brother. Is that what you would have me do? For they would leave me no alternative, you should know that. Would they have a fiesta, and a grand wedding for us? I am sorry, Carmen. I have told you that I love you. For the present I can say no more. What is there for us? And I have thought. You think I do not have dreams, perhaps, but I shall tell you that no one dreams more than I do because I am sick of this thing I see around us, this whole business of slavery—which it is. You say you have rights, well I say everyone has a right, lowborn or not. Your father can tell you who you should marry, and

91

although you think not, it is not all wrong for him to do that because he is your father. But your father could also tell me who I should marry if he wished, and if I were anyone else, I would obey, and if I were anyone else he might be after me now to marry, for it is only through families that he can rule. Every peon is subject to his whims and the whims of someone like him—did you ever stop to think of that? And can you reconcile this with the idea that the peon is the responsibility of the landowner? That the reason for arranging the lives of the peasants is not because the patrón feels it his duty to do what is best for his people, but because he is afraid that his kingdom will crumble if he does not control the lives of his serfs.

"Yes, adored one, and hear me use phrases I am unaccustomed to even hear. I love you, that I know, and do not ever think that I have not grieved because we cannot ever marry—do not for a moment think that you are the only one who can suffer heartbreak. Only with me it goes further than just losing you. I think of that unknown man who is to marry you, lying between your outspread legs, and I suffer. I think of you clawing at him in your passion, and I die. You ask me to be honest, and I tell you. A man can also feel, and a man can also suffer, and a man can also cry. But I am realistic, for there is no future for us. What would you do, fly with me?"

"You must know I would if there would be need for that."

"Would you live in a choza, with a dirt floor, with not enough food, and barely enough clothing to keep you covered from other eyes? Would you wish to see your husband kissing the ass of some patrón somewhere, worked to death for a few centavos, and then your sons, your big strong sons, suffer the same indignity, and your daughters, your beautiful, big-breasted daughters, perhaps to be used by the patrón or his sons as concubines, while we, guilty with knowledge, would be pleased that the aristocrat thought our daughters were good enough to serve them in this way?"

She said, "You are unfair. The picture you paint is not a true one. It is not as bad as that. I know that our peones are happy because my father is good to them. I know they are safe from hunger and want because my father protects them. And they would not want it any other way."

He was amazed, for he had never imagined anyone could have

92

such a thought. But thinking of Teodoro, he knew it to be true of some people.

"I do not think of marriage with the idea that we would have to go away. And yet if that is the way it must be, I am prepared to do so. I think my life would not change at all if we married, except for the fact that I would have for a husband the man I want, the man I love. That is all."

"You are naïve," he said. "Do not for one moment think that your people would consent to such a union. To them it would be an atrocity. If they even knew as much as Crispín knows, that we have a feeling for one another, the rurales would be here in an instant, and a priest, and your father would marry me to the nearest girl available. No, my guapa, it is not for us."

She was sad that he should believe this so strongly, and yet she somehow had found a happiness to know that he did love her. "I will go with you, Heraclio Inés, and have that pride of an Inés, become one, give life to more. I will live in your choza, and I will grovel at your feet in the dust, only that you do not behave like a peon—not the humility you speak of because I do not really believe that—but to have mistresses. That I will not tolerate. You think of me with another man, you say. Well, it is no different for me. I think of you and other women—I think of the women who taught you what you know, what you have taught me."

"We have settled nothing, you know," he said. "Let us be what we are as long as it is to be."

"You do not really like my father, do you?" she asked.

"That has nothing to do with it. He has been good to me and I do not dislike him."

She was now teasing again, somehow falling into her happy mood almost unconsciously. "Why do you never speak of him as 'godfather'; it is always, 'your father this' or 'your father that.'"

"I do not know. I never think of him as my godfather, that is all," he said.

"And when your brothers made the 'pilgrimage' on his birthday, you did not feel loyal enough to accompany them."

He said, and he did not know why, for she was laughing as she talked, "Do you know of one called David Contreras?"

"I think so," she answered, surprised that he should suddenly change the line of talk.

"Did you know," he asked, "that David is your half brother?"

Her voice was barely audible, her face was bloodless. "No, I did not know."

"Well, he is. And he is a sheepherder, doomed to life in the hills for as long as he lives, merely because he is your father's son. Your father is not a coward and does not run when he does things like this. Of course he is the lord of the land, and that makes it right. There are even special rules for getting into heaven for such as he, but there is no force which would make me get on my knees to a man like your father. And that is why I did not accompany my brothers."

Her eyes were full of tears. She was hurt that he had done this to her. That of her father was painful enough, but that Heraclio should tell her like this was unbearable.

She said, "Why did you do this to me? There must be much hate for me in you. What have I done that you should hate me so?"

"I simply answered your question. That is why I did not make the pilgrimage with my brothers."

"It is good that you told me," she said. And she was now composed, and all the grief burning within her was hidden. "There comes a time, I suppose," she continued, "when we discover that our fathers are human, are men and not gods." She dressed as she spoke, and stood straight, her head held high, almost posing. "And yet, I cannot quite condemn him for having done this thing, because to condemn him would be to condemn myself, and worse of all, to condemn you who are my love and my life, and who could do no wrong."

She went to her horse, and he followed. They did not speak at all on their ride back to the hacienda.

That evening, during Rosary, Carmen Becerra took a shawl and walked on a narrow, cobbled street to the house of the witch María Contreras. She could see a dim light through the celluloid pane on the only window of the jacal, and she rapped lightly.

David opened the door and stared at her. He did not speak. From the other room a voice called out. "Who is it, Daví? A client, perhaps?"

"No, Mamá," he answered. "This is no client."

94

Carmen said, smiling in a friendly manner, "Well, dunce. Are you not asking me into your home?"

"Why should I?" asked David. "There is nothing here for you, so go away."

"I want to come in," she said doggedly.

"I repeat there is nothing here for you. Go away to your peers, there is nothing but dirt and squalor."

"You are quite a boy, David Contreras. As surly and insulting as it is said you are. Now move out of the way, for I am coming in."

He looked at her and pushed the door forward as if to close it, and then he changed his mind and said, "I am being polite. It is you who is intruding. Once again now, please go. Go to Heraclio Inés, he has what you want."

She colored and he noticed even in the dim light. "What is that you say? What do you know about Heraclio?"

David laughed. "I disconcerted you, no?" he asked. Then he grew serious once again. "I know many things, señorita. Do not ask me how I know, but I will keep your secret."

She was now angry after her loss of composure. "I know some things also. And true, you cannot give me what Heraclio gives me because you are my brother, and what we can hide from the world we cannot hide from God. He would know."

He opened the door. María Contreras met her as she walked in. "Ave María purísima, señorita. A miracle to see you in my humble home."

"It is no miracle, Mamá," said David. "She lives just down the street and she owns your 'humble home.' "

Carmen sat down. "You know the saying, 'As rude as a pastor?' I finally understand what is meant by it. I always thought it meant that shepherds are always in the elements and therefore have not the graces of living in a house but it is not that at all."

"Is there something you wish me to do for you, señorita Carmen. A love potion, perhaps, or maybe you would like me to tell you your destiny."

"Mamá, for God's sake!" said David.

"No, señora," said Carmen. "I wish only to speak with your son privately." She looked at the older woman and marveled at how attractive she looked after living this way for so many years, taking

95

care of herself and her child, ostracized by her own people. And she wondered how it had been for her father and this woman, immediately being in sympathy with her because she was a woman, and again wondered if there had been love, at least on this poor creature's side of the affair. She saw for a moment two bodies in coitus because she had become a woman but a short while ago, but she blotted the vision with an effort and she felt not unlike an intruder.

María Contreras retired to the other room, and David said, "Say what you have come to say and be quick, please."

"I only come to know you. I know of you, I only recently learned who you really are and I had to see you."

"I should thank you, I suppose," said David. "Yes, I believe I should, for this is a kindness on your part—the first kindness I have ever received from the Becerras. But I want to have nothing to do with you. Leave me alone, for you could never be my sister and neither could you ever be my friend."

Carmen felt a pang of sadness, and it was reflected in her voice. "Have you really suffered so much?"

He said, "You see where I live when I am home. You know what my mother is, and yet she is the only thing dear to me. I am happy you did not speak out when she was here."

"Why?"

"Because she thinks I believe her story—that I am the son of a good man, a shepherd, who died tending his flock. That is why."

"And you let her believe you do not know? How cruel!"

He laughed. "You amuse me," he said. "You think this is deceit. Well, tell me, what does your father have to say about me when you talk to him of your half brother?"

Once again she colored. "You are right," she said. "I did not think."

"Who told you about me?" he asked, taking her by surprise, so she answered, "Heraclio."

"Whatever possessed the cuckold to say that to you?"

"I think he was trying to hurt me—I do not know why, but that must have been the reason."

Again he was rough in his speech. "You may go now. I thank you never to come here again. We have nothing to say to each other and it is as if the same blood did not course through our bodies. Now go!"

"If I can help you," she said. "At any time if there is a thing I can do for you. Please. Do not be like this, for it is not my fault just as it is not yours."

He did not answer as he showed her to the door.

Nevertheless, she decided that she would keep an eye on this half brother of hers, and, if possible, someday make his life an easier one. She had not liked him, for his bitterness was now a part of him and it was obvious that it was not a habit or a pose. She did not like him, but after all, blood meant something.

And she kept up her relationship with Heraclio until one day the coach came and she and Crispín left for Río Grande, and there took a train which would eventually take them to Seattle, Washington, a remote country.

VII

It was in May of the year 1910 that Domingo Arguiú arrived in la Flor. Since he had not been expected until midsummer, there was no one to meet him. Don Aurelio and his wife were in the capital, and the children were still away at school. The administrator saw that he was settled in his rooms, and Teodoro Inés hovered nearby to see that the guest had every comfort, for Teodoro was to be the next administrator and must take an interest.

At dinner that evening, Teodoro spoke of the fiancé of the patroncita, and Heraclio, striving to sound natural, feeling jealousy and guilt, asked:

"What is he like, Teodoro, this gachupín?"

Teodoro frowned. There was no suspicion in his reaction because, being a man without guile, he could never imagine it in another. He thought Heraclio's disrespect was merely his way, and he could not suppress a mild rebuke. "That is no way to speak of the family of the patrón, Heraclio. That word is rarely used in the house of an Inés."

Heraclio kept his silence and Teodoro continued, "Since you

ask. He is a type, Spanish to the core, although quite swarthy, darker than most. A Basque, they say, and that is a strange race, with a strange tongue."

"He does not speak Spanish?" asked Elías, and could not resist to add, "How will he and the señorita understand each other, and how will he teach her what she must do?"

"You are an idiot," said Teodoro. He was actually embarrassed, and he refused to laugh with the others, although Heraclio was still silent. "But of course he speaks the Castilian, for he is an educated one." He had not answered Heraclio's question, so he went on. "He is quite a large man, larger than our people, I should say close to two meters in height. He has a good mustache, a little soft around the middle for a man as young as he is, but that is because he does not have an active life."

"How old is he?" asked Heraclio.

"He has thirty-one years only. And his hair is already thinning out in front in the manner of the Spaniard. But I think don Aurelio has made a good choice. Good big sons they will have, and although of course they are not to reside on the hacienda because that will be the boy Crispín's realm, I am quite certain their children will spend time here." He was obviously pleased by the match and Heraclio could not keep sarcasm from his voice as he said:

"You approve of the arrangements, then?"

But Teodoro was having one of his obtuse moments and said, "Very much. You know, we who serve the patrón should take an interest in the choices for his children. It can be that don Domingo may someday own la Flor, and be our patrón."

Concho watched Heraclio, and wondered, but dismissed the thought. Juan and Elías merely thought as Teodoro did, that Heraclio was simply disrespectful and vulgar. Only Otilia, on the other side of the room with the women, watched him carefully. And although she did not like the Becerra girl, she was sorry for him, so young to have reached for so much and, of course, it had been futile.

Although Heraclio was not in a good mood, the others did not react, but maintained their high spirits, and Teodoro did what he had not done in many days. "Will you work tomorrow?" he asked Heraclio.

Heraclio shrugged. It did not really matter to him; perhaps it might even take his mind off things if he went out to the range.

"The patrón will not be here for a week, and someone should show don Domingo the hacienda. We cannot spare a man right now, and don Miguel is quite busy with his administrative duties since don Aurelio is gone. Ride around with the man, will you? Keep him company for a few days for it must be lonesome here for him."

"All right," said Heraclio, and he did not really mean it. He did not want to see this man who would take his rightful place. But because Teodoro was so civil, and because this is the way he had always wanted his brothers to treat him, he agreed immediately.

He had his hat and went out to saddle his horse. Otilia followed him to the corral.

"Do not worry, my brother," she said. "In time it will be over. In time everything is made right again. And remember, she is as helpless and as unhappy as you are. Think of her. It is really much worse in her case, believe me—no, of course you will not believe me. But it is true."

"You know?"

"I know everything and I am happy for you two, that you at least had that happiness. I was fortunate to have been in love when I married and to be more in love after I knew your brother. But there are few people like us. It does not happen often. Be comforted."

He said, and he did not want to be bitter, "There is something altogether wrong about this life. This should not be so, and yet, it is not the fault of anyone. I do not know."

He mounted his horse and rode it through the house and out into the street. She heard him gallop as she sadly walked back into the house.

He had expected the man Domingo Arguiú to be large, for Teodoro had described him, but he was not prepared to see the mountain of a man who met him at the stables behind the Big House. Domingo was huge, and yet quite handsome, dark, as Teodoro had said. He had the beginnings of a belly, huge arms and hands, wide shoulders, so that Heraclio, who was considered large in this land of small people, seemed dwarfed.

Heraclio stared, and was unwary for the first and last time before the man. He was startled by the soft, cultured voice as Domingo said:

"What do you see, boy? Is my dress in disarray?"

"No, patrón, it is only that you are so big. We do not see people such as you in Zacatecas. It is only that."

Domingo laughed. And Heraclio saw that the man was studying him closely—with laughter, obviously sincere, and yet no laughter in his eyes. He wondered why he, a peon although a jinete, could already be important to the man. It could be his guilt telling him this, perhaps, but nevertheless he would be on his guard.

"You would be too much of a burden for these horses here," he said. "Come to my house and you may have the use of my stallion."

"You own a horse?" asked Domingo as they walked down the street.

"I own two horses," said Heraclio. "But I know what you mean —the mare, I own, but it is also owned by don Aurelio. That is to say, that under the tradition here, I own the mare but don Aurelio owns me, so he owns the mare. The stallion, now, that is another matter. He belongs to me because I captured him in the wilds, unbranded until I brought him home and put the Inés brand on him."

Domingo Arguiú did not understand, and as this was the reason for having a guide, he asked:

"How can it be that a peon can have a brand? All my information has been to the contrary."

"The law of the land says that anyone who owns a beast may have his iron. Now, if someone else on this hacienda were to have a brand—and there are some who do—the brand would merely serve to distinguish one animal from another, although it gives the people a sense of ownership, for if the patrón should decide he wanted the animal, it would in an instant be his. But the Inés brand is different, for we have a few cows, and we have, each of us, two beasts we call our own. The mare, of course, is not really ours, but it is the only one, and does not carry our brand. I myself have captured four of our animals. This is a privilege the Ineses have and no one, not even the patrón, can take our animals." He had talked long, for him, and he was aware all the time that the other watched him closely.

"Why?" asked Domingo. "Why is it different for your family?"

"For some service in the past." He would say no more about it. They were at the house now, and Heraclio said to the thoughtful Domingo, "Enter your house, patrón." And he said the word "patrón" very naturally.

They passed through the kitchen and on to the corral in the rear. Domingo stopped at the threshold momentarily, to acknowledge some salutation from the women, but Heraclio went through without saying a word and he followed him.

"Take yourself a saddle from the wall," said Heraclio.

Domingo did so, and then stood dumbly as Heraclio walked to the mare and threw a small blanket on its back. He had the animal saddled when he noticed the other was still standing, holding the saddle, and so he went to him and took the seat and put it on the stallion. He got bridles and bits, then, and Domingo said:

"It is not that I expect you to act as a servant to me. It is that I have never saddled these things—in fact, I have never been on a horse's back. Even in the days when I was young and we had stables, I preferred other forms of pleasure."

"Do not have a care," said Heraclio. "It is but a small task." There was something about the man which disturbed him.

And Domingo also felt a tension, he felt he must ask more questions, for he was learning nothing about this boy. After his first lapse when he had marveled at the size of Domingo, Heraclio had allowed his features to become inscrutable, and the man did not think of the fact that he had a thousand years of experience in this art.

They were on the road to Cañitas when Domingo spoke again. "You were saying about your horse, this one, I suppose. You captured him, how?"

"From a wild herd in the mountains. I caught him and broke him so he is mine."

"When was this?"

"Over three years ago. He is getting old now—should have seven or eight years, for he was big already when I took him."

Domingo studied him again. "You were very young then. You must be quite a boy."

Heraclio laughed. "I am not a boy and these things are not rare here, patrón. It was as nothing." But he was pleased and wished he could tell Domingo how it had been that day. But he was immediately displeased as he realized that he was being lulled so that he could be questioned further.

"You implied," Domingo said, and Heraclio was on guard and the strange thing was that he did not know why, "that don Aurelio does not own you."

Heraclio did not answer.

"About the mare," continued Domingo casually. "You were saying he did not own the mare, remember?"

"Oh, the mare he owns, all right," said Heraclio.

"But he does not own you," said Domingo.

Heraclio thought for a moment, he wondered if he should simply play along, innocently telling him nothing but making him think that he was an ignorant Indian, yet defeating him, for a real Indian would have seen through him in an instant. Then he suddenly laughed loud and long. Domingo was just as suddenly disconcerted.

"Why do you laugh?" he finally asked.

"We finally had to arrive to it," said Heraclio. And he knew he could defeat him in another way, and now, in spite of Carmen, in spite of the vision of this grotesque alongside him serving as stud to his, Heraclio's, woman, not unlike the prize burros with their huge organs trailing on the ground that had been imported from Spain to service the hacienda mares, he found he suddenly liked the man. Why he was so inquisitive he did not know, and now did not care.

"We have arrived," he said, "to what you have been leading all along. You are counting your stock—or I should say, you are inventorying all that one day may belong to your bride."

"That is not so," said Domingo, losing his confidence.

"Oh, but it is. It is all too clear. Well, I will show you the lands, and I will show you many of the herds, and the flocks of sheep, and the crops, and all the vassals. But as you say, I do not belong to the Becerras. I do not belong to your señorita to give to you." He was not arrogant, he was not exultant, nor was he angry, and this disturbed Domingo.

And finally he became explicit. "What it is with you, my young friend? You are polite, and the epitome of what a host should be.

And yet, I feel an antagonism. Yet again you are friendly. I know I have been insulting you by prying, and I must say some of this is because I have a desire to know of the life here. The other is that I have the weakness of studying people, learning of their motivations, of their frustrations, of their weaknesses. It is but a habit of long standing, and I cannot control it. Most people do not even know it is happening."

"You have not been here long," said Heraclio. "In Spain, perhaps what you say is true, but here a little baby would see this thing about you."

"Perhaps. But you still have not said. Why do you seem in a mood and yet I know you are not?"

Heraclio laughed, and then laughed at his false laughter. "I was very drunk last night. Perhaps that is why I seem to be strange."

Domingo joined in his laughter. "How old are you?" he asked.

"They tell me I have sixteen years."

"And you drink? Where, in cantinas?"

"And at dances, and in brothels."

"Will you take me sometime?" asked Domingo.

"Surely. Today, if you wish. There is no brothel here and there is no music here, nor the dancing. In Río Grande, now, that is different."

"Well, let us go tonight," said Domingo.

"It is three hours if we canter, and I fear your ass will be in pain long before we get there. Tell the coachman to get us a vehicle. Tell him I will manage the mules. Do you have money?"

"Very little. I departed on an impulse before the money arrived. I barely had enough to pay my passage."

Heraclio laughed. The man would someday own all of this as far as he could see and here he did not have the price of a woman. "You must have something they want very badly. Did they measure you?"

Domingo was agreeable and said, "Not the way you mean, but in another way they did. I have a background that not all their money can buy for themselves. They can only buy it for their grandchildren."

Heraclio thought of this rare idea. Then he said, "I would not trade my background for yours and I know you must be a great thing somewhere to some people. Take no offense. I have just weighed the problem and have decided, that is all."

"I take no offense," said Domingo. "I fully understand."

"I would die for mine," said Heraclio. "I do not think you would die for yours."

They returned to la Flor the following afternoon, tired and sleepy, Domingo looking half alive. "Thank you," he mumbled, the ride on the buckboard, the dancing and the orgy, plus the ride back to the hacienda had completely exhausted him. He would sleep now, around the clock, for it seemed that even the fresh air tired him.

Heraclio left him and went home to take a nap. When he awakened it was dinnertime, and after dinner he went out to look for Antonio Rivera. Perhaps they could go back to Río Grande. He had been gay, and he had enjoyed himself, but he had not been able to forget about Carmen although he had some liking for the man who would be her husband. He had failed with the whore in Río Grande, failed for the first time in his life, and he must return to satisfy his ego.

It was not until two days later that Domingo Arguiú ventured out again. Heraclio met him by the chapel, and they walked within the walls of the Big House, through the orchard, and beyond to where the meadows for the house animals were situated.

"Does one ever get over this soreness?" asked Domingo.

"Eventually."

"What a barbarous way to live!"

Heraclio smiled. "It is our way," he said, "and it is not all bad. After a while you will ride a horse to Río Grande and not even know that you have been in the saddle."

"When did you first go to these places?" asked Domingo. He felt strange that he had as companion in carousal a mere boy. But Heraclio had behaved himself with dignity in the whorehouse, and it was obvious that he was not a stranger there.

"I went the first time before I had yet fourteen years. My brothers almost killed me making me a horseman the year before, so I thought if I were to work like a man, I might be killed like a man, and so I deserved the joys of a man."

104

"I understand you do not work now," said Domingo. "Why?"
Heraclio turned to him. "You are starting again."

"Yes, but this time I am asking you. It is not necessary that you answer me."

Heraclio looked at the older man seriously, and he said, laughing, "But I may as well answer your questions, for otherwise you will question someone else as you no doubt have been doing, and you may not get the truth about me."

Domingo laughed with him. "Since you challenge me, I cannot deny it. I have been asking questions, but it is not only that I am an inquisitive one, or that I pry—I but wish to know things. I wish to know about you not only because you will someday hold a high position on this hacienda, but so that I may know about your people. When I knew I was to come to live here, to spend my life here, I read about your country and I learned a great many things about its history, about the present México, and about the future."

Again Heraclio laughed. "Do not deceive yourself about my becoming a caporal or an administrator here. Also, why learn so much about México if you will be living somewhere else?"

"But I will not be living somewhere else, for that is a part of the marriage contract—that I establish our home in México, that my children be Mexican. Oh, we may travel to Europe, my Carmen and I, the amount of time people spend on the Continent and that is all."

The name Carmen used in that possessive way made Heraclio catch his breath, and that was the last time; and he marveled at this as he realized that it was over, and that his jealousy, intense as it had been, had suddenly disappeared. He had been thinking that this man was indeed taking his rightful place, when what Domingo Arguiú would be was not his place at all. A feeling yet remained, true, but that was all, and it was the first time since the first kiss with Carmen that he was in complete control of himself. He felt lighthearted, and he wanted to talk. Somehow, he did not know how, he felt grateful to Domingo—as if through him he had been able to overcome an emotion which was slowly smothering him.

"Again why?" he asked. "Why should the patrones insist, when there is no limit to where they can travel if they wish to see their daughter?"

"You really do not understand," said Domingo. "I am a Spaniard, and the Becerras are Spanish because they have Spanish blood. But more important, they are creoles because they were born here, and because of this they are Mexican. Do you know that when these Spaniards from the New World come to Spain we call them Mexicans? They insist that they are Mexican, and all that pride you feel, and all that love you have for your country, exists in them. One does not have to be a mestizo or an Indian to feel love for his country. Remember that, if you will. They insist that we live in México because they are Mexican, and anything else would be foreign, and they would die if they had a grandchild who was anything but a Mexican. They buy my bloodline, but they would take their money back immediately if I dared go against their wishes."

Heraclio could not argue this, for he did not know, had never thought such a thing possible. And yet it was difficult to believe what he was hearing. And if so—why the system. Why the peones, and the inhuman treatment? What kind of love was this that it was demonstrated by keeping people in slavery? He was not so young that he had not seen people whipped by the administrator's assistant, or by the rurales, those mounted police with the pretty uniforms, broad-brimmed felt hats, silver buttons on gray, with red kerchiefs and silver-embossed saddles. Good horses, they rode, and some said that except for the officer, most of these men were ex-bandits, now turned to legal banditry, a concession the government of don Porfirio made to ensure peace in the land. And there was rape and devastation in the small villages and ranchos in their wake. Haciendas they did not disturb, because they were the property of the aristocrats, the peones were included, and only when a difficult peon or an undisciplined or wayward girl was given over to them did they practice their brutality within sight of the upper class.

Why all this then if they loved México and were protectors of the poor? There was a yearning within his breast he could not comprehend. Had he known how to ask, Domingo could have explained it—a human desire for equality and justice. A human desire for his place in the universe. But now another thing was in his mind, confusing him. "The contract," he said. "What contract? Were there papers to sign like when you sell an animal?"

"Yes, indeed," said Domingo. "I was not there, of course, when my father and don Aurelio's representative, who is a relative to both our houses, through doña Gertrudes, who is really my aunt, for the Becerras have no family to speak of, worked out the agreement. It would not have been proper, in good taste, for me to be present, although I had been notified about the matter and had agreed. Very good of them to let me know they were deciding my future, but they were doing this to avoid embarrassment if I had refused. You see, in my case, because I was a wastrel, and a black mark to the family, I must marry someone of their choice, my father's choice really, but I did not have to marry anyone he should happen to find. It is complicated only because it is unusual. And the only reason I had a say in the matter was that being a disobedient son, I might take it into my head to go it alone, to refuse to obey. And they worried until the papers were in order."

Heraclio was fascinated. And yet, he measured Domingo carefully, for here indeed was a rare one. He was a snob, that was obvious—and yet, there was a certain amount of cynicism in his words. And Heraclio did not know these attitudes when they were together. He knew that a hypocrite was a hypocrite, and that an honest man—and most people he knew were honest—was simply, most naturally, honest. Teodoro was a hypocrite and David Contreras was a twisted, bitter boy, but he was honest, and if he did not succumb so readily to his candor, they might yet be friends. But this Domingo Arguiú, he was a queer one.

And that about the marriage contract . . . marriage arrangements were common among his own people, more the rule than the exception, as a matter of fact; and although there was sometimes a dowry of sorts—a goat or two, a milk cow—the boy and girl in question usually knew each other, and were already found pleasing to each other even if they had never exchanged a word in their lives. But here was a thing rarer—even more impersonal than it was in his world, and this disturbed him. He was too polite to criticize the customs of another man's country, but he must ask more, for he suddenly had an insatiable curiosity. "You are telling me that Carmen was bought—like a sow she was bought. Did your people clip her ear?"

There was no mistaking his anger. And Domingo said, "*Carmen?* You call the master's daughter Carmen?"

Heraclio controlled himself. He sensed a danger, for this man was not unintelligent. "We grew up together, she is my godsister. It is natural."

Domingo looked at him for a long moment. Some perverseness made his voice gentle. "It was the reverse. They bought me—but they did not brand me." He allowed himself to smile then.

Heraclio breathed deeply. "You signed a paper to marry a girl in a place far away from your homeland, across the ocean—why?"

Domingo laughed loud now, but he laughed alone. "But what a boy you are after all? Did I not tell you that you were exceptional? Who is asking the questions now?"

"Forgive me," said Heraclio, and he was ashamed. This was unheard of, to pry into another man's business, another man's motives. In fact, it was unusual that he should be talking so much, for a peon knew his manners, taught to him by the Jesuits for two hundred and fifty years, and then by the Franciscans for a century until the Society of Jesus earned back its grace. And he said again, "Forgive me, patrón," and, oddly, the "patrón" was still lacking in servility.

"I thought," said Domingo, "that you had stopped calling me by that absurd term."

"Tell me or do not tell me, as you wish," said Heraclio, ignoring the remark. He was very serious and he added, "I am being rude, please believe I know what rudeness is, for I can recognize it in others. But now that you have told me as much as you have, I find that I have an urgent need to know more. Forgive me and tell me I should close my mouth, and I shall do so. Or pardon me and continue educating me in the ways of the world."

Domingo was moved by Heraclio's earnestness. For the first time since he had known him, he seemed young as he really was, he was a boy and he was looking to an older man for a certain knowledge. And even as he responded to the sincerity of the youth, another thought engendered in the recesses of his mind, and even as he spoke, it came to life and grew, for Domingo was not a man of a single feeling. His emotional side was rarely in

108

tune with his intellect, and he was a student, and in truth a cynic in regard to human beings, so he wondered as he spoke, and he saw the eager, although composed face before him, and he was excited, for here was a primitive, an intuitive animal-like being who was willing to be molded. And the experiment took shape in his mind: to fill Heraclio with a certain amount of knowledge. To watch him carefully, bending him until he created an ideal in the boy so strong that it would force him into some action. That of the whorehouse the other night was fine, but he was bored and here was distraction for him. And if Heraclio did not respond, if he turned out to be less than intelligent or less than intuitive, nothing was lost, and he would merely fall back into ennui. And if, as he expected, the boy did catch on to his words, if he made a patriot of him, and supplied the mission of freeing the peon, for example, it would be dangerous but extremely interesting. And if Heraclio should die because of it, why, his was a worthless lot in any light—the life of a peon, even a horseman, was indenture.

But Domingo did not know the degree of Heraclio's intuition, which was but the intuition of the landsman anywhere. For Domingo did not know death, as Heraclio had already known it; he therefore did not know life, and he did not know of those almost supernatural revelations, those extra senses that centuries of being lower animals in that upper realm of animals give life and strength. He did not know of this. Also perhaps because he did not know of the supernatural except in fantasies on a far-off stage in Madrid, or Paris, he could not know the formidable task which lay before him.

And, also, it was impossible for him to know that an ideal was already in firm control of the boy. An ideal unrecognized, barely discernible among other feelings of rebellion. An ideal born long before Domingo's own time, and again peculiar to the underdog.

And he was speaking, kindly, sincerely with care, "I shall tell you, youngster," and he must keep him aware of this, "I shall tell you. Why did I do this thing? For a million pesetas, roughly a half million pesos which will be deposited in the Bank of Iberia in Madrid in the name of my father when the nuptials are celebrated. And for another million or two before I die. That is why. And can you begin to imagine what that much money can do?

The lands at my ancestral home will be put back into use. My father's peones will again be protected. They will have food, they will be clothed, and perhaps a few of them may be able to spare a child or two for school. It is not a sacrifice I make. It is good for the family, and we can again have a free mind because we are fulfilling our responsibility to our servants."

"Is that all," said Heraclio, and it was obvious that he did not believe this.

Domingo felt his way and was enjoying the game. "I have told you that I had no money—that, in fact, I have no money until don Aurelio returns. In my country I belong to the highest level of society. It is difficult for you to imagine what it means to have the responsibility of keeping up an appearance. Although everyone knows our fortunes have depleted, it is not talked about, and the pretense that nothing has changed is kept up by everyone. There are many of us in this situation. My parents remain in the country, in the few thousand hectares they still hold. There is a castle, a small castle but a real castle nonetheless. They do not live in it because it would cost too much to do so. Their house is smaller than the Big House here in la Flor. My father is old, my mother is also old, and I have yet at home an unmarried sister who is also growing old. That is also something that the money will do. Get my sister a husband. It is important.

"I lived in Madrid and in Paris, and I had private tutors as a boy. And I had an inheritance from an uncle which I dissipated in three years. I lived for the past seven years on the barest necessities, and it was only that I belonged to the society which enabled me to make a living actually as a stud. Like a man-whore, although we did not think of it like that, we thought of it as a strong and lovely affair of the heart—at least the woman did. And I received small favors, sometimes money, sometimes gifts which I in turn converted into money. That is how I lived, and all that time I searched for the right person to marry. There were offers, but none as glittering as the Becerras'. And, too, we are related, so it is a good match.

"You doubted that I had concern for our peones. Well, you are half right. Half right only because I have a deep feeling for the slave, be it outright slavery or not. I am of the upper class, and I would never want to be anything else, and there will always be an upper class and lower class, but it is only the blind man who cannot see that it is an injustice. You perhaps will look ill upon me because I have in effect sold myself for money—yes, even this time with don Aurelio. But it is because I know that only when the money is equal will the people be equal. I will remain where I am and I shall leave your people their will to rise to my level or remain as they are. But I will take care of them, if it comes to be that we remain here as lords of the land."

They had walked back to the Big House while Domingo talked, and they entered and went to the large room which was like a salon, and Domingo called a maid and asked for a bottle and glasses. He was excited still, but his excitement was controlled because he knew he was not in control. He wished he had thought of this earlier and perhaps have a plan of sorts. He wished he could undo some of the harm he had created by his superciliousness, and he wanted a drink and then another to make him glib, and he wanted the boy to have a few drinks to make him susceptible.

Heraclio was not affected in particular. He was anxious to have this man who was the first person from the outer world he had ever known, except for Crispín and Carmen, speak out. And he was vaguely aware that there was something strange about this talk, and he was cautious; but he did not know what it was, and it would reveal itself in time, so he put it out of his mind until it did, remaining somehow on guard, yet willing to let the talk go on. Domingo poured drinks, and sipped—a cognac, for he detested the native drink, especially after the first night. Heraclio drank his neat, in the manner of drinking tequila.

"That is a part of it," said Domingo. "With your permission, for I have no desire to offend you . . . consider the difference in the manner in which I drink my drink, savoring in sips, even in the manner in which I hold my glass. You picked it up and swilled it down. These are the niceties of the upper class."

But Heraclio was offended and said, "To sip, as you say, or to swill like a pig. It is the same with liquor. I have not really understood what you are saying, although some of the facts are clear and interest me for I do not know of these things. But this of the glasses—and believe me I would much rather drink out of the bottle—there is no significance to that of slavery or indenture or servitude. And that of being on one level, that seems absurd also, because it is inconceivable that a peon should aspire to own the Big House. I do not think a peon really thinks of owning anything, he simply does not want to be owned. But speak on, if you will favor me, but do not tell me that if I learn to drink out of a glass in the effeminate way I will rise to your level. I am not an idiot."

"If you are going to be angry every time I say something, then it is useless to carry further this conversation. Let us drink, and soon we can have food, and let us be friends." He had no intention of discontinuing the conversation, but he must not appear to be forcing it, and so he waited for Heraclio's reply.

Heraclio seemed not to hear what the man said. He was silent for a moment, and when he spoke, he returned to the original subject of his curiosity. "It yet remains strange that you came from so far away to marry someone you have not even seen."

"Oh," said Domingo, smiling. "I have seen her once or twice. Although at the time I did not know who she was or that she would someday be my wife. Of course, she must have been six years old at the time, and for the life of me I cannot recollect her features. The family was in Madrid and they spent a fortnight with my uncle, the one of the inheritance."

"Are you not curious?"

"Not at all. It does not really matter, and if I do not think about it, I will not be too disappointed if she is ugly as a turtle. And what a surprise it will be if she turns out to be a beauty."

"And it does not matter?"

Domingo laughed that Heraclio seemed perturbed, and at the naïveté of the unenlightened. "Consider, my friend, Heraclio, that the poor girl had nothing at all to say about the matter. She, the least important in the whole transaction, was but the instrument by which don Aurelio receives a grandchild related by blood to the best families in Spain, and I receive wealth. It does not matter that she gets a husband, only that a husband is needed so that she can breed, and that the husband must have lineage."

"If you permit me, don Domingo," said Heraclio, "and I mean no offense to you, especially since you are my elder, and perhaps because you are so Goddamned huge, but I wish to tell you about my brother, Teodoro, whom you met, and your right back cheek must still be wet where he kissed it. Teodoro is one of the cruel-est, meanest persons I have ever known. True, I have not known many people in my life, but there are bad fellows everywhere, and I have seen some. Teodoro is a person who can sometimes make me ill because he does the things he does. He treated me in a way that I feel no child has ever been treated, and to a point I am grateful. He is pious, hypocritical, ass-licking, and stupid; and yet, for all that he is a man. Now you, who are always asking me to consider this or to consider that, now you, my friend, Do-mingo, you mountain of a man, gachupín stud—you are very much less than a man, you are much worse than Teodoro, in fact, you are nothing more than a son of a bitch."

He said this deliberately, in a low voice, and for a moment the man almost succumbed to anger, and yet he recovered, and was happy, for it seemed that his goal would not be too difficult. Hera-clio would eventually hate him, and because he belonged to the class, he would, of course, hate the class. He did not know that, for all his talk about the aristocracy and about his royal connec-tion, he could not be thought of as a representative of the ruling class, for the most humble peon knew that a don did not spend the night in a twenty-five-centavo crib; that when a lord wanted a woman, if he did not have his own, or if he merely sought vari-ety, he took a maid or chose a girl from among his vassals and, discreetly, placed her where she would be ready whenever he needed her. He had revealed himself on the night at Río Grande, and all the courtly graces he had practiced in Spain could not recall him from so low a fall. And any serf with cause could come to him, although they were more gracious than he and would not do it unless very drunk, and say with every right, "¡Hola, Epañó! What say the gamey putas?" And all for a half-remembered, un-satisfactory hour of fornicating with an ugly, filthy, shapeless glob of flesh called incongruously Lolita, who repeated with peals of rasping laughter carrying all over the house the rare thing that a man so big and with such a physique could be so little where it counted most and with no inhibition in her speech, which is the only right reserved for whoredom, screeched out at misfortune for letting it fall upon her lot to be crushed by a mountain with no chinga and here she had the biggest cavity in all of México and the Central American republics. Already there was laughter

113

in the cantinas about the new patrón and the poor patroncita who would never know true love.

And Domingo had no way of knowing, also, that violence had barely been avoided, for the words Heraclio had spoken so quietly had been but the beginning of the game, and that he was quiet still, waiting for the return insult, which would be returned again, with more venom, and yet again for another minute or two before the two men, for at this moment Heraclio was no longer à boy, would attack each other. And violence had been avoided when Domingo decided to curb his anger, and the moment was over when he said:

"But what a boy, Heraclio." And he said it with laughter in his face. "If you had not explained that you meant no offense, I may have been insulted." And then he laughed aloud and said, "Come, another drink." But Heraclio got to his feet and walked to the liquor closet. He returned with a bottle of tequila and said:

"You drink your aguardiente. I have no taste for liquor made from grape. This is the answer—from the maguey, which lives forever, and when I drink it I feel I shall live forever and I feel almost like the maguey from which it comes, with arms extended, encompassing the land surrounding it. You would not understand that."

"I suppose not," said Domingo. "But then, I am not a poet like the Mexican."

VIII

Yet despite his immaturity, and his youthful bent toward anger, he returned again and again to learn from Domingo Arguiú. He learned about Porfirio Díaz, ruler of México for thirty-three years, but he knew about him, because half his father's life had been lived under his rule. What he had not known was that although don Porfirio was a strong man he was not the real ruler of México. There was the King of England—and Domingo made a special thing of this because he had met him once—called Bertie, he said, and his cousin in Germany called a Kaiser. These people owned Porfirio Díaz, and he was owned by a man named William Howard Taft, and earlier by someone called Teddy Roosevelt. And now there was a weasel-eyed man in México who had as much power as the President, a minister from the United States, Henry Lane Wilson.

All this was as if Domingo had said, "You see, the Mexican is inferior, lacking the industry, courage, and intelligence to change the system. And the system cannot be changed because the forces controlling it are too strong. They are as if chosen by God."

Thinking a moment, Heraclio said, "It can be changed. The system, even the Church."

Domingo, amused, said, "The Church, now, it is indestructible. Look where all the peones go after fourteen hours in the fields. They go directly to church and pray to God."

"I do not."

"So?"

"I think that the fact I do not go to church and have little knowledge means many people with knowledge also do not follow the clerics."

"You do not believe?"

"I cannot believe, because God does not believe in us."

"I believe," said Domingo, "because everything is in order. The people over you are strong, the world is run the way it was destined. Look, even the man that was to be the salvation of your people is in jail. Francisco Madero will die and things will be as always."

Heraclio did not know of these things. The political machinations of México were too remote for him.

"This man was—is for us?"

"Yes, but he is finished. I had a sympathy for that man."

"How is it that you, a don, and the potential owner to all this land, can talk this way about the government and the Church? Is it not to your interest that you defend don Porfirio?"

Domingo said, "It does not matter how much we talk about it. The government can never be defeated. Don Porfirio is too strong, and when he dies, his regime is still in power. I but speak like this because I know it does not make any great difference. Some may die gloriously to change all this but in the end it is the best thing for the nation. I, myself, do not believe in the system as such—the way it is for the peon, I mean, for I believe strongly in the rights of human beings. I but indulge in this for a time, for you possibly cannot win, and when Carmen and I marry, I will leave these ideas behind, because they are for people like you, who have a need for certain dreams and for the attainment of these dreams. My place is with the ruling class because I was born in the upper class. I know where I belong."

"And yet you sympathize with the peon, no?"

"I can see that the peon has a cause, but I indulge myself when I sympathize with something against my class. It is right that things are as they are—that there should be vassals and there should be rulers. It is an injustice to those on the bottom of the scale, but it is in the order of things, and right."

Heraclio sensed that Domingo was again succumbing to his manner of seeming to contradict his own statements. "You say," he challenged, "that you believed in the rights of man, of human beings—and that it is a form of slavery to be a peon. Yet you say that it is right that peonage exists. Can you not ever take a position and remain firm, or at least speak clearly?"

Again laughter shook the large man's frame, and then the cunning look Heraclio had come to recognize so well appeared in his face. He said, "Let me put it this way, muchacho. I can readily understand how someone like you could feel oppressed. The landowner is also a people owner, and although he says he protects you, you know he does not—you know that, but most peones do not. Most peones believe this and are content in their slavery. From where I exist, the ruling class is right, especially since most of the vassals are satisfied. I can see both sides of it, but I am on the top side.

"Now, for you it is different. If I were you, I would be prepared to go off and fight the government. I would cover myself with glory fighting against the aristocracy, liberating México for the peon. I would not have a chance in hell of ever succeeding, but I would go because I would believe that there was a chance. I have mentioned the man Madero to you. He might very well inspire an uprising of sorts. There is the man Emiliano Zapata in the south of México, who has actually organized a fight and has won battles against the rurales, and a few government troops. Of course, as soon as the election is over, he will be annihilated, since he is really becoming a serious threat. Then, in western Chihuahua there is a man, not a peon, but an educated city-bred man called

Pascual Orozco. He has, believe it or not, a force of two thousand, maybe three, well-equipped men at ready. Now this man is not exactly as nothing, for in the wastelands of the north that large a force can do a great deal of damage. But the garrisons along the railroad and Ciudad Juárez in particular have been reinforced.

"But—as I said, they think they have a chance. If I were as you, then I would too think I had a chance and nothing could stop me from joining them. I would even rob the hacienda first, perhaps make an attempt at don Aurelio's life, sack the arsenal and flee north."

Heraclio was looking at the man in awe that he should think him so stupid. "You know," he said, "you must really be crazy. How could you possibly think that you could put ideas into my head?" Domingo ignored him. "But the man I believe I would ride with," he said, "is the man from Durango called Villa. He is a terror, they say, a brute, insensate—a real killer, but with a passion for justice for the peon. Now, there is a man worth following, though he is but a bandit now and with a price on his head. But if there really is an uprising, he and his men will join the ranks. They will be pardoned by the revolutionaries, and conduct their rape and thievery on the side of law and order and reform.

"He is the man I would follow."

Heraclio was angry. "Again I say to you that you are insane. All this talk all these weeks has been for this moment, has it not? You want me to go out and get myself killed by the rurales before I could even leave Zacatecas. Or if not killed, I would be subject to the fugitive law, and shot while attempting to escape—or sent on a trip to Quintana Roo or Yucatán, there to be sold as a slave. You have not told me about that, that we have slavery in México even worse than the slavery of serfdom, but we do. We know that just as we know many things which you thought you were telling me for the first time. And we also know about Pancho Villa, a peon just like us, because there are songs sung about him, and because the traveling salesmen, the Arabs who sell junk to the housewives, they have told us.

"And I want no part of that which you suggest. From where I exist it is an impossibility at present. And we do have a chance, you shall see. And someday we will succeed—in your own lifetime, even."

"Do not be angry, Heraclio. I thought that you had courage, and also I was not suggesting that you do what I would do. I was simply showing you what I would do because I am that kind of a man—I would die rather than to live like this."

Heraclio was over his anger and was quite happy, in fact, that he had finally discovered what lay behind the man's strange manner—what it was that compelled him from the first time he saw him to be almost constantly on his guard. And to him the man was stupid, and he sensed that Domingo wanted to rule, no matter how, and no matter what he proclaimed. And he smiled because for all his worldliness, for all his knowledge, the man would never be able to deceive him.

"No, Domingo," he said. "It is not that I lack courage, nor is it that I do not care. It is only that it is not the time, at least for me."

Domingo recognized his error. The boy was not yet ready. He had been surprised by Heraclio's perception, for indeed it was true that he yearned for power. Although he had called this a game, a diversion, he recognized his need to rule. He had been born to the master class and it was important that he should rule, if only a young man's mind. Now he lost interest. He said, "I did not intend to influence you, Heraclio. I merely told you what a man such as I am would do."

Again Heraclio was not fooled. "You amuse me, Domingo," he said. "As I amuse you when I call you 'patrón.' You laugh because you are not my patrón, although you want to be; and I laugh because you are not really the man you think you are. Why should I emulate the likes of you? When have you impressed me in the slightest, except that you are so huge? No, I cannot hope to be like someone I do not admire."

"You are all wrong, muchacho," said Domingo, and he was embarrassed, for he had no real rejoinder. "But I take no offense."

Juan Vásquez, the contador, often accompanied them on their trips around the hacienda. He was always polite to Heraclio, but he still held the idea that the boy planned to supplant him one day. He had grown stouter since he had stopped going out to count sheep, and he now performed the duties of an adminis-

118

trative assistant. When alone with Domingo Arguiú, he would always manage to say something complimentary about Heraclio until he discovered that Domingo did not really like the boy. Then he criticized him with a passion at every opportunity.

Domingo was not especially affected by the man's statements, simply looking at them as private resentments, but he did not admonish Juan Vásquez, and he did not object that the man followed him in an attempt to ingratiate himself. Here, he knew, was a good servant—one who knew how to serve a patrón. And he allowed himself to be flattered, for if the contador considered him in a position worthy of flattering, he could be certain of the man's loyalty.

Although at the time the children were to arrive from the United States the hacienda was at the height of its activity, don Aurelio told his administrator to make arrangements for a fiesta. The celebration was to be in honor of the travelers—a homecoming, and also, it was time to announce the betrothal of María del Carmen. Soon also, it would be time to begin negotiations which would bring to la Flor a worthy wife for Crispín. Then, perhaps, with everything arranged, he and Gertrudes could take a leisurely trip to the Continent. It was time they saw Spain again, and Paris, and really, they should go to the Vatican.

And so a few days before the arrival of the children, vaqueros were sent into the hills to round up wild beasts. Mares, stallions, and a few bulls were brought in and enclosed in the corrals around the Big House. Hogs were slaughtered for the making of the tamales, and beef was made ready for the barbecue. Invitations were sent out, and don Aurelio went into his wine cellar with his private mozo to select the wines and champagnes which would be served to his guests. A peon was sent to Fresnillo with a wagon to bring back a string ensemble for the dancing at the Big House; a platform had been erected in a corral so that the peones could have their own dance.

The evening before Crispín and Carmen were to arrive, riders appeared from the hills—from the Rancho Grande, from the Hacienda del Fuerte, from the Rancho Colorado, from Tetillas, and even some professional riders from Río Grande or Fresnillo who came to vie for prize money or gifts in horsemanship. Also, to the surprise and joy of the peones, Father Ignacio arrived, not on a burro or even a horse, but in a handsome surrey driven by a peon. He had not come in the past Lenten period, and the people had resigned themselves to go without confession until the Christmas celebrations, but now he was here and would hear confessions.

The priest entered the Big House to the attentions of his hostess, and took a glass of sherry to soothe his throat after the dusty ride. He sat with her in an alcove, sipping his wine until dinnertime, and as they sat there, he heard her confession, and just as they were summoned to dinner he gave her absolution.

All night long the fires burned under the great caldrons, first to melt the fat from the pork, then, when the tamales were ready for cooking, fire tending became a delicate operation because the heat must be maintained evenly while they simmered, steaming for hours. Men young and old drank their fill of tequila, first standing in the long line for confession from Father Ignacio. And the priest, with an encyclopedic memory, listened to a recounting of sins, great and small, and he knew every penitent although he saw them but twice a year. There was a minor brawl, and a knifing, not serious, over near the orchard, but the two antagonists slipped off into the plains to lick their wounds and the alcaide did not get the opportunity to practice his trade.

The following morning the priest heard more confessions, and all was quiet until just before noon when the first part of the celebration, the quarter-horse races, took place. And it was noon also, when Captain Hernández and his troop of fifty rurales arrived, and with them they brought two prisoners, runaways both, and one of these was Antonio Rivera.

Heraclio was still at home, brushing for the hundredth time the stallion which he would use during the afternoon, and so was not aware that his friend was now held in the small jail. He did not go to the races because he was much too heavy to ride in these short sprints. He was in the corral behind the house when Rosa called to him that Antonio's mother wished to see him.

"What does she desire?" asked Heraclio.

"Come and see for yourself," said Rosa, and he knew that something, as usual, had angered her.

"Buenos días, doña Cuca," he said to the small, almost tiny dark woman.

"A good day may God give you, Heraclio," answered Antonio's mother. Her eyes were red-rimmed, and it was obvious that she had cried long.

"What is wrong?" he asked, instantly concerned for her.

"But just look at what has happened, Heraclio. My Toño is in the juzga'o, just this minute brought in by the rurales."

"But why?" asked Heraclio, and he found this difficult to believe. "What could Antonio have done that he should deserve to be in jail?"

"He ran away—four days ago. And he took that little mare you let him use, which makes the penalty worse." The little woman started to cry again, silently but intensely.

Heraclio felt a surge of anger, and then a strong feeling of self-castigation. He had not seen his friend for some time, and Antonio did not search him out, knowing he was keeping the new Spaniard company. He was hurt that Antonio had not told him he was leaving, then again felt guilt that he might have prevented this—or at least gone with him. Perhaps the two of them could have eluded the network of mounted police if they had pooled their strength and their knowledge of the hills.

"What do they plan to do with him, do you know?" asked Heraclio.

"No. I have seen him this moment and I told him I would come to you but he said I should not bother you. I only go against his wishes because I am his mother, you understand. I want nothing to happen to him. He is a good son—always has been, and now this."

"But did he tell you anything at all?" asked Heraclio, and in his anxiety took her by the shoulders and squeezed hard.

She gasped in pain, and he said quickly, letting go of her, "Forgive me, doña Cuca, but tell me, please. What did he say?"

She caught her breath and answered. "The captain of the rurales told him, he said, that for running away he would have received a few lashes—but for the horse, which is the property of don Aurelio, he might be shipped away to a slave camp. I do not wish him to be lashed, but the other is far worse. We know how it is there, in wild country, where they take young men and make ancients of them in but a year, and where in the second year they die. Cannot you do something for him?"

121

"What can *he* do?" asked Rosa with sarcasm, and Heraclio realized that this was the reason for her anger—that doña Cuca should come to him rather than to Teodoro for help.

He had not had a chance to answer Antonio's mother when Rosa spoke up, and now again before he could say a word, doña Cuca said, "It is because of his friendship with the daughter of the patrón. Forgive me, Heraclio, that I should talk about this, that I should be so shameless as to interfere in that which is not my affair. I talk only as a mother searching succor for her son. It is because you are the girl's lover that I ask you to talk to her. That you beg her to intercede."

"Lover!" exclaimed Rosa, and Heraclio was thankful that she was incapable of believing such a thing to be true.

"You are wrong, doña Cuca. She is but my friend, as her brother is my friend. We are like brothers and sister, the three of us, for her father is my godfather, remember? And I shall see them both —immediately, although I fear that I can do nothing for Antonio, and believe me, I grieve."

The tiny woman did not argue. "Only try. Try! That is all I ask." He walked her outside as she said this, stopping her from saying more with Rosa present, and she did not realize he was ushering her out, her concern was so great. She went home to comfort her two daughters.

Heraclio went into his room to change his clothes. He had not intended to visit Carmen—having decided it would be best not to do so. He would see her, of course, and salute her from a distance, but although he did not feel the old jealousy, he still had a feeling, and he did not want the unpleasant sensation to return when he saw her with Domingo.

They had arrived early that morning, and he had been careful to be away when the diligence from Fresnillo came in. By now the Big House was filled with guests, all in finery, and he did not look forward to moving among them. But he must, that was a demand, and so he dressed rapidly, knowing what he must do, not delaying it by even a little while. Although he dressed quickly, he was careful, for he had a vanity, and if he would mingle for a time with the aristocracy, he would let them know that even a peon could look like a don.

The charro suit was new; he had worn it but once when

he bought it in Río Grande three months ago. It had been fine then, but when he returned to la Flor, he had put it away because it was not a thing to be worn by a peon with nowhere to go. It was festival dress—and even for that it seemed too ornate. To wear it implied a skill he was not certain he possessed, for it was not dishonor to be thrown by a beast, nor was it dishonor to fail in a feat of horsemanship, but to do so when dressed like this was an obscenity. It was the utmost of indignity, and he would be nothing more than an exhibitionist, and exposed to catcalls and ridicule. He knew this, but today he would compete dressed like a charro, and he also knew that this was because Carmen would be in the audience.

He rode his horse down the street and through the zaguán to the front of the Big House. He dropped the reins over the horse's head to the ground and left it under the alamo. He had thought of going around to the side of the house, to the french windows he knew opened to her room, but in broad daylight it was much too dangerous, for he had no reason for being there. And, too, there might be a roomful of girls there, for some people had come from México during the night and it was said, although Crispín and Carmen had been there a short while, that a young lady had accompanied them—a foreigner who knew not a word of the Spanish.

He walked up to the door and let fall the great knocker. He held his hat before him in both hands, unconsciously assuming the position of humility of the peon, but although he was more than a little self-conscious, he did not feel humble and he did not speak like a peon when the mozo opened the door.

"Go tell your mistress, María del Carmen, as a favor, that I am here to welcome her to her home, don Miguel," said Heraclio, for although the man was but a house servant, he was still an older person and commanded his respect.

"Very well, come in, Heraclio," said the old man, closing the doors after Heraclio entered. He moved off to call Carmen.

The doors opened to the large salon, with an alcove in one end, and other, smaller rooms on the opposite side. Heraclio moved toward the alcove, and he waited in the dark, for the drapes had not been drawn. He was alone, although he heard voices and an occasional giggle from another part of the mansion. Sounds also came, muffled, from above.

And suddenly she was there, covering his face with kisses. "Such a happiness to see you again," she said, "such a joy!"

He allowed her to press herself against him, and then he too held her, and they kissed. He released her, hungry for the feel of her breast, seeing her naked although she was fully clothed, but the whalebone in her stays disturbed him. His reaction was strange, one entirely new to him, for he was certain his feeling for her was not as it had once been, and yet he was hot with desire and he was overjoyed that she had not forgotten. And he knew also, by the faint pain in his chest, that he had not completely rid himself of his jealousy. He said:

"You have met the ox."

She laughed at him and said, "Yes. And he is quite handsome—and big. A big man," and she added mischievously, "He does not look to me like he would be an ox."

"I have told you too many times that you are not to talk in that way," he said harshly.

"And what, Heraclio Inés?" and in her happiness she laughed yet, "What? Will you beat me here in my own house? And then, will you comfort me in your usual manner?"

"You are ridiculous," he said. "And shameless!" And he remembered now why he had come here. "Let us sit—in the center of the room preferably, before we are discovered pawing at each other like animals." It was said in jest, but he knew they should be careful, so he drew the drapes and flooded the room with light.

"But look at my Heraclio—a charro!" she exclaimed. "And as handsome as the blessed Trinity."

He was uncomfortable. "You are blasphemous," he said.

"No, I am not, because it is true!" She looked at him, from the silver buttons on the weskit, along his strong legs where the cloth clung tightly, and then moved forward and grasped the telltale bulge at the left side of his crotch and squeezed tightly.

In his surprise he uttered a short cry of pain. "You are surely a crazy one," he said, but he was pleased, and through his pleasure he suddenly knew why he could never seriously think of marrying her—why he could never marry her, why he had told her about David, and why he had tried to hurt her so many times.

124

It was saddening that the very thing which made her so pleasing, that which offered him so much joy, was a thing so unladylike that she could never be his wife. True, she did not behave this way around other people—could he really be certain? And no one knew that she was not a virgin except the two of them—himself, and that is where it counted most, with him, for he could never fool himself, and the law was firm, even for him, Heraclio Inés. He who did not believe in laws believed in this one and he could never marry a woman already used, even if he was the one who used her and his honesty made him see this, made him mourn the fact, and his consideration for her made for a dishonesty, perhaps the first in his lifetime, that he would never tell her the reason.

She was oblivious to his pain and chattered gaily. "And the design, Heraclio," and she had gone behind him, still surveying his costume, feeling with light fingers the embroidery on the back of the jacket. "With the eagle and the serpent and the cactus, no less, my Heraclio. You see, I have told you always that you are of quality, peon."

"Stop it," he said, and he was gentle. "I must speak to you."

She sobered quickly, "That is the only reason you came, was it not? I told myself, he will come, he will come—and you did not appear. I was not going to behave like this, I told myself. I was going to be demure and retiring when you came. I should have known."

"You know, then," he said, not really wanting it to be this way, wishing he could make disappear the awkwardness of their relationship with a wave of his hand, by a gesture.

"Crispín told me. He also assured me that you would be here because of the matter. It is not necessary, however, for he is already talking to my father about it." His sadness communicated itself to her. "It is true, then. You came about Antonio and not to see me?"

"Do not talk like that," he said. "It is true, but not because I did not want to see you—it is simply easier for both of us if we do not see each other. That is all." And he was not merely sad, he was angry from deep within because he was so susceptible to the rules for manhood. He was a man, he knew, and there was no reason that he should prove this to himself, and yet, he would have nothing but disdain for another man who married a whore. But Car-

125

men was not a whore. She could offer so much; she had so much love for him and it would not be difficult for him to reciprocate if only she did not have this taint. He allowed himself to think this was the only thing keeping them apart.

And if she was not a whore, then why did he treat her like one? Yet, if she had done these things with him before marriage, might she not do it with someone else? Was it that he was afraid for his life, for such a thing could lead to killing? He wanted to take hold of her, to ask her, "In these months that you were away, did you do this thing with another? With a gringo, far away, did you lay and squirm?" If he believed that this could be true, he would ask her and make her tell, for therein was his salvation—he would have no need to feel this way. He knew her answer would be no, however, and he would remain in fear, and because he would hurt her by this question, his guilt would be greater as would his pain.

She was speaking and he was not listening but it did not matter because she was but making polite conversation. He thought back to a conversation with Domingo about just such a thing as this. He did not really believe the man, suspected that Domingo was really playing with him, but he wished that at least in part the things he was told could be true. It had happened that Domingo once asked if he had a girl of his own, or if he must depend on whores for pleasure.

"It is not an easy thing," Heraclio had answered, "to find a girl on the hacienda who will make love with one. In the first place, one cannot see a girl alone, and especially after dark."

"Can they not come out secretly?"

"Never. Here on the hacienda the woman does not touch a man until she is married. That is the way of the land. And if she does, she will never marry, for no one will have anything to do with her."

"How would they know?" asked Domingo.

"Well, she would marry," replied Heraclio, "but on the wedding couch the husband would know and return her to her father or brothers in disgrace."

"How rare!" said Domingo. "What a naïve people you really are!"

Heraclio flared up that this man should criticize the traditions of his people. "Do you tell me that you would marry a woman you know is promiscuous?"

126

Domingo was quite calm, interested that he had caused such a reaction, feeding Heraclio's displeasure to probe further into the make-up of the boy. "Of course I would do so. In fact, I will say that I would much rather marry a woman with experience in the sex act, for then I would not have the trouble of teaching her, of overcoming her inhibitions about the act. Someone else would have done me the favor of preparing her for her connubial duties."

"But you are a Spaniard!" Heraclio exclaimed. "The English, I have heard it said, do not mind their women to be dogs—but a Spaniard! Every ounce of Spanish blood in me rebels at such a thought!"

Domingo, very indulgent, explained. "That is because you have not been enlightened by the education. You people have no idea of the true values in life. You are under a lord and master, who sees that you have spiritual guidance, who sees that you have food to eat, and who marries you off early for two reasons. First, to maintain the supply of vassals to meet the demand—for some die off, you know, before they can replace themselves—and secondly, to satisfy the one remaining basic need of man, which is to empty his eggs occasionally. The patrón satisfies all your needs and so you work from sunup to sundown for him, day after day, year after year, and in appreciation for his goodness, you leave him your sons to do the same after you. And so you, who have nothing to worry about, create an ideal, patterned after our religion, and make your women, your materfamilias, the epitome of purity. Virgins, like the mother of God, and if you could, your own mothers would remain virgins. That is your value, and a synthetic one it is—and utterly worthless. It is not important that a woman be pure before marriage—even after marriage if she is discreet. Why, a man could lose his life for such foolish thoughts, or, as in my case, a fortune and a lifetime of ease is in the balance."

Heraclio was disgusted and did not attempt to conceal his contempt for the man. "You can talk such pretty words," he said, "and you yet do not say a Goddamned thing to me. There is yet one ideal and one value in life. There is loyalty to honor and loyalty to your own manhood. This I have known as long as I can remember. A man who would become a cuckold for a pot of gold would be as worthless as a pot of piss! And my people, who you say are satisfied—you do not know. You do not know that they are waiting, are quiet and docile and yet look for a time when life will be worth living, and that very fact makes life for them worth while. They wait as they have waited, and they have more patience than you or I because they are prepared to wait another century or two or three!" He turned as if to go, then continued, "There is also the value of life. They, my people know this as I do. But I wish to find a meaning to this value in my own lifetime."

Domingo reddened, not because of Heraclio's words, but finally because here was a mere boy and a peasant, speaking contemptuously to him. Yet, he controlled his voice and said, "There is always one or another such as you. There is always a rebel, there is always one who would think. In the right place, with a certain amount of power, you would be dangerous, but such a thing rarely happens. Soon you will marry and breed filthy urchins, and discover that your people are right in being docile, that is has nothing whatever to do with waiting, and that you are entirely wrong. Or else you might retain your ideas and end up on the whipping post, or in the slave colonies, there to ponder on your honor and your manhood. And you would lose your manhood either by starvation and hard labor, or by your surreptitious masturbation in a dark corner with your back to the other slaves."

"You are warning me," said Heraclio calmly, though in anger.

"If you wish," said Domingo. "But I am merely explaining a truth to you. And I go back to where we began—it does not matter to me if María del Carmen Becerra has lain with ten men. I rather relish the idea that she might have."

"That is an insult to her," said Heraclio, making no effort to control his anger. "It was your mother who was a whore, not Carmen!"

"And what is that to you?" asked Domingo, now equally angry. "Why does it mean something to you that I insult Carmen? Do I detect a case of admiration from afar. A case of a mortal reaching for a star?"

Heraclio stopped his thoughts—apprehensive that he had divulged that which should never be known. He was suddenly relieved that this man could not be provoked into a fight, and he controlled his face and uttered a short laugh, then said, the sarcasm in his words barely discernible, "She is the daughter of my patrón. I merely defend his honor."

128

His answer satisfied Domingo, but he retained a suspicion about Heraclio, which was to later grow and magnify into a hatred for the boy. He had been out to show him that a destiny could be made by man, that there was nothing supernatural about life, but now he could see him only as an adversary, as a potential threat to his class. And he did not know why.

They had talked more, their attitudes now different from what they had been, each with a little more knowledge about the other, and Heraclio had finally told him that it was possible on occasion to find a woman on the hacienda. She must be a married woman, whose husband was away, or a widow. The usual case was the young wife of the pastor, who, having tasted the delights of love, had immediately lost them temporarily because her man must go out to tend flocks.

And Domingo had said, "Find us a pair, little friend. That intrigues me." And Heraclio had replied, "Although I took you to a whorehouse, I am not a pimp. And besides, I cannot be held responsible for your death, for surely if you were found out you would die. This you do not also know, that a patrón may use the daughter of a peon but he can never touch a wife. In spite of your knowledge and your intelligence, this you cannot possibly understand. In México you are with another man's wife only if you are prepared to defend yourself or to die."

And now he was in the salon of the Big House, and Carmen was not over her grief, but she talked gaily to dissimulate because now there were other people in the room. Girls from the neighboring haciendas, a few younger girls who were kept in the Big House by the nuns, and three or four girls from the capital had come in and now looked brazenly at the young charro. Carmen introduced him, and a girl, older than the others, perhaps twenty-one years old, came to them and said, "I am Blanca de la O, and Carmen purposely did not give you my name because I take all her young men away from her."

"I am not her young man," said Heraclio.

Carmen said, appearing casual, "Come, Heraclio. I think Crispín can see you now. Please excuse us, Blanca."

But the girl from Mexico City was accustomed to frivolous banter, and since she would be here for a week, she might as well make a friend, for she was aware that this could be a frightfully boring visit. "Wait," she said. "Where have you been and what do you do. You must tell me about yourself, for Carmen has kept you well hidden. With whom do you stay when you are in México?"

Again Carmen tried to draw him away. She had been concerned because Blanca might embarrass Heraclio by her speech, and now she feared that he would be embarrassed because she thought him a señorito. But Heraclio smiled and said:

"I have never been to México, señorita. But when I do go there, perhaps I can stay with you. If not, I suppose I can find someone who would keep me for a night. You see, I have no one in México."

She was pleased that he should joke with her like that. Imagine this in the wilderness of the central plateau. She said, still thinking he was of the genteel class, "Is your family abroad?"

"Yes. They are in Paris at the moment," he said.

Carmen was angry that Heraclio was enjoying the play with words. "Blanca," she said. "Leave him be. He is teasing you most atrociously."

Blanca laughed, rightly thinking that Carmen was more than a little jealous. "You know, my dear, that I can hold my own in these things."

"Not here," said Carmen. "I beg of you, desist. He is a brute—he may even beat you." And she bit her lip that she had said the last.

Heraclio said, "It is enough, señorita. Carmen is most concerned because you mistake me for a gentleman. I am but a peon, and am admitted to this house only because the patrón is also my godfather. So stop being a coquette and retire to your friends, as we have very little to talk about, you and me."

Blanca was speechless but for a moment. "Oh well," she said, "I was but amusing myself." My God! she thought. A peon! I was flirting with a peon!

And because Blanca de la O was in truth the sophisticate her role indicated—hers was the guile of obscuring the truth by acting the truth—she thought also, I was imagining the boy with me—how horrid! Or, perhaps not so horrid after all. How would it be with a peon. Something like an animal, I suppose—all smelly and all.

As she walked away, a giggle came from the side, and she turned

130

to see a young girl, thirteen years old at the most, laughing most openly, and Heraclio turned also, and the laughter subsided behind the fan of Marcelina Ortiz, great-granddaughter of the old artisan, but her large dark eyes looked merrily at him.

This is indeed a roomful of crazies, he thought. Carmen said to him as she led him out of the room, "I told you, Heraclio, that the women in the capital would be captivated by you."

He was embarrassed but he said, "That one would be ripe for anyone, I believe. Some women are like that."

"Am I like that?" she asked.

He felt a pang of guilt. "No," he answered, and at that moment he meant it as truth.

She said, "Blanca is perhaps more innocent that I am, now that I have met you. She talks this way because it is the manner in the capital. You remember how I used to be. She is really quite naïve, and is one of the favorites in the society in México. Why, she has actually been to Chapultepec to parties for don Porfirio."

"Some honor!"

"All right, be that way. I only want us to be happy for a time, since I do not know what is to become of us. You are so obstinate, and cannot see how much I love you—how much I wish I had not been born in my station. It seems that you blame me for what we are. Oh, I do not know!"

"Carmen," he said, but she was gone. He would find Crispín. Now, although she should be in attendance with her friends, she would depart for a while from the responsibility of being a young lady of the upper class. She was in tears before she reached her room.

Her grief was uncontrollable, and now she was in greater pain because she had the mantle of guilt eating at her. She had deceived him, once, but she had done it, up, way up north, in a little town called Port Angeles she had done it because she needed it and because she meant to find out if she could really substitute someone else for him and she had enjoyed only release, only the spasm which marked her betrayal, for up until then, although she moved under a man and he within her, she would have yet believed that she had not committed such an atrocity. And the boy had been surprised, had rushed her from her arrival—a big, handsome, dark-haired boy who somehow reminded her, and he was

131

shy—how could she have ever thought Heraclio was shy? He had not had too much time to spend with her because he worked to help pay his tuition, which was unusual, but he had rushed her certainly and he was so naïve when it was over he blurted, "Oh, María"—he pronounced it Mahriah—"oh, what have I done!" and he was such a fool that he did not remember that he had been surprised and frightened and in the end she had taken him and guided him into her body and he repeated, "I'll do the right thing, don't you worry!" And there was no stopping him after that time, which only happened because she had made up her mind that she should, and now he called her his hot tamale but could not really believe that she was Mexican because she was so fair, and so she did not see him anymore, but the damage had been done—more damage possibly than if she had become pregnant. And she thought, If Heraclio should ask me, or if I should convince him that we can marry, I shall tell him of this to prove to him how much I love him, but her intuition told her that this she should not do, and so she forgot the idea, and she wrote love letters to him every night and cried over them and then destroyed them, and acted very unlike the María del Carmen Becerra who had once spent a year in the capital.

She stopped crying at a knock on the door, and when it was repeated, she called, "Who is it?"

"Open the door, Carmen. I am your mother," said doña Gertrudes.

She rose and walked to the door. "What do you wish, Mamá?" she asked, standing before the locked door.

"I hear you crying, and I wish to come in," said doña Gertrudes. "Open the door."

Carmen turned the key and allowed her mother to enter the room. She turned and walked back to the bed and lay on her back, staring at the ceiling.

"What is it, my child?" asked doña Gertrudes, full of concern and already certain she knew her daughter's fears.

"It is nothing, Mamá. It is but a passing thing and I am quite all right now."

"But is it?" said doña Gertrudes. "I know of these things, my child, you must remember I once went through what you are now suffering."

For a moment, Carmen almost believed her, but then shook her head, no. It could not possibly have been true of her mother. "You do not know," she said. "Please—I am fine, now, and but need a little cry. You can understand that, no?"

"Of course, my dear. Of course." The woman hugged her daughter in a rare show of affection, but her mind was on one thought and she was, after all, a mother with a responsibility, and although it was almost indecent to talk about these things, she felt it her duty to do so. "It is not too bad, Carmen. This business of becoming a señora. A bit painful," and she winced because in spite of herself she was being crude, "and one loses her identity for a while —until the first child is born, but otherwise it is an easy thing to settle into. There is an inconvenience, of course, but I hear tell that some wives actually learn to get some enjoyment from performing their marriage duties."

"Oh, Mamá!" Carmen laughed aloud. "That is not it at all." She stopped herself from laughing because she feared she would become hysterical.

Doña Gertrudes was puzzled. "Well, then, my child, what can there be which would make you so unhappy? There is nothing in your life which would make you cry like this." Then she had another thought, and her face brightened. "Carmen, do not be so embarrassed that you cannot speak to your mother. I am a woman too, remember—and I do not need to tell you that I have an experience in these things." She gained confidence as she spoke, and said things she would never admit thinking. "It is this man-woman business after all, is it not? And it is frightening, I admit, but not an impossible thing. It is a nuisance later on, until your husband finds himself a maid or another girl from the peonada, and then it is not as often. Do not be shocked, my child, for this is the way of life, the way of a woman. It is because your intended is so huge, is it not? You see, you cannot fool your old mother on these things. You are frightened because he is so big, but have no fear. I understand that their size has nothing to do with their size, uh—elsewhere."

"Please leave me alone, Mother!" and the formal name brought a bit of anger to doña Gertrudes.

"Listen to me, girl. You must get hold of yourself and resign yourself to being used like an animal. That is in the destiny of

133

women and there is nothing we can do about it. I am solicitous because I am your mother and I carried you in my womb. But I am becoming impatient with you, for you are a lady and should accept everything with stoicism. That is our lot. The peones do it, why cannot we?"

And Carmen in turn was angry, and in her anger did not care to be cautious. "You are wrong, Mother. I have told you that you are wrong but you insist. Very well. I shall tell you! I know what it is to be had by a man. I have done these things, not once, but fifty times. And I have not been used like an animal as you say. I have been like an animal because I was taken with love and I returned it. If this is the lot of the woman then I am the happiest and luckiest of creatures—and I have enjoyed it, Mamá—I have come—that is what men call it, venir, to come, and I have loved every moment of it so much that I have counted the times. You talk like a little girl—like a dumb little girl. His size! How could his size be a factor—he is huge, as you say, but he could never be as big as my man. A duty, you say . . ."

"Carmen!"

"A duty! It is a privilege, do you hear. A pleasure! And you talk about your husband being with another woman. How can you? I would die with jealousy!"

"A gentlewoman is never jealous," was all the astonished doña Gertrudes could say.

"My God! My God! That is not it at all!"

And doña Gertrudes had recovered from her shock. This was a terrible thing her daughter was confessing. Who was this man? How? And when was the last time? The marriage must be hastened, just in case—and luckily that was already arranged. She had another fear for a moment, but no. Domingo was a gentleman. He would not raise objections after the wedding night like a common peon. The dowry had been a good one. "Who is he?" she asked, and she did not know the shrewdness of her question coming at this exact moment, for Carmen was saying:

"It is because I must marry someone else that I am dying. It is because you would never allow us to marry!"

Doña Gertrudes looked at her daughter with a wise, suspicious eye. Could it be? No, no. She was distracted from her shock. Still waiting, she felt the moment propitious, and again asked, "Who was he—who is he?"

And Carmen shook her head from side to side. "Do not ask me, please!" she whispered. "Do not ask me!"

"I must know," said doña Gertrudes. "It must have been someone like Paquito Paz, though he is eligible. Or someone up in North America?" She was giving Carmen an opportunity to lie, to keep from disgrace before her eyes by having the man be a gentleman.

Carmen still shook her head with wide eyes, pleading silently, because she could not betray him in this manner. She had done it by performing the act with someone else, but she alone knew that, and she could live with it. This would be different. To admit an indiscretion and name someone else would be more of a betrayal. And still shaking her head, she said, "Heraclio. Heraclio is my lover and I love him more than life." She was done with it, come what may.

Doña Gertrudes retained her poise. She was wounded deeply that her daughter should choose someone so common. She was hurt that her daughter had been promiscuous, but she could have been a little more selective. She said, "It is fortunate that everything has been arranged. You must have a little guile with your husband, but he is a man of the world and will know immediately. You must attribute it to a lapse when you were quite young, and he will be a gentleman. Do not fear. The banns will be published in México in two weeks, and we shall have the wedding shortly after that. We cannot take too long with these things. He has not been with you since your return? No, how could he. And what loyalty he has to your father! Yet we cannot have a scene about it, so he will go free . . . free with one exception. We will marry him off to an Indian girl. Probably before your wedding. He has had too many liberties, that brute, I can hardly call him a boy."

Carmen could not cry now, simply falling into a deep depression. Listlessly, she said, "Do not bother me with your plans. I am beyond pain, now. I will offer you no trouble, no objections. Only tell me when to do what I must and do not discuss it with me."

"You will behave in the manner expected of someone in your station. We will have no embarrassment in the house of Becerra. Is that understood?"

"Yes, Mother." She walked out and went down to join her guests.

And in another room, Heraclio greeted his godfather, don Aurelio, and received compliments on his attire.

"You are prepared to perform for our guests today, Heraclio? You will please me greatly if you ride the ride of death. It has been many years since I have seen it."

Heraclio was not displeased, and don Aurelio did not feel that his request was out of place. That of Heraclio's father had happened long ago, and this was the way of the jinete. To refuse to speak about the ride of death because his father had died that way was as ridiculous as to refuse to speak of childbirth because his mother had expired delivering him. "I have never attempted it, padrino. I have seen it but once, although my brothers have everyone done it more than once since the day of the tragedy."

"You will do it, though?"

"Certainly, to please you I shall try."

"Heraclio," said Crispín, coming into the room and leading by the hand a healthy-looking, suntanned young girl. "Here he is, dear. Heraclio, my friend, of whom I have been speaking these many months. Here he is, and you who know about baseball, and football, and whatnot—here is a true athlete. Heraclio," he changed his speech into Spanish, "I wish to present you to my wife. Her name is Susan, nee Kelley—to you Susana, and now de Becerra."

"Mucho gusto, señora," said Heraclio.

She gave him her hand, and her friendliness made him happy, forcing him to smile widely in spite of the many problems on his mind.

"I am most pleased to meet you, Hercules," she said in English, and he laughed and said, "Taddalalulalula, lúlala," and they all laughed, for that was how it sounded, and don Aurelio said, "What do you think of your friend, Crispín? I sent him to the North American United States to study how to grow crops because the hacienda needs more agriculture and he brings home a wife, thinking I meant a different kind of sowing—and rarer yet, he married an Inglesa."

They had been right, the rumor bearers, when they said she was a foreigner, but they did not know that she would be the patrona, and they erred when they said she did not know the language, for she said, in flawless Spanish, "I am a Norteamericana, not an Englishwoman. And now, I too am a Mexican. If you would find a category for me, Papá, before I became a señora, I mean, then by all means you should say I am Irish. For we Irish are also a proud race, wherever we happen to be born and wherever we may live."

Don Aurelio was pleased beyond words. This was the first he had known about her command of the Christian tongue. "Come, my daughter," he said. "Come sit with me and tell me about your people."

"Muy bien," she said. She walked away with the patrón and he could be heard saying, "Irlandesa, eh? Well, we are tied by blood, you know, for the heroic men from the Armada . . ."

Crispín said, "Spanish history is so stupid, and my father is so romantic. And yet, Heraclio, you should educate yourself in Spanish history, for it is good to know where your beginnings were."

"Come, Crispín. You know that I am a son of Cuauhtémoc. I am a Mexican, and that is all."

"But you are also Spanish," said Crispín, and really this turn in the conversation was apropos of nothing and they both knew it, Crispín with his wry smile, and Heraclio with the patience of his breed, knowing intuitively that his friend wished to communicate with him, anticipating nothing, waiting until Crispín wished to become confidential. "You cannot deny the language, the religion," and Crispín yet smiled oddly, seemingly agitated, and Heraclio had never seen him in this condition. "And romance— you like women, and you are vain, and your skill with animals might be Indian, but your way with women is Spanish—my own sister included."

Heraclio became cautious, for now he had reason to guess Crispín's motives. "I do not know what you mean," he said, watching closely, yet seeming to be embarrassed by the compliment.

"You know very well what I mean," said Crispín, and now he laughed sincerely, and Heraclio was reassured. "She has been almost crazy to get here just to see you. It is strange, for I have seen my sister around men—much older than you or I—men who have had experience with experienced women, and she has made mincemeat of them. And you, you tamed her as if she were a slightly wild mare, in fact I really think it was an easier task—and while I am on the mania of Heraclio Inés, I must say you look impressive in that uniform. And I am happy that you met my wife looking thus, for she will not call me a liar for telling her about a peasant on our lands who is a boy and yet a man and not really a peasant. I am somewhat silly, as you will note, but not from drink. I have an unpleasant task to perform and I am feeling a bit lachrymose, believe it or not—a most Spanish trait, remember that when you shed tears—and yet it is from happiness, believe me, although it is a sad task."

Heraclio did not speak, confused as he was, for his friend was not being coherent, and yet he thought, This is a day to be remembered, for I cannot think of so many things happening to make me grieve in one day in my life.

"Come," he said. "Now that you have a wife I suppose it is proper if you take a drink in the house of your father. And not that puny sherry the Spaniards drink."

"You are correct," said Crispín. "That is what I need."

"I need a drink as badly as you do, otherwise I would not have suggested it," said Heraclio. "You have no monopoly on tribulations."

They went into the large room again, and the girls were all on one side talking. They moved to the sideboard, and there were decanters on its top, but Crispín called a mozo and asked for mezcal. They drank from the bottle like peasants, and Crispín did not speak, so Heraclio also drank quietly. After a time he asked, "Who is that puta, there in the vermilion dress, with the good tetas, and hips?"

"Blanca? Would you meet her? But after we talk, if you do not mind." Crispín took another drink, and laughed. "It seems more like a wake than a fiesta. Forgive me, Heraclio. How did you know her so well, to call her a puta, when I know you would not do so unless you were certain?"

Heraclio shrugged his shoulders.

"It is said in the capital that she is all woman and wise as the ages, although she is young for a woman, but not young for an unmarried woman. She will undoubtedly marry before long to protect her reputation, for in México you can be promiscuous only

138

when you are married. For some ungodly reason that is tolerated among the enlightened."

"What is to be done with Antonio?" asked Heraclio, wishing to be over his problem while the other made up his mind whether to talk or not. "Can we talk to your father in his behalf?"

"I have already done so," said Crispín. "It is not important that you talk to him also, for he knows your wishes. Although Hernández of the rurales is also a circuit judge and has a free hand in these matters, with the sacerdotal advice of Father Ignacio, I am sure my father can have him released. He told me that he will turn him over to you after allowing him to sweat a little in the jail. You will have him in your custody and see that he does not run away again. Of course, my father is shrewd in this because it means that you must stay here, and believe me, he wants you here 'to keep you out of trouble,' as he says."

"Antonio will not sweat, be it in that little shit of a jail or at the whipping post," said Heraclio. "But I am willing to stay if it means that he can go free."

"Well, then he will," said Crispín.

"I cannot thank you enough," said Heraclio. "You are a true friend."

"It is you who are the friend," said Crispín. "You are giving up something, I am not." He was thoughtful for a time. They drank, long drinks, and the liquor was burning pleasantly in their bellies. "My sister," said Crispín, "we were talking about my sister."

"You were," said Heraclio. "I said nothing."

"Well, then, I was. She worships you and I did not know. Susana told me first, from her talk she realized it and I thought she was mistaken, but women communicate somehow without speaking. And I tell you this only because it saddens me that because I am going to do what I am about to tell you, there cannot be a chance that you two could ever get together." He stopped again and looked at Heraclio, and Heraclio waited, not knowing what to make of this, and yet not seeming to be in a hurry to know. "Forgive me, Heraclio, if I offend you. I have learned a great deal this past year. Things I have never really formulated in my mind. I am nineteen years old, almost three years older than you are, and yet I know that you are much older than I—in many ways. I say these things to you, knowing well that you do not feel

139

for my sister the way she feels for you. You would not allow your-self to yearn for her, to lust for her. I but say that if the situation could be remedied, you might find a love for her, for she is good. Believe me."

"I know she is good," said Heraclio, and he too felt the need to cry, and he did not know just why, and it was not the drink.

"I have learned many things in the United States, as they call it, thinking they are the only united states in the world. For in spite of their many forms of slavery—never called this, just as we never call the hacienda system 'slavery'—there is a place where if you work and work industriously, you are rewarded with equality. Of course, and you undoubtedly do not understand all of this, it is economic equality which brings about social equality, but the fact remains that it is possible. This is the year one thousand nine hundred and ten, and do you know that for fifty years now, that nation to the north has not had real slavery. Slavery such as we know in the Isthmus of Tehuantepec, let alone the slavery we have here in the hacienda. And yet they do have this kind, I must be fair. There is a man named Samuel Gompers, who talks about the coal mines, where there is a tienda de raya, and the eternal family debt, very much like ours, keeps the workers there forever, and their children inherit the debt, again very much in the way it happens here. But I am convinced that they will do away with this, and without a war, which I feel we will someday have.

"I tell you this only because at the moment it concerns Carmen. If you had the inclination to be her husband—and again let me beg you to forgive my voicing this and perhaps embarrassing you —it would perhaps be possible if I remained in la Flor, for that is the reason for all this talk. I am leaving—forever, except for a visit or two someday. And because I leave, the responsibility for the hacienda will fall on Carmen and her husband. If I were to stay, I could somehow help you, if you were so inclined, to go away somewhere and marry, and when I became master here, all the doors of the hacienda would be open to you, for I find that I love you, Heraclio Inés, and although I love humanity, there are few individuals I feel for.

"But I must go because I could not be a patrón in the manner tradition demands. I would go against my class, which is nothing to me, believe me, but they would not let me do it—to treat peones as human beings, and give them back some of their land. And my wife would suffer; that I could not stand. You have seen her—she is as good as she looks, and so we are to go to Spain, and later, after a year in Europe, we will live in her home state. I am fortunate that she is almost as rich as we are, and if my father should prove obstinate, it will not matter greatly. I am to leave, and yet I must know. I must ask you, how do you feel about Carmen? Nothing more, for I know you have been alone together a great deal, and I believe in love, although I have never thought about it greatly before this. What of Carmen? Can you tell me? For I must know all the hurt I create—I must know every sacrifice I make with my decision. Tell me, friend Heraclio, my brother."

"What can I tell you, Crispín. That you would at the risk of degrading yourself call me brother—what can I say but the truth. And because you are a man and deserve the truth. I have loved your sister. The word is awkward in my mouth, but I have truly loved her. And then I dominated this love because of the futility. Can I love her again? I do not know. And I tell you more, because you say you understand these things, and because I am only now beginning to see them myself. Have I lain with her? Yes, yes, yes! And we are both better for it. If you would slay me, do so, and I would remain immobile while you did it. And this obscenity which has come here to become her consort. Can you imagine my feeling? Can you?"

"I can imagine," said Crispín. And he cried silently because he must run away.

And now Heraclio could no longer fool himself. Because she was not a virgin and because she was unattainable he had made himself believe that it was over. Now he knew, and the pain of jealousy engulfed him as if from a physical blow. And there was no answer for him—what was taking place in his life was as final as death. He must suffer. He knew that at this moment he was as much a slave as the most humble peon. He walked slowly out the door to his horse.

In the jail, which was a simple adobe building with doors made of madrone and with a single barred window, Heraclio talked to Antonio.

141

"They will release you," he said, "in my custody, which means I must take care of you." The last was said as an attempt at humor because he knew Antonio would object.

"They can all go fuck their mothers," said Antonio. "I will not take you into slavery with me."

"It is not so," said Heraclio. "It is only that when you go again I go with you. And why did you not let me know? Together we might have eluded the rurales."

Antonio clasped his friend's hands through the bars. "It is as I have said. I do not want to compromise you. You are free, but if you should help a peon escape, then you commit a crime. I want no part of that."

Heraclio felt a frustration such as he had never known. Although he knew his friend would be freed on the following day, he wished he could knock the walls down at this moment. "If I could only get you out of here!" he said. Then, "What is it, Antonio? What is it that suddenly drove you to make an attempt?"

"My sister Sofía. The baby—thirteen years old, barely, and the administrators told my mother that on her fourteenth birthday, she is to go to work in the Big House. I do not want that man, your godfather, Heraclio, to get his hands on her. He is a good man otherwise, and I suppose if we found ourselves in the position where we could pick our screwing we would do the same thing —yet, if he touches my sister, I will kill him—mark my words. I swear to you, my beloved friend, that I will kill him. And if I cannot do it by myself I know someone who will help me. Although it would be patricide. Your friend David, I speak of—and it is said that he has run away. Of course it was a simple matter for him, for he was tending sheep ten leagues from the hacienda when he decided to leave, and it was a good ten days before they knew he was absent."

"David gone?" asked Heraclio, and he felt a pang of regret that he did not even know what his old friend was doing, and, along with this, the closer feeling that he had neglected Antonio also. With David it could not be helped because he rejected every effort on Heraclio's part to be friendly—but Antonio—to spend the days with Domingo Arguiú, as a feeling of duty, really, rather than take the time to visit his friend, made him feel guilt and remorse.

"And yet, Antonio, what did you expect to accomplish by running away?"

Antonio felt foolish, and yet felt justified because at least it was an effort on his part to avert that which he feared. "I was going to work somewhere, or join a band of outlaws—I did not really know. I simply decided that it was time to try to get the money to pay my father's debt to the tienda de raya. If I could have done it, my mother and sisters would leave and go live in the city, and we could find a happiness."

"How much is it? The debt that you wish to clear up?"

"Eight years ago, before my father died—or I suppose it was right after he died, the administrator came to my mother to tell her that although her man was dead, the debt was still in the books, and that when I grew up, I would have to pay it or she and my sisters would also have to work to undo the commitment. At that time it was placed at nine thousand pesos. Let me see, at forty centavos a day, six days a week, it comes to with the time off, it should take me but sixty-five years or so to pay it off—that is if I do not eat for those sixty-five years."

"And you were to work and earn that amount?" asked Heraclio in disbelief.

"I cannot lie to you, Heraclio. I was going to steal the money. I calculated that in six months, with a bit of luck and no drinking where I might lose it, I could get it. I have a few months. I really believed that I could do it."

"Tomorrow you will be released," said Heraclio. "After that wait a while and see what will happen. Perhaps you will not have to go away, but if you do, I shall go with you, I promise you."

Antonio objected. "I do not want that, Heraclio. I wish in no way to harm you or your position."

"Nevertheless, I want it that way." He moved away to give the good news to Antonio's mother.

IX

THE QUARTER-HORSE RACES WERE OVER and now the people of la Flor moved to the large corral behind the Big House, the corral where Heraclio had broken his first horse. Temporary stands had been erected along one side, and the permanent reviewing stand had been newly whitewashed, and its roof framework had been covered with palm leaves to provide shade for the landowner and his guests. They, too, arrived, and now all the celebrities were present. The president of the city of Fresnillo, the alcalde of Río Grande, friends and relations from the capital, and Captain Hernández, circuit judge and leader of the troop of rurales, were in attendance. Captain Hernández's men were dispersed in the crowd, as civilian spectators, with orders to do nothing more than flirt a little in the traditional manner with the belles of the hacienda. They could drink, but the man who imbibed more than his capacity could expect a lashing for his crime.

It was a scene of gaiety all around as a fiesta should be, and women of the hacienda offered food to those who would eat. Tacos, freshly made, tamales, birria, and native gruels called atoles. There were also cheeses and the yogurt-like jocoque, cool and strong from earthern jugs. And it was for the asking, for don Aurelio himself paid for everything except hard drink on days of festival.

And the beautiful girls, the most ugly person being beautiful on this day, gaily dressed, and carefree laughing, adding luster to their comeliness. And the game began, the young sports giving low whistles of admiration, and an exchange of double-entendres which could be made only in the open like this. Mariachis strolled here and there, playing and singing, and occasionally a girl was serenaded to the joy and hoots of those around her, and in this way, a parent might discover where a match could be made for his daughter, who was now perhaps sixteen and would soon be a spinster.

And in the reviewing stands, the dons were seated, also savoring antojitos, reveling in the songs and spirit, and for a moment, except for the fact that their shade and cushions and their dress marked them as different, they were a part of humanity. The marching band shared the comfort of the dons, except that it did not have a roof overhead, and it led off with a raucous rendition of the *March of Zacatecas*.

In the chapel, Padre Ignacio heard an endless stream of confessions. He had developed an ability to mentally record every speech, almost word for word, and as he was in his cubicle for so long, he could clearly distinguish every penitent and on occasion asked his name.

The first event was the "run at the cocks," and the riders rode their own horses. Each rider, before he participated would go to the stands if he had a favorite girl, and somewhat in the manner of a torero, would declare that his ride was dedicated to her beauty.

The Ineses stood by themselves, always quiet, almost taciturn, not being affected by ritual, for they were here only to show their supremacy, and in their mind it was not a gamble. Others might dedicate and hope to excel—the Inés man knew he would because he must. And they had mozos, every one. They had a groom to hold their steeds and they each had two, and for the present, they did not make a first attempt, for they were allowed two tries at the cocks.

The riders were grouped at one end, to the right of the stands, and at the other end of the corral, five roosters were buried to their necks in the soft dirt. They were in line, and, to expedite the activity, five riders would take a run at once. They would be judged on time elapsed, but mainly in their manner of execution. During the run, those who fell were eliminated, and those who either took the bird or touched it were given another chance. The Ineses stood next to their mounts as the action began, giving them every possible moment of rest, and of the first five riders three of them went on their heads, and the other two failed to come near the cocks. The fallen sat on the dust, and good-naturedly took the howls and jeers from the crowd, and the girls who had received their favors were embarrassed and then indignant, and tossed their heads to show it did not matter to them. And another wave of riders moved, and then another, until all but the brothers Inés had ridden once. There were some very good ones, especially from the Rancho Grande, and one or two of the professionals, and now it started once again, and because they had not as yet tried, Heraclio and his brothers went first, and they sped across the runway in front of the stands, neck and neck at first, their mounts almost identical mares, their bodies also alike, and then Elías moved ahead, and then came Juan and Concepción, then Teodoro, Heraclio being last, but with less than a horse length separating them. They went down along their animals' sides together, right hand extended until it lay palm up less than an inch from the ground, their mounts moving at top speed, and the fingers of the hand opened wide as they neared the cocks, and each took his bird from the ground cleanly, hooking it in their fingers as they sped by, but Elías was not only faster but had better form. They trotted before the stand, holding their prize aloft, and the band broke into dianas, and the drummer beat a flourish. Elías took first place and a professional came second and then Juan. The prize was twenty-five pesos, and the Inés men went to their women and gave them the roosters, mauled but still alive. And the headless cocks which had been decapitated by a not gentle competitor were taken to the Big House and immediately dressed.

Now the band played *La Modesta* while the cowboys of the hacienda made preparations for the second event, which was the Mexican equivalent of bulldogging. This time the participants waited on the left, for the bulls would be run from left to right, along the barrier, with a rider outside to see that they did not swerve out. This time one attempt was allowed and only those who considered themselves superlative in the art competed. There were new entries and some who had competed in the first event retired for the present. The tradition of allowing guests to ride first was observed, and every one of the visitors threw his animal, and then the men of the hacienda took their turns, and only two failed, and then Elías, Juan, and Concepción threw their animals very well, and Heraclio came down the runway on his huge stallion, pounding hard, nearing the bull, and in the manner he had been taught so long ago reached down and grasped the tail, holding it for three strides and at the right moment, spurred his mount and pulled, then hooked the tail near his hand with his right foot, adding leverage, and the bull went up and over on his back, slid a few feet with legs straight up, and Heraclio sped by. He received his dianas and applause as an animal was made ready for Teodoro, who sat his horse lazily, with a sober face, and extremely pleased that it was his little brother whom he must defeat. His horse stood still yet trembled a little, its ears lay limp, its head hung a bit, looking nondescript, small even for a mare, for Teodoro preferred mares for his work. Heraclio came by him, also with a serious face, although he was pleased inside that he had done so well, he had a twinge of admiration, almost affection for his brothers. Others might perform better than Teodoro at some things, certainly not at this he was about to do, and no one knew horses as he knew them. He sat on a true cowhorse, one that knew it was on earth to work cattle, and one that preserved its strength at all times. There was nothing showy about Juguete, as Teodoro called his animal. It did not prance, nor did it toss its head, and never expended its energy until it was required. And somehow, Teodoro was the same way when on a horse.

The bull was let loose, and immediately the mare moved its feet, needing no command, not even the light touch of a spur, and it was like a streak, man and horse seeming as one, and when immediately behind the bull Teodoro brought his left leg up and over, and he sat his mare sidesaddle-like, hooking a leg on the saddle horn, and then reached down, dropping his reins, and the bull veered to the right, but the mare followed him in and Teodoro had the tail, leaning far, as if tying a shoe, then took a half turn on his right ankle with the end of the tail, another jump, and suddenly he kicked up, his left leg went over the horse in a great arc, like an acrobat, his right leg brought the animal's rump up even with his saddle, and his feet were in the stirrups even as the animal was in the air. He turned around and walked back to the riders, the mare once again assuming its lazy stance, relaxed like its rider now that the task was performed. Heraclio and Juan had received second and third places.

Lesser events followed, such as bull riding, and the Ineses did not compete, for this did not involve skill with a horse, and the professionals, who did this often in the city where it was a favorite sport, took all the prizes. But when the roping competition came on, again the Ineses took three places, this time Juan and Concepción and Heraclio winning, and the other two not far behind.

And then the cowboys began to rope while on foot, and the activity seemed to increase. Calves were thrown and hogtied, and after that, mares were driven into the huge corral, thrown and held down while a rider straddled it. In this way, both the roping and bronco riding were done at one time. Some jinetes roped and then mounted their own animals, and in this event the brothers Inés took the first three prizes.

147

The first place money gave Heraclio twenty-five pesos, and it was not enough for what he had in mind. He would attempt the "ride of death" but would get no money even if he succeeded because he had been asked to do it as a favor by don Aurelio. So while young boys made crude passes with their jackets at young bulls, he went to Teodoro.

"I need another prize, Teodoro," he said. "I have need for some money."

"Why?" Teodoro would have answered brusquely, but the boy had pleased him by his work this afternoon, and so he was pleasant. "What need do you have for money, boy?"

"I wish to buy me a gun."

Again Teodoro would have laughed or dismissed him, but he was forced to look at his young brother, and, looking at him, he could not but agree. "You are correct," he said. "You are grown, my brother, and you should have a gun. But there is no need to buy one, for tomorrow I shall get one for you at the arsenal."

Heraclio said, "A man should have his own weapon, Teodoro."

"You are correct once more," said Teodoro. "What would you attempt for more prize money?" There was always prize money at these events for the horseman who would do something unusual, a thing beyond what their profession demanded from them. And yet that which was attempted would not be a foolhardy act, for there was no prize for failure, only ridicule. And a true horseman had his pride.

"There is one thing," said Heraclio, "but it seems such a simple thing that I am afraid the patrón would not consider it."

"And what is that?"

"To down an animal while on foot by roping it by the neck. We have all done it—you yourself taught me how."

"But of course," said Teodoro. "But these people do not know the simplicity of these things. Prepare yourself; I shall tell the patrón."

Heraclio seemed reluctant yet. "All it takes is a good eye and a good hand," he said.

"And balls," said Teodoro, and smiled one of his rare smiles. He clasped Heraclio to him, and Heraclio, looking into his brother's face, also smiled.

Teodoro walked away and Heraclio waited where he stood. The

148

band blared raucously once more, and he was a bit giddy with emotion. Looking at the stands, at the men who lived with horses, smelling fresh horse dung, and the band and that of being an Inés—that, most of all—for the first time really, being accepted as a part of the family of Inés, reliving every moment of the afternoon in his mind, seeing Teodoro, whom he hated most of the time riding his Goddamned mare, and the others, quiet, taciturn, yet magnificent with beasts, and he himself, competing with men, with less experience and showing so well. It was suddenly a great thing to be alive, and for now, at least, he could almost believe Teodoro. He walked across to the other side of the corral, walking in front of the grandstand, knowing that many eyes were upon him, very straight, with dignity, controlling himself so that he would not appear smug merely because he was alive.

It was, as he had told Teodoro, a simple thing to win the twenty-five pesos. He stood in the sun and took three turns around his middle with his reata, and the animal was driven across in front of him from his right. He cast a soft throw even as the horse was abreast of him, then moved forward as the noose fell true, and waited for the moment, and when the moment came, he allowed the slack to be taken in, making the rope taut. The horse placed its feet on the ground at this very moment and was twisted violently to the side before it could spring again, and now, off balance, his own momentum threw it over. Heraclio moved quickly forward along the rope, but the horse did not get to its feet. Its legs moved spasmodically as it lay on its side, its neck no longer sloping but at an angle, its eyes wide, expressive with pain and fear. Teodoro walked over and put a bullet into its head.

The carcass was dragged from the arena as two professionals twirled reatas in an expert exhibition, and Heraclio walked to the entrance of the corral, and outside, near the zaguán, an Arab had his wares spread on the ground. Two small mules were tethered to a mesquite, and down a ways, yet not too far so that the peddler could not watch his property, was a two-wheeled cart. A few women were bargaining with him over the price of a piece of organdy, and young boys lurked all around, looking for something they could snatch up on the fly.

The peddler winked at Heraclio as he made his sale, and Heraclio's face did not change in the least. "I come for the gun, Arab, that which we spoke about earlier."

"Of course," said the peddler. "It is a very good gun—the best on the market today. I got it from . . ."

Heraclio interrupted the stutterlike accents of the peddler's Castilian. "I do not come to bargain. I have fifty pesos, you have the gun. Let us exchange."

"But that is not the way to do business," said the Arab.

"That is the way I do business," said Heraclio. "Do you want the fifty pesos or not?"

"Very well." The peddler's tone showed that he was disappointed that they would not haggle, for this was an enjoyable thing to him.

It was a beautiful gun—a Colt, forty-four caliber—and Heraclio admired it as he walked back into the corral. All was quiet; the bandsmen waited patiently for the word that they should break into music once again, and before the reviewing stand, don Miguel López spoke out loud and clearly, that, as administrator of the Hacienda de la Flor, he declared the equestrian events terminated, and that the dancing would begin immediately after the next event, which would take place only if there was somewhere in the gathering a jinete willing to attempt the ride of death.

Teodoro walked to the administrator and talked to him, for Heraclio had already indicated that today he would attempt this, and in the tradition of the family, because there was no father, Teodoro was in attendance and spoke for him.

Two other jinetes came forward then and spoke for themselves. One, from the Rancho Grande, had placed well all afternoon, and the other from a ranch called Guadalupe. They were in their twenties, and it was obvious in the manner they sat a horse and in the way they walked that they were of the range.

Don Miguel López spoke to the audience once again. "We have three men here who will entertain us with another exhibition of the art which makes the Mexican the greatest horseman in the universe. We have Rafael Muñóz from the great ranch to the west, the Rancho Grande, whose distinguished owner, don Juan Molina, has graced us with his presence. And we have from the Guadalupe, Eulalio García, master of beasts. And from our own

150

beautiful la Flor, the last of the Ineses until another generation, Aurelio Heraclio, godson to our lord, don Aurelio Becerra!"

"We shall have the arena cleared, please, and bandmaster, give us once more the *March of Zacatecas*."

The riders left the corral, dispensed with their animals, and returned to the stands. On one side, Heraclio's brothers gathered with him, Teodoro the only one talking, Heraclio nodding very much like the day when he had his first trial. All of them surrounding him made him want to cry out to them that indeed he did love them, that they did have a birthright, and to tell them they did not err at this moment when they knew he was not afraid. And Teodoro's words brought him back to his father's image, and he thought many things at once, because Teodoro said:

"You must forget about your own mount—that is the trick to this one. If your horse is worth a good shit, then he will do for you, if not, you must adjust before you prepare to jump." And it had been the horse, and not his father's error, he thought, and he knew Teodoro must feel this, but Teodoro was still talking and was saying, "Once you make your move, you must not hesitate— like the horse whose neck you broke, it was only at one instant that you could get him, so it is with this. You may change your mind once, twice, or even three times, but this is before you move to spring. Once you start, there is a place of no return—you must follow through no matter how badly you leap. To change your mind at that time will mean that you fall between the beasts. Badly you will fall, on your face if not on your head. Understand, boy," and he pushed Heraclio in the face with his hand open, and stood back and grinned widely. And the others talked to him then, and did not talk about what was to come, and Heraclio was grateful that they were not participating because they were giving this day to him and he also knew that if he failed in any way, another one of them would do it. It was impossible that the family should lose to a horse.

As he walked away to get his horse, one of the professionals asked, "And what does that child think he is doing in a man's world?"

"It is that here in la Flor, every baby thinks he is a jinete," answered another, a stranger, someone from another ranch.

"Shut your mouth," said Juan, who was nearest to him.

151

"The baby you speak of," said Elías, "is out there, playing his life against his skill. You are sitting here, enjoying your food and your drink and with your finger up in your ass."

Teodoro walked to the first man, the ever-present quirt in his hand, and would have struck him but said instead, "Pacify yourself, señor, for you are our guests. It would not look well if we gave you a turn around the corral at the end of our reatas, which we will most assuredly do if you do not shut your filthy mouth."

The brothers continued at their pace, having done all their talking without hesitation.

There were others who spoke up, for it was early in life for Heraclio to exhibit himself in this way, and he was not even a true jinete, for he did not work the range, but no one said anything within earshot of the brothers.

In the stands Blanca de la O said to Carmen, "But what peasants you breed out here, María del Carmen! Is he really going to attempt this thing you say?" She had been watching him all afternoon, and her initial repugnance at the idea that she should admire a peon had completely dissipated as she saw him perform —in fact she was very much attracted to his brother called Concho, also a peon, but Heraclio had youth in his favor, and youth was attractive to her because she considered herself old at twenty-two.

"He is not going to attempt it, my Blanca," said Carmen. "He is going to do it. Watch."

And beside her, Domingo Arguiú said, "He is quite a boy, this Heraclio Inés, my dear, is he not?" And he was wondering about this Blanca, who was more like the women he had known in Europe—not wondering about her really, but wondering when it would be that they would be together.

"He is not a boy," said Carmen, almost in anger, losing her poise in the tenseness of the moment. Both Domingo and Blanca looked at her but she did not notice them.

In the center of the arena, Heraclio joined his two adversaries. They stood next to their horses, whose reins fell to the white ground, again an indication that their masters were centaurs. They embraced and wished each other luck and God's help. They then walked forward, their horses remaining where they had stationed them, and stood abreast before the stand.

152

The charro from the Rancho Grande was a talker, and he had a girl friend in la Flor, a second cousin who would someday be his wife. He moved to where she sat and dedicated his ride to her honor in elegant and yet ostentatious language. His face was flushed when he returned to his place.

The jinete from Guadalupe had no one he knew present, and in the tradition of the land dedicated his ride to don Aurelio Becerra. And don Aurelio, pleased, said, "The winner of this competition shall have the beast he dominates without encumbrance of any kind, and I shall add fifty pesos for his gallantry."

The patrón from the Rancho Grande could not be left out and he said, "I shall increase the prize by another fifty pesos, and I wish to publicly wager don Aurelio fifty Rancho Grande mules against a like number of la Flor mules which are far superior, that the charro from Rancho Grande wins it all." He made as if to sit down, then rose again and quickly said, "Not that I mean to offend the talent of the young jinete from la Flor."

His last words were drowned by the hoots and laughter of the people.

Heraclio moved forward, and he stood before the barrier and looked up to Carmen. He was going to say that this was to be in honor of her coming marriage, a hope that she should have many sons, but only because he did not really have anyone to whom he could dedicate his ride. But now, looking at her, seeing her beauty, which was greater because she was unattainable and because her return gaze was undisguised, he could not do this, and so he said, "For you, María del Carmen Becerra, in honor of the love I hold for you, I dedicate this demonstration of my skill," and because he did not wish to compromise her and not because he was afraid for himself, he added, without pause, "my sister."

There was a great cry of approval from the crowd at such a natural thing—that a godbrother should love a godsister. And Carmen suppressed the tears which came to her eyes, and Crispín was joyful at Heraclio's audacity, while doña Gertrudes seethed with anger and at this very moment decided that her husband must be told as quickly as possible.

The first cornettist stood up and in clear, mellow yet loud notes played the opening passages of a paso doble as the first outlaw horse was brought into the arena. Two jinetes began the task of positioning it for the run, while a peon placed a pennant near the far end of the stands. This marked the point which disqualified the rider, and therefore they had but fifty yards in which to come alongside the bronco and somehow get over onto its back. The man from Guadalupe was the first to try, and the bronco was worked forward, making a sharp turn to get onto the runway, then got away from the drivers, and they followed it across the great corral and once again brought him in. Then he was on the runway, and the jinete waited, moving slowly, but his mount betrayed him and lost a stride, and as they sped along the barrier it was obvious that the man would not overtake the wild horse, and before they reached the flag the bronco veered out into the center of the corral. The disgusted rider walked his animal back to where Heraclio and the Rancho Grande charro waited, and they offered him their sympathies. Since he would not be allowed another attempt, it was now a contest between the two. Again the custom of precedence was honored, and the man from Rancho Grande slowly walked his beautiful bay toward the starting point, and the drivers had the wild stallion in position, and he picked him up perfectly as he came by, racing alongside for three or four lengths and then making the change seemingly quite easily, and his bay fell back to give his master room, and the charro was screaming to his bronco, digging deep with the rowels, and the animal refused to stop its headlong flight for the far wall, but here the wall curved out instead of being at a right angle, and the beast turned at last, too short, stumbled and fell, crashing against the stone fence, but the rider was already on his feet and moving toward the wall, which was good, because the animal was up in a moment despite its tremendous fall, and the rider climbed over the wall to safety, for the stallion was a killer.

And now, Heraclio had seen the elimination of his competitors, and the stallion was driven out and another was brought in, equally as large, a magnificent animal who would attack the drivers, but they moved him into position, and Heraclio gave his own stud his head, and his range-smart animal moved as if to cut the other horse from a herd, knowing he must come alongside and follow the other animal whenever it deviated from a true course, and Heraclio was thinking only of the animal's broad back, where

154

he would land after his leap, and that this was a hell of a place to attempt this when a circular corral was needed, and he thought of the rider who had just failed, and why, all this in but a moment, and he was alongside, and between the horse, timing his move intuitively not knowing when he was safely on until he felt the rocking of the horses gallop, and his own mount, unaccustomed to this work, moved ahead and veered in, making the wild animal slow down for a moment, and it was all it needed to change its mind, and it turned almost slowly, and moved to the center of the corral in a series of short bucks before it began to twist and leap, hurting itself in an effort to remove the tenacious being from its back. There was no order to its gyrations, no series of moves, no pattern to its attack. And on its back Heraclio gloried in the moment, and he thought, if only he does not get it into his head to scrape me off on the ground, he is mine. And the horse did not, and soon Heraclio did that which he had seen so long ago in a corral in Toribio, and because the blood is that way, had he seen himself, he would have seen his brother Concepción, making the horse do his will, first making him turn to the left, and then to the right, working him gradually until they stood immediately before the reviewing stand, then, throwing his right leg over, he slid off the horse, and the animal remained there at his side for a moment, panting, wondering.

X

The fiesta continued without interruption, for not one household in la Flor served supper this night. The dance, held outdoors in one of the corrals and which was to continue through the night and part of the next day, began immediately. Heraclio talked for a while with his two competitors and promised to visit with them someday. He then took a bottle of tequila to the jail and sat for a time with Antonio, sharing his drink with the two other inmates. The drunks who had been locked up during the afternoon had been taken to their homes to recover in time to get back for some dancing.

After a time, because he had been asked to do so by his godfather, he went to the Big House. He was almost to the door when

he heard a sound to his right, hesitated, then unmistakenly heard
a voice say:

"Here. Over here, señor—quickly please!"

He moved to his right, around to where the new wing had been
added, and stood at the wrought-iron grille. A slight figure in white
stood in the shadows, and he waited a moment until it moved
forward, and a face became discernible.

He recognized her immediately, and asked, "What do you wish,
señorita?"

Marcelina Ortiz, plain of face, but somehow made beautiful by
her large black eyes and comely manner, laughed. "I have never
been called that, I suppose, but I am happy it was a man who first
uttered the word in my presence."

He waited. "I have been out here for such a long time. I thought
you surely would not come."

Finally he asked again, "What is it that you wish?"

She laughed again, as if her mission was humorous to her. "I
come on a commission," she said. "To deliver a note to you. A love
letter, I suppose. You know from whom."

He also laughed. "Do I?"

"But of course. She told me I should be very discreet. I should
not let the señorita María del Carmen know of this."

He was surprised. He thought the note might be from Carmen,
and yet he knew she did not need to write to him, for she could
speak to him at any time.

The young girl held the piece of paper in her hand and he wondered if she wanted him to ask for it. Finally she pushed it
through the iron bars. He did not look at it. "Why did you make a
messenger of yourself?" he asked. She amused him, and in a delicate manner attracted him, which was a surprise.

"I do not know. Perhaps I wished to get a good look at you?
I do not know."

"Well?"

"Well, what?"

"You have had your look. Are you satisfied now?"

"Very much," she said. "I never knew that a man could be so
beautiful."

"Thank you," said Heraclio, and at this moment stopped teasing her. "I must go," he said.

156

"I know. Go with God," she answered.

He moved to the porch, and in the light, before he knocked, he read the short note. He smiled, was warm with pleasure and feeling very much a man as he walked into the Big House.

Inside, dancing was in progress, although at the moment not many couples were on the floor. The young men were in one corner speaking, some in agitated tones.

Crispín stood with his new wife alongside him, giving food for gossip to the young ladies because she was so different. But really because she had removed from their midst and their dreams one of the most eligible. All the young men were from good families, and all from the National Army. The subject under discussion was war, which meant very little to them, for it would last but a month, they said, if something should materialize. And their only wish was that they might be in a position where they might see some action against the bandits from the north. They did not seem to realize that this was the north.

"Don Porfirio may retire, after such a long and gallant service to the nation," said one, "but there are others who could replace him—many who know the importance of our class, and who would rule to our advantage. There is, for example, the Limantour."

Crispín, angry and yet polite because he was a host, said: "They are all alike. And you need not worry too much for your class. It will survive. I wish only that there would be a revolution—a real one, for that is the only way human rights will be restored in our country. But I share your sentiments—such a thing could never happen." He saw Heraclio and called, "Here, my friend." His face broke into a wide grin.

Heraclio was congratulated by everyone on his fine performance of the afternoon. One of the guests, a year or two older than he, came to him and said:

"Tell me, my friend. You who are one of the underdogs. Tell me, how do you see this business of the presidential succession?"

Heraclio smiled easily. "I did not think," he said, "that a thing such as a presidential succession existed in México."

Laughter came up at his words. The young man flushed but was not discouraged.

"I mean it, Heraclio, that is your name, is it not? I should like to know how your people feel about it."

"I do not feel about it one way or another," said Heraclio. His eyes saw Blanca de la O looking at him from across the room, and barely perceptibly he nodded his head to her as he spoke. And, certain that she had caught his message, he faced the young man. "I have no concern whatever about what happens in the capital," he added.

"You see," said Domingo Arguiú, who, hovering nearby, had not spoken before this. "You see how futile it is for you to wish to know the feelings of the peon? You can easily see what could happen if there is suffrage—if these ignorant people are given rights and have a hand in the forming of a government."

Crispín would have spoken but Heraclio placed a hand on his arm. "Do not do that, Domingo," he said. "One time, because we are under the roof of a friend I might ignore. But do not speak to me in that manner again."

Domingo did not reply, he merely smiled his supercilious smile, and the other young man retired, confused as to what had made Heraclio so angry. Heraclio frowned and turned away from Domingo.

Upstairs, in another part of the house, Padre Ignacio sat in his bed with a bottle of aguardiente on his night stand, and held a copy of Candide in his hands. He was tired, for he had been enclosed in his cubicle hearing confessions for two days. And now, only a few minutes ago, he had come from spending the better part of two hours with the captain of rurales, and with the administrator, and with the good don Aurelio Becerra. He was pleased, thinking now, because his memory had been so good. He had made his report with clarity and conciseness. But there had been so many people he had heard that now he felt a slight headache. He wished he had a girl, if only to feel her nearness—he had not been near one this year, but these things were difficult in the provinces. And so, he chose to retire. After the second drink his headache disappeared and he settled back to enjoy his book.

Down in the salon, don Aurelio mingled with his guests, accepting compliments on the la Flor manner of holding a fiesta. He spoke to Heraclio. "You have pleased me, boy. But why did you not take the prize money?"

"Forgive me, Godfather. I do not mean to offend you or your

guest, don Juan Molina, but I did not take that last ride for money. I did it as a favor to you, remember?"

"I understand, of course," said don Aurelio. "It is only that I took fifty mules away from don Juan merely on your skill."

"It was my pleasure," said Heraclio.

"I shall tell you," said don Aurelio. "I shall see that two good milk cows, with papers so you may put your own iron on them, shall go to your corral. You may be taking a wife one of these days and shall have need for an animal or two. And the stallion?"

"Have Teodoro tame it for your son-in-law to be. It is surely big enough for him. I shall accept the cows, though, but only to please you."

Don Aurelio placed an arm about Heraclio's shoulders. "Thank you. You are a good boy," he said.

"Thank you, sir," answered Heraclio. Carmen passed by and called, "We shall dance, you and I, Heraclio."

"No, my life," he said. "You should know I cannot dance."

As she went out of hearing range, don Aurelio said with a jab into Heraclio's ribs, "Those places where you go—in the evenings, you know—you dance there, do you not?"

Heraclio was embarrassed that the man should joke with him in this manner. "One is usually more than a little drunk in those places. And the ladies are too, so I should not call that dancing."

Across the room, doña Gertrudes spoke to Crispín. "What is that peon doing here? Who told him he should come?"

Crispín was startled by the vicious sound of her words. "My father asked that he be here. I am sure he would not have come otherwise." He wondered how his mother knew what he had been told only this morning. That she knew he was certain.

"Get him out of here! Immediately! I will not have him in my house!" Crispín exercised his rarely used prerogative, that of a grown son speaking sternly to the women of the house, any woman, even a mother. "It is also our house, Mother. And your screeches are making people stare. You are a lady, so control your passion, or if you must make a scene, go to him and tell him to leave. Then contend with my father for your bad manners."

She felt humiliated by the rebuke, but she was a lady and held her tongue. It did not matter greatly now, for she saw the hated

159

jinete walk out the door. Immediately she went to her husband and said a word, then he followed her into one of the alcoves.

Later that evening, when the strains of the music had finally died out, don Aurelio sat in his rooms, and held his head in his hands. And he thought how age had mellowed him, that he could not make a decision, when his house had been dishonored. He liked the boy, truly, and he wished with all his being that he could have chosen him for his daughter—this was something he would not have considered even five years ago. He sipped jerez, for he had never been a drinker, and he wished suddenly that he could drink. What to do with Heraclio? He did not think of Domingo Arguiú—the dowry was enough, if the man chose to be a fool, he would increase it or even break the contract. He pulled on the bell and a maid came immediately. There was a look of surprise on her face, and she waited for him to speak.

"Bring me a bottle of tequila," he said. Then, as she turned, "No, forget it. I merely wanted to tell you to retire. I do not want you here tonight."

"Very well," she said. She showed neither interest nor disappointment.

She was to have come a little later, for this was a day of fiesta, and don Aurelio had been in a high state of emotion all day and had need for her. He particularly liked her, and she was ripe at the moment, two months with child, his child, and although he had destroyed three others before it went this far, he had suddenly wanted to father a being—perhaps for the last time. He had not known any of his scattered children since the boy David, born of María Contreras. And, ironically, it was she who had kept him supplied with abortive herbs all these years.

As don Aurelio paced in his study, which was off the bedroom, Captain Hernández, with a detail of men and the administrator to show him the way, was rounding up those men that Padre Ignacio had selected for incarceration. There was little space left in the jail, and so the prisoners sat on the ground in the corral, cold and frightened, while their guards warmed their hands over a small fire.

Don Aurelio stopped his pacing. He would marry Heraclio off, and soon. Perhaps it would be better if he were sent away—but could he make him leave without resorting to the slave camps, or should he have him hanged, which was really what should be done? No, he knew he would not harm him physically. He heard a noise outside his study, and, there being no light in the small room, he was able to stand at the french windows, and he saw a shadow move. He felt a constriction in his chest, as he recognized his daughter, but no, the moon was strong tonight, and the figure moved away from the trees, and he could see clearly it was the flirt from the capital. He watched for a moment, and would have stepped out to talk to her, but there was another sound, and he remained where he stood, and now a horse moved delicately through his grounds, and the rider reached an arm down and clasped Blanca de la O by the waist, and lifted her to his horse's neck.

Don Aurelio was suddenly angry. The Goddamn boy again, and he was but seventeen years old! What the hell! They are all putas! he thought, and then he thought of his own daughter, and suddenly had a rare thought, that Heraclio was betraying his little girl, and this put him almost in a rage until he thought about himself and about his maids and for certain he had too much sherry tonight, for he was seeing things honestly, and he was not thinking the right things. He wished he had the bottle of tequila, but did not wish to disturb anyone at this hour—even that thought was different for him. He thought of his wife's unattractive body —once a month he covered it with his own because of his marriage vow which he could not remember, but he thought this was demanded of him. And he knew how he would punish Heraclio when it was almost dawn, when his thoughts turned to the activity of the morrow, which he must witness and yet, perhaps because he was aging, he did not wish to happen, but he could do nothing to stop and because at this moment, when the night dissipates and the day is not yet come, and time is as if in limbo, he again heard the soft hoofs outside his window, and Blanca de la O came home, he suddenly knew how he would get back at Heraclio and he fell asleep. He did not know how well he had selected his punishment. If he had, perhaps he would not have done it.

In the morning, bright, in the sunlight of the corral where the jaripeo had taken place the previous day, Captain Hernández sat on his sorrel gelding and read from a paper to a group of prisoners huddled against the barrier. To his right, a whipping post had been put up that morning, and as he called a name, the peon walked to the post, where he was bound by the wrists up high, and administered the amount of lashes Captain Hernández had decided was suitable punishment for his offense. For everyone, no matter what his crime might be—poaching on the private orchard, stealing a hen, or some goods from the tienda de raya—it did not matter what the transgression might be, here was his price for absolution. And the punishment was taken stoically, with rarely an outcry, and the family of the accused were also stoically resigned. Only when the rider who had been brought in with Antonio Rivera was sentenced to be shipped to the territories to be sold as a slave was there a cry from the womenfolk, and then Antonio Rivera was brought into the corral. He who was to have been released this morning was dragged to the post and bound, and he received twenty-five lashes, and only that many because the mare he had taken did not belong to don Aurelio but to Heraclio, and when he was cut down he was unconscious but had not uttered a sound, and Heraclio carried him home in his arms like a child.

He had a hatred now—one he had not known could be with him. That don Aurelio should have talked to him in the manner he did a few hours ago, and then to do this! He did not stay to see the last case—the case of one Tiburcio León, who had six months ago taken a hundred kilos of corn from the granary in the night and had not even left a trace that it was missing.

"You are accused," said Captain Hernández, "of having stolen one hundred kilos of corn from your benefactor, don Aurelio Becerra. Do you deny this fact?"

And Tiburcio León spoke. "I cannot deny it, my Captain, for I have confessed it to the man of God."

"For this crime it will be my sad duty to see you hang—and this is not merely punishment, but a lesson for the people of this Hacienda de la Flor. To steal from a master is not now nor will it ever be tolerated."

Tiburcio León's wife and daughters would speak for him, but they were silenced. That their man's credit at the tienda de raya was too meager for the needs of the family did not matter. That he was merely doing what any man would do, try to bring something home so that his people might live, did not matter.

Tiburcio León spoke just once more. "I am ready," he said.

He was walked to the zaguán, and then through to the chapel and around the other side to the cemetery. There in its center stood a knarled oak, a tree foreign to this region, and yet formidable as the very earth from whence it sprang. The noose was ready, and without ceremony whatever Tiburcio León was swinging from a creaking limb, to remain there the entire day, for he was a much better lesson if visible.

In the evening, after vespers, male relatives of the family came to cut the body, now stiff, features forever grotesque with thick tongue, and bulging eyes, and twisted neck. And in the Big House, the disturbed don Aurelio sat at the head of the table, slicing from the cheeks of a barbecued calf's head, while the Padre Ignacio told the guests about his recent trip to Guadalajara where he had visited the archbishop.

It was not until the following day, when Padre Ignacio had gone on to Fresnillo, and Captain Hernández and his rurales had departed to the north, and all the guests with the exception of Blanca de la O, who had decided to remain for the coming wedding, had left that Heraclio was summoned to the Big House.

Crispín waited for him at the door. "I am sorry, Heraclio," he said. "Believe me, I did not know until it was over. I am truly sorry."

"Why?" asked Heraclio. "Only tell me why."

"Because they know about you and my sister."

"Only that?"

"Only that," answered Crispín. "I shall see you once more before I leave?" he asked, and as he received no answer, he added, "I am ending my visit now, tomorrow at the latest. I am sorry for Antonio, but I am more sorry for the other, the man who hanged, and the other whippings—the men who were sent into slavery. I cannot remain here now, not after this atrocity. I have heard of these things—I did not know that it also happened here. I ask you, Heraclio—my father and mother wait for you, and she feels that they are to put you in your place once and for all. Do not be too harsh on the old man. He can do nothing about these things,

163

in fact, he did not order them—only the whipping for Antonio, that was his order at the insistence of my mother."

"What could I do to him?" asked Heraclio. "I do not like him but certainly I cannot harm him."

"You can hurt him. That is all."

"I shall see you," said Heraclio, and moved toward don Aurelio's study.

They sat quietly waiting for him to enter. Don Aurelio sat at his desk, his wife in an easy chair beside him.

"What do you desire, patrón?" asked Heraclio without even a semblance of friendliness to his face.

"I wish to speak to you, sit yourself."

"I shall stand."

An order came to don Aurelio's mind, but he decided he would seem foolish since the boy did not in any way seem offensive. "You know why you are here?" he asked.

"No." And now the "sir" was excluded.

"You have wronged my house," said don Aurelio. "You have made me grieve, for I have loved you as my own, and expected better treatment from you. And now I must do something about it."

"Be quick, then," said Heraclio, and although he spoke calmly, had seemed polite, his words denied this.

Don Aurelio was not in anger, and he doubted that anything said here could make him angry. "I have decided that you should take a wife. It is time. Crispín is married, Carmen will soon be also married. I think you understand that an unpleasant situation could be avoided if you take a wife."

"I understand nothing," said Heraclio. "Especially I do not understand why you should punish another because I lay with your daughter. I can see your concern, your fury even if that were to be—but having another person flogged for my transgression, that was an inhuman deed. I know, I should not talk to you like this, but it was so. And now, you would marry me to someone so that I would not touch your daughter. That is the humor in this foul thing we are playing. As if that would stop me if I desired to continue with Carmen. Has it stopped you? Were you not married when you sired the unfortunate David Contreras? Or has it stopped you since with only you know how many of our sisters?"

164

"You are insolent!" said doña Gertrudes. "We should recall the rurales to take you away."

Don Aurelio was white-faced and would not speak. "For what reason?" asked Heraclio. "Because I exchange a few truths with you, you would have me sent to Yucatán? You are mistaken. And I shall tell you. I shall marry only when I desire to do so. That is a thing you can do with some others but not with me. You have no hold on me, except that you can injure those I love. And I shall continue with your daughter if I wish it so—I should really marry her as she desires, but I do not control lives as you would. I think we have nothing more to say to each other, so I will go."

Don Aurelio came from behind the desk, an arm extended, not knowing what to say, yet beseeching, but Heraclio was gone and doña Gertrudes stood up and shouted, "You let a peasant talk to you that way? What kind of a man are you? Your common blood has finally shown itself!" And for the first time in his life, Aurelio Becerra, lord of la Flor, struck a woman, and he did not do it gently, for he was but a novice at these things, and his blow knocked his wife across the room and into the wall with a force that left her almost senseless. He looked down at her dispassionately as she bled from the mouth and nose.

It was not for revenge that Heraclio resumed his meetings with Carmen, for it was impossible for him to wish to hurt anyone. Although when he did inflict pain, he did not suffer remorse nor did he think too much about it, he was not insensitive to the fact. Those around him were lives such as he himself was a life, and they were subject to the ills and wounds of time. This was the manner of things on earth, and it was only when deliberate and thus unjustified pain was inflicted did he object.

Therefore, it was not a matter of vengeance but again a thing which must be as long as he remained in la Flor, and yet, it would not have been again as it once was, except that after Antonio's whipping he did not strive to avoid it.

He did not work at all now, and was considered somewhat of an oddity—a man who would not work—for he was filling out into a man's body. But no one said a word to him. He was surly these days and he had a gun. And he roamed the range, a recluse on horseback, thinking—always thinking.

For Antonio, he had smiles when they talked together. They talked about leaving and how soon. With Carmen he was happy, and they knew joy again, and then again.

"Heraclio, my life, I shall have you," she said. "For a time, to be sure, but I shall have you and you shall have me; and I will not think of this thing you are doing to me nor why."

"Thank you," he said, truly grateful. "But why? You should be angry—castigate me and reject me."

"But I would be depriving myself also, do you not see? And we have so little time."

Her impending marriage hung heavy, shroudlike over them; and then, too, like a welcome release, for there could not be a forever to this thing. In this way it was one day, but a few weeks before the nuptials, when they had loved strongly, having been away from each other for a few days—it was in this way, anxious to see each other that they had been careless and Juan Vásquez, who had always suspected, followed at a discreet distance.

They were finished and lay side by side when he heard a foreign sound. Instantly he was on his feet and although the plain was devoid of cover she had time to gather her clothes and hide herself just as the contador came into view.

Juan Vásquez caught a glimpse of the disappearing form and was both sad and happy that he had not seen the full, young body more plainly. He saw just enough, for to have seen more would be dangerous, and suddenly a smugness filled his chest. If it had not been so perfect his destiny would be different, but now he had a lever on which to raise his station, and his exultation made him careless. Because he was full of apprehensions about his position as a servant of the hacienda, he believed that everyone had similar fears, and in his mind, his knowledge of the great transgression which had been committed gave him a power over the boy. And so when Heraclio ignored his strong rebuke, and the rebuke became a diatribe, even as Heraclio calmly put on his trousers and boots, the contador came forward and with his quirt struck the boy across the shoulders and the back of the neck.

And Heraclio, who at that very moment was reaching for his blouse, pulled from its folds the gun he had so recently acquired, and turned to Juan Vásquez, whose arm was upraised and whose face was distorted, looking like a scarecrow except that he was too fat, and the distorted face became surprised, yet remained purposeful in the desire to punish while the arm was raised interminably and the boy tried to fire and could not.

Juan Vásquez did not move, not really afraid, suddenly believing very strongly that the boy would not fire because he really did not want to do so, even as he heard the boy, for he was a boy still to him, cursing that he had not practiced with the weapon because shells were dear, even then he did not believe and he was almost smiling now, opening his mouth to say something to Heraclio—what he was to say he did not know, but he meant to tease a little, and his mouth was open when the boy finally pulled back the hammer and the bullet pushed him backward violently as it tore a hole in his great belly above the navel and as he was falling he remembered that he heard a distinct sound as the bullet entered him even above the explosion. He sensed pain, but sensed it only because the second shell ripped his throat before he hit the ground and he did not hear, nor did he know that Heraclio stood over him, firing three more times rapidly, nor that his body moved a little with each shot as the boy mastered the instrument in his first killing.

XI

SOMEHOW HE HAD ALWAYS KNOWN that he would leave in this way—a fugitive; just as he had known he would have no feeling whatever for the dead man he would leave behind. And it could be only as a fugitive that he could leave because now he had no need to choose a destination, no need to come to a decision about where to go. He must get away. He must keep away from ranchos and haciendas or he would be lost. This was his only destination, except that at the moment he must stop at Cañitas, near the railroad, to get a bedroll and some meat and hardtack from his mother's people. With luck, he might even get some ammunition.

He rode hard and yet he remained calm, not frightened, only knowing that he must get to the village and out of it as quickly as possible. The hue and cry would not come for a while, but he must ride while he still had daylight.

And he felt that it was not a romantic thing, this flight. Not like in the songs. The ballads always made it romantic and the people always sympathized with the fugitive, especially if there was a love affair in the story, but his love affair had nothing to do with the killing, although the killing made it tragic.

He had gone to his horse and Carmen waited fully dressed.

"He is dead?" she asked.

"Yes."

"And now you will go?" She was calm, yet poised to break down at any moment in her grief, more concerned about the end of a part of life which she thought was all her life than about the man who lay dead but a few yards away.

"I cannot stay," said Heraclio. He held her, for she was suddenly everything that he would leave behind. Then he helped her mount her horse.

"Good-by, my lover," she said, resigned to her fate. "May God watch over you."

"Adiós, gachupina," he said.

And so he fled for his life, not frightened even a little, but surely he fled for survival.

In Cañitas he went directly to an old aunt's hut, then went north along the railroad tracks, in the direction of Peñuelas. He rode for perhaps an hour before he turned directly eastward, traveling between mesillas, turning southward every so often. In this manner he made a great circle and by nightfall he was moving in a southerly direction. He stopped at a water hole, ate some meat, and rested his horse. He continued for another three hours before he bedded down to sleep.

He was up before daybreak and saddled his horse, for he was dangerously near a ranch called La Colorada, and he must go south and into the mountains before he could feel safe. He had seen no one since he left Cañitas and he hoped no one had seen him as he veered away from the railroad. If he had this good fortune he would have no trouble escaping—in a few short hours he would be lost from the rurales, depending on how far away they were when summoned by don Aurelio.

The identity of Juan Vásquez's killer would be known the instant the body was found; he only hoped, for Carmen's sake, that the events leading to the killing would never be discovered.

And so he began to climb the mountains, because it was the most unlikely route he could take. Everyone knew all fugitives fled in the direction of centers of population, and it was only when in groups that wanted men roamed the hills.

The sun was high but he felt secure and continued until the hour of midday before he tethered his horse and went to sleep. A foreign noise disturbed him and he opened his eyes. An Indian sat on his haunches, four feet away, staring impassively at his face. Heraclio did not move his head, but his eyes looked cunning as he listened, and through the silence he heard soft sounds of breathing behind him as he lay on his side. He looked at the Indian once again, dark, fierce, with lank hair, and ugly. He was perhaps the ugliest man he had ever seen, and he wore a single bandoleer across his chest. A rifle, stock down, was held stafflike in his right hand.

To remain tense was tiring, useless, and wasted effort, so Heraclio suddenly relaxed as completely as if he were alone on his pallet at home.

The Indian had not moved, did not speak.

"Well," said Heraclio, laughing lightly, "this is what happens to those who sleep late." He looked the man over carefully, and said, "You are Indian and yet you are not Indian."

"We are all Indians, are we not? Unless we are gachupín," said the man, and he did not speak the Castilian of the Indian.

"How true," said Heraclio, "but you have the fortune to have more Indian than some of us. What do you desire from me?"

"Your horse and your gun, for now," said the Indian, "and your money belt if you have one, which you must, for your dress, your saddle, and your beast show that you are a don."

Heraclio was amazed as he suddenly realized that this man before him was an old man. He appeared to have perhaps fifty years but his speech somehow revealed that he was an ancient. He smiled and said, "No, old one. I have a good horse because I am a jinete and had my pick from the range. I found him not too far from this place. My saddle is good because our artisans are good, this one has the blood of princes heavy within him just as you do. I have fine clothes because I have at one time or another won a little money in competition with beasts and because I once was vain. But I have no money belt, in fact, no money. And I am not a don." He lay on his side as he had been when he was awakened, knowing he must not move until told to do so. He was annoyed, waiting for the old man to speak, and the old man decided to study him a while. Heraclio became angry, and just as suddenly his anger left him. He could remain in this position as long as the old man could sit on his haunches, and he knew this could be hours.

The Indian finally spoke. "I think we will simply take your animal and your gun and let you go. I am not in the habit of killing for nothing, and a few hours' walk could get you to La Colorada."

"Who are you? And who is we?" asked Heraclio, although he knew he was surrounded and the other knew he knew.

"I am called Ysabel Pulido."

"I have heard your name mentioned but no one described you, nor did they say you were so old. The women in my land think you ride a white charger like Emiliano Zapata, and that you are young and handsome. They should see your handsome features."

They laughed together. "Look around," said the old man. Heraclio rolled over and two dozen armed men were there, relaxed, yet ready, some sitting and some standing. They were expressionless, waiting for a word from their leader, and among them was David Contreras, unrecognizing and as inscrutable as the others.

"Hola, Daví," said Heraclio, happy to see his old friend even in the gravity of his position. "So this is where you have been."

"What trick is this, Heraclio?" asked David.

"Always suspicious, and even more bitter," said Heraclio. "It pains me, David, that you refuse to be my friend again." They might have been alone on the range somewhere, or with their flock, the way they spoke.

"Bitter?" said David. "You think I lack the right to be bitter! Hah! And suspicious, you say? Should I not be? Of you, the precious godson of my father?" Some strange compulsion made him refer to don Aurelio as "father," and Heraclio smiled.

"And why not suspicious?" David spoke loud in anger at his slip and because Heraclio's smile was supercilious to him. "You allowed yourself to be taken so easily! You have lived in these hills, you know how to sleep out here—I have seen you on your feet when a pebble has been disturbed by a lizard!"

Heraclio spoke because now he must. "It is not so, Daví." He was thinking because the bandit leader, who he knew was still on his haunches behind him, was silently listening to the exchange deciding at this very moment Heraclio's fate, and that was one thing these outlaw leaders did quickly. And Heraclio must stop the talk coming from the hurt and angry David. Stop it forever, and there was but one way to do it. "It is not as you say, Daví," he said again with scarcely a pause. "I am here because I killed a man and am a fugitive. Juan Vásquez, the contador, I killed only yesterday." Then he added subtly, thankful that he was not facing the old leader, "And as for my being caught unawares, I was careless and how should I know you carry Indian trackers with you. These people walk two inches off the ground."

David did not speak, still suspicious that Heraclio had been sent to find him, and yet slowly believing because he knew Heraclio.

Ysabel Pulido spoke, and Heraclio kept his back to the old man. "You have led the rurales to us, boy?"

"The rurales do not know where I am. Not yet, at least. And they should not know unless someone has seen me, and even then, if I was observed as I fled, the one who saw me might not talk."

"Nevertheless," said the bandit, and he sighed in annoyance although this was a great and serious thing that the rurales should know his whereabouts, "the situation exists, and it has saved your life for the present, I suppose, for I was going to allow David Contreras to decide your fate." He stood up and motioned that Heraclio should do the same. "I do not want to leave this area at this time, for they look for me over that mountain which is in the state of San Luis Potosí. We cannot bury you and we cannot take your body with us, and we could not send you back to tell that we are here, so you must join us. The thing to have done was to have let you sleep and hide from you—imagine, thirty-two men hiding from one," and Heraclio saw that indeed there were more men coming from behind rocks. "But we have you with us now. Certainly you did not come out here to get one of us and then die. Unless, of course, you wanted to come after David badly enough to pay with your life."

"You talk very much, old one," said Heraclio, "but you reason well."

Ysabel Pulido did not choose to hear him. "And I do not think you want to kill David, although it seems that he would want to do that to you."

He gave the order then, and they mounted. Heraclio rode alongside the man. "Why do you not take my gun, patrón?" he asked.

"If you say you are not here to kill, I believe it. What need then is there for me to take the gun?"

They rode a few paces. "I like your ways," said Heraclio. "I think I should like to ride with you."

Ysabel Pulido merely thought.

They rode side by side in silence for a time, and then Heraclio fell back carefully, knowing that the men behind him were watching him closely, knowing also that he would die at the moment he made one suspicious movement. And as he came into position near David, he had his first opportunity and would have escaped, but he was in fact attracted by the Indian Ysabel Pulido and remained. He was certain now that if he must, sometime, he could escape from these people.

"I let you go there," said David in a low voice. "Why did you not run?"

Heraclio looked to him in surprise. "You really want me killed," he said. "I did not know it was like this."

After a time David spoke again. "Why did you kill the contador?"

"Because he attempted to whip me."

"For what reason?"

"Because that was the kind of a pig he was."

David thought a moment, but then was satisfied. "Do not speak any more," he said. "Don Ysabel does not like us to talk on the trail."

They camped in a box canyon so narrow as to be almost a ravine. Its sides were steep yet thick with scrub oak and underbrush and huge boulders. At the closed end was a trail, steep also, but passable. Beside the narrow path, water trickled gently from above, forming a small pond at the base of the cliff before it slowly moved toward the entrance of the canyon until it disappeared into a crevice in the rock.

"People have been here," said Heraclio as they dismounted.

"We stay here sometimes," said David. "It was here that I joined these people."

172

Two men came down from the high walls above the entrance to the ravine. And then a rider came in through the entrance, driving a calf before him which, once well inside, he roped and hogtied immediately. He then slit its throat. It was the jinete from Guadalupe who had lost to Heraclio in the ride of death.

He walked toward them and embraced Heraclio.

"What are you doing here, my friend?" he asked.

"You know how things are," said Heraclio with a shrug. "And you?"

"I was recruited by a friend who in the end lost his courage and turned back."

Heraclio turned to David, "And you, Daví. You have not told me. How did you come to join Ysabel Pulido?"

"It does not matter how. What matters is that I belong to the band of Ysabel Pulido, I am a part of something for the first time in my life, and it makes me well. Here there is no talk of bastards, nor of birth, nor of witches. Here I am David Contreras, outlaw, and am respected as such. Once I belonged to a group— the peonage, and within that group I belonged to the sheepmen, and then within that group, I belonged to the society of illegitimacy. The first two groups were too large. I was lost. The third was a department of society which is too small. I was alone. Now, here, I am happy."

"Then I am happy for you," said Heraclio. But he feared for what would happen when David found himself alone once again.

It had happened that one day David's colero had fallen ill, and Juan Vásquez came and took him away to the hacienda. Because he had not anticipated this, there was no one to leave with David, and the contador split up the flock, parceling out the animals to other shepherds, and leaving David with but five hundred sheep for a few days.

David spent the night where he was, and the next morning, although there was good pasture nearby, he allowed his animals to walk where they would. They led him out around the Rancho La Colorada and to a place untraveled for so long that the land merged with the stone fence of the hacienda, and it was an easy thing for them to scramble out onto open range.

They moved slowly, grazing, yet steadily, and it was the water which attracted them to the box canyon. And David did not attempt to deter their movement in any way, for he was in a mood of depression rare even for him. He was in the mountains and yet all afternoon he could see the higher ranges of San Luis Potosí ahead of him and he allowed himself to be drawn along, climbing always, through short, narrow passes, and then wider ones. Dreaming. Thinking that he would simply keep walking, on, away with his flock until he reached the city of México—how far? And he knew, of course, that he would not do that but just walking south was something, getting away from his pain and his frustration, and to climb made his spirits soar for a while, for the higher he went, the farther away from the world it seemed he could go and so tomorrow or the next day he would return to the hacienda range to meet the contador at the designated place.

The mood, the feeling of being alone on earth, remained although he could see that someone had been in this place not too long ago, for he must maintain the illusion that he had broken away from the hacienda because he was now very nearly resigned to a lifetime of servitude.

He had said to María del Carmen, his half sister—she had insisted that he speak to her on his last visit to the settlement—"If you are determined that you should do something for me, I shall request that which is not possible to obtain, but I ask it anyway because life as I know it is insufferable."

"What is that?" she asked, eager now that it seemed she had penetrated his thick shell of bitterness. "Tell me quickly what it is you want and it shall be done!"

"Ask your father," he said, hurting her, for he steadfastly refused to utter his father's name, "talk to your father and ask him to set me free. Tell him to write off our debt at the tienda de raya so that my unfortunate mother and I can go into the city and make our lives where we are not known. Ask him for that only and you shall make me happy."

But Carmen's face had changed. It was she who was now sad. "I cannot do that, David," she said. "Oh, how I wish I could but I could not possibly do that!"

"Why?" His question was devoid of inflection, without emotion.

"Because to do so would be to admit that I know about you. I could not hurt him like that."

174

David could laugh at this because his anger toward the land-owner had dissipated through the years. There remained yet a hatred, but a passive sort of a hatred, and he could laugh that this man could feel hurt by the knowledge that his peccadillo of sixteen years ago was not a secret to his daughter. And he laughed loud and long because the thing was even more confused, more dishonest than Carmen could guess.

She was near tears in her compassion for him and now sudden anger defeated her grief and she asked, "Why do you laugh? It is true. It would hurt him terribly and I could not bear that."

"I believe you," said David, "and I do not laugh because he would be hurt. It is that for a moment I saw something—a ridiculous thing clearly in four or five distinct ways. And it is important only because it is about your father and about you, and because you do not want to hurt his feelings. You are both frauds, you and your father, although he is the bigger one because you really do think of him. You believe that it would cause him grief to know that you know because of his concern for your own pain, no? And yet, he could very well know you know. And more than that, he may also know that you know he knows you know. As long as you do not speak about it, you may fool each other into thinking you are fooling each other."

"I do not know what you are saying, talking around in circles about knowing and not knowing knowing, and you are confusing me no end. All I know—and there, I am doing it also—that it would be a sorrow to him if he should learn that I am aware of his slightest imperfection. That is all." She seemed perplexed, for she was too young to know of defenses such as he was inarticulately describing, let alone to build them deliberately. And she lacked the perverted guile necessary for such a thing.

"It is clear to me," he said. "It is as clear to me as the fact that you love your father and the fact that I hate him is clear. Look, the thing he did when he made me was an atrocity far worse than your knowledge of it could be. It is with him like a man with a wife who has lain with another. The husband discovers it but does nothing to make her aware her transgression is known. She learns that he has knowledge of her betrayal, but they do not speak about it because he loves her, lacks the courage, or cannot live without her because he could not get another woman or any such reason. If it is brought out into light, he cannot remain a man and yet do nothing. On the other hand, he is incapable of doing anything for the reasons I have just mentioned. And so they both remain silent and he retains his manhood. But he knows that he lost that manhood the moment he discovered the facts and did not discard her at least, or killed her or her lover, or both. And he will refuse to think the truth, which is that he had never really been a man, else his wife would not have been forced to turn to another. That is the way it is with you and your father—yes, and me, also. The bad thing about all this was committed years ago. It is merely to forget the great sin that we give importance to the lesser sin—sort of make it bigger."

She reddened, not angry but bashful, for the allusion to her love affair with Heraclio, although not intended, was nevertheless obvious. "You do confuse me," she said. "David, I love you. To me you are my brother and someday, even in my own father's lifetime, I will recognize you as what you really are. That I promise you. But now, about this fidelity and honor. This I do not understand—I see not the analogy, but then I am only a woman and do not think much about anything. You have time to think out in the pastureland. I did not know you were concerned with manhood, nor with honor, in fact with anything having to do with people. I am not happy with the things you think, but I have now seen that you are one of us and for that I am pleased. Now, if you are really honest, and if you truly believe in manhood and large balls—that is what you men call courage, is it not?—then you go and speak to our father. Go and ask for your release. And do not flinch when I say 'our father,' for that is a physical truth like having two arms and two legs, and we are being honest today."

And David said, "I will," not because he had been dared, nor because he could not refuse to do so gracefully, but because in that moment of lucidity when he spoke to her about deceit, while attempting to explain his revelation, he had recognized his own dishonesty.

He knew it was not to be even as he stood before the man in his study, and felt the awkward indescribable sense of fear exude from the man, for don Aurelio believed in God in the Christian manner of accepting an eternal hereafter, and here, incarnate,

176

was one of his mortal sins. And in the moment of salutation, David felt strongly a compassion for the man, seeing closely his features, growing old, death near he looked, and now there was a side to David, objective, looking down upon the tableau, slowly merging with his self, achieving complete identification with don Aurelio, for after all he, too, was a man, potent, with carnal desires on occasion, sometimes for his own sister although the horror of such a lust was easily disposed of because he never thought of her as a sister and this man, his father, had done only what any man might do, David included, and suddenly the misfortune was that he had planted his seed that was to create David in María Contreras' choza and not here in this elegant house. How different it would have been, and he did not know that it would not have been David, if the sperm had been in a different egg, if the fetus had nurtured in a different womb. Yet, now, he grieved once again for he in a moment had renounced his mother and all these thoughts were in moments between words.

"What is it you want, boy?" asked don Aurelio through an unsmiling, pale face. He, too, was thinking, looking at this fine son, What have I done? What have I done? For he had such thoughts these days.

"May I sit down, patrón?" asked David. He had not meant to call him that, but that much he must give him, if only because he had given him life. He would not speak of the relationship—he would spare him that.

"Certainly," said don Aurelio.

David sat. He, too, sometimes had the desire to go to a whorehouse. With Heraclio he could go anytime, or even alone, except that he never had the money needed for such luxuries. And in the brothel if he went and he might as well be a frequenter of such places since he thought of it so often, whose sisters, whose mothers would he violate? And Heraclio? Was not he also a violator of sisters?

Heraclio, whom he loved yet in spite of himself—Heraclio, who was kind to him always and whom he wished to alienate, to hate, but could not—not unless he forced him into battle and then one would be killed, perhaps himself, though he was not afraid. What had he ever done to deserve his ill treatment, just as this man, now soon to be an ancient—what harm had he ever really done to him? "A request, patrón," he said, and he spoke like a peon in the tones of servility, "with all respect I come to speak to you."

And the lord looked upon him and thought, Forgive me! The boy was Iberian, had come from his own loins. "Well. What would you have?"

"My freedom, patrón. For me and for my honored mother. A clean slate so that we can go away." He had the feeling that he should not have said it, that he should have walked out while he still had good thoughts. Giddy feelings and good thoughts, though sentimental, but he asked and don Aurelio laughed. It was a forced, tight laugh, but a laugh nevertheless—a necessary laugh because he was a patrón and his role in the scheme of life could not change and to change for one would be a danger to the system and somehow to all systems. To make an exception would disturb the universe.

"Are you crazy, boy? Is it that you have lost your mind to think that you should have to ask me that? No peon is held against his will. Once you pay the debt of your family of your father, who was a good servant before you, you are free to go where you will." He was safe, and that of a moment ago was the sign of an early senility.

David at that moment was imagining this man in union with his mother and vaguely the vision aroused him, but now he forgot this and became David Contreras once again, although seemingly older than a day ago. He had been prepared to abide by the rules of tact. He had felt a need for this man, a hunger to know him, the beginnings of what could be called love. But when he refused to play the game, his father had again become just another man.

"I will not salve your conscience. I will not be a part of your filthy deception. I ask of you that you allow us to go, to save myself embarrassment and humiliation, and perhaps to save you some of it also. It is not as a peon begging for surcease that I come. It is as your son. I beg of you, yet I hold my head high. Let me go!"

"Impossible!" And don Aurelio showed the beginnings of rage. He would not admit he had heard the words, and yet for this one time he must allude to the fact. "To let you go would be an admission to the world that you are different. I cannot have that."

Why to him, Aurelio Becerra, should this happen? Why of the millions and millions of men did he have to be the one who must answer to an indiscretion?

David spoke calmly, and for him this, too, would be the last time he spoke to his father as a father. "Once this was not necessary. Once I could stand the cruelties of voices because I was a child and children are indestructible. Now I am a man and it is not the same for me. The only real difference, however, is that I do not hear the voices now, though I know the talk goes on. And my unfortunate mother—the idiot witch, they say, and it is not true. The black arts she does practice—you know that—but she is as normal as you are. Not an idiot nor is she backward at all. Let me remove her from this, I beseech once again!"

Although still firm, don Aurelio allowed his voice to become gentle. "I know what your mother is, boy. And I know that you have suffered far more than she has. But I insist I cannot let you go. These things are just not done. Something else—ask me for some other thing. Would you work the range? Or here, in the Big House?" He must be touched indeed to even suggest the Big House, he seemed to lose control in his effort to somehow please this boy who came of him.

David laughed a bitter laugh. "The range? No. It is much too late for that. At one time there was nothing I wanted more than to be a vaquero, but now the time has passed for that."

"Perhaps," said don Aurelio, more anxious than ever to make David's lot a better one, "perhaps you would like to work with the contador. He could teach you much, and also, you have seen the work a contador does many times so it would not be difficult for you. In two years or three you could take his place since Juan Vásquez does not go out to the pastures much now anyway. How would you like that?"

David shook his head sadly. "I accept what I knew when I came here, patrón." He rejected his desire to make the man aware that Carmen knew about the relationship. "You see, it would be far worse than if you allowed me to leave. People really know I am your son, and we would not be allowed to forget that, whereas if I went away, in a short time it would pass over. I could not live here if I should receive special treatment."

179

"Perhaps you are right," said don Aurelio. "But I can offer nothing more."

"Then I must refuse and return to my flock."

And so he had wandered aimlessly that day, as if one of the sheep, allowing himself the luxury of not caring, and although he yet maintained the hope that one day he would escape, it was not now the vigorous knowledge that he would, but merely a hope. He made his camp in the box canyon, after the sheep had drunk their fill, although there was but little pasture, but the flock had grazed as it moved and it did not matter. He stationed his dogs at the entrance and at the foot of the path which led upward, and at dawn was awakened by the furious barks of the dogs and was startled into fright by the ferocity of the barking. Something foreign was nearby and he could not see where.

Suddenly the dogs behind him, at the foot of the trail, began also to bark and snarl; and he knew there were men around because an animal could not surround one. He had feared a wild animal, perhaps large, because there was timber up above. Somehow he did not fear men.

They appeared, five or six of them at the entrance, their horses shying and skittering at the fierceness of the dogs' cries, and the dogs waited for David to give the word and they would die attacking these strange beings.

"Call them off!" shouted one of the men. David gave a long, low whistle, and the barking stopped although the dogs remained stolid, the hair along their backs standing straight, their faces set indelibly in a snarl, uttering soft, gurgling sounds from deep within them.

"Get them back," repeated the man, "or I will surely get me a dog this morning." He drew a gun from beneath his sarape.

David was moving slowly toward the group of riders, his sling with a rock in its pouch hanging loosely from his right hand. He said, "You harm one dog and I will break your head."

The man, who was a townsman and had been a small-time thief until he had been run out onto the plains, dared laugh at the ridiculous figure of the youth, standing in huaraches, seeming smaller than he was in the ragged sarape with a head hole and holding the strange instrument in his hand which he felt was protection and talked like a man. "Watch," he said.

But Ysabel Pulido raised an arm and said, "You watch, Mercedes."

A small, unfortunate owl, driven down out of its element by an unknown impulse, with eyes tightly closed against the light of the dawn, its beak looking more like a petulant lip, sat immobile on a stump of sage dead many years, a full forty yards away.

Ysabel Pulido pointed and said, "Knock him down, boy."

David's missile caught the bird in the center of the chest and knocked it ten feet beyond. The man, Mercedes, stared with wide eyes and slack jaw, and when he turned again to David, the youth held his sling as before, a stone exactly as the other in its pocket. Mercedes had not known of the people of the hills who tended sheep.

"You see, Mercedes," said the outlaw leader, "you could not shoot that straight, perhaps not even that quickly."

David looked at the man who sat slouched on his horse, a huge sarape wrapped around his shoulders so that only his face showed. And he knew that he was old, very old, and he saw the dark, ugly oval of a face and was instantly overjoyed, for there was kindness there. His joy was not of relief, for he was unafraid, but the man seemed to have lived forever and David saw this in every line in the wrinkled yet strong face; and suddenly he felt, also, that he had loved this man for a long, long time although he did not know who he was.

He murmured something to the dogs and they withdrew. He moved forward, reaching out a hand, and the old man took the hard yet youthfully soft hand in his own gnarled one as the youth said, "David Contreras, to serve you, señor," and he kissed the old, dry hand, kissed it as if this man was his father or a close uncle. The old man looked down understanding with the wisdom of his eighty years.

"I am Ysabel Pulido, you know of me, boy?"

"No, señor."

"It has been many years since my hand has been adored in that manner. My children have all expired. You bring back memories, thank you." And he added kindly, "But it is not necessary to ever do that again."

David continued to look at him, a slight smile, seemingly reluctant, in the unaccustomed face.

"You are a good one, boy, to revere age. And you are not afraid?"

"Why should I be?" answered David. "I have nothing but five hundred sheep and two goats that do not even belong to me, and which you can certainly have if you wish. There is no reason to be afraid. The dogs, now—the dogs would die for me in a minute. I would be helpless without them so I have no fear to die for them."

"Once, as a young man—well, to you it would not really seem young since I had thirty-two years at least at the time—I tended sheep in the highlands of Jalisco and I used the weapon you carry there to fight off the jinetes who were mostly Spaniards then and who had an aversion to sheepmen for some strange reason. It is no wonder that you have not heard of me, although to be honest, my fame is small. The shepherd is isolated. It has always been so, and when Maximilian was executed at Querétaro, I did not know for three or four months that the pig was no more."

"I suppose you are outlaws," said David.

"Bandits, we are called, with a price on our heads in five states," said Ysabel Pulido, and laughed softly.

"Will you accompany me as I break my fast, don Ysabel?" asked David.

"Gladly," said the old man, and although they were in the wilds, this was the boy's home and he removed his hat, very serious and added, "Thank you."

Since David was providing the meat, Ysabel Pulido insisted that his men prepare it, and as one man milked the goats, others built the fire, and still others slaughtered and dressed a large ewe.

And David sat on a rock, smoking, detached from the group, and there in the new-risen sun told the old man his story.

He made one request when Ysabel Pulido asked him to join his band, and that was that the goats be killed, for they would suffer much with no one to milk them, and the request was so unexpected that the old man was touched and had the entire flock driven ten kilometers into the hacienda land, to be left where other shepherds might find it. This because the sheep would be prey for wild animals if they were left in open country.

And thus it came to be that David Contreras followed Ysabel Pulido, calling him always don Ysabel, through the mountains of

San Luis Potosí in the eastern Sierra Madre, through the states of Guanajuato and Aguascalientes, touching a portion of Jalisco, and back into Zacatecas. As they moved, they robbed municipalities, rich estates, and fought running battles with rurales. They lost men, but as the ranks depleted, new faces appeared, and all this time David saw that indeed the old man was a kind man. He killed only of necessity, and always, except for that needed to get the bare necessities of life, Ysabel Pulido gave his money away and forced his men to contribute a part of their share for distribution among the needy. And when the need came, the old man was also a veritable tiger. He had the loyalty and respect of all who followed him, and once, when a young, strong man attempted to take command, the old man proved the stronger and the would-be usurper died while on his knees begging for mercy.

And in spite of the fact that he, too, gave his money freely, David had money enough to buy his mother's freedom by the time the band swung back into the state.

In the beginning the thought of looking after the old man, doing tasks for him which might prove too burdensome. Soon, however, he saw his error, and now he rode always near, but as a man and thinking of his chief as a strong man, and Ysabel Pulido smiled to himself and was pleased.

They returned to the box canyon because David wanted to see his mother; wanted to somehow get the money to her, and before they arrived they found Heraclio Inés.

David and Heraclio sat together, leaning back away from the huge campfire. Across from them, unseen, a man strummed a guitar, and in a high tenor sang ballads of love and honor, and death and tragedy.

They had eaten; now satisfied, they talked, hesitantly at first, but, sharing a bottle of sotol, they were soon speaking hurriedly in a torrent of words, making up for the many silent years.

"You were wrong back there, Heraclio, a while ago on the trail," said David. "I did not want you killed. If I had wanted that, I would have merely asked that you die, and don Ysabel would have had you staked to the ground, naked, on your back with legs apart, and we would leave you to die in your own good time, but the vultures would arrive long before you died and the first ones would feast on your eyes and they would not even hear your cries, for they are insensate, and yet the pain would not be so great that you would not feel the stripping of your gonads."

"You have nice thoughts, Daví," said Heraclio. "Now I wonder how you think such things. And he, the ancient one, he would do such a thing?"

"Certainly. If I had asked it."

"He is really a man, then, without a doubt. To be able to do such a thing when he is really a kindhearted one."

"You saw it too?" asked David quickly.

"Yes. And I wonder why he chose this life and at such a late date."

"No one knows," said David. "Some personal tragedy, perhaps, but he does not say. Anyway, I wanted you to leave, to get away, because I was afraid that you might take my place at his side. I did not want you dead." He said this looking down at the bottle he held between his legs, averting Heraclio's gaze, and now he raised the bottle and took a long drink.

And Heraclio felt strongly his friend's sentiments, for he knew that only the strongest feeling for the man would make David admit such a thing. "I am sorry, Daví," he said sincerely. "Sorry that I misjudged you. I was quick to do that since you might have been doing it for old friendship's sake."

"I have not been overly friendly recently," said David, dismissing Heraclio's apology as needless.

"You like the old bandit that much?"

And now David finally turned his head and with enthusiasm spoke directly to Heraclio in a way he had not done in years. "I love him, Heraclio. I love him as I have loved you—with filial love, and yet, there is something more. Rationally I think of him as a father, as the father I never had, but sometimes, more often now, it seems that he is really my father. That I have been searching the earth for him and have finally found him is my thought. I look at him sometimes and it is almost as if I remember him from long ago, hazylike, and yet real. "You know," he said, thinking Heraclio could not believe him, "you know how it is when you find yourself in a strange part of the range, a place you are certain you have never been to, and yet of a sudden you are aware of familiarity. Suddenly you recognize everything around you—the

184

landscape, a mesquite there, a mesa quite distinct in the distance just where it should be, a manantial that even when you press your face into it you remember the coolness of the water and having done that another time. Well, that is the way I feel when I look upon Ysabel Pulido—he is familiar and I have known him."

"I understand," said Heraclio. "And yet, that of seeming to know a thing that is foreign to you, it has happened to me, but I always feel that perhaps in my childhood someone has taken me to the particular place."

"So did I, at first," said David. "But I know it is not true. And, also, it is improbable that I was taken to this man when I was a child."

Heraclio was silent for a moment and took the bottle from David. "True," he finally said. "But Daví, you know, there are many strange things which we cannot explain. Like the things your mother does, for example. She does something in la Flor and a man or a woman two hundred kilometers away gets a stomach-ache of all stomach-aches, or else begins to fret and sweat and to lose weight. Now how? Perhaps she has charmed you—but no, it is unlikely that she would do that to you. And she divines, too, you know that. When someone loses something of value, she tells them where to look—she tells fortunes and they usually come out true, just as she has said. If a woman is barren, she can help her have a child, and if a woman does not want a child she is going to deliver, your mother can take it away from her, but of course, the last is more like poison."

"Yes, and a sin, I suppose," said David. "You know, Heraclio, that sort of thing that my mother does almost makes you believe in the little angels, and in the dark Virgin, and in God. And you know, although that of deliberately aborting is a sin, my mother is not really a witch because she has never killed anyone. Sick yes, she has made them sick in bunches, but none were made sick enough to die like some other practitioners we hear about now and then do. She is also a magician of sorts, and I cannot understand how in hell she did not get us our freedom through her prestidigitation. And about this business of believing in God and don Ysabel—you know how I feel, Heraclio? It is as if I have lived before. I have the feeling, although I know that we live but once, that at another time I was on earth with this man my father—

185

that perhaps that is why I did not have one in this life. Certainly he is old enough to have been my father in another age."

They were relaxed yet disturbed by this talk of the supernatural, gazing into the flickering flames, lulled and somehow apprehensive, and they were startled by the voice of Ysabel Pulido directly above them.

"Diverting yourselves, boys?" he asked in his soft voice.

David jumped to his feet and stammered apologetically. "You frightened me, sir."

Heraclio was a little angry. "You should hang bells on yourself, old one! You pussyfoot around like a thief and scare the wits out of the innocent!"

The bandit leader laughed. "I began to think with the full stomach and the warm fire," he said. "I would like a word with you, David—with the permission of Heraclio Inés."

"Certainly," said Heraclio, and moved away, adding, "I would probably not hear you anyway."

When he was out of hearing range, Ysabel Pulido said, "A good boy?"

"Yes, don Ysabel. He is a good one."

"And courage?"

"Of ten men."

"I thought as much." They spoke for a time of unimportant things, of the meal they had enjoyed, of their mounts, of the peacefulness of their hideaway.

David was curious but waited patiently for the old man to speak what was on his mind, happy only because they were speaking intimately.

Finally the old man said, "I have thought that it is time to do a little fighting. We run altogether too much, too much, but if we can kill a few rurales, things can be a little easier for us. Can this Heraclio Inés be trusted?"

"He can."

"Then call him here so that we can talk."

Both boys now waited for the old man to begin again, and finally in his soft voice, almost as if he were talking of anything but death, he said, "It has always appeared to me that this cajón can be a beautiful place for an ambush. "You, boy," this to Heraclio, "sleep for an hour or two. Then go to La Colorada and drink

186

and wait. Two days only, do not remain longer than two days. Then on the morning of the third day, before the sun, move out. That will give the Judas, whoever he will be, time enough to get word to the rurales and for them to get to La Colorada. Make arrangements to be seen as you leave, and once away from the ranch, wait until you see the police coming for you. Lead them here, by devious ways so they do not suspect that you are deceiving them. But get them here by daylight, nowhere near if it is dark."

And in his wisdom the old man sensed that David was slighted and he added, "Now I want you to know that I should send David on this little errand, since he knows the land as well as you and because I am sure he can be trusted. He is not a horseman, however, and might fall into the hands of the police. But he has vouched for your honor, and if you fail, although I hold much affection for him, he will forfeit his life. This you must think about. Now go."

"Very well," said Heraclio. He removed himself from the group and slept.

The Rancho La Colorada, although much smaller, was not very different from the main settlement at la Flor. And although the ranch itself was on land which belonged to the hacienda, its owner held title to it under an obscure decree dating back to colonial times. Here, too, was a Big House—not as elegant as don Aurelio Becerra's, but overshadowing any house within the ranch. There was a small herd of good cattle, but most of the property was used for agriculture. The crops were taken by wagon to the market at Río Grande and sometimes to Fresnillo. Once a year don Gabriel Ramírez traveled to la Flor to deliver a tithe to don Aurelio Becerra because the yellow parchment which made him a ranchero told him he must.

Heraclio had been there twice during the days he rode the range. And he had been to the home of Aquiles Cortez, whose mother had been an Inés of his own family. He came to this house, now, before the noon hour.

"I have been expecting you, Cousin," said the man, giving him a quick embrace. He looked out the door, closed and barred it, then peered out the windows. They sat at the kitchen table and the women of the house brought food for them.

"You know, of course," said Heraclio.

"The word is out. And the usual reward of thirty pieces of silver. I wonder what distorted humor set that price—that is, of course, until the fugitive becomes an outlaw and the price is raised. Strange, is it not, that there are countless in the mountains worth more than Jesus Christ."

Heraclio smiled because he had looked upon this relative with disdain as he ran around old-womanlike peeking out of the doors and windows. Now he understood the man was merely cautious, and his strange manner was pleasing. Aquiles wore white breeches down to the calves, revealing strong, well-muscled legs. His shoulders were powerful. He had a full mustache, and the machete hanging at his side gleamed from constant use. The man suddenly looked formidable as he tore pieces of meat with his strong jaws.

"Primo," said Heraclio, and he was embarrassed to call him cousin, almost as if he was now accepting him as an Inés, and embarrassed also that now, when he needed help, he was being intimate with a man whose table he had shared and with whom he had barely exchanged a word. "Tell me," he said once again, "how safe is it here?"

"Not safe at all," said Aquiles, chewing methodically. "You will hide here this afternoon and part of the night. Then it is better if you ride. Go north, because the word is out that you will go south in a circular fashion to get to Fresnillo. And they may be here tomorrow."

"With your permission I will remain another day or two. That is, of course, if I am not imposing," said Heraclio.

"This house is yours, Cousin. What do you think? What is this of impositions?" asked Aquiles. "I think only of your welfare."

"I need a little rest," said Heraclio.

"Sleep. Sleep the afternoon. I go to the cane field, otherwise someone may find it amiss that I am not present. My connection with your family is known—makes it difficult for me at times—drunks try to get me to mount a horse and that sort of thing. I have a hard enough time staying on a burro."

Heraclio laughed. He was taken through a bedroom into another large room with a door facing the plains. His horse, saddled and laden with food, stood near his bed.

"Can you not keep it outside?" asked Heraclio.

"No. It is better that the beast is not seen. It would be a difficult thing to explain."

"But he will shit in the house," he said.

"It is a good smell," said Aquiles, "the defecation of grass-eating animals. A strong odor of the earth which is not offensive. And then, too, we can clean it out later."

Well, Jesus Christ! thought Heraclio. But he took the saddle and bridle and the mochila off the horse before he went to sleep. The last thought he had was a fear that the horse should decide he had to scratch and should roll on the floor. Serve the "cousin" right if the beast kicked the Goddamned walls out.

"What is it that you wish to prove, Cousin," said Aquiles in the evening, "that you must go out to frolic and tell the rancho that you are here?"

"Prove? Why, nothing," said Heraclio. "I simply wish a little diversion. Now if you do not wish to accompany me, I shall find my way alone."

"No, no," said Aquiles quickly. "If you go, I go also. After all I am of the family and I shall fall with you. I only wonder if perhaps you are too young for fame. It makes one dizzy, fame does, they say, and it seems you want people to look at you."

Although he knew by now that this man was no fool, Heraclio was instantly wary, careful that his desire to be exposed would not be as obvious to others.

"I shall tell you, Cousin, although I am embarrassed because of your age. The truth is that I should have more respect—being here in your house, and you a mature man with a family," and he thought to himself how he was beginning to sound like the cousin. "Well, the truth of the matter is that I will be in the mountains perhaps a long time and I am thinking that I should have a woman."

The other laughed long. "Well, look what a boy! What a boy!" This he could understand, yet Heraclio was not fooled. The cousin was not really deceived.

"Is not that thing cumbersome to carry about?" Heraclio

189

pointed to the machete hanging from Aquiles' waist. They were at the brothel now, a large house with a dancing room and narrow hallways leading to smaller rooms.

"Now," said Aquiles, "what if someone should decide to make a reputation by breaking me only because I am connected with the family of Inés?"

Looking about, Heraclio made no reply as he studied every face, noted every hint of recognition. The word had traveled fast indeed.

"Go ahead," said Aquiles.

"Go ahead where?"

"Take yourself a woman so that we can get out of here. There are only four, and if you go now she will be fresh, not used first by one of these dirty field hands. Go now."

Heraclio looked at the man, attempting to show disbelief. "You have no sense of romance, Cousin," he said. "No, we are not in a corral, although it might seem so. It is impossible to merely mount a woman. Let us drink, and dance a bit, and get into the spirit of things."

Aquiles shook his head sadly. "You are my guest," he said, and sighed as if he wished he could defy custom. "I suppose you have your reasons, I only wish you were not my guest so that I should suggest something."

Heraclio felt a kinship with the man, and for the first time felt that which he should have known earlier. The man's family was in jeopardy, his life also, for his having harbored a wanted man. But the damage was done the moment Aquiles took him in and as of now there was nothing Heraclio could do to change it. He placed a hand on the man's arm with kindness, almost tenderly. "Thank you for your courage and for your selflessness, mi primo. Let us have one drink or two only and I will be done here. There is no harm since it is already too late to avoid that which you wish to avoid. I am sorry, believe me, that I did not think—I have compromised you."

Aquiles would have spoken, would have objected, but instead simply nodded and in turn took Heraclio's arm strongly in a cautioning gesture. He moved him toward the end of the room where the bar was situated. A bottle was placed before them, and two glasses, and Heraclio turned his back to face the room as Aquiles poured.

"Salud," said Aquiles, and they took up the tumblers. The man was before them as they half turned again, a horseman obviously, in this ranch of agrarians. Heraclio shifted the glass to his left hand.

The man smiled. "The gun is not necessary, boy," he said, for he was a mature man in his middle twenties. "I come to congratulate you, Heraclio Inés, for it is not every day that we can see a killer, especially a killer of a near administrator." He offered his hand and Heraclio refused it. The man seemed unaffected by the rebuff. "Present me to your relative, Aquiles. You have the manners of a backwoodsman. Tell him who I am."

"This is Bernardo Arnaz," said Aquiles quite seriously. "He calls himself the lion of Colorada for some reason or another. Intimidates a few youngsters and some of the weaker men around here, but otherwise has nothing which would make one admire him, much less like him.

"You are both nervous and testy," said the man, still in a friendly voice, but a rigidity showed in his face. "You will not provoke me, Aquiles, for we are friends. But do not be unfair. The horses. Tell about the horses."

"Oh yes," said Aquiles. "With horses he is quite good—really the best around these parts. That much I must say. And now it is said so go away."

But Bernardo Arnaz would speak and he ignored Aquiles. "It is said you are a jinete. Difficult to believe, knowing your age and now seeing you. But I should like to meet with you in competition."

What the hell! Heraclio thought. And this was the reason the cousin was warning him! And as if reading his thoughts, Aquiles said, "Yes, I must say he rides well—and he talks much."

"You do not interest me," said Heraclio, and turned his back to pour another drink.

"But I can interest you," said Bernardo Arnaz. "I come to tell you that I admire what you did, and that I wish to go with you, for I too hate the rurales. There is no limit to what you and I can do together, for I am like a tiger and fear nothing."

"You are sick," said Heraclio, "and it is you who are the boy."

191

"Very well, if that is your nature, very well," said the other. "I shall leave you alone, for now—but only for a little while."

Aquiles spoke once more. "Do not do it, Bernardo. I know your father and he is a good man, and I respect him. So for that, do not do that which you plan."

And Bernardo Arnaz said, "Do not do what, crazy? What do you say? The boy does not wish to speak with me and that is all—that is all of it, why do you say I plan something? And what?" His smile was back but Aquiles also turned his back.

"Stay," said Aquiles as they arrived at the house. His peculiar manner left him for a moment. "The harm is done, so remain here."

Heraclio slept for an hour, then saddled the horse and rode away. When the sun was high, he returned riding openly, showing that he was not in the house of Aquiles Cortez, and he found the house which was a cantina for the ranch, and broke his fast there on broiled kidneys and a bottle of mezcal, then drank leisurely until a parched drunk brought him the news that the horse troop was visible in the distance.

He gave him what was left of the bottle as a reward, tightened the cinch on his saddle, and rode slowly out toward the east. And an hour later he was on the first ridge and he looked back to see them riding hard, remained in silhouette to ensure that he was seen, then cantered along the ridge for a time to disappear on the other side.

It was too long a time to play like this until the following morning, and so he led them in a direct line until he was but an hour's ride from the box canyon where Ysabel Pulido waited, and suddenly he veered away again, making his trail give the impression that he was confused, then just as suddenly he lost himself and it was dark. He moved around until he was behind his pursuers. In the early hours he retraced his steps, coming out into the open directly before them, running back and forth to give the impression that he was trapped, then headed for the hideout, hoping with all his power that those waiting for him were ready.

The most dangerous point was at the entrance to the box canyon, where he must allow the rurales to come close enough to follow him into the trap. But fortunately the police did not fire, for they would take him back alive and hang him publicly, because these were troubled times. And as he neared the entrance, he dug his spurs deep, striving to lengthen the distance between them in the few paces remaining, knowing that the trap into which he led them could very well be his own. He had made no preparation for escape if he should suddenly find himself alone. He knew only that at the end of the canyon there was a trail—where it led he did not know—a footpath really, and he must dismount and lead his horse up through the brush. He would be able to move but slowly, but he must have his mount unless he could evade the rurales until nightfall and then lose them until he could find a wild beast somewhere.

These things he thought as he went through the opening of the canyon galloping strongly, veering to the right as he followed the contour of the floor, with the single thought suddenly that he must reach the trail. There was no sound other than the hoofs behind him and his own mount's, and he feared. But as he reached the abrupt end of the canyon, the rifles of Ysabel Pulido opened fire, crisscrossing murderously upon the forty men of don Porfirio.

He swung his horse around and drew his gun, but he again forgot about the single action and could not fire, then in his fury, threw the weapon away and took his lariat as one soldier galloped in an arc, invulnerable to the fire from the canyon wall, shooting at him, Heraclio, his one visible enemy. And Heraclio roped the rider cleanly around the chest, pinioning his arms, but his own horse, prancing, wild-eyed and frightened, did not brace itself as the rope fell true, but rather moved away and to the side, and Heraclio heard the snap as the ankle broke, for a moment saw the exposed tendons and flesh extended. The body twisted off the saddle and the man screamed once before he hit the ground and the foot remained in the stirrup of the running horse.

He felt somehow unfulfilled. He had not done well, and that about the rider he had roped he did not like. He had meant to kill, true—he had meant to kill because one did not think while killing about the human destroyed. But it had not been his desire to mutilate, for any reason. He had done this because his horse betrayed him, and yet, the horse was not at fault, for it had been frightened in its first action. He could not use this same excuse for himself.

And this of the killing of men. Enemies, true, and yet not personal ones. There had been an exhilaration to the whole of it; the flight and then the fight. This he could not deny. And before, earlier, so long ago, now, when he killed Juan Vásquez, he had no feeling after the act. He remembered no remorse, no special pleasure. But that man had done a harm to him, making the affair one of honor, and he had behaved like a man when he killed Juan Vásquez.

But here?

Ysabel Pulido came to him as he sat thinking. "I have brought you a gun, and a rifle," said the old man, "since you have no interest in looting the dead like the others. Later, you can find yourself a scabbard for the carbine."

"The rifle I thank you for," said Heraclio, "but the gun I do not want. It is exactly as the one I threw away. It will not fire."

The old man laughed. "You must teach yourself about firearms, boy. The guns are alike except for one thing only—look!" And he fired the gun easily toward the canyon wall. "The señores Colt have now a double-action weapon."

Heraclio was embarrassed that he had not known. "Thank you, old man," he said. He took the gun then, and knew that he would practice with the rifle and with the pistol as diligently as he had once practiced with the rope. He had crossed a line and could not turn back. He sensed that for his lifetime, now, he must defend himself.

"There are twelve prisoners," said the old man, and though he seemed emotionless, there was a crafty smile discernible to Heraclio. "They are yours, since you brought them here so unerringly. What do you wish to do with them?"

"Let them go," said Heraclio.

"Why?"

"Because they are such as we. Because they are people who can do us no harm. Strip them of their horses and guns and let them walk away."

"You are truly a buck," said Ysabel Pulido. "It shall be as you wish."

They rode three leagues to the east after the prisoners were released. They ate their meal before riding on, and Ysabel Pulido spoke to them.

"All this time, these last three years that I have been doing these things," he said, "I have had a purpose. I have robbed because I must eat, and sometimes I have robbed to help others who also must eat. But my rancor is with the government because it has used me ill. And until this day, outside of a few minor running fights with the rurales, I have not really done an act against the government. Nothing at all against these beasts who come mounted upon beasts, who call themselves police and protectors of the people. Today we have dealt a good stroke to the pigs and will now be doubly wanted.

"There is really nothing that we can do here to harass our enemy and I feel that it is time to move to the far north—to a place where a rebellion is destined to be born. I go now to join the man called Villa, a man very much such as I, but a man much younger and more fierce. I ask only the two boys to come with me. David and the new one, for it is a far journey and it will be long before we return—if at all we do return. The boys I am asking, and hope they will accompany me. The rest of you, I thank you, but you have families somewhere. Perhaps you would like to take up once more your peaceful life. Or perhaps you would choose a leader from among you and continue to annoy the civil police. That is your choice to make and you have only until we have eaten to decide, for I leave this night."

In the end, only three went with the old man. David and Heraclio because he had asked them and because they wished to remove themselves from this place, and the charro from Guadalupe, who felt he would like to go with Heraclio, and perhaps, too, wanting to leave these parts.

They would go to la Flor, said Ysabel Pulido, so that David could see his sainted mother. But Heraclio asked that they stop at La Colorada, for he must see for himself what harm had come to the family of Aquiles Cortez because of his own stupidity.

"Who walks?" A feminine voice answered his knock.
"Heraclio Inés."
The bolt was quickly drawn, and he walked into the kitchen.

He started to ask the woman for her husband, but Aquiles walked in from another room and quickly embraced him.

"I have been waiting for you to return," he said. "Until the morning I would wait and then go after you, for I, too, must flee."

"Bernardo Arnaz?" asked Heraclio.

"The very one. He reached Cañitas very fast, brought the rurales with him and remained here when they followed you."

"And your family?"

"Nothing, except that I must leave them for a time."

"Are you prepared to leave?"

For an answer, Aquiles opened the door. He had already made his farewells.

"We shall get a horse for you in la Flor," said Heraclio. "And perhaps a gun. Where is your machete?"

"I buried it with the cuckold's head," said Aquiles.

It was midnight when they arrived at la Flor, and although it was late, it was strange to find every house in darkness. The boys felt the unnaturalness more than the two men because they had lived here, knew that there was always activity, and now they had come home for a moment to find a ghost town. David went directly to his mother's house to leave the money and to take leave of her.

Although he had not thought of doing so, Heraclio also went home. Concepción and Otilia were sitting up before a small fire in the brazier.

"Somehow I knew you would return tonight," said Concepción. "When we received word the rurales had left Cañitas, I knew you would lose them and return before going away."

Otilia kissed Heraclio on the mouth. "Are you hungry, my brother?" she asked.

"I have supped."

"I told you," she said, "that the fair one would be dangerous for you."

He made no reply to her. "I am going north," he said to Concepción. "I go to where the revolt will soon begin."

"The revolt has already begun," said Concepción, "but not in the north."

"Started?"

"This morning, or during the night—down south, a man, an important man named Aquiles Cerdán and his sister have been murdered by state police. He was an active man and sympathetic to one called Francisco I. Madero, and it is said that this is the beginning. But you are right, there will be fighting in the streets to the north."

"Come with me, Concho," said Heraclio, suddenly wanting very much that this one of all his brothers should go with him. "Our cousin, Aquiles, from La Colorada, goes with me—he is outside. Will you come?"

Concepción put an arm about his wife. She would speak no word, nor would she hold rancor toward Heraclio for suggesting this, but she feared greatly that her man would go away and Concepción reassured her first with the gesture, then with his words that he would not do it.

"I cannot go with you, Heraclio, because my life is complete. I cannot leave Teodoro, you know that. I would need his blessing and he would not grant it. And most of all, I could not leave Otilia to go fight in a war I know nothing about."

"I understand," said Heraclio. "She would be very difficult to leave behind." He smiled in pleasure because here was love. "I must go, however, even if I were not a fugitive, I would go. I know I must be a part of this. It seems that I have nothing whatever to do with my life, that I live according to a plan made up for me long ago by someone else. Everything seems so inevitable, somehow. He looked at the two for a moment longer. Then he turned away. "You would need a blessing from Teodoro. Odd that I do not, but I shall say farewell to him before I go."

"No, no!" said Concepción quickly. "Do not see him, for it is in his mind to hold you for the authorities. We are fortunate that he could not believe you would come back so soon. At that he may wake at any time."

"There are no rurales for miles," said Heraclio.

"But there is yet authority here. There is still the alcalde and the two gendarmes."

Heraclio laughed. "Those washerwomen?" Then he had a sudden thought. "You would help him, Concho?"

Concepción moved toward him. "They would not harm you,

Heraclio. Merely hold you for a time, and then they would let you go. You know we would allow no harm to come to you."

"You have not answered me."

Concepción faced him squarely. "If Teodoro ordered me to do it, I would."

Heraclio passed a hand over his eyes. "A moment ago I forgot that day in the corral. I saw you only as I had seen you in another corral in Toribio so long ago. Strange that I should make such a mistake." He looked at the floor and was very nearly weak. "No," he said, "that is not it at all." He said this about what he was thinking, not of what he had just uttered. "The mistake was not in what you did in Toribio, but that I forgot about the day Teodoro made a man of me. I used to think about Toribio. I thought about it in the way I thought about my first horse that day, about Teodoro groveling at the patrón's feet, about the duty and responsibility of being who I am. It all seemed so ridiculous. My father died for no reason. You dominated the beast that killed him for no reason. None of that was important. Tradition—it was and is tradition, and we live on within the tradition. We are Ineses and we are better. Are we really? Or is it only that we were taught that to make us feel free. The truth is that we are men, and we are human, and for that reason it was important that my father die, it was important that you ride that horse. He played his life against his art and lost. You won. It was a deliberate thing, and it was the closest thing to a decision we are allowed. Because the thing about bondage that is unbearable, be it bondage to tradition or in the physical sense our neighbors are slaves, is that we do not have the right to make a decision.

"I did not know this until the day you left me on the range alone, to take a horse or to walk. I did it. And I do not have to tell you how dangerous that could be. I decided to do it— not because I feared Teodoro's whip, not because I wanted to please my brothers, but because I chose to do so. And it was then, in the open, when I knew that to be thrown could mean death, for the stallion would surely attack me, that I knew that my father had to die, that you had to do what you did. I had a moment of clarity that we must get only a rare time in life. An act when deliberate is a choice. And one thing that no one can do to me as to any human, is to fuck with my life. Neither Teodoro with

198

his warped mind, the patrón with his tradition, or the government with its rurales can stop us from dying if we wish to do so. If I decide to die for what I believe is right, no one can stop me. Just as you and my father did what you had to do. And my going away is a deliberate thing. I may die, and it will mean nothing to humanity, but it will mean something to me. It is the only thing we have—this right. I believe in the rebellion to come, and I may begin another Inés tradition, to stand up for our rights, for the rights of man. I do not clearly understand this, but I feel it."

He had placed his hat on the table, and now he took it, dropping the string behind his head, and pulled the brim low on the forehead. "Keep him, Otilia. I rid myself of these my brothers once. I do not know why I return to them time and again, but I shall never do it another time."

"Heraclio, wait!" said Otilia. "Understand your brother, I beg you!"

"It is nothing," said Heraclio. "It matters not," and he went out the door. But there was a sense of loss as well as disappointment and now, walking along the alley to his horse, he was also disillusioned, aware of the unlighted houses, the bolted doors, and aware also that inside the chozas few slept, for they were afraid. To his young mind it all seemed wrong. These, his people, should be singing out in the open, with torches held high and spirits straining to the glory of this day. Instead they cowered in the darkness as they had cowered for so long, and his brothers? He had almost said something about the darkened houses to Concepción and the why of it, but if would be as if he questioned Concho's courage, and of course there was no such question. No, his brothers would lose no sleep but they might as well be as the others. But how beautiful it could have been—the five of them riding away together to help rid the nation of the vermin.

He was surprised to find that he was near tears.

"The fight is on," he said to Ysabel Pulido. "That is the reason for this blackness on this day of joy. The meek are in their holes, so let us go deliver their homeland for them. The revolt began this morning."

"Do not be so bitter, boy," said the old man. "They will come out, the meek, as you call them, and they shall be as a wave of tigers, and there shall be no stopping them, perhaps no controlling them. You are young, but there is much time, much time."

Heraclio regarded the old man's wisdom. "I am angry because of the complacency, that is all," he said. "I do not know very much, but then, I do not have many years. Perhaps you are right. I hope so."

"You shall see," said Ysabel Pulido. "Consider yourself now. You have ceased to think about that of this morning. The twenty-eight rurales who died this morning are no longer on your conscience because a revolt sprang up a few hours earlier. You have glory of sorts—suddenly you are not a bandit but a revolutionary fighting for freedom. So will it be for these people who now hide —time will also change things for them."

Heraclio was embarrassed that the old man had known all along, and yet he was not surprised. "You are right, old one. The idea of a moral lapse for that of the rurales has left me. Now I am a rebel—true, and I know that it was never meant for me to be a bandit."

David came to them, and with him was Antonio Rivera. "I knew you would want him with you," David said to Heraclio.

"Welcome, friend Antonio," said Heraclio. He led them to the armory. "I did not intend to do this, but we are at war now, so we are forced to take arms where we can."

While Aquiles and Antonio carried rifles and ammunition to the street, he took David behind the Big House and hitched two mules to a wagon. He said to David, "Take the wagon toward Río Grande, but first, after you load the guns, stop at the warehouse and take a few sides of dried meat and some sacks of corn. If I am not with you when you approach Río Grande, veer left and away from the town. We must find a hiding place before daybreak."

"Very well, Heraclio," said David. "Say good-by to my sister, will you."

Heraclio paused, for there seemed to be a warning in the casual remark, yet not a warning about Carmen. It came to him then that David was apprehensive because Heraclio was giving orders, and was thus a danger to Ysabel Pulido.

"I will," he said. "Go now." He was too impatient to humor David at this moment. Later, on the trail, David would see that he meant nothing by taking the initiative here.

He rode his horse through the garden directly to Carmen's window, not concerned about making too much noise because he knew that they had already been heard. He did not have to call, and she came to the barred window, and clasped his hands.

"Where do you go?" she asked.

"To join the revolt. I had to say good-by to you. I came to wish you happiness."

"How can you say that when you go to fight my people?"

"Your people?"

"When it comes to a thing like this—a war—the killing of people, then I must say that they are mine."

"México belongs to the Mexican," he said. "We have waited much too long."

"We are also Mexican—but Heraclio, do not fight with me! Please! I wish to tell you something. I wish to ask you to remain here. Do not go, for it is not too late for us to marry."

He shook his head. "Carmen—do not waste time like this. You know that is impossible. We have discussed it a thousand times."

"And I tell you it is not. My father is like a different man—I know. And if I speak to him I can have you, forever, not for minutes at a time such as we have known."

"And the contador? What of Juan Vásquez. They would still call it murder, no?"

She spoke quickly. "My father will send you to México for a while, there to remain with friends, and after a time I shall follow and we can marry. Perhaps we can go to Spain until this is all over, and then return here. It can be done! I know it can be done! Only, speak now and say you will. Come with me."

"I cannot! I simply cannot do this. It is a dishonorable thing you ask me to do and I am incapable." It was out of his hands. He had not been forced to make the decision after all.

"Then this is really the end," she said, "for in a week I marry Domingo. When you leave me, I will become the mistress of la Flor to you as to any peon."

"That is the will of God," he said. "Good-by, Carmen, I love you."

He moved out of the garden, across the front of the Big House, then circled the corral and rode away at a gallop.

The Second Book

The Campaign

THE MULES, TIRELESS, pulled the wagon around the town of Río Grande and, once beyond, picked up the railway again, following it westward on a two-rut road until the railroad began to twist and climb, and the trail dissipated gradually until they were moving on the open plain, yet ascending.

In this way, the small group moved into the state of Durango daring now to travel on the open road, skirting only cities and large towns, for the rurales had disappeared and most Civil Guards were sympathetic. And as they moved, they were joined by men young and old, singly or in small groups. Those who were unarmed were given guns until the wagon was empty save for some staples, and these too were distributed and the mules were unhitched and given to two recruits who were on foot by the time they reached the thickly foliaged mountains.

The old man led them, not unlike a patriarch, wrinkled, lank-haired, yet clear-eyed and stately proud in the saddle, and he was patient, as were those who knew him. And it was two days after moving into Chihuahua that word from Villa arrived in the form of an old man leading a pack burro. He was old, incredibly old—more ancient than Ysabel Pulido—and the two ancients sat on the ground cross-legged for three hours and talked and yet nothing was said, but the next morning, first one man on horseback met them, soon thereafter another, and then two more, until there were fifteen strangers in their midst weighted down with bandoleers and sidearms, fierce-looking men much like Ysabel Pulido, and finally they came to a place where there were a few houses and a corral.

Three men walked from the house which faced the corral. As Ysabel Pulido dismounted, David and Heraclio quickly came to his side and flanked him. One man stepped forward, in cowboy dress, twin bandoleers, and his spurs jingled as he moved. He was lithe and tall for these people, red faced with small black eyes, a full mustache, also black, and perhaps in his middle thirties. He picked his teeth as he spoke.

"You are Ysabel Pulido?" he asked.

"At your orders."

"Your fame is known to us. Come, give me an embrace."

Ysabel Pulido stepped forward and the two men clasped each other.

"I am Celestino Gámez," said the man. "Lieutenant now—in the forces of my Captain Villa."

"There has been an amnesty, then?" asked Ysabel Pulido.

"On the part of the Revolutionary Forces only," said Celestino Gámez. "Francisco Madero has pardoned us and we are in the ranks of the Colonel Pascual Orozco."

Ysabel Pulido nodded toward the enclosure. "That is for us, no?"

"You must forgive us this, don Ysabel," said Celestino Gámez. "You know the life and must surely understand."

"Do not be disturbed," said Ysabel Pulido. "Truly I do know the life, else how would I have known?" He anticipated the next request and turned to the two boys. "Have the men dismount and unsaddle their beasts. Leave saddles, guns, and ammunition on the ground and move into the corral. They may keep their mochilas."

"They may keep nothing but the clothing they wear," said Celestino Gámez.

"It will be cold tonight," said Ysabel Pulido quietly. "They need their bedroll and they must eat."

"Then they must be searched."

"Do you doubt my word?" said the old man, still calmly.

"Very well." Celestino Gámez was embarrassed by the old

man's gaze. He spoke and now he was not embarrassed and laughed. "You are a strange lot," he said. "An ancient for a leader with two children for lieutenants."

David and Heraclio had returned to Ysabel Pulido's side after unsaddling their own animals. They looked upon the man's face impassively.

Ysabel Pulido chuckled. "Watch my children grow," he said.

"Come into the house," said Celestino Gámez. "And bring your children with you. Tomorrow I shall take you to my chief. I am sorry I have not the authority to accept you into our ranks."

"I understand, but I should like a favor."

"Declare it."

"There were six of us who started out together," said Ysabel Pulido. "I should like it if we could remain together. I want them to accompany me on the morrow."

"It shall be," said Celestino Gámez.

The horses were already being driven away and the arms and saddles were loaded on two wagons.

In the evening, after they had eaten in the house, the old bandit and the two boys went out to the corral to sleep with the men. It was late, and Ysabel Pulido said:

"Come, David, sleep by my side."

David Contreras was overjoyed and rolled himself in his blanket alongside the old man.

And that night, Ysabel Pulido died in his sleep.

It was in itself a miracle that Ysabel Pulido had brought them so close to Federal strongholds without encountering any opposition. The hideaway where Celestino Gámez held them prisoners was but a few miles from the guerrilla leader's bivouac and but two days' ride from the towns of Santa Rosalía and Camargo, Villa's next objectives. And, too, in every center of population in México, the peasant was up in arms. With machetes and rifles and knives, the peon slaughtered the rich where he could, indiscriminately looted and raped—and for the first time in almost four hundred years had no one to stop him from doing his will and he did it. As a result, towns hastily set up civil defenses and the poor people now fired upon any horsemen who should appear and thus they fired on their own.

And that morning, with Ysabel Pulido, now stiff, still in his bed-roll, and David Contreras on his knees beside him in deep grief kissing the cold, marked face, Celestino Gámez scratched his bushy head and sighed.

"What a misfortune!" he said to Heraclio Inés. "The old one had to expire and now what shall I do. I am to bring only the leader and a man or two of his. And now who is to be called the leader?"

"Why, that shall be I, my Lieutenant," said Heraclio Inés, until that moment not having given that possibility a thought.

"You!" And Celestino Gámez laughed. "Don Pancho would for certain have me shot for wasting his time with children! No. I shall talk to the men and have them select a leader. That is the only way."

Together they walked to the corral. The men were murmuring, restless. They had come many miles to fight in the great fight and instead here they were corraled like animals, and now the sun was coming up and there was no shelter. The scene was most unmilitary as the lieutenant addressed them. Most did not bother to even stand up. But Celestino Gámez was one of them and he spoke, not as an officer, but as a man of the mountains.

"Your jefe is dead and you must select a new one so that we can negotiate. If there is a disagreement, I will supply two of you with fusiles and separate you by thirty paces so that you can decide." He grinned widely now as a perverse humor took hold of him. He looked at Heraclio and gave him his gun. "I have one leader here," he said. "We shall form a line for those who disagree."

Heraclio checked the gun and moved away a few paces to the side. Why he was doing this he did not know, except that he would follow only a man who was at least his equal. He waited calmly for the lieutenant to send someone to meet him. But perhaps because he had been with Ysabel Pulido in the beginning, or because in truth no one had a desire to lead, there was no objection, and Celestino Gámez said, now that his pleasure would be denied him:

"But what a passel of men we have here! I do not know that we wish to have alongside us men who would allow a mere baby to treat them in this manner! What say you? Is there no man among you who would lead a troop?"

But once again no one answered and Heraclio walked to him and returned the gun. "Lieutenant, I should like the same request you saw fit to grant don Ysabel. The men who were with us in the beginning—when we set out to find your people—I should like them to accompany me when we meet your captain!"

"Very well," said Celestino Gámez, and he spat disgustedly before him in the direction of the men.

And now, Heraclio Inés, with Antonio Rivera, the cousin, Aquiles, and the charro from Guadalupe—David would not leave the body of Ysabel Pulido—waited for an audience with Villa. The man was eating, they were told, and he would see them presently, but a man came from a thatched lean-to and said:

"Send them in."

He sat on a field cot, eating beans from a deep dish and with blunt, strong fingers tore pieces of meat from the ribs of an animal. He had reddish hair, near auburn, thick, and a thick mustache. Everything about him seemed thick—his shoulders and arms powerful, his face and jaws strong, and yet he was not a tall man. His eyes were gray, expressionless, and he looked up at the newcomers and said while chewing:

"And is the old man such a great one that he must send messengers?"

"His heart stopped in the night," said Celestino Gámez. "The long ride north was too much for the ancient one."

"Do not malign the dead, Celestino," said Villa. "Especially when they have been men. And from all reports this Ysabel Pulido was such a one. It must have been his time." He looked at Aquiles Cortez, and Heraclio quickly said:

"I am the one, my chief. I have seventy-five men—most of them horsemen—and we offer ourselves up to become your soldiers."

Villa turned his full gaze at Heraclio and his expression was one of mirth. His mouth grinned wide, the flesh at his temples and around his eyes crinkled, but the eyes showed nothing. Heraclio feared at this moment more than he could ever fear again, and he understood how David could have such devotion for Ysabel Pulido, for here seemed to be his own man.

"What a dandy, what a dandy, just you look," he said to his men. "Is Zacatecas such that a child shall lead them?"

"Zacatecas is such," said Heraclio, "that it needs leadership of any kind."

"Even a hairless one like you?" But this was not true, for although a week's growth of beard on Heraclio was not much more than barely visible down, his mustache was now almost full, though not as full as Villa's.

"The thing of it is, my jefe," said Heraclio calmly, "that I am not a child. There is nothing your men can do that I cannot do. Some things I can do better than any of them. I am not immodest. I merely tell you what is true."

Villa laughed once again, and although he asked questions, his judgment was not based on the questions and answers. "And me?" he asked jovially. "Would you stand up against me?"

"I do not know," answered Heraclio, "but I suppose so. I do know, however, that it would not be difficult to die for you."

Villa stopped his jesting. He said, "To die is never difficult."

"To die for someone other than oneself is," said Heraclio.

Again Villa seemed to be humorous. "And how many years have you, my guerrillero?"

"I shall have eighteen in a month."

"And how many men by your own hand have you stopped from living?"

"Only two," said Heraclio, and now he felt in himself mounting anger. And he added, "If that is not enough, my jefe, I shall go out and shoot a few more until I qualify."

And now Villa laughed loudly. "Do not have anger, my dandy. I mean nothing, it is only that I must know certain things." He called to one of his men. "Hey you, you who has said to me that you have the power of handwriting. Get some paper and fix it so that this little boy—what are you called?" he asked Heraclio.

"Heraclio Inés."

"—so that this muchachito Heraclio Inés is a second lieutenant. And bring it over to me so that I can affix my signature—I can do that, you know," he said to Heraclio for no apparent reason. He added, "I do not have the arms for your men, although we got a few mausers when we took San Andrés."

"We were well armed when we came to you," said Heraclio.

208

"Celestino, you have the teniente's arms?"

"Yes, mi capitán."

"Return them to him." Heraclio received his sidearm and his rifle. "Where do you carry your shells?" asked Villa.

"Where else? In the pocket of my jacket."

Villa turned to one of his men. "Give him your carrillera and get him a gun belt," he said. "I will not have my officers looking like civilians on a grouse hunt." He took the bandoleer and personally put it over Heraclio's shoulder and across his chest. "Go back," he said to Celestino Gámez, "and bring the teniente's men. Give them their arms and welcome them to the mob. Leave the boy here—I would talk with him."

They faced Camargo and Santa Rosalía beyond it on the plain. It was cold, and their horses, now at a standstill, shivered in discomfort, while they, the men, wore sarapes for protection and those who had them wore bandoleers over their bulky clothing. And Heraclio was impatient now that he had come this far. He wondered how it was to be, not the least bit afraid, but he did not know what to expect. The man had said that this he was to do —to be a part of the main force attacking; and Heraclio had but thirty men now, for half his people were assigned elsewhere. He knew that this was not the main force because there had been at least five hundred men and here were but a hundred. And three lieutenants led them.

In a moment he would ask, for he was tired of waiting and a bit annoyed. This was all new to him. When he had fought first he had been running and now to attack a stronghold of a thousand men with their small force seemed folly. But Celestino spoke to him and said:

"You shall ride to my left, infant, and do not overtake me but fall a little to the side and back." He turned to the other officer. "You do the same, Guadalupe, on my right. And keep an eye on me, somehow, no matter how it goes out there, for when I give the word, I want your men to turn and run a ways, and turn again and fight for a short while, then once again retreat as if disorganized. We shall do this even if we return to this point from where we start. Fight and retreat, fight and retreat—they shall follow us and then you shall see. You shall be on your own then, to stand and watch or come and share the blood. Go now to your men, for we move of a sudden—but first, give me your hand, Heraclio Inés, and you, Guadalupe Morales, for after this if we can pull it off, you are no longer children."

Heraclio shook the hand of Celestino Gámez and then that of the other youth, who was perhaps two years his senior, then moved several paces to his left. He sat his horse and waited for the dawn, flanked by Antonio, David, and the primo Aquiles. The charro from Guadalupe was now with Celestino. He sensed the impatience of the men behind him, the restlessness of his own mount beneath him, and tried to think why they had such strange orders. Nothing made sense, and yet he had a knowledge that this was the right thing to do.

His men were ready, as unafraid as he, for what was death, after all? They knew it well whether they had been violent men or not, because to their people death was but a part of life, a small part. From birth they had been aware of death, and in their familiarity, personified it and insulted it. The only fear they knew was that of the unknown—that of confusion.

Now, at that moment when dawn becomes the day, when all is quiet and time is still, Celestino Gámez screamed as if in sudden labor, a scream of pain and yet of pleasure too, and then, as the horses, frightened into movement, lurched, bared his teeth wide and shouted:

"It is the time for it, boys! A *chingar la muerte!* Let us go fuck death!"

Somewhere before them there was infantry entrenched, to remain out of sight until the very last. And as they moved, Heraclio veered away and his men followed and fell back. Across from him, Morales did the same until they formed a screaming, shouting phalanx four hundred yards wide. Then the men behind came up, refusing to fall back, the hundred men now spread upon the land and they came up to the trenches as a line.

The fire from the defenses was rapid yet deliberate, and now the screams were screams of agony and men fell and were trodden upon and the living came together as if this would give protection. Many did not fire, did not even draw their arms, their Winchesters 44-40 sheathed useless in their scabbards. Others there were who, not being horsemen, dropped their guns to use

210

both hands in an attempt to control their animals. Horses and men fell together and some, untouched by gunfire, were kicked to death by the flailing hoofs of animals in their death throes.

The retreat began without a word from the leader. An ebbing of flesh, out of individual control, and Celestino somehow broke out ahead and turned around.

"Back! Back!" he shouted. "About and at them, you sons of bitches!" But his orders were unheard and he lashed out at them with his sabre as they went by him, and then enveloped him, carrying him with their charge. And now Heraclio, too, broke free, and spurred his animal forward by a hundred yards, and turned to face them. And he, too, screamed and shouted, flailing with his quirt at the first few that reached him, and then in impotent anger drew his sidearm and slew three of his own men. They had run awhile and had slowed somewhat, and Heraclio moved from one side to another, shouting obscenities, threatening, clubbing, while on the other side of him, Celestino, too, had slain a man, and now with Guadalupe Morales chastized and whipped them into line.

They had run so far there was no need to charge again as they had been ordered, for the Federals had climbed out of their trenches and followed them, shooting, laughing in gratification for such a quick victory. And they talked to those they pursued, talked to them in low voices as they paused to reload or to fire, and when their enemy was out of range, they turned and fired ineffectually at the thin line of pickets on their right flank.

But now among the pickets, far over, closer to the trenches than the defenders, appeared a stallion barely trotting, and Pancho Villa pushed his hat high on his forehead and looked down upon the skirmish. He raised an arm almost casually and grinned widely. "It is time, my little ones," he said. "Eat them up, my little boys." And with a short wave he sent his four hundred in from the flank and the Federals were naked on the plain.

And they devoured them. With rifle fire and small arms, they slew the government, and then with machetes and knives they hacked and slashed, and finally, with their horses, they trampled them. Some ran into the plain but only for a while, for although the breastworks were now reinforced, there were but two hundred soldiers remaining, and fifty of these were guarding the municipal palace.

The assault group sat and watched the action. They had regained some order when the attack from the flank began, but Celestino, still swearing and chastizing, threatening, did not send them down until the end. The prairie was strewn with bodies for four hundred yards and the horsemen of Francisco Villa regrouped for the assault, and the bandit leader raised his arm again. Celestino moved them down and Heraclio thought:

How foolish! When all we have to do now is to go around and enter the city unmolested from another side!

But before Villa could give the word, the commander in the trenches jumped out and moved forward, waving his arms and finally his hat, and his men came out also and threw their rifles down, and Villa rode his stallion slowly down onto the plain.

In the municipal palace of Santa Rosalía, Captain Francisco Villa received a committee of townsmen loyal to the cause as occasional bursts of rifle fire reverberated from the rear of the building where city officials and captured Federal officers were being executed. At that moment, south of the city, troops destroyed the railroad, pulling up sections of track and blowing up two trestles. Communication lines were cut and the garrisons of don Porfirio to the north, Chihuahua and the border town of Juárez, were isolated from Mexico City.

A new municipal president and city officials were appointed by Villa with the admonition that thievery and malfeasance would not be tolerated. The city was returned to the people.

Later, the victorious officers sat in the dining room of the chalet of the deposed mayor. Francisco Villa and his lieutenants, ex-comrades in banditry, feasted regally. Celestino and Tomás Urbina, compadre and long-time friend, others who had been with Villa in the beginning, none had known such sumptuousness. And Heraclio Inés and Guadalupe Morales, newcomers, yet already beginning to find a place.

The men were jocular, and with the exception of their captain, they all drank hard liquor as they ate. He poured buttermilk from a gourd and, wiping his mustache with the back of his hand, said:

"A good blow, boys," and he laughed loud. "A good blow. And

212

Celestino, you enticed them outside so perfectly, only"—and the eyes looked coldly upon them—"for a time your deception was such that it seemed to me that you were really in a rout."

The men were silent. And Celestino said, "We were, don Pancho. It was the first action for many of the men. Some, I think, have never been on a beast—why it was a miracle that we controlled them at all, for it seemed they would run all the way to Mexico City."

"And the two young ones," asked Villa. "You went beyond the range of my vision and I wish to hear how they behaved."

Celestino said, "The older one, now, there was no great problem because his men, I believe, are more disciplined. They have been together longer and they know him. His struggle to avoid a panic was much like mine, but the young one—he had much trouble in the real sense, for his people have not had time to know him for the man he is. You may send him with me whenever it pleases you."

"That is a high recommendation, Celestino," said Villa, obviously pleased. He could not remain annoyed for long on this day. And after all, there had been a reason for the wild flight, and Celestino had accomplished his mission.

"Well," said Celestino Gámez, and he uttered a short laugh, "now he can tell you that he has killed by his own hand five men."

Villa looked full upon Heraclio's face, quite coldly, in study, and murmured as if to himself, "So that was the way of it, was it? So that was how it was?" And then he was jovial once again and said, not speaking to Heraclio but for Heraclio's ears, "Now here is one to be my very own, muchachos. This creature was a born cock, for some things come to one—such things one does not learn. To kill a comrade in arms is as necessary sometimes as it is to die for some sometimes." And now he spoke to Heraclio: "Tell me, boy, what made you kill your own men?"

Heraclio was cautious. He did not really know this man Villa; did not know when the sarcasm in his voice was in tune with his words. For here, things quite serious were said in jest, and Castilian lent itself to double meanings, and also, he was still somewhat confused. The action of the morning had been complete confusion for him until he took command of his men. He had been a center of things—everything was outward, swirling around him, and now sitting here in a fine mansion in a dusty mining town in the north, he thought of the movement all over México and how everything outside this little populated area was also a swirling mass as far as they were concerned. But there were men who made sense of such things, he knew, even Pancho Villa could, for that which had seemed to him so misconducted, the taking of Santa Rosalía, had had a sense of order to it. He had thought how fortunate for them all that Villa had erred and not sent all his men into the frontal attack! He had judged it as a stroke of luck, rather than that of genius—but only for a short time and because he did not know of these things. But then he saw that although the initial action had disintegrated in disorder, the entire operation was a plan, and since they were victorious, the plan was sound. The larger operation, the rebellion, would also be disorderly, he knew, but it too had a pattern—it must.

But now, looking at the men around him and finally into the eyes of the guerrillero, he did not know what the man wanted from him, and suddenly he felt an outsider, and he had the feeling also that he might very well die in this town if his answer was not a good one, and he had the resolve that he would speak the truth and only that, and if he was to die he would die here in this room and one or more of these men would die with him. He was prepared to kick his chair back at any moment as he answered Pancho Villa.

"It was not a killing in the ordinary sense, mi capitán," he said. "I did not kill my men, I executed them. I was angered, for they became a threat to our cause. Suddenly they were a danger to my very life, and so I killed them. The others stopped after that. But at that moment I would have killed more if they did not obey my command. Did I do wrong?"

"Wrong?" Villa roared the word. And then he teased Heraclio by mimicking him perfectly. *"Did I do wrong?"* He laughed and stuffed meat in his mouth with his finger. "But look here, boys, at my little dove. Have you in your sainted life ever seen balls such as this one carries? They drag. I swear they drag along the ground! Did he do wrong! Take an example, boys, take an example. The boy knew what to do and why. The objective is the thing. And when you have a doubt as to whether lives are worth an objective, deliver the lives, for if it were not worth it there would be no doubt and thus no objective. Now you imbibers of the weed —one of you toast a tequila to our new mascot, for I feel within me that he brings luck—like a hunchback or an idiot, but, do not mistake him for an idiot. Compadre . . ." He looked at Tomás Urbina, who sat to his right.

The squat, swarthy Urbina, with a bleached-out mustache and soft-looking body, looked more like a well-fed clerk than a man of the mountains, which he was, stood up and said, "To our warrior, Heraclio Inés. May he live long and slay many, and may most of them be of the enemy."

The men laughed and raised their glasses high. "Salud, Heraclio," they said in unison.

Villa spoke again. "How will they ever stop us?" he asked of no one in particular. "What saint is there who loves me so that he sends me men such as you?"

And to Heraclio's surprise, the man began to cry. Tears rolled down his face as he spoke, and Heraclio looked to the others, but they seemed unaffected; this was not a new thing to them. Villa continued, "Why, they can never stop us. You, all of you, and I will show them who I am—they will know that Pancho Villa is the father of them all, and they will know it soon." He regained his composure as he spoke. "You are a jinete?" he asked Heraclio.

"Of the best," answered the youth.

Villa smiled and shook his head. "We are going north, boys, to rendezvous with the Colonel Pascual Orozco. He was repulsed in an attack on Casas Grandes, which was a stupid move, but has taken Ciudad Guerrero. Francisco Madero is with him now, and although he is a great man and should do all the thinking and talking in the movement, he should leave the fighting to those who know about such things—they now propose to attack the city of Chihuahua, another mistake because it is well fortified, as you well know, and they are five thousand men waiting, just waiting to kill us. Now the place to attack is Ciudad Juárez. It is not necessary to take Chihuahua if we have all the area around it.

"And yet, it may be possible to take Chihuahua. Certainly we shall try, eh, boys, if don Francisco Madero insists?"

"We shall travel more slowly now that we have an infantry." Almost two hundred captured Federal soldiers had been given the choice of joining the rebel forces or facing the wall, and Pancho

215

Villa would go north with seven hundred men. "And you, boy," and now as he talked to Heraclio the jest was gone from his voice, "you take your seventy-five men and even as we move, you make them run and maneuver on horseback. Teach them to ride at least a little or take their beasts away from them. They can become of the infantry, those who cannot handle a horse, for we will never run away again."

Outside Ciudad Guerrero, once again alongside a stream, this time the Río de Haros, the army of the north encamped. In the center of the camp, a row of tents stood, facilities for the general staff and distinguished visitors. Pancho Villa stood in the sun before the largest tent, talking with his superior officer, Pascual Orozco.

Orozco was a slender man, not overly tall, with light red hair and mustache. He had been a storekeeper and had been considered a superior in his community, and although he appeared to be a gentle man, here in the field he made his superiority felt. He believed in México, but he also believed in classes, and being one of the few in the upper middle class, and having an education, he did not think it difficult to be of the elite. He could not conceive of a peon as his equal, and, thus, his tone was always tainted with superciliousness. He did not wear bandoleers, the mark of the rebel peon; instead, he carried two cartridge belts around his waist. He did not carry a sidearm and, oddly, usually wore a white shirt and tie with his battle gear.

He spoke to Villa in anger, yet seemingly merely in mild rebuke, "But sir," he said, "what you did in Santa Rosalía—that is not done. But what authority did you execute those Federal officers and those civilians?"

Villa looked at him calmly, his eyes again feelingless. "I was the ranking officer present. The men were criminals and I had a prerogative," he said. "I merely exercised it."

"It was not your prerogative, señor," said Orozco with mounting anger. "These men were gentlemen, on the wrong side, but gentlemen, nevertheless. You had no right to kill them. Men like you can give the revolution a bad name, for you tell the world that we are no different from those in the government we are trying to overthrow."

"No, mi coronel," said Villa, and his anger was visible only by the calmness of his voice and the deliberateness of his speech. "I shall do it again, for what, after all, is the revolution? Are we to retain these people, and give them back their old positions so that they can rob and pillage and murder the people again?"

"They are experienced, educated men, from good families. México needs these men for the reform."

"Well, señor, it seems to me," said Villa, and he laughed as if dismissing his superior officer, "that you and I are fighting on opposite sides. You seem to feel that the great fight is for the parasite. No, sir, to me, it seems that if I could kill a Federal officer and a corrupt city official a day, that would be reform enough."

"If you do it one more time," said the Colonel Orozco, "You shall be court-martialed." He turned and walked into the largest tent.

Pancho Villa stood in the sun for a moment longer, then followed his colonel into the headquarters.

In the tent, the guerrillero sat on a field cot to one side and listened, watching the leaders of the revolution make plans. Villa was allowed to be present as a courtesy, for he had no political knowledge and as yet no real leadership in the movement.

Seated around a table were Pascual Orozco, now named military head of all the revolutionary forces, Francisco I. Madero, who had proclaimed himself President, two of his brothers, who had sided with him against the wishes of their family, José María Maytorena from the state of Sonora, Colonel José de la Luz Blanco, and Giuseppe Garibaldi, the grandson of the Italian liberator.

Madero was speaking. "This, sirs, is the beginning of the end of this great tragedy. That we should kill our brothers and that they should kill us is indecent. Poor devils! It is not their fault, for they have been conscripted, but this is the only manner in which we can do this thing.

"Now all we have to do is take the city of Chihuahua. Our people in Washington, D.C., assure me that Dr. Limantour will meet with them there before he goes on to México to report to don Porfirio. The feeling is that the government is preparing to capitulate. Díaz will step down, it is said, although is has not been offered yet.

"But the time is past for merely that. Before the election, the removal of the President would have satisfied us, for it would have been a bloodless step forward. Men have died now for reform, and these dead have earned us other guarantees, but a victory at Chihuahua will give us the power to demand. We shall have a new cabinet and a general cleaning of the Chamber of Deputies.

"And that, señores, is why we take Chihuahua. For those who have died and for those who shall survive—for a better México."

Villa had been watching the man, listening patiently. He was fascinated by the manner of the little man, by the wen on the right side of his face moving above the ridiculous beard, by his little arms gesticulating. As was his custom, he appraised quickly and liked the man and trusted him. But he considered him misguided in military matters; and although he was out of order, he would speak, for he did not believe in self-deception.

"For those who have died, you say, your excellency," he said, "and also for those who survive. But you forget, or have not considered, those of us who will be killed in the attack of a worthless objective. And I do not know that we can take the city."

There was a moment of shock, of silence, and the men clambered to their feet, each talking, but the handsome young Italian leader of a company of renegade Americans was the one who managed to raise his voice and address Villa.

"How dare you, sir," he said in indignation. "How dare you address your supreme commander in that manner."

Villa merely looked at him, in a quandary, caught between anger and amusement.

Garibaldi was now enraged and he said through livid lips, "I demand that you apologize to Señor Madero at once. At once, do you understand?"

Villa looked upon him coldly, no longer amused, and he said, "Remove yourself to the far side of the tent, Captain. And do not speak to me like that again. I am speaking to don Francisco, if you please."

And Garibaldi would talk again, but Francisco Madero said, "He is correct, señores. Captain Villa, as one of our military commanders, deserves an answer." And speaking softly, indulgently as

218

if to a child, he said, "Do not concern yourself, please, Captain. We know what we are doing here. I have faith that we can capture Chihuahua because my commander-in-chief has assured me that we can. The Colonel Orozco, who will shortly be called General, is in full accord with our plan."

"But the plan is as foolish as the attack on Casas Grandes, and the result will be the same. There was no reason to attack Casas Grandes, a city isolated and far from the stream of things, just as there is no reason to attack Chihuahua. The logical objective is Ciudad Juárez, on the border—cut the government off from the gringos and we have won the war."

Madero smiled. Here was one of his people, a mestizo, a step above his little children who were the Indians, but a child also. "The reason for the attack on Casas Grandes, foolish as the act might seem to you, was a very good one. He had to show the people, and in particular the United States, that we were taking the initiative. We knew the odds were overwhelming. We did not expect to take the town—although I must say also that we did not expect to be defeated so decisively. A stalemate is what we sought."

Villa was incredulous. "Do you mean to tell me, señor," he said, "that you stormed that garrison knowing you would be repulsed? Without any hope whatever of gaining a victory? Now that is not the way to do things. And what of the gringos? Why should you kill our people to impress them?"

Again there was movement among the men, but Madero was a patient man. "I detest killing," he said. "I detest the idea of wars. But in war, death is inevitable. And the lives of a few hundred men are as nothing to the recompense, which in this case is the eventual recognition on the part of the United States. Our new government must be recognized by the United States. That is the way of things. That is why it was important that we impress those people. Consider this, my Captain. In your attack on Santa Rosalía, as it has been described to me, you sent men to certain death to draw your enemy. This was no different. The objective was a different one, that is all."

This Villa could understand, and he felt a wave of gratitude for this man, an educated upper-class individual, an aristocrat, who took the time to listen to him and then patiently explained the way of things. And yet, the attack on Chihuahua could not possibly be justified, and he attempted once again to dissuade Madero.

"Thank you, señor. But I must still insist that you consider once again the mistake it would be to storm the garrison at Chihuahua. An idiot can see that it is wrong!"

And again the young Garibaldi came to his feet. He spoke to Pascual Orozco. "I insist, mi coronel, that Captain Villa be censured for his behavior! It is abominable that he should criticize the President's judgment and our actions!"

Madero placed a hand on Villa's arm, but before Pascual Orozco could speak out, the guerrilla leader said to Garibaldi:

"I deeply appreciate, señor, that you, a foreigner, come to help my México. But I wish to tell you that I am not accustomed to give warning even once, let alone twice. Speak your mind if you wish, but speak civilly. Convince me that I am wrong about Chihuahua, and I will follow you through hell."

Garibaldi's face was white with fury. And Madero said, almost with benevolence, "Giuseppe."

"Very well, your excellency," said the young officer. And he spoke to Villa, and as he spoke, the tremor in his voice diminished until he was in complete control. "The taking of Chihuahua is not that difficult, Captain. The enemy has thirty-five hundred men, four thousand at the most, and we now number at least five thousand."

"Yes," said Villa, "but they have fortifications, and we have not one piece of artillery. It will be the same as at Casas Grandes—their cannon will cut us to pieces." He chuckled, and continued in a friendly manner. "We will run, as you did in that other place. I understand your American Legion was the first to bolt. This time they may not stop until they cross the frontier."

Garibaldi flushed but was not offended. "This time we will not run," he said. "This time we will close with the enemy so quickly their cannon will be ineffective. It is a difficult objective, true, but Juárez would be much more difficult. It, too, is fortified—but beyond that, there are but three sides to the town. The north side is American territory. Fighting that near the border can cause serious harm to our cause, for the Americans have twenty thousand troops on the border, waiting for a violation. Stray shot can do irreparable harm to what we are trying to accomplish."

"What you say is true," said Villa, "now that don Francisco has explained the thing to me. But, yet, I see us annihilated in Chihuahua, and also see a good possibility for a victory at Juárez despite the obstacles."

Pascual Orozco spoke up now. The tension which had hung heavily in the room, the awkward atmosphere which the man of the mountains had created, was over and Orozco said, "What the Captain Garibaldi has said is correct, Captain Villa. Juárez is much more difficult because of the gringos, although, as you say, it should be the next logical objective. Chihuahua is a formidable garrison, and yet, we must attack, and quickly, before the garrisons along the line are all reinforced. This time we do not attack for political reasons. It is a military necessity and it will be a bloodbath—a costly victory, but we mean to take Chihuahua. And we will enter there with the knowledge that we will have victory. I believe we can do it. I really believe we can defeat them."

For the first time, Orozco had spoken to Villa like a commander to an officer. Perhaps because in the group, among aristocrats, he felt a closer kinship to the peon of the north, his earlier manner was changed and he was neither condescending nor supercilious. And Villa could accept him as a man and now as a leader, for he understood that they alone in this gathering were of the military. The others, in uniform or not, were really political.

"Very well, Colonel," he said. "We shall take Chihuahua as you say." He chuckled and added, "I am damned if you have not convinced me that we can do it. We may yet be men enough."

But in the end, it was not to be, for even as this council of war was taking place, the government was repairing the railroad at Santa Rosalía and Camargo, and as the rebel forces made ready to deploy for their advance upon Chihuahua, word came that the garrison had been reinforced by two thousand men and twenty cannon. And, thus, it was out of their hands and so they skirted the city, and marched steadily northward, for Juárez was now the only possible objective.

In the vanguard, the Villistas spread wide, continually reconnoitering, engaging in a few small fights with units of cavalry sent out from Chihuahua to harass them. And the railroad was destroyed every few miles as they traveled. Heraclio now led fifty men, and everyone, with the exception of the cousin Aquiles, was familiar with beasts. Heraclio had turned over more than twenty men to Villa, to be integrated with his now growing infantry. Aquiles he would keep with him, for he had developed a love for his kinsman and admired his courage.

And Aquiles practiced and drilled long hours on horseback, although halfheartedly, for he, too, wanted to remain at Heraclio's side. He thought it strange that he should become so close to this the youngest of his many cousins. Fate had thrown them together, had made him, Aquiles, a killer at the advanced age of forty-three, although, thinking back, he wondered how he had lived so long without being forced to kill. But he must remain with Heraclio because he loved the youth, and now for another reason. The evening after the fight for Santa Rosalía, he had talked with Antonio Rivera.

"Look here, negro," he said, and Antonio smiled at the manner of the man.

"That which is black has beauty, my mother has always told me," said Antonio.

"Mothers always say such things—when their children are ugly, they will say they are filled with goodliness. When they are born idiots, they say that God has touched them and that they are saints. But look here, boy, I wish to ask you something because you know both David and the cousin much better than I do. Is there rancor between them?"

"On David's part, perhaps," said Antonio. "Although David is a strange one who seems to hold rancor against everyone."

Aquiles rubbed a huge hand over his eyes. "Would he fire at Heraclio?"

Antonio looked on him calmly, saw the concern in the man's face, and said, "Then you saw it too, so it must be true."

"I could not be certain," said Aquiles, "for I was struggling to stay on my beast, and I was afraid and running. I do not mind telling you that for once in my life I was afraid. And I thought I had a glimpse of David, shooting at Heraclio's back as he raced forward. And he did not look frightened. That is what made me think I was mistaken, for in that maelstrom, the very devil would have been frightened and it seemed to me that David was not, so it surely must have been a hallucination."

"It was not a fantasy," said Antonio, "for I saw the exact thing in passing also. I only thought that in the confusion my eyes deceived me. I know now that it was only that I could not believe such a thing possible. I knew what I saw, but then David disappeared and I could not believe it. So he did try to destroy Heraclio."

"I have been thinking that he did, because at first, seeing Heraclio in what I thought was flight and in my fear even envying the beautiful manner in which he runs a horse—it is a terrible fear to not know where one is; that is what happened to me—and I saw Heraclio run and thought he too had panicked, but then he turned around and he knew what he was about because he killed those men directly before me and would have shot me too, except that he recognized me and instead gave me such a whack in the ribs with his weapon that he almost unseated me. And the blow and the sight of the open plain before me made me stop and as I fought to quiet the horse and catch my breath, my courage returned and so I followed him and banged a few heads with the flat of my machete. So it was possible to retain courage in that mob and David did try to kill Heraclio, and now what are we to do?"

"David is mine, Aquiles," said Antonio.

"I am thinking that I should do it, since you have all been friends from childhood."

"No," said Antonio. "It is my duty as I see it. If I fail, you will have your chance."

"If you fail!" said Aquiles. "How could you possibly fail against a coward who would shoot a friend in the back like that?"

"Do not mistake yourself, Aquiles," said Antonio. "David is no coward. You, yourself, saw he was not afraid at Santa Rosalía."

"I suppose you are right. I am believing that I was the only one who fell apart there—but then, why does he not face Heraclio openly if he has a reason?"

"I do not know. Perhaps he fears Heraclio because he loves him. But he will someday decide he hates Heraclio and then he will face him. But what am I thinking, we cannot break him, not if we esteem the other."

"Because it would displease him?"

"Because it would grieve him."

"Qué caray!" said Aquiles, in a quandary because he could not simply kill David. "These complications! I suppose all we can do is talk to David."

"That is all we can do," said Antonio. "I only wish it were not so, for it is dangerous."

They searched for David together. The towns of Santa Rosalía and Camargo adjoined each other, and drunken soldiers brawled in the streets, spilling over from one town to the other, looting stores and cantinas, occasionally firing at one another. Through victory and drink, they had regained their courage, and even those who had been in the wild flight of the morning had now forgotten the shame of having run. And David had been among the revelers.

They found him in a group of men, all drinking quietly, cleaning guns and rifles and loading bandoleers. "Have a drink with me," said David, seeming friendly and quite happy.

Antonio took the bottle and drank, then handed it to Aquiles. "Did you break into an armory?" he asked.

"We went out there and took them from the dead," said David. "I now have two sidearms, bandoleers, and a good rifle. There were two Federals out there who were still alive. I gave them the shot of grace," he added, laughing.

"What the hell has come over you?" asked Antonio. "What ghoulish business is this—those things you carry came from our own dead."

A man in the group spoke up. "They had no further use for them," he said.

Antonio ignored him. "And that of the shot of grace, David. You seem to have found joy in doing that. What enjoyment do you get from shooting wounded men?"

"They were dying," said David. "I merely put them out of their misery. And what is it to you? Are you now suddenly my keeper? Has Heraclio designated you as my guardian?"

The stranger sitting with David spoke again. "If you have no stomach for these things, boy, you should have remained behind with the women and children. Go away."

Antonio stood before the man. He looked even younger than his eighteen years. His body was slight so as to make him seem frail. His small, sharp face was very dark and his body shook as he spoke. "Have respect for that which does not concern you, señor. Speak to me in that manner one more time and you shall die."

"But just look," said the man, "just look at this young one! I shall die, he tells me!" He started to rise and David laughed.

"Sit down, Lalo," he said. "He is right, so sit yourself. If you get to your feet he will surely kill you. He is quite a panther, my Antonio."

The man sat back.

Now Aquiles laughed aloud. The man had obviously been bluffing and now looked at them warily, shifting his eyes from one to another. "Did you ever notice, Antonio," he said, "that those who have no balls usually end up together?"

Antonio, still in anger, did not answer.

But David Contreras said quietly, "Be careful, Aquiles. Because I do not intimidate."

"We came to warn you, David. Do not do again that which you did this morning," said Aquiles. "This time you got away with it. Next time will be your last."

David was on his feet. "You come to warn me—together? What was that you were saying about brave men, Aquiles?"

"No, David," said Antonio. "I come alone. You know me and should not have to be told that. I do not know what goes on in that crazy head of yours—but do not try that of this morning again or I shall break you without feeling other than I would have to go back to your mother and tell her how you died."

"And why do you warn me? Because we have been friends of sorts?" David uttered a short, bitter laugh. He made no effort to deny the accusation. He said, "You know me also, Antonio. I am ready when you are, and after that I shall take your friend there who carries the big knife. How would you have it? Guns or knives?"

"If I had come for that, David, I would not have been as polite as you are being. I came to tell you that I know what you did, and only for that, but if you initiate it, why, we shall go to it."

"Heraclio does not know?"

"I did not want him to kill someone he loves," said Antonio.

They were very near to a fight to a finish, and yet the words they exchanged were not angry ones. It seemed almost that they were sadly jesting. "Heraclio would not kill me," said David. "At least not now—later perhaps he will. But right now he will remove me to the infantry, perhaps, or at any rate to another troop."

"Will you stop now, David?" asked Antonio, and his tone was kindly. "And shall we forget about the other?"

"Drink with me," said David. "If it comes to that another time, I shall meet him in the open."

Antonio was satisfied, but Aquiles did not know David and was unable to accept the promise. He was careful that Heraclio should not suspect it, but he became companion and bodyguard to him.

II

Ciudad Juárez, in April of 1911, was in a state of high activity. The citizens of the border city milled in the streets, excited by the idea of the coming battle which no one believed would really take place. Tourists from El Paso mingled with the natives, sharing the excitement, feeling highly adventurous as they gazed upon the preparations made to defend the city.

For if the people and the politicians felt a mild danger only and yet believed that it could not happen here, the ancient General Navarro, who had fought alongside the man for whom the city was named, and who only recently had decisively defeated Pascual Orozco at Casas Grandes, had the mind of a soldier. He built up his defenses to save the town. Visitors streamed across the border daily, feature writers for tabloids and photographers had a field day, and they all laughed as machine-gun emplacements were erected on the roofs of the tallest buildings and sandbag entrenchments were stretched across the main streets, and barbed wire. The people of the town laughed with them. In the evenings it was like a time of carnival, the brothels and cantinas flourished, and the people sang and danced and loved in the streets.

But General Navarro would soon be surrounded. The rebels would come from three directions, and on the north, he was fenced off by the international boundary, the Río Bravo. He could not communicate with México; he knew only that he must defend the garrison, that he would defend the garrison, which he now thought of as his own. And his energy belied his eighty years, as first he erected his defenses within the city, and then he directed the building of bulwarks on its perimeter.

The rebels came from the south and west, and their numbers were augmented by small bands of guerrillas which arrived day by day; so that when the siege was laid, almost six thousand men were entrenched in a semicircle around the city, facing only a hundred yards away a similar line of trenches which formed the outer defense of Ciudad Juárez.

On the southeastern side of the city, covering the area to the very banks of the shallow river, the seven hundred men of Pancho Villa waited in their trenches, occasionally calling out to their enemy, exchanging friendly insults. Behind them, in a hastily built hut, a demolition crew worked long hours, making hand bombs out of bottles, tin cans, and any container available; crude instruments of death, the store of explosives grew, and yet Villa urged them on. Other men were at work sewing satchels to be used by the grenadiers. And although this was a conglomerate force, not well trained, it was well disciplined, better even than some of the Federal conscripts.

And now, to the east and south, a mile or two from the outskirts of Ciudad Juárez, a tent city sprang up. Francisco Madero with his political advisers, his brothers, Captain Garibaldi, who was now commandant of Madero's guard of honor, and reporters, both American and Mexican, awaited the arrival of Limantour. On April 22, Madero and the besieged General Navarro agreed on a truce of fourteen days while the negotiations took place, but Limantour's demands were too great, and at the end of the period of armistice, nothing had been resolved. The truce was extended, and Limantour, who offered nothing but the removal of Díaz, and in turn wanted the revolutionary forces to disband, found his position stronger with each day. It was plain to everyone but Madero and his civilian advisers that if the rebels did not attack the Revolution would end, having been nothing but a spark, a flare of resistance by the people.

Orozco pleaded with him, his own favorite, Garibaldi, and Villa, now a colonel agreed with the general, Maytorena—all strongly advised that they should attack, but Madero was steadfast. A treaty was in the making and would come to be without bloodshed. And his officers were loyal and obeyed. But they had not anticipated the guile of Pancho Villa.

While the conferences were taking place, his men continued in the manufacture of grenades. Somehow, every day, a new supply of dynamite was brought in, and now, along with the crude missiles, sticks of the explosive were wired together, caps were distributed, instruction was given. All this was done over a period of days, and all kept secret from anyone but Villa's men. And on the morning of the extension of the truce, Villa returned to his men from a meeting of the high command and gave his instructions.

He had spoken first to Pascual Orozco, and for once pleaded with the General that they take action, and Orozco said, still in his overbearing manner, "You have your orders, Colonel. Obey them. We are of the military and do not meddle in the politics of the matter. Respect the truce, and see that your men respect it!" He did not add that he agreed with him.

Villa had said, "I worship the little man, don Francisco, but he is in error. It is time that we, who are stronger, take a hand in this." He failed, and decided to act contrary to orders.

"I am not in the vicinity," he said to his officers. "No matter who comes to call me, when this thing begins, I am somewhere else. That is understood." His men were picked, at ready, knapsacks over their shoulders, fifty men, among them Heraclio Inés and the primo Aquiles.

And Colonel Villa gave the word and it was seven o'clock in the morning when the word was passed from mouth to mouth to the foremost trench, and a man jumped out in the open.

"Federal motherfuckers!" he called. "Are you not tired of sitting there on your fat cheeks, accepting money from the government? Do you not have anyone there with balls, who would make you fight?" He went on, insulting, conferring obscenities, pacing back and forth along his trench, waving his arms. "Is there one of you who knows how to fire a fusil? Who taught you, those nuns you have for officers?" And although catcalls had been exchanged before this, the man was making a target of himself, daring the enemy to shoot him, and at that moment someone did, hitting him in the temple as he turned to walk another time.

And a few shots rang out from the rebels' side of the field, and

228

there were answering shots, and now the rifle fire across no man's land was intensified.

Villa came forward, then, and spoke to Celestino Gámez. "A fusillade, my comrade—until we get up close. Then wait for us to throw our bombs and follow us. We must take that trench before we do anything, and we must do it quickly before don Francisco comes to stop us." The field before them dipped in the center, and when Villa and his fifty men were on their way, the entire trench was a sheet of flame, and they were not really seen until they were almost to their objective, then the machine guns opened fire, and men fell, but now they were near enough, and with cigarettes or cigars, matches, they lighted their fuses, and the grenades fell into the bulwarks with devastation, leaving gaping holes in the line, and pieces of human beings splattered the landscape.

And the horde from behind them bore down, screaming, yelling, firing, and they were swept into the trenches before them, and in close they clubbed and fought with knives and some with bayonets and a few machetes.

And now the first objective was secured and all along the line the rebels attacked, while don Francisco Madero, furious, attempted to stop the fight, but now the very people he sent to order a cease fire entered into the action. Pascual Orozco, now that the deed was done, drove his troops furiously from the northeast, Maytorena and Garibaldi from the south, and Heraclio looked upon the body of the cousin Aquiles at his feet. He had seen him once, without thinking about it, for he had been too preoccupied in battle, and Aquiles was like a lion with his machete, but someone had come to him from behind and slit his throat as if in an unguarded attack in the night. He had died very quickly and had lost much of his blood. His face was now white in the sunlight and Heraclio turned away.

He had said to him a few minutes ago, "I know what you are doing, Primo. Protecting me from David, I suppose. But do not forget to look out for yourself, for what will I do with a dead bodyguard." And the other had not spoken, and Heraclio laughed. "I but wanted you to know that I am aware," he said, and gave the other a grateful pat on the back. "It is not necessary, however."

Now they were at an impasse. The buildings of the city were

before them, and the machine-gun emplacements were unattainable. "It is time, boys," said Villa, "and you who remain behind, give them hell, and move ahead. We will help you from the other side."

Of the original fifty grenadiers, but half of them remained, and they gathered the explosives from the dead and slipped over the bank of the river. They hugged the side, along the water line, and snaked forward. They arrived to a point where the bank was too steep, and they slipped into the water to their crotches, yet moving, now almost under the International Bridge, and still unseen except by the Americans on the opposite bank of the river. Slowly, quietly, as they knew how to move from their years in the mountains and in hiding, they one by one crawled up the bank and slipped upon the Federals from behind. The grenades tore into the emplacements, a part of the bridge disintegrated, and with a yell the small band was on the move, this now their second objective.

Down the street, machine guns were trained on them but were not fired because their effectiveness would be across the border in the streets of El Paso, and the commander waited, and waited too long, for the men disappeared into the nearest side street. And now from a building across from them, the fire came down upon them, and hastily they ran into the nearest building. And out of a knapsack came a hand drill, and the one demolition expert luckily had not fallen, and he quickly drilled and put a charge, and the wall came out. Quickly, they wriggled through into another room, and then another, sometimes blowing a wall right onto a huddling family. They reached a street, and then through another block of walls, and this time they were behind a barricade, and with a yell, again they loosed grenades, and fired still utile guns, and came upon a square, near where their men were advancing, and thus joined them, having an open entrance to the heart of the city.

In the northeast, Pascual Orozco moved forward, and to the south, the bullring, main bastion of the southern defenses, fell to the rebels. And by evening, the taking of the city of Juárez on the international boundary was completed.

On May 10, 1911, General Navarro surrendered to the rebel forces, and that very day, Francisco I. Madero personally walked the Old Campaigner to the International Bridge, affording him safe-conduct into exile. Villa objected strongly, and, oddly, General Pascual Orozco joined him in his demand that the Porfirian general be held in custody.

"We are honorable men," said Madero. "The General has been a national hero in his day, and it is only fitting that he should be allowed to retire now in his last years." And so arm in arm, victor and vanquished walked to the border, and General Navarro was met by friends from El Paso.

Negotiations, long drawn out, now resumed, and the Revolutionaries, whose bargaining power was made stronger by the military victory, again saw their position strengthened by the news that on the twelfth of May the garrison at Cuautla in southern México had fallen to Emiliano Zapata. And a few miles outside the city on the twenty-first of May, at ten-thirty in the evening at a table illuminated by the headlights of three automobiles, Limantour signed the Treaty of Juárez. Díaz and Limantour would resign, and a provisional president, one Francisco de la Barra, would hold office until an election could be held. It was understood that Francisco I. Madero would be the next president of the republic.

III

IN MEXICO CITY, President Madero had decreed that the new Federal Army must be uniformed, and tailors throughout the capital were commissioned to outfit the officers. Thus, Heraclio Inés arrived at la Flor resplendent in a captain's uniform. And the people of the settlement came to him and shook his hand and some of the very old wept as they embraced him.

Later, in the house, Teodoro said, "Very pretty indeed, in your new uniform, but that is all over and tomorrow you must go out on the range."

Heraclio looked at him in surprise, and then he understood that Teodoro must try. "I will rest tomorrow," he said, "and the day after that, and perhaps the day after that I shall go away. I do not know. It may be that I will go to Río Grande for a few days until I decide where it is I wish to go."

"You must also go to the Big House and report to the patrón

that God has returned you safely to us." Teodoro chose to ignore Heraclio's remarks.

Heraclio laughed. "Surely he must know I am here already. And what of the son-in-law—the big one?"

"*He* is the patrón," said Teodoro. "Don Aurelio has taken doña Gertrudes to Spain, and the señora de Arguiú and don Domingo are now in the Big House." And he added with pride, "I, of course, am now the administrator."

Señora de Arguiú, thought Heraclio, and in spite of himself felt a sharp pang and a loss. Carmen, as she had predicted, was the mistress of the land, and for certain he could not remain here now.

He thought of the war, and here on a cold day, in the glare of the sun on the white ground of la Flor, he could see starkly that all went on as before. In the Big House, a few paces away, the patrón and the patrona were sitting themselves to their noon meal, with mozos in attendance, and in the hills to the east, countless sheep were being watched by pastores, some as young as he had been. In Toribio, jinetes were breaking horses, in Peñuelas they would soon be branding, and to the west the field peon followed his yoke, not much more a buck than the oxen leading him. And in the tienda de raya, a clerk was at this moment putting a cipher down in the book after a name which had been written a hundred and fifty years ago.

And all this he thought about, and he knew, without a doubt, that the war was not over. He thought of his brothers and tradition, and sensed now that, although sometimes they could be wrong, traditions were essentially to maintain the male dignity; and with or without custom, to have dignity was a necessary thing. And because dignity was not measured by man alone but also by those around him, to be judged by others was perfectly valid. He decided at that moment that he would visit Carmen. Somehow, if he should do this, he would maintain his own dignity.

"David is gone," said Antonio, and Heraclio did not hear him. "I said that David has disappeared once again," said Antonio.

"David?" He seemed distracted. "I wish he had not, because we will be mobilizing again before long."

"I am quite happy he is gone," said Antonio. "He will someday get himself killed if he stays around here."

232

"You do not understand David," said Heraclio.

"I have always told you I am not good with animals," said Antonio.

She was in the sitting room writing letters when he was admitted by the mozo. She looked no different, but there was a stiffness to her body, turned slightly away from him, for she was now a matron and a landowner. She walked toward him, very sober, and he almost laughed, but said instead, "How are you, Carmen? It is so good to see you."

She said, coldly, "I am señora to you as to any other peon."

"A thousand pardons," he said, and he was angry and would have walked out, but she was unperturbed and turned to greet her husband.

"Dearest," she said, linking her arm through Domingo's, "come welcome Heraclio back from the wars and in a magnificent uniform."

"Hola, Heraclio," he took the youth's hand, "welcome home, savior of the nation. And an officer, too—I had no idea that you had influence." He clapped his hands sharply for the mozo. "This is an occasion for a drink," he said.

"In our army we were not judged by the people we knew," said Heraclio.

"Good point," said Domingo. "Acts of valor, impetuous actions, eh?"

He sipped his drink, intrigued by these two suddenly, and resisted the impulse to leave.

"Tell me," said Domingo, "does my señora seem much changed?"

"She does not smile much," said Heraclio, and could not explain to himself why he should be rude.

"You are impertinent," said Carmen.

"Come now, my life," said Domingo. "After all, Heraclio is a friend of your childhood. He has some liberties." To Heraclio he said, "It is the responsibility. You understand. When you went away she was a young girl, now she is a wife and a patrona, and she has the welfare of how many peones? on her mind."

"I understand," said Heraclio. "But I saw you two in México.

233

For a lark I went to a ball with friends, but when I saw you, I left. You did not smile there either," he said to Carmen.

Domingo was amused. "Why did you leave the ball?"

"It was not a dignified thing to do, to remain there with my betters," said Heraclio.

Now there was an embarrassed silence, and Heraclio once again prepared to leave. But Domingo broke the silence once again.

"A fine uniform, Heraclio, but much too fine even for the work I have in mind for you."

Heraclio laughed, again surprised. "You know I do not work for you."

Like Teodoro, Domingo ignored him. "It has been my idea that you should accompany me on my rounds. Although your brother is the administrator, you could be a sort of special assistant to me."

"To keep you informed, I suppose," said Heraclio. "If there is informing to be done, Teodoro will do it, even if he must inform on himself." But he must end this talk. "This thing must be settled once and for all, Domingo. I do not know why you people think that things are different from when I left . . ."

"I once told you that things would never change," said Domingo.

". . . and because they are not changed I am also unchanged. I will not work on an hacienda again in my life—any hacienda. I am not obligated to work for you, and, too, I shall be leaving again soon for the wars."

"The war is over, you young fool," said Domingo Arguiú, losing his patience.

Heraclio sensed the man's strong dislike for him and wondered why they all insisted that he should not leave the hacienda. "It is not over," he said. "You and those like you are still here."

"And we shall remain, because that is in the order of things. Your Madero will go phpht"—he snapped his fingers—"one day soon, and responsible people will run the government. And the only hostilities will come from people like that bandit, Zapata, in the south, and in time they, too, will be exterminated."

"And Villa."

234

"Villa is finished," said Domingo. "They do not even have to buy him off. You know he is in prison?"

"I know." Heraclio was close to hate. "He cannot be bought," he said.

"Any man can be bought."

Heraclio moved toward the door. "You err. Gravely, you err. And you shall see one day." He paused a moment and added, "Of all the things you have ever said to me, there was only one thing with truth in it, and strangely you meant it as a lie."

"And what was that?" asked Domingo, and he no longer smiled.

"About Villa," said Heraclio. "You told me he was the man to follow."

And he meant to leave the hacienda, leave forever, and wished to be forgotten. In México, he had again met Blanca de la O, married now to an old Colonel Magallón, who would soon be a brigadier until he died. The old man was on the staff at the National Palace, and Blanca had time on her hands, and Heraclio knew her again. It was with them that Heraclio had attended the reception in honor of someone or another, and had seen Carmen.

"Stay here in the capital," Blanca had said. "You are so young and well on your way in the army. My husband will help your career. Those in the army will inherit México. Remain, and if you would leave the army, there are other ways for you to make your fortune. Only say that you will stay."

But to remain in México, in or out of the army, was out of the question. If he were to remain in the army, it would not be in a city post, with Federal people, but with his General Villa, out in the hills where he could breathe, and to remain in México as a civilian was a worse fate. Only now, here on the hacienda, and after his talk with Domingo, México seemed once again attractive. And, too, his general was in México and he did not know how long he would be held in prison there. México seemed like not a bad idea.

But as he walked from the Big House, he stopped to pay his respects to the old artisan, the saddlemaker, and everything was changed for him. The old man greeted him with an embrace.

"Well done, my boy! Well done!" said the ancient one. "My old eyes have waited long to see this happen. Only now, you who are young must not let victory elude you. I remember when the North American pigs occupied our glorious capital; remember the dog Maximilian, the noble Juárez, and the despot Porfirio Díaz. Every time it seemed our México was free, a glutton came along to gorge himself and his followers on our blood. And now God has seen fit to grant us one more chance and we should not allow the opportunity to slip away from us." He rambled on, but Heraclio was looking at Marcelina Ortiz, who sat demurely on her great-grandfather's only chair, and she looked back at him with her great brown eyes.

It had been a year and yet she seemed to have grown entirely in that short time. She sat and he could see her shapely ankles, she was still extremely slim, but now her blouse revealed the contours of her small though developed breasts, and for some unknown reason the idea of this small bosom excited Heraclio, and he saw her slight brown face, and he knew in that moment all her goodness. He had no doubt and now he must stay, for it comes only once to a man, and if he is a man, he knows, and he cannot fool himself, and he can have a hundred women and know love for every one, but there is one who will be different and she might be a bad partner in the act of love, might be a bad housekeeper, might in fact be a bad woman, but she will be special because she is not quite real, and the ideal becomes the strongest love.

"You are a woman," said Heraclio, ignoring the old man.

"Will you look at me now?" she said.

"I will look at you now, and I will come for you soon," he said. And that was the extent of their courtship.

He went with Teodoro because for her sake he would do the thing in the accepted manner, and he must speak to her great-grandfather because her father was away in Torreón with his woman.

"We should wait for the priest," said Teodoro, "and have the hand of God on this from the beginning."

"That would take too long," said Heraclio, "and anyway, I want as little to do with those clerics as possible."

"You will have to wait for the priest anyway, and he can do this and marry you at the same time." He was displeased that his

236

youngest brother should have this attitude, and yet he was over-joyed that he was finally marrying, for this should settle him.

"I know a priest who is now in Fresnillo. He will come to marry me."

"And how do you know this curate?" asked Teodoro, not really curious.

"I have dissipated with him. In the army."

"Dissipated?" Teodoro would never really believe these things. But his brother had been "outside" and there were things that he would never know because he would never leave the hacienda, and of a sudden he was curious about what happened elsewhere, and he asked, "How dissipate? What do you mean?"

Heraclio smiled to himself. "The cards. Drink. And of course, women."

Teodoro was aghast, half believing that Heraclio was but torturing him. "This priest, he did these things in your company? Is that what you mean?"

"Innumerable times," said Heraclio. "As a matter of fact he did it more than the soldiers. I suppose because no one took him seriously as a man of God. When he learned that no one would hear his Mass he became quite a good fellow. There is an association, or a cult, or something—the President Madero is a member—they call themselves Masons. Well this priest belonged to it, and found many such members among the politicians. But do not disbelieve, he is a wonder with the cards and with the ladies."

"Incredible," said Teodoro. "But of course, it can be explained. He is not a good man, and should not wear the cloth. That is all. Everywhere a bad man can be found, the Church is no different."

"On the contrary," said Heraclio. "He is a wonderful man, although he cheats at cards. But come, for Christ's sake, will you go to the ancient one and ask for her hand, or shall I take her at this moment to Fresnillo and marry her there."

"Do not be hasty," said Teodoro. "I will go."

Dressed in their best clothes, they entered the old man's shop, and don Guadalupe knew immediately why they had come.

"This is no place for sacred discussions," he said. "Come to my house." In his jacal, he insisted that they have an aguardiente, and Heraclio was impatient that they must follow these formalities.

"Tell the old man, Teodoro, for God's sake! What a waste of

237

time!" he whispered hoarsely, and Teodoro waved a hand to quiet him.

Teodoro cleared his throat, and Heraclio was surprised that his brother was actually nervous. He looked amazedly at Teodoro as he spoke. "As an oldest brother, in lieu of our sainted father, I come to tell you of the great love, affection, and respect that Heraclio, my youngest brother, has for your great-granddaughter." He stopped because he had forgotten her name.

And it was too much for Heraclio. "Look, don Guadalupe," he said, rising. "I am now sorry I tried to do this in the way it is done. The truth of the matter is that I wish to marry Marcelina. We will marry whether or not you give your blessing. I only come to you out of respect for her feelings."

The old man would not be hurried. "We are Christians here, and things are not done in this way. In a moment I shall refuse to speak to you until another day. If you do respect her, then by all the saints be patient and respect the tradition. And anyway, why all the rush with you? Is it that you have been with her already and must hurry the nuptials?"

Old people disturbed Heraclio because of their candor. "Why you old bastard!" and he was livid with anger. "You are insulting the woman who is to be my wife, even if she is your great-granddaugher! I shall show you what I think of your stupid little act of formalities! We will simply go away and marry!"

Teodoro was on his feet, grasping Heraclio strongly. "Sit down, Heraclio, Goddamn it! There are certain things don Guadalupe must ask. And when you have a daughter you will know about this —not until then!"

Heraclio sat quietly for a moment, then he spoke out. "Forgive my rudeness, don Guadalupe. I should venerate your age. I am quite sorry."

The old man was very serious. "I shall this time accept your apology and forget your outburst, but only because your brother has a sense of propriety. You say you want to marry. Have you spoken to her and has she accepted you? For I am not one who will give away a great-granddaughter unless she desires it. I am much too old to arrange marriages."

"She knows, don Guadalupe," said Heraclio.

"You have asked her?"

238

"No, I have not asked her," and Heraclio again was angry, but he held his tongue. "I have not asked her, but she knows."

"Then perhaps," said the old man, "you should go ask her. She is in the other room mending some of my things. Your brother and I will make the necessary arrangements, since you are certain she will not refuse you."

"Yes," said Teodoro, almost pushing Heraclio out the door. "Go speak to your chosen one, and we here will take care of the matter."

"One thing only," said Heraclio. "It is to be as soon as possible. We do not wish to wait."

Before he closed the door behind him he heard don Guadalupe say, "I have three milch cows of my own that she will receive when she marries . . ."

She looked up to him and put her sewing down. It seemed to him that she was the quietest, most unobtrusive person he had ever known, even when as here they were alone.

"You heard?" he asked.

"I heard voices, only that," she said, and her voice was musical.

"But you know why we are here?"

"Yes, I know," she said, and because she knew he wished to know, she added, "I am very happy, Heraclio. Very pleased and very proud that you should want me."

He reached down and pulled her to her feet now, and she seemed like a child alongside him. He touched her hair along the temples, and then her face. "How many years do you have?" he asked.

"Fifteen. But do not concern yourself. I am quite ready for you." She had no need for tact, she was so honest, and he was pleased.

How gentle I must be, he thought. My God, what a gift—and she was there all along. "We will marry soon, in a week, or two at the most."

"So quick?" she asked, but did not object.

"So quick," he said. "And too, this of them talking in there, it is only because I want you to feel right about it. People will think badly of you if there is no formal request for your hand. I suppose I can say the same thing about the ceremony itself because I do not really believe too much about the saints and such although I live with them. We will be married by a priest because it is done that way, but in mind we were married the moment I saw you again. Do you understand?"

"I think I do. And I should like to be married by a curate because I do believe very much, not because people would not approve. Do not concern yourself about things like that, because I do not care what people think, I care only about you and me."

And he believed her because she could not lie. "And about marrying so quickly. There is no reason to wait, no? We will be together a very long time, for all our lives, Marcelina. So why wait?"

"As you say, Heraclio. I want it to be today," she said, and she blushed. And gently, for the first time, they kissed.

In the night he went to the house of María Contreras to inquire about David.

"I do not know where he is," she said, drying her eyes and quickly stopping her tears. "He wanted me to pack my belongings and go away with him. But of course that was impossible. I have everything I want here. Thanks to my son, I have paid the debt of the family, and I earn enough to keep me. Why should I go? I would not know how to live anywhere but here."

"It is unfortunate that you could not go," said Heraclio. "David has lived for the day he could take you away from here."

"The people are accustomed to me here, Heraclio. At one time, I, too, wanted very much to get away—but to go to a new place and be ridiculed and unwanted, perhaps driven away. I do not think I could do that. He knows how people feel about one who practices the true arts. He simply will not understand."

"In this case, I suppose you are both right," said Heraclio.

She continued, now as if talking to herself, "After all, I am almost thirty-six years old, and it is much too late for me to start my life in a strange and perhaps hostile place."

Heraclio looked at her as she stopped her pacing. Indeed she was still young and a comely woman. He wondered why no man was at her side, and then thought of her sin which was David, even though she had probably been forced by don Aurelio, and of the fact that she belonged to the black arts, and he did not wonder. "I must go," he said, before his thoughts could dominate him.

240

She saw it in his face. "Please stay for a while, Heraclio. It is good to have some company. I am truly so lonely sometimes."

And he knew she spoke the truth, for she lived always entirely alone, but he also knew she at this moment sought more than companionship. And he did not want to stay—for himself and for David he did not want to remain here.

She said again, "Please!" Her face was full of yearning, yet a yearning devoid of lust, and for a moment he felt secure, and said, "Very well, doña María. I shall visit for a while." She moved slowly toward him, still with the strange look on her face, sad, perhaps afraid, as if this would be the first time for her.

"Turn the lamp low, Heraclio," she whispered so he barely heard. "Turn the light low and come and touch me here." She took his hand.

In a cantina, in the city of Zacatecas, David Contreras sat morosely over a bottle of tequila. He was at the bar, for to sit at a table would mean that a woman would join him. He did not know whether he wanted a woman; he only knew that he must not throw away the few pesos he had left. As it was, he was sleeping in his sarape in a gully in the outskirts of the city. He had many things to think about, and all on the same question—what to do?

It was now almost a week since he had come here, and he had been unable to find any kind of work. The city seemed full of young men and old men without employment. And all of them were city people, with some knowledge of the trades. It had not taken David long to realize that he had run away from the only thing he was able to do. And so he attempted to persuade someone to take him on as an apprentice and had no success. Tonight he knew he must find a ranch or an hacienda which would take him as a shepherd, and the ranches were not large enough to have many sheep, while to go to an hacienda would be not much better than to return to his own. He thought he might even go on to a larger city, perhaps even to México once again, but he sensed that his poverty would be immeasurably greater in a large metropolis than in the hills which he knew and where he would be free although not free.

He thought of Juárez and perhaps of jumping the line. Many were doing it, and the border was open, but, too, many were returning with tales of mile-long fields of cotton and oppression despite the dollars. He did not know, and he must find himself, and he was all alone.

He sipped his drink, weighing personal freedom as opposed to freedom from hunger, when a hand came down heavily on his back and the words, "Well, look at this! A miracle it is to see you again, Contreras!"

He turned in anger, with disgust and hate at a human voice and the human touch. A sallow face, mustached, gap-toothed yellow, grinned at him. It was the man Lalo, who had led him to strip the dead at Santa Rosalía and Camargo.

David said dispiritedly, "It is you, Lalo."

"*It is you, Lalo,*" said the other. "Such enthusiasm for an old comrade in arms! Yes, it is me, Lalo. I wondered often what had become of you."

"I am here."

The other's face grew serious. "Look, amigo," he said. "It is obvious you are in a mood. Offer me a drink, or I shall get a bottle and share it with you, or simply tell me to go away. Eulalio Solís will not remain where he is not wanted."

David pushed the bottle toward him but yet did not speak. Lalo called for a glass. "What goes?" he asked.

"Nothing goes," said David. "How is it with you?"

"The same," said Lalo. "A short time back I very nearly returned to Torreón. But there I worked for a blacksmith and it is not in me to return to a job now that the war is over."

"You are fortunate and do not know it," said David. "Would I had the opportunity to work for a blacksmith—to work for anyone."

"You are insane, to think of working for anyone," said Lalo. "Why should we have to work for others? We are heroes. I have been thinking of something. What would we be doing if the war had not ended?"

"On a campaign somewhere. Or in a warm house in a town, with much food and drink, and money, and, of course, a woman."

"Right!" exclaimed Lalo. "In the army, when we had need, we took, no? I have never lived as well as when we were with the mob. The spoils of war spoiled me, you might say. And I am thinking we can eventually join a band in the hills. Or else we can

242

find some boys and form our own band. There are many like us, only waiting for an opportunity. After all, if Zapata can do it down south, why cannot we do it up here?"

David laughed. "And you call *me* insane! Zapata, you say. Why, Zapata is not a bandit, but a guerrilla. And he can fight the government and the rich because he has hundreds of soldiers, even thousands if you count all the small groups he has scattered throughout the southern mountains. This Zapata is a patriot, not a night rider!"

"I still insist *you* are the crazy," said Lalo. "Patriot! They are all bandits—it does not matter who they are. They are bandits on both sides and they stick together because they are bandits. But they set an excellent example for us, and so we must take ours while there is yet time. Come with me in a few minutes and I shall show you what I mean."

"Follow you where?"

"Drink up and come with me," said Lalo. "I have been watching something for over a week, and if you have courage, we will do something about it tonight."

"What is this about courage?" asked David. "I have courage enough for anything, only I must decide for myself. You will not convince me, for to take the career of the outlaw, I must decide to do it forever. That is what it seems to be outside the law, forever, unless one can save some money and go to a place unknown and get a piece of land or a business."

"You make up your mind while I am telling you this," said Lalo. "There is a man. A dealer in fresh meat and at present the only one with access to beef in the city. Of course the bastard also sells horses for beef—dead horses that people like you and I sell him. So you see, he is a bandit also and does not care that some get sick who eat his product. In a few minutes he will leave his shop and carry his profits to the strongbox in his home. It is not necessary that we go into his house because there is nothing in the strongbox, but in the darkness near his house—it is the only place where there is enough darkness—we can take him."

"How do you know all this?"

"I tell you, I have watched. Now he has a gun, and that is why there must be two of us. Are you with me?"

And David knew that was not the only reason there must be

someone with Lalo, for he remembered his cowardice at Santa Rosalía—his cowardice on the field and also later with Antonio Rivera. "Then what?" he asked.

"We shall divide the money and separate. The train for Torreón leaves before morning. If possible, board it. There is a woman here where I am welcome. If it seems too dangerous, I shall wait a day or two, but look for me in the market place in Torreón. Only look for me and I shall find you."

"Let us get on with it, then," said David, coming suddenly to his decision.

The house of the merchant was on a steep hill. They waited for him at the ruins of an old house, away from the cobblestoned street, and they heard him long before he was visible.

"He will appear about there across the street," whispered Lalo. "And at the point he appears, he will start to cross the street. Remain here and he will come within three feet of you. When he passes, take his arms from behind, I shall do the rest." He moved a few yards toward the house and was lost in the shadows.

The man hummed a tune as he approached, and David wondered what he must be thinking at this moment, then smiled at the thought of how surprised the merchant would be in a minute.

He took but two steps and gripped the man's forearms strongly from behind. Lalo leaped quickly and his knife entered above the pelvis and slashed upward to the sternum. David felt the body convulse, then sag, and did not know until he saw Lalo clean the knife on the man's clothes.

"Goddamn you!" he said. "You had no need to do that! A smash on the head would have made him sleep long enough!"

"Help me, quickly," said Lalo, as he dragged the man farther into the shadows. The man had not released his satchel and now Lalo took it from the lifeless fingers. David hesitated, thinking insanely that he should attempt to do something for the merchant. "Come on!" said Lalo harshly. "He will die very soon."

In an alley, the money was divided in approximately equal amounts, Lalo whispering all the while. "There, David, you would work twenty years merely to earn that much." And as David did not speak, he added, "That was a part of the operation. Something I decided a long time ago. He had to die, or else he might somehow identify us. A victim should always die."

244

David remained silent. He thought it would have been impossible for the merchant to remember anything in that darkness, but it was Lalo's project and everything had come off as he had told him. They separated and David did not know he had almost three thousand pesos under his sarape.

He had no difficulty in boarding the train, even though the station was crowded. It seemed that many people were going north these days. He sat in the third-class coach smoking, his hat low and his sarape close about him. He knew suddenly he should have taken the gun from the merchant and hoped the body had not yet been discovered. Peering out the dingy window, he looked for Lalo. He was apprehensive because for certain the train was delayed. This was not a long stop and he had been aboard more than ten minutes now.

The car was almost full. An old man slept alongside him, while in the seat before him two men dozed, opening wide their eyes at intervals. He thought of feigning sleep and suddenly had the urge to move from this place. Casually he rose and walked forward. All around him people slept and there was no seat empty. At the very end of the coach, next to the toilet, a young girl sat with an infant in her arms. Another child slept against her hip, and a third lay on the seat before her. Gently, David moved the child's feet and sat down. The woman's eyes opened instantly, although she had been asleep and while asleep clutched the small baby in her shawl.

She smiled at him, her face Indian, lovely. "A thousand pardons, señor. I should have moved the child and made room for you. I must be tired that I did not notice we were stationary."

"Do not concern yourself," said David. "I am perfectly comfortable."

"Where are we?" she asked.

"Zacatecas."

"Another day and a night," she said wearily. Her child whimpered and she slowly rocked forward and back.

"All the way to the border," said David. "You have been there previously?"

"Oh no," she said, and laughed like a child. "I have never been out of my village in Michoacán." Because she sensed his curiosity and he could not ask, she told him, "My man is there. I go to meet

245

the father of my children, who is a conscript although I have had no word from him in many months—since he was home last. He has never seen this one," she indicated the child in her shawl. "He is to be released from the army in Juárez and we are going to go north into another country. Fidel does not want his sons to ever be conscripts."

David felt a sudden sadness for her. She would arrive at Ciudad Juárez, alone and knowing no one, probably having but a few cents, and there would exist no Fidel. For Fidel was already across the border, or with a woman of which there were many in Juárez, or else dead these many months when David himself had fought there.

"I go to Torreón," he said, "to make a new life there. Now that the war is over, I have left the hacienda where I was born."

"Our village was free," she said, "but very poor. It is said that in the new country everyone lives like human beings. I shall like that—for Fidel and for the children." She thought a moment and added, "For you it is almost like us. It is almost as if you, too, go to a new country."

"Well, the life will be different," said David. The train had not moved, and he was very much aware of this. He was at the point of going out to make an inquiry when he heard activity outside and thought that they would now depart. The child now cried in the woman's arms, and she pulled back the shawl and opened her dress. Her breast lay bare and she gave her child suck.

"I wonder why we have not moved," she said.

"I do not know," said David. He stared into her eyes, feeling that the slightest lowering of his gaze would indicate that he was aware of her bosom. He was very strongly affected by her and all the while his ears were tuned to the noise outside.

At the woman's side, the other child was now restless and sobbed softly in sleep. The woman patted the small form, but the child half awake now cried aloud.

"Permit me, please," said David, and leaned forward to take the child in his arms. "It is probably cold for him."

"She is a girl," said the woman. "The other two are bucks."

He held her close to him and wrapped the end of the sarape around her body. She stopped crying, but whimpered yet a while, and David was quite happy. He had never known that this could

246

be a pleasure. To his mind came a half-forgotten lullaby which had once induced sleep in him, and he crooned softly.

They entered then, from both ends of the coach, not gendarmes but soldiers, so the murdered man must have had influence. David was startled, and then angry that city noises had dulled his senses. He could never be taken like this in the hills. He moved the child to and fro and looked up at the soldier. At that moment he knew that, come what may, he would not resist.

"Your destination?" asked the soldier. And David without thinking answered, "Juárez, and then to North America." He dared not look at the woman's face.

"And you come from . . . ?"

"Morelia," he answered, giving the first place he could think of in Michoacán, not knowing why it must be Michoacán except that she had come from there. And still no word from her, and now he looked. She seemed removed somehow, like a good wife intent only in feeding her child, not intruding in the business of men. When he looked up, the soldier had moved on. He watched because it would be unnatural that he not be curious, and everyone in the coach was searched. Why they had not been disturbed, he did not know. Even the woman's carpetbags had not been touched.

He was safe now, and he asked, "Why did you help me?"

"Because you are good," she said.

"Do you have any idea of what they were after?"

"No," she said. "And I do not want to know what you have done. But it could have been nothing, for this is the manner in which my man was conscripted. The soldiers simply came and took him away."

He looked at her in wonder. "You are a good man," she repeated.

He bought their breakfast in Cañitas, and stared somewhat mournfully toward the tetillas, and, quite conscious of the children about him, thought of his mother with compassion. And before they arrived in Torreón that afternoon, he thought of going on to Juárez. He wanted to follow this young girl who was a woman, and be present when she found need for him. This could be soon, he knew, for she would not find her man. Within a few short weeks this would be his family if he should decide. This was the way of these things, the way a man and a woman were joined together. And they could go to that far country she spoke about. But no, for Mexicans would gravitate, and one day without a doubt if the man had survived the battle of Juárez, he would come and one would die with heartbreak for her either way. This, too, was the way of things. Of course, it did not have to be the North American United States; it could be Sonora or one of the territories not yet too populated, like Baja California, where he could get a piece of land and raise his greens and have a few animals and survive with this delicate thing before him.

And now he felt relief that Lalo had killed the merchant, for he felt free and it could never be that way if he feared every strange face. So here, while teasing the children, he decided that he should let her go. Go your way, he thought. And remain pure, for only thus can you find happiness.

Aloud he said, "I do not mean to offend you, but I have had good fortune recently with the cards. I want you to take some money."

She said, placing a soft hand on his, leaning toward him, "Please, no. I need no money, truly. And my husband will be with me shortly."

Again he thought of going on with her, but he had made a choice in Zacatecas. "For the children, I ask you," he said. "There is much confusion in Juárez. You may not see your husband for a few days, and they should have food and lodging."

She looked at her children and understood, but would not speak aloud his knowledge which was her fear. "For the children, then," she said. "Only for the children." It was bad money, she knew, but what was to become of them otherwise? She smiled at David, and to him her hand was almost hot as it pressed his own. He handed her some bills, how much he did not know, and said good-by.

He could not control his destiny. He had made a choice because he had no other, but he would not be a robber in the city, for quickly he would fall on unknown ground. For a few days he would be a citizen, law-abiding, but then to the mountains. He thought of Ysabel Pulido suddenly, and just as suddenly removed him from his mind. He had a fancy that the old man would not have approved. Then he thought of the hills again and was impatient.

IV

To the house of Teodoro, Heraclio Inés brought his young bride one day in April 1912. She was frightened—not because this morning she had been a young girl and now when darkness came she would become a woman, but because she was in a houseful of strangers. Strange men although their faces were familiar, and strange women—women she had never seen until today.

One, the aunt Timotea, came to her and clasped her frail form to her large body. Crying loudly, she said, "It is over, now. The last one is grown and married, and my task is finished. Witness, Marcelina," she almost screamed, and for a moment the young girl was startled, thinking the woman addressed her, but she spoke to her dead sister-in-law. "Witness. I have fulfilled the vow I made at your deathbed! Aurelio Heraclio has now taken a woman and the house of Inés is filled!"

Marcelina shuddered. She had often prayed to her dead mother, who must indeed be a saint, but in the intimacy of her room, quietly. This was so strange! And then another came to her, and her beauty was quite startling to the girl. The voice was soft, seemingly caressing her, and although the blue eyes glistened with tears, there was no outcry from this one.

"Welcome, my sister," said Otilia. "I have waited long for you and we shall become closer than sisters, you shall see."

The oldest of the wives, looking dry and bitter to the girl, spoke up. "It is better for you, young lady, that you pay little attention to that one. She is much too frivolous, and you must now learn the duties of a wife. Overly protected you have been, I have been told, and small wonder, living in the Big House like a fine lady. The metate is in the corner and you may as well begin by learning to knead the corn, if your tender knees will allow you."

"Rosa," said Otilia indignantly. "Give the child enough time to remove her wedding gown!"

"Enough of that," said Rosa, equally angry. "You know I do not tolerate your impertinence, Otilia. Hold your tongue!"

Otilia's face was red and she hung her head. Heraclio laughed and took his wife's hand. "There is time enough for the instruction, Rosa." He turned his back to her. "Come," he said to Marcelina. "I will show you our room."

It was his old room, except that he had bought a bed, and against the wall a chest of drawers with a small oval mirror stood.

She looked at her reflection and turned suddenly, burying her face against his chest, her arms tightly around his body. "Are you really mine?" she asked.

"For all time."

"But I am not even pretty, why me?"

"You are beautiful," he said, and he took her arms. He had an odor which was his own and she did not want to release him. He sat with her on the bed, half turned to her. "Do not allow anyone to bother you. You are my wife and only I can ever say anything to you. Will you remember that?"

"I will, Heraclio." She touched his face, timidly. Her hand caressed his eyes and then his lips. He took the small, smooth-soft hand in his own. "I will help, though," she said. "I will learn to be a wife."

"Of course," he said. "But you will tell me when you are abused."

"I do not want to be a crybaby," she said.

He smiled. "You do not understand. Here, Rosa is the mayordoma of the women because she is the wife of Teodoro, who you know is my oldest brother. Only sometimes Rosa thinks she is Porfirio Díaz. I know her well. So you tell me when things are not right." He reached out and placed a hand on her small breast. She looked at him, her eyes wide, her body rigid. "I have longed to do that for many days now," he said. She nodded, and he kissed her below the ear. She shuddered.

"This dress," he said. "I told you it was my mother's wedding dress, but I did not tell you that you are the only one to wear it after her. She had a form like yours, I am told, and none of the other wives were small enough to wear it. To alter it would be a sacrilege, so it has been saved these many years just for you. Odd, too, that her name was also Marcelina."

"I am pleased, Heraclio. Pleased to have been able to wear your sainted mother's dress."

"Change your clothes," he said. "And come out to the corral—I have a gift for you."

250

In the corral a small mare was ready for her. "The saddle is old," said Heraclio, "because none of the women here ride, but I shall have your great-grandfather make you a new one. The mare is your own; and she is very gentle."

"Oh, thank you! Thank you so much, Heraclio." She was overjoyed. "And I can ride, you shall see. My father, when he was in the hacienda, rode with me." She walked around the animal, admiring its golden coat. "What do you call her?"

"Beast, that is all. I have no name for her, you give her one."

"Like a piece of gold," she said. "That is it—her name is Grain of Gold."

"So be it," said Heraclio.

As they cantered away, in the house Rosa shook her head and asked, "What shall become of these little women when their own husbands encourage frivolity? She shall awake one of these days and Heraclio's house shall have no discipline."

It was a fortnight now since her marriage, and although she could not remember an unhappy day in her life—except, of course, for the state of being motherless, without a mother she could not possibly remember—she could say now that she had never been happier. In the sunlight of the morning she carried the wash to the creek behind the orchard. She held her basket on her shoulder, certain she would never learn to carry things on her head. Many things she could never learn, she thought, and was suddenly a little sad that she was not good enough for her man. She had been totally unprepared for that first time, and yet, how could she be anything but naïve? She had no way of learning things other than through him. She had believed that a man had but to touch a woman in a certain place to make life. The euphemism *to be used* had told her nothing. And that of being touched was not unreasonable, for the feel of his hand on her breast was enough to make her feel life quickened within her. And it was enough for her to be held close by him on their bed, his hands on her body, unmoving. And now her sick days were approaching and already she was embarrassed, for he would surely know.

As she walked through the streets of the hacienda, she saw a cock chasing a hen. She colored. That, too, was strange. Why had she never noticed things like this? And living in an area with so many animals about, why had she not seen what life was? Even this very week, two or three days ago, she had seen a group of dogs waiting impatiently for their turn at a bitch.

And the first time he had not been with her, she knew that he had lain with another. Although that did not have to be true, as Otilia had told her the next day upon sensing her sadness, "It is all right, little one. Everything is the same, believe me. It is only that it cannot happen every night." She was aghast, and could only nod and blush. Although Otilia thought her sadness came from the fear of being unloved, the information was welcome— but she knew what he had done. And she knew that was a privilege which he had and she could never have. But she had no desire to be with anyone but him. She knew all these things but could not be unfeeling. And it would be like this always when he did these things; she would always grieve a little.

This was the third time she had been to the creek, and she found she enjoyed being out there with these women. Knowing who she was, they welcomed her the first time, and taught her how she must pound the clothes with stones to cleanse them. She walked into the water without hesitation, not like the first time when she had been ashamed to do this, and sat so that the water came above her waist. All the women did this, fully clothed, and talked and some washed their hair.

It was then that Heraclio rode up and she was embarrassed that he should see her at something which she could not do well. She stood, then waded out to meet him.

"What are you doing here?" His voice was harsh, in anger, and she had never seen him angry.

She lay a hand on his leg and he sat his horse. "I am but doing the laundry. I am sorry, Heraclio, that I was not home and you had need for me."

He slapped her hand away. "What do you mean by this—washing clothes? My wife does not wallow in the mudhole pounding garments!"

And the women called to him, for he was in an area reserved for women alone, very much like in the kitchen. "Bully!" they called. "Leave the girl be, abuser, for how else can clothes get clean—by themselves?" And they hooted as women will.

252

He turned on them, his face livid, "Neddlesome biddies! Shut your Goddamned mouths!" And thought, Christ! I am arguing with harpies!

She faced him bravely and her voice was calm. "It is true, Heraclio," she said. "The garments must be washed."

He did not know. He had not thought about it, for a man does not think of such things. He was sorry and looked down at her. Her wet skirt clung, outlining her legs and thighs, and he transferred his anger. "Is it in that manner that you walk home, displaying your form to any man's eye?"

"Heraclio," she said, and for a moment he was certain she laughed at him and almost struck her. "I wring my clothes out when I am finished—while they are still on me," she added quickly. "Then a few minutes in the sun and I am the only one who knows that they are damp."

The women still called insults, and he spoke down to her in a voice only for her. "It is my fault, my life. I did not think of this— but you shall not do this again. You shall have a woman to do your wash. I did not think."

"It does not matter," she said, and smiled, happy that all was well between them. "If you wish to hire a woman, it is all right, but I do not mind, really. And anyway, these are not our garments. Rosa sent me to do her wash."

She knew immediately she had again said or done something wrong. He reached down and picked her up, placing her before him on the horse's neck. In his fury, he was speechless, and she cried out as they galloped, "Heraclio, the clothes! I cannot leave Rosa's clothes."

He placed her on the ground, then rode the horse through the house to the corral, not bothering to take the saddle off. His brothers were at the table, for they had been out in the early morning hours. He came in, breathing heavily, and strode to Rosa, who was at the fire. Everyone turned to look at him in amazement, and Marcelina stood at the door holding her hands fearfully.

"Listen to me, woman," he said. "You are never again to order Marcelina that she should do your work for you. You have a basketload of shitted diapers waiting for you in the creek. Never, do you hear? She is not your washerwoman, nor is she your charwoman, nor your nursemaid!"

253

Teodoro came to his feet also in a rage. "You have something to say to my woman, Heraclio, you say it to me, or answer to me!" he shouted.

"Do not threaten me, older brother, for I am unnatural. I speak to her because she is the martinet here with the women. She intimidates my brothers' wives and even my aunt, but she shall not intimidate my woman, I warn you."

Rosa recovered from her momentary fright, for habit was strong with her. She came to Heraclio, drawing in a great breath for her harangue, but he anticipated her.

"Do not speak, Rosa. I know what you will say. With sarcasm you will say, *She is so delicate, so sheltered! Is she with child already that we should pamper her?* That is what you wish to say. And also that she is lazy. You see, I know all your pretty speeches, and if you say one of these things to me I will surely knock you down." His voice was now normal, and he said, "And you, also, Teodoro. You would say that I am young and do not know how a wife should be treated. Let me say that I want no wife I must treat like an animal. Nor will I allow you to treat her like one. She is here to please me, and she cannot please me and be a beast of burden also."

"The authority of the house," said Teodoro sadly, "it is breaking up."

For the first time, Heraclio laughed. "I should not tell you your business, Teodoro. But the authority you speak of is too rigid and there is a sore need around here for a little justice, a little understanding. I feel no disrespect because I protect my wife. The right for respect is lost when the need to protect or be protected arises. I must protect mine, that is the way it should be although not according to pattern." He sat down and said to Marcelina, "I will eat."

She moved toward the fire and knew not what to do. Only Otilia, with a slight smile on her face, went to help her, whispering directions and beginning the rhythmic patting of the tortillas.

At the table, Elías, Juan, and Concepción looked at Heraclio with resentment born of guilt. He knew, and thought, Am I to someday have to fight them all? And he said as he ate, "Teodoro, send me to Peñuelas there to work."

254

And for once Teodoro did not argue. He knew that this was the only way. "Very well," he said. "When?"

"Tomorrow."

In the night she cried against him and he said, "You are unhappy because you leave your great-grandfather?"

She shook her head. "It is that it hurts me to see a family at odds. I am unaccustomed to it. And because it is your family, I grieve. That is all."

"The others do not fight, do not talk back," said Heraclio. "I am the only one. It seems to be my way of life."

"It is not because of my great-grandfather—that I am leaving him, I mean," she said. "I do not cry for that. My place is with you, always. And anyway, we will still be on the hacienda."

In June, a rider came to Peñuelas to tell Heraclio that he was wanted in his brother's house. There was a man there, the messenger told him, who had come to see him and was waiting even now to talk to him.

"What is he called?" asked Heraclio.

"I do not know," said the man. "Teodoro sent me to fetch you. He came in a carriage, with a driver, and from the direction of Fresnillo. I know nothing more."

Together they left Peñuelas.

In the house of Teodoro, the stranger and his coachman sat at the table with Heraclio's brothers. Although Teodoro did not drink now, a bottle of tequila was on the table, for there were guests in the house. Antonio Rivera leaned against a wall, smoking.

"He is here," said Teodoro, and smiled. "But I have told you, he will not be interested, for he is now married and has a responsibility."

Heraclio deeply resented that Teodoro spoke for him, but he would not insult him before strangers, and he said, "You wished to see me?"

"It is this gentleman, an old friend of our father, who wishes to see you," said Teodoro. He turned to the stranger, who came to his feet. "I present you to my youngest brother," said Teodoro.

The man took Heraclio's hand firmly. "Pánfilo Natera, to serve you," he said.

"Heraclio Inés, at your orders," answered Heraclio. "Sit yourself, please." He pulled a chair and sat away from the table. He reached forward and took the bottle, then offered it to the man. He drank and then Heraclio drank.

Pánfilo Natera was not a large man, but he was muscular and had a strong chest. A man of the plateau, he was, an outdoor man although now dressed in the casual wear of the city-bred.

"I had the honor," he said to Heraclio, "to know your father, God give him peace. He would come to my hacienda, and although I am a pastor, we were acquainted and became good friends. He was older, of course, and yet he esteemed me. It should not be necessary for me to tell you that I held the same affection for him. This I tell you to explain what pleasure it would give me if you are agreeable to what I have to say." He paused—puffing on a cigarette, thinking.

"Go on," said Heraclio.

"I shall tell you," continued Natera. "I am recruiting men for the great fight that is to come. I have come to get a pledge from any and all men, but especially I come for you. Your brothers have refused me, everyone. Your friend, Antonio Rivera, waits for your decision before he makes his."

"And why me?" said Heraclio. "And is it that certain, now, that the war shall erupt again?"

"It will start up again," said Natera. "I shall tell you about that in a moment, but first, let me explain what I propose to do and thus, why I want you. In the last skirmish, I operated as a guerrilla in the mountains to the east and in San Luis Potosí. When I returned to my hacienda, I did not feel it in my heart to be a shepherd again, and have been in the city. The war accomplished nothing, it seemed to me, and I went to México, there to make up my mind whether things would eventually improve or not. I saw and heard enough to know that it is but a matter of time—months, perhaps weeks before hostilities.

"Now, although I believe in the importance of a central government, I am a Federalist by philosophy, and feel strongly that in the end, a modified federal union is to be desired or we are open to despotism or anarchy. The states must be strong of themselves, or the central government will not function honestly or properly. I have support from state officials from the governor on down, and am building an army of Zacatecas. Three thousand men in

256

the beginning, but eventually not less than eight thousand. We will defend our state, and when the Revolution takes up again, we will side with the people who are in the right—those who will truly bring reform."

"And you shall decide who is right?" asked Heraclio.

"I, and the governor, and other learned men in the state. We are fortunate in Zacatecas that our state is in the hands of men with no personal interest whatever other than the good of the people and thus the republic. Many men are pledged, but unfortunately, very few of them have seen action, have seen war. You are young, but you have been a leader, and a good one. We need men like you and I am prepared to commission you a major immediately. I have such authority."

"How do you know about me?"

"We know of every man in Zacatecas who fought against Porfirio Díaz. As you see, Antonio is here. Your friend from Guadalupe is already in the hills with a group of my men. Your other friend from here, David Contreras, has lost himself. But I want you—I need you."

"I cannot go," said Heraclio. "I think I would like to, but I cannot."

Teodoro had a wide grin on his face. He was proud that Natera thought so highly of his brother, but was also pleased that Heraclio had refused him.

Natera said, "Unfortunately we have not the power to conscript for the state militia, for surely we would draft you. But listen, boy. I, too, am married, as are many of our men. We but fulfill our responsibility to our families by fighting for a better life for them. That is also a responsibility, to create a good world to live in."

"You need not explain that to me," said Heraclio. "That is the reason I went in the first instance, and I understand that quite well. And it is not that of having a wife, although it will not be an easy matter to leave a bride of a few months. It is only that I wait for my General Villa. When he calls, I shall go. Not until then "

It was Natera who now smiled in pleasure. "I should have thought of that," he said. "While in México I visited your general where he is held at Tlatelolco. He is a man we feel will be on the right side, if he can ever get out. His sentence has been set at five years. Much can happen in five years. He is in full agreement that we must fight again, and in prison has heard of a plot to overthrow Madero. He gave me leave to speak to you, and to tell you that you are free to join me if you wish so."

"Five years!" exclaimed Heraclio incredulously. "Five Goddamn years! And Madero does not help him—why?"

"Perhaps he does not want to help him. In any event, Madero can do nothing to help him."

Heraclio drank again, and Concepción brought another bottle. As usual, the brothers were silent, but they were drinking, and Juan brought out the guitar. He sang with Elías in harmony, a ballad of themselves, of the Ineses while their father yet lived, when Heraclio was but a child.

"It is still the same," said Heraclio. "I am sorry. My general gives me leave to go with you, but I do not give myself leave. You see, I ride with him because I choose, and not because he orders me to do so. I shall wait and he will one day call."

Natera said, "I pray that he escapes. He can make the difference, I do believe. I wish you could see it differently."

"He will escape," said Heraclio. "By this time he must see that it is the only road to take."

Natera tried again. "All the things I have heard about you are all good. A week ago, in Sombrerete, I spoke with the Major Celestino Gámez."

"The Tiger," said Heraclio, and smiled in affectionate recollection. "And what is he up to?"

"The same as I," said Natera. "Keeping in touch with his boys, he said. Although that seems far south for him. He is back in Chihuahua, but in the mountains. However, I mention him only because he spoke so highly of you. Much man, he said of you. Of the best, a bravo. And he described your action in detail."

Heraclio said, "From a man such as Celestino that is the highest praise one can receive. I am grateful to him, for it is not for nothing that they call him the Tiger." He thought back for a time, and Natera did not speak, but Heraclio finally said once again, "I am sorry, Señor Natera, but my decision still stands. Come, enjoy yourself. Drink and sing us a song from your parts."

"Thank you," said Natera. "When I receive an answer from Antonio Rivera, my business shall be over. A pity if I must leave here without one man."

258

Antonio walked over and took the new bottle. "I shall save you from grief, my General. I go with you."

Heraclio was surprised. "I thought you were to never leave again?"

"It does not take long," said Antonio, "to tire of work when one has not done it for a time. I suppose it is because nothing is changed, because the tienda de raya still keeps books. And if I go with Pánfilo Natera, I will remain in Zacatecas, near my mother."

"Well, good!" said Natera. "Now we can be festive."

"You will stay the night here, of course, in your house," said Heraclio, although this was Teodoro's home. "I fear, however, that there is no bed for you."

Natera laughed. "A petate is fine. Remember, I am a pastor."

"A pastor was I also," said Heraclio, and laughed with the man. "But I never had a coachman."

Later in the night, after a bowl of menudo, Heraclio excused himself. "It is two hours at a gallop, and I must arrive in time to go to work," he said.

Antonio left with him. He led his horse as he walked with his friend. "You will have no trouble getting away?" asked Heraclio.

"Of course not," said Antonio. "Although the books exist, times are still troubled and anyone can come and go. Your brother did not like it that I am going. Will he make trouble for the General?"

Heraclio said, "It is natural that he would not like it. A peon, going off to fight the landowner—that he does not understand because he cannot believe that the system should be changed. But he will not attempt to harm the General, because in spite of our differences, Teodoro is a man and Natera is a guest in his house. To treat him other than honorable would be a breach of tradition, and Teodoro would sooner die than abuse a tradition."

"It is true."

"Good luck, Antonio," said Heraclio, and they embraced. "It saddens me to see you go, but it is the only thing to do, I know."

"I grieve to leave you, too, my friend," said Antonio. "But it may be a long time before you mobilize. And like you who waits for your General Villa, when you want me with you, you have but to call."

"I know, Antonio. I love you," said Heraclio, and laughed lightly.

"And if you have love for me, you will allow me to leave my horse here for a short while."

Antonio laughed also and said, "You are a bastard."

Heraclio slipped through an alley and moved to the house of María Contreras.

Through July and August, Heraclio worked out of Peñuelas, waiting patiently for the new call to arms. Marcelina bloomed, already showing her first child, and Heraclio had a woman in the house to help her. They were happy, and yet she had a sadness because she knew that one day soon he would be gone. He had told her to expect it, and that when this happened she would go to her great-grandfather there to remain until his return.

And it happened quite suddenly in September. One moment she was lighthearted, giving him his dinner, and the next, her world collapsed around her, for a rider arrived to tell Heraclio that a stranger looked for him at the railroad stop of Cañitas.

Heraclio offered the boy some money but he said, "No, señor. I have been paid. The stranger gave me a hundred pesos to find you."

He talked to Marcelina. "You must make yourself ready," he said, "to remove yourself to la Flor in the morning."

"I have thought," she said, "that perhaps you will allow me to remain here."

"I suggested it only because there you would be with your old one."

"That is true, but here I have women friends, and even the midwife is my friend and would be near when I deliver your child. I should like that, and Tula is here to help me."

"Well, good," said Heraclio. "I feel better also that you remain here, and for the same reasons." He called the domestic. "Tula," he said, "I shall go away, perhaps tomorrow. I want you to move your petate in here and stay with the señora when I am gone."

"Yes, sir," she said.

He dismissed her and spoke to Marcelina. "I shall never be so far that I cannot come to see you," he said. "Be of courage and we shall be together again before long."

She said, "I am brave, Heraclio. I only fear that you shall die far away. I shall have a candle burning to the Virgin every day you are away."

"If it pleases you," he said. "But I have no fear that I shall not return."

She grasped him strongly. "Take care, my love! Oh, take care!"

He asked, "You have the gun?"

"Yes."

He had given her a small revolver and had taught her to load and fire, to take it apart and clean it. In these times one could never be certain, and he would not be around to protect her.

He asked, "Do you remember what I have told you?"

"If I must take it up, I must use it, and I must shoot to kill."

"Can you do that?"

"I can do that," she said quietly.

He looked at her brown face and into her black eyes for a moment, then kissed her almost brutally. He could not remember when they had kissed so passionately.

"I shall be back later tonight and will be leaving early," he said.

"You will not return tonight," she said. "Do not attempt to convince me, please. I know you leave now."

Perhaps, he thought. It was not the first time the intuitions of those around him as well as his own had come true. It was not yet dark as he took the trail along the railroad to Cañitas. And he led a spare horse.

The General Francisco Villa sat in the railroad station at Cañitas on a chair tilted back against the wall. He wore a jacket, unbuttoned, a felt hat, and low shoes. He looked like a cattle buyer or a commission man as he half dozed while he waited. He opened his eyes to slits at the sound of spurs.

Heraclio entered and went directly to him. "You asked for me?" he said.

"If you are Heraclio Inés, I come about the cow."

"Well, I do not have it with me, but I have brought a horse for you if you can ride."

Villa smiled. "Well, muchacho, it has been some time," he said, "but I shall try." They stepped out and Villa asked, "What is it like in that direction?" pointing toward the tetillas.

"Prairie, and finally mountains—a little north are Sain Alto and Sombrerete," said Heraclio. "Not the safest way."

"As I thought," said Villa. "And to the east—you know the trails?"

"I made them," said Heraclio. "I brought you a carbine but I did not have a spare sidearm." The General did not wear a holster, but somewhere on his bulk, Heraclio knew, he had a weapon. "There is also a mochila for you on your horse."

"What a boy you are," said Villa. "Is there a store in this forsaken place? I must get a hat. With this one, I feel like a gachupín."

Heraclio laughed. "A chinito has a store, but there is no need to buy one. I shall give you one when we get to my house."

Villa was serious. "We do not go to your house, boy. It will not be safe."

"I doubt," said Heraclio, "that there is real danger here. Look yourself—no one pays the slightest attention to us."

And true, although there were a few people in the streets, each seemed to be in his personal world. But Villa said, "I have been very fortunate evading those who want me. And it is when it is most quiet that I must be most aware. It can happen here."

Heraclio looked at the man and he saw fear and was astonished. For this was a brave man here—the bravest, most audacious, strongest man he knew. Christ only knew how he had escaped from Santiago Tlatelolco, how he had escaped the capital, how he had arrived here. There was something here with Villa he did not know. He thought suddenly of Antonio Rivera and his courage. He did not dare think about himself, about his own.

Villa turned to him with a sly look. "Muchacho, I sense you wonder about my balls. It is not a lack of courage for a man to be careful. It is the mark of a man to admit that others may have the strength and the cunning to take him."

Heraclio was embarrassed. That must be it, he thought. Antonio did not know as much as this man and could therefore be foolhardy. That was all it was.

Villa chuckled. "Come, let us get the hat," he said. And when they left the store, he said, "Goddamn Chinese! Can it ever be that I can someday be somewhere in México and find no foreigners in business?" The horses were ready, and he said, "Muchacho, I wait here, go to the station and send a marconigram to Juan Núñez in Parral. Tell him to look for you in Saltillo. Sign your name, then we will go."

"Where is it that we are going to go?" asked Heraclio.

Villa said, amused, "What a boy, Heraclio. Always the questions with you." He thought a minute, then said, "You forgot to ask, but Juan Núñez is Celestino Gámez. I have been thinking that I am tired of running. The políticos, now, what do they do when they fall out of favor and must hide until their day is here again?"

"They go to another country," said Heraclio.

"Exactly," said Villa. "They hide in comfort, in the open, and so shall I. We will go to Texas, to a land which is legally ours but was stolen, and there remain with friends until the time to fight. There will be eight of you with me, for even there they might try, though not in force. Now, does that answer you your question, boy? Can you send the message now so that we can get away from here? We can move a long distance this night."

Heraclio was happy. "Right away, Jefe," he said.

"Well hurry, then." Villa took the carbine from its scabbard and examined it. "For we are on our way to get thirty thousand of these into men's hands."

V

AT MIDNIGHT ON MARCH 13, 1913, Pancho Villa and his eight men made their way back into México. When they rode their beasts across the Río Bravo, the offensive was begun.

From the first, as they made their way down the great desert which is Chihuahua, they were joined by men from every village, men who had been waiting, alerted by Villa's agents. At the point where they crossed the railroad somewhere between Chihuahua and Camargo, the army numbered a thousand men, of which a great many had their wives or soldier women with them. Children there were also, and the bivouacs were unlike settlements, the women cooked over their small charcoal fires, the children played helter-skelter amid the animals.

And now, Tomás Urbina, Celestino Gámez, and Maclovio Herrera of the original eight who crossed the border with Villa rode forth to find their men. And another officer arrived, one Rodolfo Fierro, who had been recruited by Villa immediately before the first battle of Juárez.

Fierro was a railroad man, switchman and roustabout, brakeman and telegrapher, and he was to become chief of transport for the Division of the North, and head executioner for Pancho Villa. He had with him two hundred men, city-bred like himself, and he had secreted his small force out of the Federal stronghold of Parral.

While the army was gaining strength, others, Heraclio Inés and Guadalupe Morales among them, went into the vast rangeland belonging to the Terrazas family, who along with the Guggenheims of the North American United States had financed Orozco's abortive attempt on the Juárez government. Immense herds were driven to the border, there in turn the money received for the cattle was exchanged for arms and ammunition. All horses rounded up were sent to Villa for his growing cavalry, and an occasional bank or estate was also incidently stripped of its wealth.

The man-woman army grew, and as it grew small Federal garrisons and outposts were either abandoned or overrun. Villa controlled most of the state with the exception of the cities, and he was impatient. The women and children were a hindrance to his movements, but he found the women irreplaceable, for aside from their value to the soldiers who had nothing but their guns and the clothes they wore, his army numbered eight thousand fighting men, and Villa had no way to feed such an army. And so the women remained to cook for their consorts.

For this reason, Villa was compelled to form a unit of unencumbered males. The elite corp was made up of eight hundred horsemen, every man a jinete lean and hard, with excellent mounts, the best armament available, and led by the young captains Guadalupe Morales and Heraclio Inés, each with his four hundred. He called them Dorados, the Golden Ones, and he dressed them in a uniform, simple after his own taste, but of a golden hue. And if his army seemed more like a mob of displaced people, Villa's Dorados trained every day and were prepared for a forced march, a sudden attack, and the quick, violent action of the guerrilla. They were to be his personal guard, and his pride, and they could not carry soldier women with them. When not on

264

military movements, when inactive, they could take a local woman or a soldadera lately "widowed" from the ranks.

In the city of Nogales, on the border, don Venustiano Carranza gathered his Constitutionalists and formed a cabinet of young intellectuals and embryonic military chiefs. From Sonora came Alvaro Obregón and a swarthy ex-schoolteacher named Plutarco Elías Calles. Unique for ambitious men, these two would never have a falling out. And among these men, at Constitutionalist Headquarters, was the hidalgo Felipe Angeles, recently escaped from the penitentiary and lately from exile in San Antonio, Texas. During the endless conferences and discussions, it was clear to him that his aid and his knowledge would be used but sparingly, for if Villa was Carranza's social inferior, Carranza and those around him were gross alongside Angeles. A man of his ability and his honesty was out of place here. He must not have the opportunity to gain prominence: he was not in the plan of things.

In June of 1913, in the dawn of a new day, Pancho Villa with five thousand men stood facing the city of Jiménez from the south. The Federal garrison was now commanded by his old ally, Pascual Orozco, who had now gone over to the side of Huerta. With his Colorados, Orozco had elements of civil defense (paid for by local businessmen) as well as a few hundred aristocrats who felt they must take a hand in the protection of their class.

For this action, Villa did not think of tactics or of maneuvers, but depended instead on his favorite manner of operation, the bold, frontal attack. This would cost him men, but men were the only expendable war material he had, and the battle would be short and decisive. Most important, he knew that, although the Federals were entrenched and Orozco's force was superior in size and matériel, it was not enough to contain his hordes. And he gave the word for the attack.

The first wave consisted of twenty-five hundred men, and the two thirds who survived returned and a second wave of two thousand swept forward even as the first were retreating. They, too, returned, but not as quickly as the others had turned back. And the wounded in the field continued their fire where they lay. The disrupted first wave, now reorganized, moved again, taking the retreating men with it toward the enemy. Villa stood as detached, keeping only his eight hundred horse in reserve until his men spilled into the trenches, and in hand-to-hand battle broke through the first line of defense; he gave the word again and the Dorados went at an angle into the streets of Jiménez.

But by now, Orozco, having placed full confidence in his defenses, was defeated when they crumbled, and moved the bulk of his force out of the city northward. The cavalry of Villa followed and slew the disorganized, and the following day, the armies clashed once more, and again Orozco was routed with great losses. With scarcely one thousand men left from the garrison of seven thousand he had commanded, the General Pascual Orozco withdrew to the safety of the city of Chihuahua.

The Villistas moved to within sight of the city; they withdrew also, destroying rail all the way back to Jiménez.

It was a great victory for Villa, and thus for the Constitutionalists, but Jiménez must now be abandoned, for here the Federals could trap his force from Parral to the west and Chihuahua to the north. But that would not be for days, and meanwhile Villa destroyed the city government of Jiménez. Every Federal officer captured and Spanish men of wealth were turned over to Fierro. The civilian authorities had already been made to dig their own graves.

At the embarcadero, the prisoners were herded into a great corral where animals were kept while waiting for the cattle cars which would take them south to México. A hundred yards away, out of their vision, the Colonel Rodolfo Fierro began to line them up against the adobe wall of a large warehouse. To conserve ammunition, he set them three deep, and a few yards before them he placed riflemen, one for each line. In this way, eighteen men would die at once, and then would be dragged to the great ditch between them and their executioners.

Rodolfo Fierro sat on his haunches, smoking, a slight smile on his face. Behind him a few hundred soldiers watched, joking and shouting insults and obscenities as the first victims were brought forward. The prisoners also joked, and engaged in repartee with their tormentors almost as if in innocent competition.

"How does it feel now that you are not behind the skirts of the drunken Huerta?" the soldiers called and hooted.

266

And one, a youth of perhaps twenty years, shouted back, "Abuse your mothers, dogs!"

Soldiers moved to tie the doomed, but the young prisoner sent them back. "Go on with your butchery!" He stood straight, unflinching.

Fierro would give the order to fire, and now as he listened to the young Spaniard, he said, "Do me one favor, boy. At the top of your voice, yell, 'Long live the Revolution!' for me before you die."

The young man screamed, "Fuck the Revolution!" He ripped at his blouse with both hands and revealed his chest. "Right here," he said, "let this be your target! Be done with it, bandits! I die for México!"

Rodolfo Fierro was furious. "The only true thing you say, Gachupín, is that you die. Not for México, for you are not Mexican!"

"A pure Mexican I am," said the youth. "More Mexican than you, peon! Now let my blood flow to my mother, Mexican earth!"

Rodolfo Fierro stood abruptly and slammed his cigarette down.

"Hold your fire!" The command was sharp and loud from Heraclio Inés, and Fierro turned in anger.

"With your permission, Colonel," said Heraclio in a voice that only Fierro could hear. "I want that man."

"That boy, there?" asked Fierro, and his lips trembled in his agitation. "That pup who is insulting me even as he is dying? No, Captain. I am removing him from the line only because I have another death planned for him. A death that will make him cry and beg for mercy!"

"I doubt very much that he will cry, for you see he is no coward. I have prior claims. He insulted me a long time ago, long before you ever saw a Federal. I, too, have plans for him."

Fierro nodded. "In that case—but can you wait so that I can witness when you break him?"

"I fear not," said Heraclio. "It is an affair of honor. Highly personal."

"You will describe it to me later—how he dies?"

"Yes," said Heraclio. "But this I can say now; he will die well."

Fierro spoke to the prisoner. "Come here!" The man moved toward them. "You are fortunate. The Captain Inés requests the pleasure of breaking you himself. You remember him, do you not?"

The youth looked at Heraclio with hatred and said, "I remember him, and he can fuck his mother also after he fucks yours."

Fierro struck him on the mouth, and the youth regained his balance. He spat red. "Pig!" he said.

"You are quite a cock, you fancy," said Fierro. "But you are fortunate that the Captain here has prior claims on you. If it were not for that, I would soon teach you to call me father."

"I am not a dog!" said the other.

Heraclio spoke, for the youth might go so far that the Colonel would insist upon the right to kill him. "Come along," he said. "Thank you, my Colonel."

He walked so that his gun was away from the youth, for he knew that in his anger he was at this moment capable of any desperate attempt.

"Shut your mouth!" he said in a rasp as the other started to speak to him. They heard shots from behind them. The executions had begun, and they met the second group of prisoners walking toward them.

The older, the civilians, were sallow-faced, but these who had been soldiers were also engaged in banter and spoke to Heraclio's prisoner as they passed. "And where to, my Lieutenant? Is it that you are to be given a feast or a woman, perhaps before you die?"

And the youth would have answered to give them more courage, but instead suddenly said, "Oh, Jesus Christ!"

Heraclio stopped, startled, and then saw the young man staring at one of the prisoners. "My first cousin," he said hoarsely. "My first cousin Paco."

The revelation came quickly to Heraclio. It did not seem possible, but it was so. "That is Paquito Paz?" he asked. But he did not wait for an answer, for it would soon be too late. Quickly he spoke to one of the guards. "Bring another prisoner in place of this one. He goes with me."

"The authority, my Captain?"

"My authority—or do you wish to take his place yourself?"

"No, sir," said the soldier, and ran back to the corral.

They walked in silence until they were removed from the area. "And why did you do this?" asked the first youth. "You obviously plan to take us to another place to die. And all this merely because I once asked you a question in the Hacienda de la Flor?"

268

"I am taking you to freedom, you Goddamn fool. That is if you will allow me to do so."

"And why me?" asked Paquito Paz. "You do not even know me."

"For the same reason I free your first cousin here," said Heraclio. "Because you are both friends of a dear friend. You must say almost a brother, for Crispín is certainly that."

The first youth said, "You saw me but once—the night of the fiesta. It is fortunate that you recognized me, but what will happen to you because of this?"

Heraclio chuckled. "Nothing, I suppose. One can never tell, but certainly whatever happens to me will not be as serious as that which very nearly happened to you. However, if you wish me well, you can decide at this moment to come over to our side. I shall recruit you, if you wish, and that will keep me from a severe reprimand."

"What do you say, Joaquín?" asked Paquito Paz, laughing lightly.

The other was again angry. "Me fight alongside a pig like that colonel back there!" He turned to Heraclio. "I knew there was a reason for this, cuckold! Take me back to the butcher! Immediately!"

Heraclio also laughed. He grasped the man's shoulder and said, "I was but jesting. Do not have a seizure. I knew the idea was repulsive to you."

At this moment they seemed like three young men jesting, almost as if their short walk was not a dangerous one. They came to a building where some soldiers lounged in the street. Heraclio called to one of them, for these were his own men.

"Mauro," he said, taking him a few paces away. "Take these two men out to the western edge of town."

"They are gachupines, mi capitán."

"Of course. Is it that you think me blind?"

"No, no." The man Mauro did not wish to offend his superior.

"Take them," said Heraclio once again, "to the western limits of the town. First give them jerky and hardtack, and then find the two strongest beasts you can get your hands on in a hurry. Let them go. And Mauro, this did not happen, can you remember that?"

269

"Yes, mi capitán."

"You understand," said Heraclio to the youths. "I cannot give you fusiles because you might use them against my people. But the horses you have with my compliments. Do not fight again, if you can help it, for I may not be able to do this for you another day."

"Thank you," said Joaquín. "We are indebted, and you are a man."

Heraclio said, "I think that if you had not been a man back there I would not have done this."

He went to the stables to check that his groom was caring properly for his own horse. He had but one horse here, and the march would be hard. He stopped for a time to talk with some young officers who had liquor and women, and a few drinks, then went to headquarters to see what his orders would now be.

Villa sat on a heavy leather chair which had belonged to the newly dead municipal president. In the room were Urbina and Maclovio Herrera. Across from them were Celestino and Rodolfo Fierro. Calixto Contreras and others of the high command were also in attendance.

"Qué hubo, infante?" asked Celestino Gámez, addressing him as he had always since that day back in 1910.

"Nothing, my Colonel," said Heraclio. "I but come to see how we break this inactivity."

Villa spoke slowly, soberly, and he was displeased. "It seems to me, Captain, that you have already found a way of destroying inactivity—by going about the business of releasing prisoners. What have you to say to that?"

"They were friends, mi general. Old friends."

"But you interfered in Rodolfo's pleasure."

"He had three hundred," said Heraclio. "What difference to him if he kills three hundred rather than three hundred and two?"

"I say he should die in their place," said Rodolfo Fierro, moving forward.

"Here you have nothing to say," said Villa, harshly and with a look of anger. "Here I say—only I say, understood?"

"Yes, my General."

Heraclio stood before his general, and now he too was angry. "I was not weakened by a feeling of humaneness toward the enemy. I tell you, my General, they were only two and they were friends."

"And now they will fight us again another day."

"Not these two. I guarantee that they will go to México and there remain or even go to Europe. They will not fight again."

Villa spoke in disgust. "You are a Goddamned fool, boy! They do us more harm in México, for they have money which will be used to buy arms for others, or even to buy soldiers. And even if they are only two, they can do us harm if they remain in the field. How many men have you killed?"

Heraclio was confused. "Do you always have to ask me that? I do not know. Thirty, perhaps."

Villa allowed himself to smile. "The last time I asked you that you had only killed two. You are growing in this business." Heraclio did not speak, and so he continued. "Consider, boy. If you have killed thirty, and before the war ends another thirty, that makes sixty of the enemy you have destroyed. Now, you are a real killer, for I have seen you, and I do not expect a mere gachupín to match you, but say that between them they kill sixty of ours. Does it not occur to you that one of their victims might be one of us here in this room?"

"The manner," said Fierro, and Villa looked at him again but listened. "The manner in which he took one away from me, making me think that he meant to personally execute him. That I do not like."

Heraclio said, "Mi general. I did not have the time to come to you about the matter. It was the only way I could save him, and I had decided. It was but expeditious that I lied to the Colonel. I assure you, however, that if I had spoken to you and you had explained what you have just this minute told me, I would have made no effort to free them. I was a fool but the deed is done."

"I should think," said Villa, "that all my officers should have the privilege of pardoning a friend or two. In this mess, we may someday see our own brothers face our firing squads—who knows? We cannot kill them all, and yet we cannot feed them, and also, we cannot keep them out of the fray if we let them go. Next time this happens, you tell the officer in charge the truth. That is all. We cannot have this Goddamned subterfuge between my command. That is intolerable!"

"It shall not happen again," said Heraclio, still in anger. "The Colonel Fierro can kill every son of a bitch between here and México, and I will not interest myself in his doings."

"And now you are close to an insult," said Fierro. He was also in anger, and he said to Villa, "As his superior officer, I demand that he should be censured or even degraded to the ranks."

Villa still spoke quietly. "The Captain Heraclio Inés is quite valuable to me, Rodolfo. Contain your anger, or if you insist, reprimand him yourself for lying to you. What would you do, flog him?"

"I have your leave?"

"You have my leave."

"Well, then," said Fierro, and moved forward, his hand moving slowly to his sidearm. But Heraclio had his gun in his hand and said, his voice cold and cruel:

"Move only a little more and I shall blow you up. I will kill you in a second," he said as Fierro hesitated, "and if you do not know that, those in this room can vouch for me."

Fierro put the gun away, but Heraclio held his before him, waiting for the other to speak. Finally Fierro said, "I was but placing you under arrest for a few hours. To teach you manners."

"Take such ideas out of your head," said Heraclio. "I have business here—I came to war with my general to help in a much bigger fight, and I cannot be troubled by the petty feelings of a mediocre and a half-sane colonel. I warn you to keep clear from me, or you shall surely die."

Villa laughed. "Put the gun away, Heraclio. There is no need, for the Colonel will not disturb you in any way. I tell you that. He had his opportunity, and failed. So now, let us stop this little play." And yet laughing, he said to Rodolfo Fierro, "Did I not tell you the boy is a killer? This is my warrior, Heraclio Inés. One of the best. See to it that nothing happens to him." The last was said in the same tone, but Fierro understood and said:

"Very well, my General." But he would remember his humiliation.

"I have been told," said Villa, "that among the executed there was a man not Mexican." He followed habit without thought and in his simple statement even the Spaniards were Mexican.

"An English," said Fierro. "An old man, perhaps a septuagenarian—claimed he was a newspaperman, at least that is what the men were able to understand. A journalist, he said, he was, and that he had been a soldier in his younger days, in a great civil war in his own country. He was but simply trying to save his life, for what was he doing with the enemy?"

"An English?" asked Villa. "Or a North American?"

"English, North American—what difference."

And Villa stood up. "Difference! You dolt! What was this man like? Did he have a gun when captured?"

"He admitted that he had a gun. In the heat of the battle, he said he could not resist taking part. What was he like?" said Fierro. "Why, he had white hair and blue eyes. That is what he was like."

Villa paced the floor. "That he had a fusil. That may make it all right. You must understand, all of you. That the killing of North Americans must cease for a time. We cannot kill gringos, for we must have the embargo lifted by the United States or we have no arms. We must be politic for a time—we cannot disturb the colossus at this time. Every gringo is an important man—so from now on, only Spaniards go to the wall. Is that understood? Now about this one today, perhaps no one will know. If he was important, they may trace his movement to Jiménez, but none of ours saw a gringo. I did not see one. My compadre Urbina did not see one. So, we can rest easy, but it must not happen again. Yet, if he should be traced to us, he died in action, killing our people, for he was armed. That is all."

And the assault force went west into the mountains, there to join Villa's reserves, and whereas they had numbered five thousand before the battle, they were now eight thousand, for many of the vanquished joined their ranks.

The rustling continued and Villa's coffers filled. Because twenty thousand Americans were now along the border to enforce the embargo on arms, his army was inoperable, with only the Dorados in action, attacking strongholds along the railroad, winning every engagement although usually outnumbered, but always retiring into the mountains or the desert. As the days and then weeks passed, Villa paced impatiently, an animal in his lair, and now before too long it would be winter, and winters were white in this northern region. The cold weather would be cruel to his people living without shelter, so he must take a town somewhere, a town he could keep for three months, or he must move south into Durango.

Thus it was that on a morning in November 1913, the Division of the North, now numbering eight thousand men, massed for the attack on the city of Chihuahua, having ammunition for only a few days' fighting. They had come from the north, because Juárez was barely two hundred miles away, and they must know if a large force came at them. And the fortifications were all on the north side of the city.

The General Mercado had seven thousand excellent troops, artillery, and machine weapons in vast quantity. And he had constructed and added a line of defense, digging trenches outside the city and placing heavy artillery on the hills commanding every approach.

On the plains, out of range, the army gathered. And on a hillock, on a cold gray morning, Pancho Villa gazed quietly at his objective. Today he sat a pale horse. In a moment he would give the word and he knew what was before him. Of a sudden he seemed to shake his head almost sadly, and he turned his steed and cantered away, then pulled it short and turned to look another time, not unlike an animal that backs away not knowing whether to fight or run. His sudden indecision saved his army, and in that moment of reflection, an inspiration forged his battle plan. He laughed aloud.

"Get me my compadre and the other boys," he said to an aide. And he returned again to his vantage point.

They came to him and there on horseback he held his council of war. To his compadre, Tomás Urbina, he said, "Leave me here a few boys to watch the activity, although I am quite certain they will not come out to fight, why should they?"

The others laughed easily and it seemed that they were anything but a group of guerrilla leaders intent on a mission of death as they casually discussed their plans. Maclovio Herrera, a man noted for his courage, mostly Indian and intuitive, said calmly, "It is obvious that they will not come after us: so there we must go . . . but, has it not occurred to you folks that"—and he turned to look toward the city—"those people over there with those great big

274

guns could, with one well-placed round, blow us all to hell and end the Revolution?"

"What caution! And from you!" said Celestino Gámez. "If the destiny says it is my time, why I shall go. Did you forget the destiny?"

Villa, amused, looked upon them and spoke before Herrera could answer. "All of us know of the destiny, but Maclovio is more Indian than you or I and perhaps even talks to the destiny, or gets messages through the soles of his feet. You have a feeling, Maclovio?"

"It is not caution, my General. I have a feeling."

"Well," said Villa, and he moved his horse. "A Mexican never discounts a premonition. Let us remove ourselves to the other side of that knoll there, or the war will be over." And as they galloped away, they heard the first shell land where they had been gathered.

"It was but a feeling," said Maclovio Herrera, and laughed at Celestino.

"But," said Villa, "since the destiny is hand in hand with us, we must give the destiny a little help. Rodolfo," he spoke to Fierro, who was now his chief of transport.

"Mi general."

"Take yourself those town-bred railroad people you call soldiers, and remove me thirty kilometers of rail about midway to Ciudad Juárez. The trestles, also, of course. We do not want the Federals to come up on our rear, for they would murder us all in this place."

"Very well, my General," said Fierro.

Early in the afternoon, Villa said, "Well, they are not coming out, so as Maclovio predicted, we shall go in after them." He grinned, and it was obvious that he had known all along what must be done, and how it would be carried out. Playfully, he teased. "This has been a day for Maclovio. Twice now he has been right. On a day like this he could practice witchcraft."

"But witchcraft is a nighttime art, my General," said Maclovio, also in good humor.

"But I *am* speaking of the nighttime," said Villa. "Tonight, in the darkness, you will work your witchcraft on the defenses to the

275

east. Your witchcraft shall consist of five hundred mausers—Heraclio's four hundred and another hundred jinetes selected by you."

"In the night?" asked Maclovio Herrera, and his humor was turned into surprise and consternation. "Attack in the night?"

"And why not?"

"It is not done!" said Celestino Gámez. And Maclovio Herrera said, "Truly, it has never been done. The nights are not for warfare. They are for a little tequila or mezcal—a song or two, perhaps, and a fire. And then, perhaps, a little good screwing. It is traditional that only those things and love are for the nighttime."

Villa laughed. "You, Maclovio, speak of love? Can you not see yourself? Black as liver, your hair is like John the Baptist's, you are filthy as a newborn foal, and ugly. You have extraordinary balls, true—but other than that, what to make you speak of love?"

"Only that and the feeling, my General."

And Villa laughed. "All screwing is good, Loco. And it has nothing whatever to do with love. And this of not fighting at night is merely a bad habit . . ." But at this moment, Maclovio and Celestino thought of love. And about how this made Villa a different thing—although they loved him, this was a flaw; a flaw much worse than his brutality, his psychotic behavior at times—a thing they did not understand but would not question because he was a man. But the lowliest, the most backward peasant knew love—knew it over and over again with a mistress or with the most horrible, grotesque whore. He knew that when his organ filled with blood, whether it was love for humanity, for life, or merely for the love of copulating—it was love—and he could not explain it. But then again, he could not deny it. And Villa was saying, ". . . a bad habit that we will break and surprise those people over there who would destroy us. You remember, compadre," he said to Urbina, "these two have forgot the old days, but you remember when we were bandits and fought rurales. Did we ever make an attack in the daylight? We fought by light only when forced to defend ourselves or when we were stronger. Why not now?"

Urbina said, "I remember, compadre, although I had not thought of attacking at night either, but as you say, why not? This mania of it not being tradition is, of course, so much caca. I am certain that Maclovio and Celestino would—and have—bedded

276

a woman in daylight as well as at night. Would you lose the moment with a woman because you must remove your spurs or your hat, only because these things are not done with your spurs on? If one can die fully clothed why not function with them on? Eh?"

It was understood that they—all of them—were not questioning Villa's words, which were conversational but were orders. Objections were but academic—they would fight. And Celestino Gámez said, "I also remember. But I think the same as Maclovio. Then we were guerrillas, although bandits, whereas this is a battlefield. We are a large army, here we are as all the glorious heroes of México were—perhaps stronger. At that time we were forced to fight to survive."

"The same reasons are here," said Villa. "That man over there is no fool. He knows his trade. His people are entrenched and armed to the teeth—Christ, they are impregnable. As you say, we have an army here, but we do not have the ammunition for the type of fighting which would give us Chihuahua. In the old days we were at a disadvantage—we are at a disadvantage now." He was now animated. "And so we will make them pregnable by pushing their Goddamned perimeter back into the city. Then we will see what can be done."

Gámez and Herrera were convinced and grinned self-consciously. What a lark to fight at night—and really why not? Villa continued, "Now that we have everybody's permission to conduct a war at night, you can go about the business of getting out of the way every little routine that you conduct at night. You can build yourself a fire, Maclovio, in the prairie; and drink yourself a little tequila and sing yourself a song. And then, do that other thing you spoke of. As for me, tonight I sleep while you work."

In the night, the plain was dotted with campfires, and on the hillsides near the city, there too were fires, and at the trenches, the Federals were out of their holes and cooked their food and ate. They would sleep there tonight, but now was a period of truce. Between the two suns there was no need to be watchful, for tradition was strong, had been for four hundred years.

And the Division of the North, spread out across the prairie, was like a gathering at a carnival, or like an immense crowd of pilgrims stopping for the night. There was singing and there was a little dancing—even drinking though not much of this, for a drunk would pay with his life for the pleasure. And gradually, the noises died and the fires disappeared by twos and threes. The silence of nature in the night, as heavy as the din of day, enveloped the army, and to the east and south, Maclovio with Heraclio's troop and his own hundred made ready for a frontal assault. While to the west and south, Celestino Gámez took a thousand infantry over the hills to get at the gun emplacements. And all the while, the General Villa slept.

Near midnight, Maclovio Herrera gave the familiar, "'Hora, muchachos!" The assault was on.

The Division of the North withdrew on the following morning. During the night, it had taken the perimeter completely around the city, but it was impossible to hold these positions, exposed as they were to the fire from the fortress. Villa must attack, but the bulk of his ammunition was found to be defective. And he cursed the Saxon businessman—honorable man of profit—who had taken the gold Mexicans had bought with their lives, and in return had given them cartridges filled with white dust.

And so he withdrew toward the south, then later to the west, men, women, and children climbing steadily into the mountains. Maclovio Herrera and his force fell gradually behind and veered away to lead the pursuing army from the main force. For the General Mercado, who had lost ten men for every rebel killed during the night, believed somehow that he had won a brilliant battle, and sent word to México that Villa was in disorganized flight, and dispatched two thousand men along the railroad to slay rebels as they fled.

Maclovio teased and ran, and led the two thousand Federals, crying joyfully of their victory, out into the desert. Then in a gigantic arc, he sprinted his five hundred horse and struck the column at its flank, broke through, then waited for the enemy to close ranks and struck again, up at the forward end this time. Now he did not hesitate, and quickly hit the center once again, but by now the Federals were in full flight, and the rebels killed on the run until they saw the walls of the city.

In the mountains to the west, near the Haros River, the army came together once again. And there all ammunition was collected and examined, and eight hundred men filled their bandoleers. With the General Villa at their head, they moved toward the railroad between Chihuahua and the border. Day and night, they moved, and nowhere, as they traveled north, did they see signs of Fierro. The railroad was intact. And then, less than a hundred kilometers from Ciudad Juárez, they were met by the red-cheeked colonel who would tomorrow be a brigadier.

Villa was angry that his orders had not been carried out, and in a moment would give the order that Fierro be executed. But he would hear what the man had to say.

"Everything is wired, my chief," said Fierro. "In one moment we can destroy you the thirty kilometers you asked for; we but wait for a train, for why expend good explosives without doing a little killing, no?"

"And it is impossible for a train to get through?" asked Villa.

"Absolutely," said Fierro. "Also, we have captured the station up ahead and the marconigraphist has died so one of my boys is operating his instrument. A train is coming through this afternoon for Chihuahua—now that you have been defeated and Mercado has sent messages in all directions that he has crushed you. It was my idea to blow up a car or two, and since there is a Y at this station, turn the engine around and fix it so that it will blow up in the center of Ciudad Juárez."

But Villa was now grinning. "Blow up the track," he said, "beyond the Y, blow it up and then we shall see. I have myself an idea, and if we pull it off, I shall call you General, my friend."

The railroad was destroyed a mile south of the station. The telegraph line to the south was also destroyed, and the rebels waited for the train from Juárez.

Since the line had been cleared of the enemy, the supply train had but a hundred men to guard it. Not a shot was fired, as the guard climbed down to begin the laborious work of repairing the rail. It was immediately surrounded by the rebel force. Given the choice of walking on to Chihuahua or becoming rebels, the Federals quickly changed sides, since they were conscripts anyway. All but the Lieutenant. He was shot in the head by Rodolfo Fierro as he handed over his arms.

And the engine was turned around and placed at the other end of the train. Villa went to the station house and dictated a message to the commandant of the garrison at Ciudad Juárez, clearing the train for entrance into the city. He was sending reinforcements, he telegraphed, and he signed the message simply, "Mercado." The supplies on the train were loaded on his horses and sent to Tomás Urbina at the bivouac, with word that the people should move north toward Juárez.

After dark, Villa rode in the engine with Rodolfo Fierro. In the box cars, his eight hundred men sang gay songs, and the train moved across the desert, an iron horse due in Ciudad Juárez at midnight.

In Juárez, four thousand Federals celebrated the victory of the government at Chihuahua. There seemed nothing to fear for the forces of Huerta. Obregón was hopelessly stalled in Sonora and the offensive that Venustiano Carranza had promised was killed with the destruction of Villa's forces. In the Municipal Palace, General Noriega had to dinner and a later reception members of the Terrazas family—land and cattle barons of the north—representatives of the American businessmen who would now be friendly to the Huerta government which was an evil but now, since Chihuahua, the strong element and thus right.

The border was open to tourists now that it was safe, and Americans streamed along the main streets, into the cantinas— men with their wives, partaking of the special thrill of revel where men had died, where civil strife was imminent but not tonight. Men alone, equally stimulated by a feel of adventure from a danger that could not possibly be actual now. And women, driven by the intuition which tells them where men need women, where they could sell the only thing they had left, joined their duskier sisters in the street and on the softness of a grassy plaza, against a wall in an alley, and occasionally in a dimly lighted room practiced their trade. To lay with a gringa was somehow a great desire to the dark sons of Cuauhtémoc, such as it was to the fair-haired Saxons of the north to mount a hot tamale señoreeter.

They played in the night and they reveled and had joy, while quietly, the train from the south coasted into the railroad station. Villa waved an arm and a crew ran from the cars and overpowered the men who had been sent to meet it. Boldly, Villa moved his men to the barracks where half the garrison slept at this hour. The rebels burst upon them, screaming, "Viva Villa!" and the Federals woke to the nightmare of big-hatted, dirty, bandoleered mountain men, with carbines firing, and those of them who did not die ran into the night in their night clothes.

In the cabarets, the firing was heard and caused some alarm, but in the Municipal Palace, the General Noriega smiled and said, "A few drunken rebels creating a nuisance—the boys will round them up," and bade the music to continue.

Of a sudden the fire became intense, for the Villistas had encountered a stronghold of a hundred men who were truly for the government and were willing to fight. These were destroyed and the rebels moved toward the International Bridge, where hordes of men, women, and Federal officers stampeded into the safety of El Paso.

In isolated areas, the government resisted, but it now had no leaders and in the end abandoned the fight. The rebels broke into the palace where the waltzes had been stepped off a few minutes ago and they found it empty. Noriega and his staff had somehow made it across the Bravo in the early morning light, while on the other side of town, two thousand regulars had run pell-mell into the desert to save themselves. Some of these but partly clad would die from exposure; others would join Villa's army.

Before the fight ended, riders were sent to Urbina, and through that first day, the people came into Juárez by the hundreds, as did the demolition team Villa had left behind his troop trail to destroy rail.

VI

IN A SMALL ROOM in the cellar of the customs house, Villa slept on a field cot, while Celestino Gámez, Maclovio, Fierro, and Calixto Contreras talked quietly. Heraclio served as a personal guard while the General slept, although it would be impossible for a single man to break into the room.

The General had his back to them and he opened his eyes as they spoke, listening to their conversation, already testing for an indication of their disloyalty. But they talked of other things—of

281

horses; and Rodolfo Fierro talked of his days as a railroad man, when he had been a peaceful, home-loving paterfamilias. He was uneducated but of the upper middle class because he earned a high salary. He wore now, as he had then, a civilian jacket, and he had carried his lunch in a pail, saluting his neighbors on his way to work, keeping from them a thing he did not know himself —that he was an insensate killer, a sadist, and a psychopath.

And these were things felt by the men around him as he spoke quietly of his peaceful days, sensed by these men who were killers and fearless even of him. In their minds they marveled at such a man as he spoke nostalgically of his little house, his good wife, and, quite sincerely, of his children, who were precocious as all parents' children are.

Villa, who was only a paranoid, smiled that he, too, could not understand this man. But how invaluable he had been already— how invaluable he would be. To think that only yesterday he almost had him shot. The other three seemed indifferent as Rodolfo Fierro talked, but in Heraclio, Villa sensed a hatred, controlled, but a hatred nevertheless—and a wariness.

"Brigadier," said Villa, and only Rodolfo Fierro knew he was being addressed.

"Mi general."

"You will precede us this night. Go over the mountains, and for your sake do not get yourself lost. Somewhere between here and where we took that train yesterday, you will send a scout down to the railroad and he will find the General Mercado coming to attack us. Proceed a good distance behind him and destroy rail back toward Chihuahua. Continue as far as you can safely, then return here again through the mountains, for we might fail, and prepare to help my compadre Urbina defend this city. If that is not necessary, begin repairing the line for our offensive south."

"As you say, my General," said Fierro. And he sat as he was, waiting for Villa to resume. "Well, get to it, man!" said the General, not in anger. "Somehow, get your people on horseback, for you go twice the distance we will."

Fierro moved out, and Heraclio said, "It is for certain that the Federals come?"

Gámez and Maclovio laughed. "What a boy," said Villa. "But of course they will come. It is imperative that they should regain

282

Juárez. And they estimate our strength at under a thousand men, and they must crush us, for today, our army is for the first time receiving international acclaim. People who have called me a bandit are today saying I am a brilliant general, and Victoriano Huerta is calling Mercado an imbecile, an incompetent, and a few other things. He cannot waste the time to call Noriega anything because he is safe in Texas. I feel he will send half his force, Mercado will, perhaps a few more in an effort to annihilate us, but we shall surprise him."

"We cannot wait, my General?" asked Celestino Gámez, not unlike Heraclio. "We cannot entrench ourselves and wait for them to come?"

"We do not do things in that way," said Villa, "for they would not fight and wait for more troops and then for more troops. They would starve us and in the end defeat us. Now is the time for us to strike, not only because we will surprise them, but because even the North American politicians and the businessmen are watching us. They have their little doubts as to which side they should help. And so, to make up their minds, we shall overrun this army which would eat us, and roll into Chihuahua. Then they will come to me with arms and ammunition in bunches. They will sell me anything I need to get to México."

"How far are they?" asked Heraclio, and almost added, "If they are really coming?"

"Somewhere between here and there—where we started yesterday," said Villa. "That is why I had Rodolfo's boys place those bombs along the way. They are slowed now, repairing rail, but they think they have much time. We will engage the enemy wherever we meet, be it day or night."

Villa chuckled. "The surprise," he said, "is that they are being attacked. We shall go," he said, "four thousand of us—half cavalry."

A noise outside the room stopped their talk. Heraclio moved to the door, gun in hand. He spoke inaudibly to someone, then opened the door and two soldiers entered, leading, half dragging a young girl between them.

One spoke out. "Here is the diversion you asked for, my General. My lieutenant said we were to bring you this one—young

283

she is, but mighty skinny. My feeling was to bring you something with a little meat but my lieutenant . . ."

"Let us see," said Villa, curious, although he knew he would send her away. He had no desire for this now. Earlier, a troupe of performers had been brought into a corral, she among them, and after he had ordered their release, he decided he wanted her but at that time he had no idea that he would march tonight. "Let us see her," he said again, and sat up on his cot.

She was pushed forward and a lamp was lighted. Disheveled and very Indian, she looked upon them. She was clean, everything about her seemed clean, and Villa laughed. "What are you called?" he asked, and she did not answer. Her fear was well hidden and she gazed upon them with haughtiness. Villa's features were serious. "I asked a question, little girl—and by the way, how many years have you?"

She wore Tehuana dress, odd for this far north, but understandable because she was an entertainer. She decided she must speak. "I have fifteen years," she said.

Villa waited, but she was again quiet, and he said, "And your name?"

"Xóchitl," she answered. "Xóchitl Salamanca."

Villa laughed once more, and he gazed upon her in good humor. "Now, that is better," he said, and since he knew she had been taken from a circus, he was curious and asked, "Tell me, what do you in the circo?"

She was thin, but her blouse was filled in front, and she stood now proudly, her fear gone with the knowledge that she was a woman in a roomful of men, and although she must submit to a thing she had no knowledge of, her intuition told her she was superior because she was wanted. And somehow she knew that any one of these strong men could become undignified, could reveal himself through her. She smiled, barely, and gained strength, and spoke. "I worked on the wire. I did many things, but mainly I worked on the wire."

"Well," said Villa, and he scratched his head. "Just what is that of the wire? We are mountain people here and do not know of the sophistications of the city. Do you know, Celestino, or you, Maclovio, what it means to work on this wire?"

"No, mi general," answered the men, also perplexed.

284

And the girl actually laughed aloud. Then she became extremely animated as she explained, her hands moved gracefully as she gestured to give emphasis to her words. "There is a wire," she said, "a strong, thin wire stretched between two poles a few meters apart and ten meters in the air. I walked on the wire with a bamboo pole for balance like this," she picked a carbine from against the wall to demonstrate. Heraclio took a step quickly and snatched the gun out of her hands. She was startled, and looked at Villa in time to see the tenseness leave his face, and she understood, and continued as if nothing had occurred. "Anyway, I walked on the wire and I performed tricks like throwing my feet over my head and regaining my footing on the wire. Things like that."

"But what a girl!" exclaimed Villa, wanting to disbelieve. "And what if you had fallen?"

She shrugged her shoulders and went on, "And sometimes my father joined me and I would climb atop his head and he walked to and fro on the wire, back and forth. We are acrobats, also, and oh, we do many things."

The men were quiet now. That of being atop her father's head made them not believe any of it, and, to tease, Villa said, "You know what will happen to you now, little girl who walks on wires?"

"I have but an idea," she said, and she added with no evidence of concern, "I knew when I was sequestered that my fate would not be a good one. I am not afraid of death, you know," she said matter-of-factly, "but, no matter, I know I am not to die."

"And how do you know that?"

"Because I am a woman and am worth more to you alive." She shrugged again and wondered then, although she did not know what it would be to be mounted by a man, whether the others would remain in the room while the General took her. And suddenly she was frightened. Her eyes darted from one to the other, stolid, expressionless faces, except for Villa's, which displayed a sly but unmistakable mirth. The idea which had brought her terror was that they might all mean to use her, one after the other, and why, in a city with many women, would they want to do that? She looked toward the men who had brought her here, hoping that perhaps they might decide to take her with them, but they were detached, she saw, not really a part of the others, remaining in the room only because they had not been dismissed. She saw this at a glance, then her eyes were on Heraclio, the youth who had so harshly taken the carbine from her, afraid that she might shoot someone, and his face as he stared in return was also inscrutable, and his eyes seemed to be looking beyond her.

Villa watched and enjoyed her changing emotions, first the fright, and soon now the shock, and then, of course, would come the tears which would result from resignation. Then he would give her freedom, but he must enjoy himself, for he had a minute to spare. But as he watched, she regained her proud stance, and her own expression became as theirs, devoid of meaning, devoid of attitude. He was amused, still, and he thought, Goddamned Indians! Who would have thought this little piece would show her heritage like this? He had known she would break down, but she did not, and pleased him. So, it was over and she would be delivered safely to her people, who were now across the Bravo.

But she spoke, almost arrogantly, and moved her head so her full hair swirled on her shoulders. "If I must be raped," she said, scarcely aware of what the word meant, "I would much rather that it be done by your young soldier here," and she moved and grasped Heraclio's arm with both hands. "He is so pretty—with him it would not be near bad."

Now, without her knowledge, she was in danger for the first time. And contrary to her reasoning, she was quite near death, for she had startled the General Villa first by her speech, and then had struck deeply at the vanity of the man by suggesting he would be repulsive. And to lend credence to his sudden thought, Villa raised himself slightly and broke wind, a prolonged, high-pitched squeak emitted, and he said in anger:

"You think, then, that another man could please you more than I?"

She sensed her error then, but she was committed, and said saucily, "I suppose that is what I meant, although I have no way of knowing whether it is a pleasure to be violated by anyone. It seems only that with this good-looking boy it might not be as difficult."

And Villa turned his glance to Heraclio, who had disengaged

his arm. "And you too, my warrior—do you believe you are a bet-ter man than Pancho Villa?"

Heraclio was suddenly tired. He wanted no part of this, had been disinterested, in fact, except to see that the girl did not sud-denly go mad and attempt to harm the General. Now he was sud-denly in the center of an unpleasant situation. He said, looking full into Villa's face, "I follow you, don Pancho. I could not fol-low anyone who is a lesser man than I am."

Villa chuckled, satisfied, and said, "You hear that, little girl, from his own lips an admission that I am the man? So accept the fact and become my woman for a while."

She said, "So be it. But man or not, I would much rather he took me."

Villa was on his feet, his face livid. In his rage he thought sud-denly that she had conspired with Heraclio. "You are against me!" he shouted, pushing her aside as he moved toward Heraclio. "Where have you spoken to her before this?"

"I have never seen her before she entered this room," said Heraclio. "And I wish I had never seen her. What is she to me that you should castigate me so, my General?" This is a fantasy, he thought, and in a minute he might be forced to defend himself— and because of nothing, for although he would die for this man he loved, he would not die like this. Not for this farce and without resisting. He was deeply disturbed, aside from his immediate con-cern, that the General could be like this. It was a flaw he could not deny and could not begin to understand. It had happened be-fore this that he had seen men led out to face a firing squad be-cause the General had a tantrum such as this one. No, he could never understand it, but Villa was a man, despite this, and because he was a man and because he loved him, Heraclio accepted him. For Heraclio, too, was a man and a man must take his friends with and for their weaknesses as well as their goodness and manliness.

Villa changed suddenly and almost whined as he said, throwing an arm about Heraclio's shoulders, "Tell me the truth, boy. You saw her first somewhere and made your arrangements—so she is yours, for you saw her first." And whereas the General had been unarmed as he slept, Heraclio noticed now that he held a gun in his free hand, his arm hanging loosely along his thigh.

He felt a chill along his arms and legs because he had been so careless as to not see Villa take up the gun as he left the cot. He felt the General's body alongside his, pressing against his own sidearm, and he eased himself away, casually, as if he had not noticed, and said, "I tell you again, my General, I do not know the girl. Put down the gun, there is no need for it."

Villa laughed aloud, his mood changing once again. His face transformed itself to show mock guilt. "But look at this," he said, shaking his head from side to side. "How did this fusil get into my hand just like that?" He turned away and said, "Take her, Heraclio, and do it right for the both of us."

The moment of danger was past, and Heraclio felt a quiet rage. He looked at the girl and wished to knock her down, for she had caused the thing, and then he spoke. "I do not feel that I insult you, my General," he said, "by refusing a thing you wanted, for I know you did not really want her. Send her away as you had planned all along."

Villa was amused once again. This was the impulsive Heraclio talking, and he sometimes enjoyed seeing the boy behave like a boy. A moment ago, in his anger, he did not forget for an instant that Heraclio was not a boy and was dangerous. At this moment, he was a boy and indignant, and the General found it humorous.

"Well," said Heraclio, "I do not want her. Unless, of course, you are ordering me. But I have no desire whatever for the Chichimeca and if it is an order, can a general order a penis to become rigid?"

"I am not a Chichimeca!" said Xóchitl angrily, not really hearing the end of Heraclio's statement. "I am a Maya from Tehuantepec!"

"Shut your mouth!" Heraclio very nearly screamed. Christ! I am doing it too, he thought, and quietly said to Villa, "Send her away, my General. I truly do not want her."

"What a boy," said Villa, and turned to the men who had brought her. "Get yourselves away from here. The Captain shall escort the lady." He then turned to Maclovio and Celestino. "But what do you think of the boy?"

The two men laughed and Celestino looked at Heraclio with sincere affection, although a minute ago he was prepared to shoot him down if he made a move against Villa. "The truth of the matter, my General," he said although he yet looked at Heraclio, "is that the infant, here, cannot carry out the order. He is too sensitive, too young to be able to take a slip of a girl who quite obviously is a virgin. Give me the duty to perform, my General, and I will take care of the matter in quick time."

Heraclio looked at all three and their laughter was suddenly a din to him. He grasped her shoulder strongly and pushed her forward. They went through the door that led into an alley. And Villa called to him as he was disappearing, "Remember, my warrior. You have but an hour to tame that mare." And the laughter came out into the night.

Outside, he walked ahead of her, in quick, long strides. She stumbled frequently as he increased his pace, but retained her footing. To Heraclio, everything since she came into the room was ludicrous. He moved along, purposely not looking back so that she could get away. His anger was intensified because she was struggling to match his pace and he marveled at her stupidity. She said, "Wait for me, please! I cannot move as fast as you do."

They were on a lighted street now, and he suddenly knew he would take her to a room. Yet, he felt no attraction, but she had caused him embarrassment and discomfort—even fear. For that, she must be made to pay. He slackened his pace and took her arm as they approached a hotel.

The clerk was fair-skinned and light-haired. He averted his eyes as he spoke, for they were hazel, and he enunciated his Castilian like a Mexican. He was fearful lest he be taken for a Spaniard.

"There are no rooms to be had," he said. "Absolutely every room has been taken, and I perform no function here, for no one bothers to register and no one pays. But my employer said I must remain or else when the peace comes I will not have my job."

"You will get me a room at once," said Heraclio.

"Perhaps an occupant will share a room with you," said the clerk. "Or find a spot in the lobby, here. Everyone else seems to be sleeping in it."

Heraclio grasped his throat with one hand. "You will come around from behind there and bring that key you have which opens every door!" He released him, and the clerk was quickly at his side. He scurried forward, Heraclio and Xóchitl following. He stopped at the first door, but Heraclio pushed him forward, to the end of the hall on the first floor. French windows opened from the hallways into the patio and Heraclio said, "This one," pointing to the corner room.

Loud noise came from within the room, and the clerk, after knocking a few times, inserted a passkey and pushed the door open. A soldier appeared immediately and pushed him in the face. "Now just what the Goddamn hell are you doing, man?" he asked. Inside, there was a sudden silence.

"Get those people out of there. Quick," said Heraclio.

The other looked at him and laughed. "Boys," he said to his companions. "Here is one who wants to die although he is on our side." In the dimly lighted hallway, he could see only the twin bandoleers across Heraclio's chest, and now Heraclio moved, and the golden uniform was visible as were the epaulets, and the soldier said, "Caramba, mi coronel! I did not know you were an officer and one of those Dorados!" Once again he called into the room, "Let us find other quarters, boys. There is a general or a colonel or something here who will use our room. With your permission," he said to Heraclio, and he went into the room again. They came out then, two men and three partly unclad women, carrying their clothes, and the first soldier followed carrying bottles.

Heraclio took one from him as he was passing. "Here, wait," he said. "I shall pay you for it."

"No need," answered the soldier, and his humor was refreshing to Heraclio. "It is all free anyway. Everything is free in this town, have you not learned?" And he looked meaningfully at Xóchitl. "Tequila, women, even the room is free." He paused for a moment. "You know, my Captain," he said, and Heraclio smiled that he had known all along his rank, "I have never stayed in a hotel in my life until tonight. In fact, I have never even seen one."

Heraclio's anger was completely dissipated. He felt more than a little guilty that he had forced them out, but the man added, "We were finished with it anyway—the room, that is. You know, a man is only so strong and no more than that."

The clerk, who had disappeared, came running up with clean linen. "In a moment, my General, and you shall have a fresh bed."

Heraclio drank from the bottle and did not answer. Quickly the man was finished and was gone. Heraclio was already removing his clothing. "Well," he said to the girl.

She stood in the center of the room, and she was afraid. She did not attempt to disguise it now. It was not a fear like terror, but a deep quiet fear.

"Come here," he said almost kindly. Although he had been angry, he now felt almost sorry for her. She was a child and a woman, both deserving of compassion. He took her hand and sat her next to him. And now he looked at her and was suddenly reminded of Marcelina. Rare that they should be so much alike, although this one—this Xóchitl—was more beautiful because she was here. And he had a sudden yearning for his wife, for this was not unlike his wedding night.

"You were very stern and harsh with the clerk," she said, and almost giggled in her nervousness.

"I was not myself," he answered.

"I knew you were not like that."

"How did you know?"

"Because I am Indian," she said. "My mother has told me about it. Indians know things when other people do not."

He was intrigued by her, and he had the wild thought that he would merely hold her to him for a while, and then release her, while yet unharmed. And he would tell her so, but he knew that was not true.

"You know I am afraid?" she asked.

"I know. But do not feel that way. There is nothing to be afraid of." Again he thought that he would not cohabit with her.

She said, "How would you know that? You have obviously never had this done to you."

He had no answer. Instead, he asked, "Would you like me to turn the light out while you disrobe?"

"No, no," she said quickly. "I know you have little time and I shall be but a minute. I hold no anger toward you, after all, I chose you—in fact, I forced you, I suppose. I am afraid, and I am embarrassed, and I mean you ill will by this, but I must disrobe before your eyes, in the light, for I want that you should see that which you will violate."

She stood up and moved away, and somehow she caused him to be embarrassed, and he quickly stepped out of his trousers and slipped into bed before she could turn around. She kicked her huaraches off and undid her full skirt so it fell to the floor. The blouse came off then, and the chemise, and finally her full drawers. The undergarments seemed startlingly white in contrast with her brown skin. And she stood, despite her fear, as proudly as she had stood up to Villa.

"Look at me, you, what-is-your-name-you. Look well at what you ravish," she said.

And as she had brought on his embarrassment a moment ago, her words now freed him from it, and he spoke easily. "I am called Heraclio Inés," he said.

"Heraclio," she said. "That is a pretty name, Heraclio." Her voice lost its quality, quavered.

"Come here," he said, "or surely you shall catch pneumonia and end up a phthisic."

Like a small child, she said, "Extinguish the light now, please. I wanted you to see me and I worked on my courage, but it has left me. Turn it off and I will come." She seemed lost and pathetically small. Heraclio placed the palm of his hand against the opening of the chimney, and the lamp went out slowly. But he had seen her, and though he knew that he would never see her again after this night, he would never forget the sight of her.

She was alongside him, and he placed his hand on her belly, above the pubis. She was rigidly tense, her arms up close on her breast, her hands formed into tight little fists were under her chin. He slipped his arm under her head and turned her toward him, then ran a hand along her back. He stroked her from her head down to her buttocks and the outer thigh.

He took her arm and gently tried to pull it free from her body, but she held it fast, and so instead he kissed her. Her face was lifeless under his and slowly he opened her mouth, and now she struggled, for she could not breathe. What crazy thing is this, she thought, a man's tongue in my mouth? And she pushed at his head with both hands, but now she had no thoughts as she was near panic until suddenly her lack of air made her inhale deeply through her nostrils, and she thought she did not even remember she had a nose and yet she held his head in her hands, but she was relaxed and his own hand went in under her arm and clasped her breast so she felt something within her like an unuttered gasp she had never known existed. She put her arms around his neck because she did not know what to do with them and now he spoke: "Beautiful Xóchitl—beautiful, beautiful," the one word over and over again seemed delicious to her ear and she wished he would kiss her again but did not know she wanted him to kiss her, did not know anything really and it was only because in her confusion she moved her face near his, that she suddenly opened her mouth to him and now his knee came against her legs slowly; gradually she allowed it to part them until she was over the upper part of his leg as if astride an animal and he moved the leg slowly back and forth rubbing softly against her and now she felt his own body, hard against her belly and whimpered this time with fear that so huge a thing should enter her. She was now terrified but had no will, no control over her body.

And Heraclio was with his wife. In the darkness, the slight body in his arms was Marcelina, and he tightly closed his eyes to will it so, but his hand caressing her breast made him return for a moment, for this breast was large and taut—like Marcelina's, only now that she was big with child but the child was born by now, he thought crazily, and they are small again and he felt a rush of love for his wife and he himself now uttered a cry and forgot Marcelina completely as he turned over and covered Xóchitl's body with his own.

"No one told me that to be raped would be that pleasant," she said.

"You were not raped, idiot," said Heraclio, but she did not hear him, marveling still at the feelings she had just experienced.

"Always," she continued, "it was a thing to be feared—to be taken by a man by force. Always it was the most terrible thing that could happen to a woman. It is not that at all!"

Heraclio wished suddenly that he had not done the act. "I am sorry, Xóchitl. I am truly sorry I took you."

She touched his face. "Oh, do not say that, my guapo. I am not sorry. I am sorry only that I have lost my family—that I shall never again see my mother and father."

Guilt feelings about these things were entirely new to Heraclio. He turned to her in anger. "Why did you not run, for God's sake?"

"Run?"

"On our way here I purposely gave you an opportunity—but

no, stupid as you are, you actually ran after me so that I could do this thing to you."

She came up on her elbows and looked into his face. Then she laughed. "No matter, Heraclio," she said. "You wish to blame me for what you did? Very well, I accept the blame. I raped you, yes?"

He was a fool, he knew, and he felt more of a fool as he said, "You are as guilty as I am, you know, for I gave you a chance for freedom."

She threw an arm across his chest and placed her face alongside his, speaking into his ear, almost as if she knew how to make love to a man. "Take the frown from your forehead, big, stern Heraclio. It is you who do not think. If I had run from you in the darkness, how far would I go before another dirty old man like your general would take me? Hey? Answer me that. It was just as I told that filthy man—I feel safer with you—after all, it is not every woman who can select her ravisher."

"I wish you would stop saying that!" He was yet angry. But what she had said was true, and he thought about that. And he thought how at this very moment she could very well have been on another man's bed or on the hard ground somewhere in the darkness with a group of drunken men taking their turn at her, and he felt a fear somewhere within him that such a thing had almost happened and then he wondered that he could feel so strongly about this when he had never been disturbed by the sight of such things. Then he laughed at himself because he had spoken harshly to her, but his words had not been harsh. Now he turned and held her against him. He talked, their faces almost touching, and he said:

"I did want to blame you, I suppose. And it was my doing— mine only. But I can say that I should not be blamed because within a few hours I will be in battle and I may die. I can say, 'It is only fitting that a man should have a woman before he dies.' But of course I will not die."

She was silent and her eyes were wide, and he was alarmed that she again showed terror. She said, sensing his concern, "It is not what you think. Truly, I could never be afraid of you again. Now I fear for your life."

"You should not bother yourself with such things," he said. "If you can forgive me, then try to forget what happened."

"How can I forget such a thing?"

"In time, as you grow older, you can forget many things. Come," he said, springing out of the bed. "Dress yourself and I will take you to the bridge so that you can go join your people."

"No!" She surprised him with the vehemence with which she uttered the word. "I go where you go now. I wish to be with you, for I belong to you—and, too, I cannot go to my people to face my father, for I am no longer virtuous."

"It is not necessary that they know."

"But I know, do you not see?"

She was right, but it could not be that she should follow him. She must go back and she must tell her father what had happened. Perhaps he would forgive her; after all, it had not been her fault. "You cannot go with me," he said. "I am fighting a war; it is impossible."

She said, "I can come with you. I have heard of soldaderas who follow the army. They take even their children along—I can do that far more easily because I do not have a child."

"There are many who do that, it is true," said Heraclio. "But I am not allowed women in the campaign. But come quickly. I do not have much time."

She dressed as she spoke. "It was destined to be, Heraclio. Yesterday I was but a child, waiting to cross the river to go with my parents to New York and then to Europe. There I was to begin my formal training on the trapeze. That is something—the trapeze. I was to be the last generation of Salamancas to fly, for I have no brothers. But it was not to be, you see. One more evening, the impresario told my father—one night performance, even, for he did not have an act which could replace us and because my father believes in the tradition of the entertainer, we remained and this happened. You understand how the destiny works. All this was so that the Salamanca name should die as a circus family. It simply had to be this way."

They were dressed and he grasped her shoulders strongly. "Listen to me," he said. "This is nonsense, all of it. You are a young girl and you have a long life to live. Go after it—you shall someday see that I am right."

She shook her head sadly. "No, my buck. I do not have a long life to live. Tonight, here with you, I received the knowledge that

I will not live long. What time I yet have remaining I wish to spend with you." Then she seemed gay once again. "Find me a place where I can wait for you. A place where these pigs cannot get to me—where I can be safe until they learn that I am your woman."

He took her arm. "I am taking you to the bridge and am sending you across the border. Go home where you belong." But he was sad that she had sensed her death. If she had this premonition, it would, of course, come true.

It was not until four days later that the Division of the North met the Federals barely eighty kilometers south of Juárez. The railroad men of Fierro had carried out their task of destroying rail too well, demolishing trestles, setting fire to ties. Now they repaired the railway in the direction of the enemy, even as the enemy did the same toward them. And by this time, the survivors who had fled Juárez had joined the Federal force, bringing its number to over seven thousand.

On the morning of the clash, the Federal army broke its fast leisurely, ten troop trains lay stalled for another few hours. And suddenly the quiet of the morning was disturbed by a succession of detonations to their rear, muffled but audible nevertheless. A feeling of alarm ran through the General Staff. It was impossible that there should be firing to the south—and yet, the sound was unmistakable. It must be investigated and the commander was at the point of giving the order for a scouting party when a junior officer ran into the car.

He had ridden hard a distance of over two kilometers, from where the labor details were at work on the railroad.

"Your permission, my General," he said. "A force has appeared out of the desert to the north and is at this moment preparing to attack us."

"It cannot be too large a force," said the General Argumedo.

"I believe it is large," said the junior officer.

"How large?" asked Argumedo. He was incredulous yet calm.

"It is difficult to say. At first we believed it to be but a dust storm—but then, of course, we recognized it for what it was. It seems that there are three forces perhaps ten thousand meters distant when I left."

296

"Guerrilla tactics," said Argumedo. "He is impetuous, that Villa—three forces of perhaps two hundred and fifty men each," he waved an arm to an aide and the man hurried out of the car. To another the General said, "Send a detail to scout our rear. See what is going on back there." Strains from the bugler came into the car and shouts and orders were heard from without. The brigades were being assembled.

"We shall finally teach him a lesson, this bandit," said Argumedo. "Perhaps he believes he is attacking a stronghold of stragglers—refugees from Juárez. What a surprise when he finds seven thousand well-trained troops!" He laughed with pleasure. "This shall be the end of him," he said.

Aside from his personal aides, only his chief of artillery remained with him, waiting for orders. "Leave the cannon on the flatcars," said Argumedo. "We shall only have to load them again —a nuisance when surely we will not need them." He dispatched an aide to alert the horse troop. When he cut the attacking force into shreds, his horse would chase the remnants out into the desert. He was gleeful, for he had been a general for don Porfirio and now for Huerta, and as yet he had never won a battle. Small as this engagement would be, he would kill or capture Villa; his future was bright.

His mount was brought to him and he mounted, then walked his animal slowly toward the front.

At the moment, the labor battalions were arriving, running pell-mell, spent from their flight back to camp. He could not help but smile at their fright before he scanned the horizon. Slowly his pleasure changed to alarm. There were three distinct forces, becoming more separated as he watched. He realized his error immediately. Here was not a guerrilla force, but an army. And he was vulnerable on the plain. He turned to the artilleryman. "Quickly, make the guns operable and let them taste shrapnel. Do not wait for my word!" He spoke to another officer. "Send riders quickly to the scouting force. I must know what activity is behind me!"

His army was now in a semicircle, having deployed as the enemy maneuvered. For perhaps ten minutes there was silence, except for the activity around the flatcars as the gun crews worked hurriedly to get their guns into position.

And suddenly, Villa attacked on three sides, his cavalry coming in from the flanks and Tomás Urbina's infantry in a frontal assault. The return fire was brutal and the cavalry was repulsed, but Urbina, with Villa alongside him, although bogged down, continued the attack while the cavalry regrouped.

Now Argumedo's artillery was moved up and employed against Urbina, cutting gaping holes in the line. But the second charge of the horsemen penetrated the line. A few jinetes broke through and they lassoed each a small fieldpiece, dragging it away into the desert.

A rider came to General Argumedo, saluted despite his skittering nervous mount. "The railroad behind us has been destroyed, my General! The bandits were away before we arrived!"

There was no retreat. And Urbina's men, with wild screams, charged all along the line. The cavalry was now prepared to charge again, and Argumedo gave the order to his staff. With five hundred of his cavalry, he deserted the field and moved south.

The Division of the North swept the desert, and when finally they moved south, it was now a force of nine thousand men. Federals by the hundreds took up the cry, "Viva Villa!"

In the city of Chihuahua, the General Mercado raged, but he did not direct his rantings at Argumedo. His frustration was that he had no trains with which to take his troops south and he must defend the city with three thousand troops, begin a forced march to Torreón, or surrender to Villa. And oddly, Argumedo would now stand and fight, arguing that they could hold the city until reinforcements could come from Torreón. A large force would then be sent to retake Juárez and Villa would be back in the hills in the same situation he had been these past months.

The argument was sound, but Mercado would have no part of it, and he was the ranking officer. In the end he took his army and with loyal civilians—men, women, and children—set out across the desert in a direct line to Ojinaga, a border town across the river from Presidio, Texas. It was the nearest haven, but to be reached only after a brutal march.

Villa came into Chihuahua and ignored the fleeing army. He knew the desert well—it would do his killing for him. He arrested Spaniards and enemies of the people, and because he was thinking of Mercado he did not execute, but sent these people south, along the railroad into the desert to make their way to Torreón, the nearest Federal stronghold, almost seven hundred kilometers away. The road south through Camargo and Jiménez was dotted by crosses marking the graves of children who perished in the heat, and occasionally by the bones of a human, gnawed clean by animals, and in one day bleached by the sun.

VII

In Chihuahua, in the western part of the city and south, where the artisans lived, Xóchitl Salamanca, now calling herself Inés, although only for a lark, for she believed in the fact that people should know that she was with a man for love, swept her one room and small kitchen, waiting for her captain.

She had come on the first train from Juárez, after Chihuahua had been secured, dressed as a boy and riding on a baggage rack because there was no space allotted to women soldiers. She was not disturbed because no one really looked closely at a sleeping boy among other sleeping children. It was cold and she had been given a mackinaw by an old woman who had lost her family, and she covered that which would divulge her identity as a woman with the heavy, loose garment. Once in Chihuahua, she gathered with other familyless youngsters around a fire, and eventually they were fed by women who were mothers and had a feeling for orphans. Then, satisfied, she went to the Municipal Palace to wait. She reasoned that, since she had met him in Villa's presence, there she would find Heraclio.

But Heraclio was not in Chihuahua, having gone to Ojinaga with the forces of Pánfilo Natera. These were Zacatecas people, and he accompanied Antonio Rivera and the charro from Guadalupe. And so in this way she lived for the time he should return, grubbing for meals, sleeping in the elements among the many dispossessed, happy all the while because soon he would return.

She learned where those who followed him were living, and made friends with one called Mauro—slow-witted but devoted to his captain. He, too, waited—and now it was not as difficult for her to get food.

He came then, haggard, with a few days' beard, exhausted from a forced march through the desert. He did not speak to her and he was angry, she knew. For a time he watched his men as they groomed his mount, then he moved to the headquarters and she waited outside in the sun. When he came out, he still did not say a word for he was yet angry, and would not castigate her before his men. She took his arm, completely unconcerned about his anger, and for a time they walked. Without knowing it they were in the section where men and women wove baskets and tapestries, and where father and son painted on canvas. And there they found a room for housekeeping and Heraclio's anger had dissipated, for it had been born of guilt, and he had by now embraced the rationale that he had done what he could for her, had made right whatever wrong he had perpetrated when he took Xóchitl to the International Bridge. Now she had, contrary to his wishes, contrary to his advice, followed him . . . well, how could he be blamed? In fact, he felt the pleasure common to man when he is wanted. There, where his anger left him, away from the noise and activity of the army, they looked for a room where they might live. And he brought to her a small, dark, monkey-faced young man who was Antonio Rivera.

"This is my most intimate," he said. "A brave man and a good man. He can dominate anything on this earth except a horse. With a horse he is as a child."

She gave her hand to the stranger and said, "Xóchitl Salamanca, to serve you," not adding the Inés for fear he would take offense since he must know Heraclio's wife.

He said, removing his hat, "Antonio Rivera, at your orders," and he placed his hat back upon his head of long, lank hair, all the while holding her hand and looking into her face. He dropped her hand when she could scarcely stand his look and said in the kindest voice she had ever heard, "I, too, love him, señora."

They were friends; intuitively she knew that they were as if they had known one another for years. He called her señora knowing that, although she was unmarried, she was not a virgin, and she felt no shame. She knew instinctively that he felt a sorrow for her.

"At my orders," she said gaily, although the mood at this moment was not for laughter. "Always the custom is to say, 'to serve you,' or 'at your service.' Is it really so? Will you obey my orders?"

300

"You have but to order," said Antonio, and he did not smile.

"No pity, then," she said. "No grief for me, for I know what I have. I have made a choice and am satisfied."

"No pity, no grief," said Antonio, and now he smiled. "Does the señora wish anything else?"

"Yes, one more thing," and she reached out to touch his cheek. "Watch over him."

Antonio Rivera nodded.

"Let us have food," said Heraclio, "for Antonio and I go on an errand tonight."

Silently, she placed food on the table. She did not want to question, to make him feel that he was not free, but she yearned to know where he would go. And she felt pain that he would rather be out in the street somewhere or in a cantina—for where did men go in the night?—than here with her. She padded quietly about the room and Heraclio laughed and pulled her by the wrist to set her full upon his lap.

"What gestures you make your face make," he said. "I but go for three days or more—to carry out an assignment for my general." His hand, hidden from Antonio, touched her breast.

"It is not my place to expect explanations from you for what you do," she said, showing annoyance toward him in her guilt.

"But you wished to know."

She looked into his face and said, seriously, "You must help me to be a good woman for you. Out here, in the campaign, I am your wife as long as you will have me. And I must behave like a wife although I do not know the how about it. No matter what I feel, I must keep my grief well hidden—that is the manner of the Mexican woman, my mother told me, and since I am Indian, it should not be difficult."

Heraclio knew not what to do. And he was slightly embarrassed before his friend. He pushed her off his lap and self-consciously patted her buttocks as she moved away. "I shall be back soon, crazy," he said, and looked up to the sober face of Antonio. He knew his friend was laughing raucously.

Torreón, Coahuila, in the year 1914, was a city of forty thousand people. Situated on the basin of the River Nazas high on the Central Plateau, it was the center of the most productive agricultural area of the republic. It was a city surrounded by smaller, thriving communities and was the railroad junction for Saltillo and Durango, for Chihuahua and Zacatecas.

Earlier, some months ago, when the fight for power was still undecided in México after the death of Madero, Villa had easily occupied Torreón with but a small force. But when Huerta took full control, he sent an army to garrison the strategic city and Villa removed himself.

Now, in the month of February, the General José Refugio Velasco had ten thousand rested, well-trained troops within the city. Disciplined and strongly armed, they made the objective impregnable, and the terrain surrounding was also heavily entrenched, guarding all approaches to the city.

In the town of Bermejillo, twenty-seven kilometers to the north, Benjamín Argumedo lately from Chihuahua and Ojinaga, commanded the most northerly defenses of Torreón. Under his command was the entire Federal cavalry, and on the hills to the west of the village, he had infantry burrowed in row upon row of trenches crisscrossed, and he had cannon and Gatling guns dug into the slopes.

In Chihuahua, it rained. The month of February ended and in March the sun shone bright once more. And Villa gathered his troops. His plans were unannounced and unknown, but there was a festive air among his officers which carried over to the ranks. The men were happy. They would go to war—and soon. Villa yet did not speak, but lived each day as he had lived the last, and one week passed of March before he called together his command.

His superior, Venustiano Carranza, in Sonora, had for some time now attempted to undermine his efforts in an attempt to keep him from becoming too powerful. He had let him have the former Federal general Felipe Angeles, because he, too, could prove dangerous if allowed to be too successful. It was to the advantage of his Constitutionalist army that his hand-picked General Obregón be the first to enter the capital.

They congregated—the fat and short Urbina and the tall, lean Celestino Gámez, Maclovio Herrera, and Rodolfo Fierro, who still looked like a small merchant, very ordinary, and a group of advisers, civilian and military. Guadalupe Morales and Heraclio Inés were there because they led Dorados, and Antonio Rivera, the only enlisted man inside the room, because he and Heraclio might have to retell what they had already reported to Villa.

The generals sat at a table, the two young captains standing near the door, Antonio beside them. Felipe Ángeles sat to the right of Villa, Calixto Contreras, guerrilla and veteran Villista, alongside him. And Villa spoke.

"This time," he said, as if they had known all along his plans, "and from this moment on, we confide in no one. Carranza need not know that we will move upon Torreón. He has made a race of our dedicated struggle to gain the capital and now we do not know if he is friend or enemy. It is time that we moved. We have the ammunition and the guns—and we have fifteen thousand fighting men. What say you boys?"

One voice spoke, and that to ask the simple question, "When, my General?"

"I do not know, I rightly do not know," he said, "else I would tell you now. I but know that for a little time only must we have to wait." He gave his first orders. "Compadre," he said to Urbina. "This day, when we are finished here, you will isolate Chihuahua from the world. The last trains are en route from Juárez. When they arrive, no train shall leave the city, no wagon, horse, or man on foot shall leave. Place sentries and patrols around the clock and pass the word to the populous that none shall travel, for none outside shall know what we are up to here. For twenty-four hours, send all travelers back into the city. After that, those who would attempt to leave are either spies or fools. Shoot them on sight."

He paused and looked about him. "Rodolfo," he said. "Make inoperable the marconigraph in every direction. I want this city sealed, that must be understood by all of you. The trains must be made ready. Every engine, every car, everything that moves on rail shall be prepared to move. General Angeles, load your guns on flatcars—if there are not enough of these, Rodolfo will make flatcars out of coaches if he must. The rest of you all make ready. Act as if we leave tonight sometime—we may at that. Prepare your troops."

His generals looked at him, as he, now silent, seemed to be far removed from them. They waited patiently with respect, and knew that he was at this moment seeing that which would be lived

within the next few days. Ángeles alone of all these men an educated one, a don, an intellectual, also respected, and he marveled
at the man who dominated them completely. He thought of the
primeval genius in the man—what supernatural gift had been be-
stowed and why on this man who was in fact an animal? And what
would he have been with training and direction, for, semiliterate,
he knew things about warfare that years of study did not teach
many men. And suddenly he saw that which he had known but
had not recognized. Why it was that he loved and respected and
followed this man who should be inferior and distasteful. He
was crude, uncultured, rough—with a deep-rooted potential
within him ready to explode. Here was México, crude and uncultured, gifted with latent energy, and the uncontrolled energy
of Villa was the México to come; his weaknesses, even his foibles,
as well as the unleashing of his force through war—all this was
México. And to the General Felipe Ángeles, Villa, despite his
inferiority and, to be truthful, his superiority, was a prototype—
he was the image of the fatherland under a big hat, behind
mustaches, and cruelty and sentimentality. And that was why
the hidalgo, Ángeles, followed him.

Near the doorway, Heraclio also knew these things, but he did
not think about them. He had never questioned his feelings about
Villa, and knew he never would, even if he should grow to hate
the man. He had recognized this at the moment he met the General although Villa annoyed him then. But some men know things
without the need to reason.

On the sixteenth of March, the relative quiet of Chihuahua was
broken by the bawling of orders, animal noises as horses were
loaded onto cattle cars, and the shouts of men and soldier women.
And the sky on the southern end of the city blackened with the
smoke of many engines. The Division of the North entrained for
the coming battle.

Mile upon mile of troop trains moved. In the forefront were
two construction trains to repair rail; Felipe Ángeles moved his
artillery on fifty flatcars, then came Villa's new addition, a hospital
train with doctors and nurses—he was becoming a sophisticated
warrior. Behind all this came the troop trains, some with cavalry
and horses, more cattle cars loaded with infantry. Thousands of

women and children had been left behind, to follow and seek their men in any way they might, to find him and, if not, to take up with his comrade in arms. But some women, for the most part those without children, with carbines strapped across their shoulders and some with bandoleers, rode atop the converted cattle cars or boxcars, with small braziers burning and their ever-present sheet of tin over the coals, made their tortillas, and cooked their beans while exchanging ribaldries with their neighbors. Then came the headquarters train with a red caboose which was now Villa's private car, and last, the reserve trains with ammunition and supplies.

And the horizon was littered with horses, mules, and men.

That first day, the army traveled as far as Yermo, barely one hundred and ten kilometers from Torreón, and here they waited for the stragglers to catch up. Yermo was a desolate desert station, now windswept, and the women and the children who had been secreted aboard made camp. And once again, in the desert night with campfires flickering in the wind, the people sang and danced, played guitars and joked—those who would soon die as well as those who would survive were festive before the clash. But late in the night, as the fiesta increased in tempo, a sandstorm disrupted what death and privation could not, and the Division of the North suffered through the night.

It was not until the twentieth of March that the cavalry moved out, followed by the trains at a slow pace, and the infantry. The women and children brought up the rear. The cavalry moved for forty-seven kilometers and met no opposition. They camped then, until the remainder of the army could gather. But in Bermejillo, the General Argumedo sent mounted scouts out, thinking that they might find a small reconnoitering force, never dreaming that Villa had already begun a full-scale offensive. And Villa had once more fooled the enemy by sending two men to reconnoiter, to tell him the things he already knew by the strange means of communications of the people. He had sent Heraclio with Antonio, dressed as sheepherders and actually leading a flock into the slaughterhouse in Torreón, so that he could know from one of his own that the information he had received was true.

And so, as the army came together, the men of Heraclio Inés and Guadalupe Morales led fifty Federals into camp. Villa, unkempt in a rumpled suit, a soiled, sweaty shirt, and with blood-shot eyes, for he had been to a wedding dance the previous night, then ridden directly to the bivouac, gave the order to move into Bermejillo.

He said to Angeles, "Do not unload your guns, don Felipe. But get your mare and come to see the fun. Would that the full length of the road to México were to be as easy."

In Bermejillo, as he prepared for dinner, Argumedo was suddenly told that an army was but minutes away, and it seemed to him at the moment that his life was one of sudden surprises—always when Villa came he was unsuspecting. And he had seen the fury of the rebel attack, knew he could hold out for a time, but also knew the folly of such a course, and ordered the withdrawal of his troops. They would fight at Gómez Palacio. In his haste he did not notify Torreón of his retreat, leaving his communications to the city open.

Villa came into the village, and happy in an easy victory, perversely called Velasco by telephone, telling him that he and his officers would be spared if they turned Torreón over to the Constitutionalists within twenty-four hours.

The astonished General Velasco slammed the telephone down. What manner of adversary was this, he thought; a man who should resort to childish pranks such as this. And where was the God-damned Argumedo? He felt a surge of confidence. Why the man Villa was an idiot, and to defeat him would not be difficult. He thought of the stories he had heard about the man, and he felt that he had traveled this far by sheer luck in having had inferior officers to face. Argumedo was obviously an incompetent, Mercado had behaved like a frightened dolt at Chihuahua, running into the desert like a fool. Navarro at the first Juárez had been an old man, senile, and the second time at Juárez the man—he could not even recall his name—had been a drunken satyr; had been in fact between a woman's legs when the city fell!

But here, by Christ! He had fourteen thousand men within the city, another six at Gómez Palacio, for that was where Argumedo must be. And at Lerdo and Avilez, at Sacramento and Tlahualilo, another three thousand in all, expendable troops these last, to slow down the enemy, and capable in their position of destroying half the rebel force before they themselves perished.

306

At the very moment Velasco soliloquized in his glee, General Francisco Villa held Mapimí, had dispatched a strong force to take Sacramento and Tlahualilo, then sent Calixto Contreras directly east and then south to cut off any escape toward San Pedro de las Colonias. And the Constitutionalists moved toward Torreón. At the railroad station of Noé, barely twelve kilometers from Torreón, the army must stop, for the railroad from the point had been destroyed by the Federals. And Rodolfo Fierro's people began to repair rail.

On the twenty-second of March, Villa's forces were reinforced by three thousand men he had garrisoned in the city of Durango, and the rebels moved toward Gómez Palacio and Lerdo. The fighting to the point had been in favor of the rebels, but now the more difficult task of attacking the strong Federal entrenchments commenced. The Constitutionalists attacked Gómez Palacio and Torreón simultaneously, on three fronts, with Villa personally leading the center thrust. For three days, the action was heavy, in assault and counterattack, the fighting concentrated in an arc of one hundred forty degrees. On the night of the twenty-fifth, Villa returned to his guile of night warfare. His troops had been decimated, although they had destroyed a third of the Federal fighting force. Ángeles in a brash move had placed his guns too near the fight, and he was sent back with heavy losses; then when he could bear his artillery upon the enemy, he discovered that, although his ammunition had been manufactured in México, supposedly to his own specifications, most of his shells were duds which fell harmlessly, leaving the troops of Villa naked of the support they had expected.

The attack in the night was on all fronts, in the Villa manner of directing wave upon wave of peones. Villa sat his horse calmly amid it all, well within range of the enemy and exposed, over and over again sending humanity to its death. To his left, Celestino Gámez attacked the outskirts of Torreón proper, Villa being in the center between the two cities, and to his right, the compadre Tomás Urbina, made for the Cerro de la Pila, a hill overlooking both Gómez and Torreón. The Pila was the best fortified Federal position in the republic, with perhaps three thousand troops entrenched, with light cannon, and automatic weapons in such quantity that they were visible although dug in along the hillside.

307

Heraclio had suggested to the General, when he and Antonio returned from their scouting mission, that perhaps the hill could be bypassed, and indeed Antonio had argued with Heraclio, although he did not say this to Villa, that the hill could not be taken. But Villa would not have this much firepower at his back, and Urbina took his infantry to the base of the hill, and there let them sing and joke a while, then sent them up to die. Seven times that night the Pila was lighted by the fire of the enemy as the shouting, screaming rebels clambered up to overpower by sheer numbers what they could not see or fight. And there was no retreat that night, and the attackers were allowed to move almost upon the first row of trenches before they were cut down, and then another wave followed the first, until when dawn was breaking—when there was light to discern shapes unmoving—seven windrows of dead could be seen clearly around the almost circular Cerro de la Pila.

But in the night, about the time of the third attack, the commander of the forces atop the hill succeeded in convincing his General Velasco that he could not hold out indefinitely, for there seemed to be no end to the fodder being thrown at him. And at that moment it was true that to hold the hill and inflict such losses on the enemy might win the entire battle, so Velasco sent two thousand men to reinforce Gómez Palacio and in that way help his people on the Pila. But Villa's men, who had been going forward a hundred meters and retreating ninety, broke through suddenly, and there were some who were surrounded before they could withdraw, and among those were a few, a very few, who escaped back to their lines and lived to tell what they had seen. And Villa sent for Maclovio Herrera, who was with Celestino on the left.

"Get yourself and your men on beasts at once," he said.

And Maclovio would answer, for at this moment to find his men was all but impossible because they had been all fighting on foot and they were, those who survived, all nearby somewhere but all was confusion. But Villa anticipated him. "I want at least five hundred men on horseback within a half hour. How you do it is your business. The enemy has about a five-kilometer walk to get to where it is going, so if you do your duty, you will engage at the halfway point and in the open."

At one point he had seen Xóchitl in the midst of the fighting and now at this moment saw Guadalupe Morales and had him brought to him.

"Mi general," said Morales, and saluted.

Villa waved an arm toward him in response. "Look for the little Indian," he said, "if she has not gone to hell already, and ask if she knows where Heralcio is at this moment." He did not speak angrily, did not seem to be in anger, but he was in a rage that he should know exactly what it was he should do, and could not place his hands on the men he wanted. He knew at this moment everything of the battle, where every brigade was, how much ground it had advanced—but he did not know how his key officers were dispersed, the line of attack was so concentrated.

And Guadalupe Morales said, "It is not necessary to make a search for her. Heraclio is where I was this minute. Why he chose to remain there when everyone withdrew, I do not know, but he had that little monkey man with him and will not leave until they come en masse to retake their ground. He will appear in but a little while."

At that moment, Heraclio and Antonio Rivera appeared, crawling on their hands and knees, then coming to their feet and running hard.

Villa had given Maclovio his orders, and now Heraclio and Guadalupe Morales went with the General Herrera to put together a force of infantry. The word was quickly passed along, and in ten minutes Herrera had eight hundred jinetes preparing to mount. Antonio was alongside Heraclio as they made ready to move.

"Do you think you can remain on the beast?" asked Heraclio, and laughed, pleased that his friend would ride with him.

"If I cannot," said Antonio, and laughed in good humor, "I shall walk or crawl to where we are going."

They moved obliquely to their right, through the troops who were preparing another assault and who would move when they did. Yet another ten minutes they waited, poised, their horses nervous beneath them, and then Maclovio said, "Vámonos." He was flanked by Heraclio and Guadalupe Morales. Behind them were four lieutenants, older men than the two captains, and in the forefront was Antonio, who would remain near Heraclio if he could. They moved slowly at first, and then they cantered for a time, and suddenly they stopped. The word was passed that there would be no talking and they waited once again. Behind them they heard the shouts and screams that meant a rebel advance, and to the right, again the Pila seemed afire, and Heraclio reached forward beyond his rifle and unsheathed his machete. For this he would not need his gun—he would have shells to fire tomorrow. And he suddenly thought of the primo Aquiles, and felt a quiet rage within him; although these people before him had not killed his cousin, they somehow represented that which had. Behind him others had machetes also, and Maclovio held his saber high.

They were on high ground, and below them, although still quite dark, shadows were seen perhaps a furlong distant. They watched a while, and Maclovio knew, for he had vision in the night, that four abreast they marched, the Federals, as if they were on a parade ground. There was no sound, he merely dropped his arm, and for half the distance, only the hoofs of horses were heard, and suddenly the shouts and curses of those who came to conquer and the obscenities of those who were surprised. They passed right through the column, trampling as they went, then swirled around to hack them to the ground, but the Federals fought courageously; they dropped and fired steadily. And yet the rebels hacked away and drew their arms and also fired. The noises changed, to screams of pain and futility, to shrieks of death, as in the dark the armies clashed and no one really knew which way the battle went.

The fight continued, for not one Federal tried to escape until the end, and but a handful made it back to Torreón. Maclovio followed them as far as he dared, then took his men back to his general, who was at that moment seeing his attack thrown back.

And now at near dawn, at the annihilation of the seventh wave on the slopes of the Pila, Villa called Ysabel Robles, mountain man of his own breed—made general of his own in the hills as a guerrilla after having been a bandit also—and said, "Bring me your Indians." And from the left flank, from the troops of Celestino Gámez, who held the same position he had held three days ago, five hundred barefoot Yaquis in breechcloths and henequen shirts which came down barely over their hips, carrying spears, and knives, and bows and arrows, trotted to the center of the line where Villa kept a headquarters in between assaults.

310

And the peasantry, those who had not seen these people yet up close, looked upon them with awe. They had eyes and noses and mouths, these people, but they had no faces, for there was not a sign of emotion to them. They showed neither joy nor fear nor humor nor surliness. And the legend about them was well known —they had no fear of death—the bravest men in México, it was said—and one could kill ten thousand of them and the last one would stoically come forward to die. This was the legend, and this made the peones marvel—and also, because the rebels, even the most backward and illiterate of them, were Christians, they marveled, for these Yaquis were heathen—they were savages and were unable even to speak the Christian tongue. But Ysabel Robles knew the Yaqui tongue, and he had brought a thousand of these people from the mountains of Chihuahua and Sonora. Only it had happened that five hundred had already perished alongside the dead of Celestino Gámez, and the people who had fought with them knew that they could run away as fast as anyone.

Now in the half light of dawn, Villa was to send these five hundred up the slopes of the Pila. Not in a charge, but in the stealthy fashion of the Indian, dispersed, not in an organized frontal attack. And each was to kill one man up there, and as they performed their task, another charge, twice the size of any of the previous night, would overrun the hill. And Villa moved to the base of the hill, there to talk to his compadre Urbina, who now, although still pudgy, showed lines of strain along his cheeks and eyes. And together, along with their men, they looked in wonder as Ysabel Robles sent his Yaquis up the hill. No one stopped to think that the men who had died on the slopes through the night—who had been sent up not to come back—were as brave as these men who were different; that no breed of man is braver than another, that every man is brave, for every man must die in the end and yet he lives with that knowledge.

Slowly, the Yaquis moved up the sides, taking cover from the dead and from some wounded, and there was no sound from above, and Villa watched the first ones clamber over the trenches, and then they were all standing atop the small mountain, and Villa swore a violent oath. He had erred gravely, he knew immediately. For the Federals on the hill had withdrawn the moment they knew their reinforcements had been destroyed, leaving their gun emplacements as they were, and Maclovio could have had them all if Villa had not sent him back to Celestino Gámez.

They went around the mountain then as the Yaquis climbed down the other side, and in minutes they walked into Gómez Palacio, for the troops there had also withdrawn into Torreón. That same afternoon they were in the city, fighting from house to house, moving slowly block by block and paying heavily for every step they won. This was the twenty-sixth of March, and on the following day, the rebels were once again outside the city, having been repulsed during the night. And this continued for seven days, and each day the rebels penetrated at least once into the center of the city, fighting around the main plaza, and each day they were driven all the way to the gates once again. But the toll was heavy on both sides, and much heavier on the Federals. It was a certainty that another day or two would see a rebel victory. The General Velasco, although guilty of overconfidence in the beginning, was a general, and he would save what troops he had and as much matériel as possible. And he moved at the moment he was expected to offer his last full-scale resistance.

On the morning of April 2, he gave his orders to his officers. Alongside him was the General Argumedo, whom he had so mistakenly, he knew now, called an incompetent. Argumedo had yet to win a battle, but it was through his efforts in the main part that the Federals yet retained the city. He had lived up to everything required of an officer, and had impressed Velasco greatly in defeat. And it was his advice on how they should withdraw that made it a success. He had fought Villa now so many times, and it was to him as if he knew the man's mind. Here, in Torreón, Villa had not outgeneraled him. Here, the rebel chieftain had crushed them with brute force, and Argumedo prayed that Villa should follow his usual pattern—that he would obey his instincts and react on impulse as was his habit. If he should, Argumedo would motivate him to act.

And so, on the cold morning of April 2, barely two hours after the Federals had driven the Constitutionalists out of the city for the last time, the remaining artillery was brought to bear upon the western edge of the city. It was a concentrated, intense barrage, inspired of desperation, and light automatic weapons were also brought to bear from the roofs of buildings. And in Urbina's ranks there was chaos, for they bore the full brunt of the barrage, and he was indecisive, for he could not attack at the moment, which was the first thought which came to his mind, and he ordered his officers to move their men back, retreating more than two kilometers.

Now it was Villa's turn to howl with glee. "I did not expect this until tomorrow or the day after, boys, but we have them now! Now they will attack, for they cannot get out—and it has been my wish all these days that they should decide to come out into the open. We have them boys, let us go eat them up!" He pulled every brigade under Celestino Gámez and Calixto Contreras over from the eastern sector to support Urbina, and he himself took his troops behind Celestino's.

Velasco and Argumedo received word that Gámez and Contreras had pulled their troops, leaving the route to San Pedro de las Colonias and Saltillo open. Argumedo could not be certain yet, but he had reason to think Villa had taken his bait, and told Velasco that they must gamble and make their move. Already men, animals, and supplies had been crowded toward the eastern part of the city, and so leaving only five hundred horse behind to harass Villa should he pursue. The Federal army moved out of Torreón. The artillerymen would be as expendable as their guns.

The barrage had continued for two hours and more, and now, although yet heavy, it had noticeably decreased. The Federals had reached the point the rebels knew so well, only a few rounds remained. And at that moment, as if guided by some supernatural power, a violent dust storm arose in the desert to the east, and the General Velasco drove his five thousand survivors into its vortex.

Villa, waiting for the Federal charge, suddenly had misgivings, although he did not yet know he had been fooled. And the artillery yet fired toward and upon them. Now the very instinct which had betrayed him suddenly made him act once more, and Villa did not question and gave the order for a mass attack. And the Division of the North, though not without losses from the last gasp of the cannon before them, broke into the center of the city of Torreón.

And the city was empty, even the citizenry hid in their houses or in holes burrowed weeks ago. And suddenly, a few buildings,

313

warehouses obviously, and stables, burst into flame, and the silence was ended by the shots of the rebels and by the belligerent curses of the Federal soldiers before they expired with torches still in their hands.

Villa was as a child in his rage. He cursed himself for having been a fool, and cursed the Goddamned idiot Velasco for having outwitted him. He paused only long enough to leave the city in charge of Urbina, and moved his troops across the city to go into the desert. And whereas he had cursed himself, he now cursed his God, which he had not had since he was a child.

"But who are we to fight for our noble cause when even the Lord is against the little people?" He ranted and cried great tears. "To set up a cover of dust so that son of a bitch of an Argumedo with his father, Velasco, can escape us?" And his rage was over as suddenly as it had come on. It was a mystic thing to the Mexican Villa, as it was to his men, that the dust storm had come up at just that time. But it was fate which was but a side of the destiny, and the destiny is never questioned because it is a futile thing to question the destiny, and so Villa controlled himself. He left his army there prepared to march, and with a few hundred men rode back into the center of the city.

As was the custom, the rebels rounded up all foreigners and creoles—businessmen all. And as Villa and his men arrived, Urbina's men were toying with a large group of Chinese. First they made merry by cutting all their queues, and then they shot a few, and Villa, laughing all the while now, said, "That is enough. Let the little monkeys go where they will," and so they were herded to the edge of town, those who yet lived, and buffeted and spat upon, were sent to go their way. There was only one way for them to go, and that was south, along the railroad, and they walked, talking in their strange tongue. And they were hardy, although rich city-folk and thus of the ruling class, and most of them would survive to begin anew a business somewhere, and earn their revenge by owning peones in twos and threes in their own fashion.

And in the embarcadero at the south end of the city, in a corral, four hundred men, captured soldiers and creoles, were executed by the hand of Rodolfo Fierro.

The cavalry moved that night, but it was two days before the army began its journey east. It was slow travel, for the Federals had done a complete job on the railroad as they moved along, and the construction crews worked night and day. It was forty kilometers distant where they disembarked because the cavalry had made contact with the enemy and Velasco had traveled to Viesca, a town seventy-six kilometers south of San Pedro. The Division of the North moved southeast. Once more Velasco held them off, and on the third day, despite his heavy losses, escaped again and moved his army north.

Villa followed relentlessly. The Federals could not escape him forever, but at San Pedro de las Colonias, the Federal General Joaquín Maas had arrived with fresh troops to defend Torreón. He was late, but he had lingered in Saltillo after driving the Carrancista general Pablo Gonzales out of that city by his mere presence. He had eight thousand fresh troops, regulars, and with the five thousand Velasco brought into San Pedro, he was prepared to fight a major battle.

The Division of the North arrived and Villa knew immediately that here he might yet lose. He was short on ammunition and his army was vulnerable. How many men Joaquín Maas had with him he did not know, but the report said it was a force of some size. If the Federals chose to come out to attack him, there was nowhere he could take his men. The railroad, where he had left his trains, was destroyed for fifteen kilometers. The enemy was a superior force in numbers and arms, and he made plans to send Natera back to Torreón with his four thousand, there to prepare to defend the city. But first he must be audacious in an attempt to keep the Federals on the defensive, and he ordered an assault on three sides.

In the town of San Pedro, Velasco threw his men into the breach and helped Joaquín Maas drive Villa back into the desert. And the balding Maas, with white side whiskers and deep blue eyes, commended his men and congratulated himself and Velasco.

But Argumedo was more of a general than either of these two, and had already spoken to Velasco.

"We must postpone our congratulations until later, General," said Velasco to Maas, "until we crush the enemy."

"We can hold our position indefinitely," said Maas. "Let the bandit come and we shall crush him, as you say."

"We shall not sit here," said Velasco, and he was annoyed at the older man. "Prepare your troops for action, for we attack

315

within the hour. And if the General Villa attacks before we do, we shall follow him out into the desert when we drive him out, and there do battle and annihilate him." There was a certain manliness about Velasco, a certain code illustrated in that he recognized Argumedo's worth, and now, in that he called Villa "General," he was respectful of an able adversary.

"We will remain here and tear him to shreds," said Maas stiffly, his face flushed, revealing his own anger. "We will send him back if he comes once or if he comes twenty times."

Velasco did not attempt to hide his disgust. "If the General Villa and those wild people out there return only three times more, we are finished. But out there in one great clash we can defeat him."

"It is as the General Velasco states," said Argumedo, for although he was outranked by the two, he was also a general and could speak. "It is imperative that we attack, and at once, for every hour we give him will help him escape or will enable him to bring in ammunition if he has it somewhere, which is all he needs at this moment."

"No, sirs," said Maas. "You have been chased and beaten in the desert by this rabble, and yet you would return to be ground underfoot once more."

Velasco was livid, and Argumedo spoke strongly. "I resent deeply your implication, General. It is more than two weeks now that we have been fighting every day and every night also, for these people have no regard for the protocol of warfare. We have been overpowered, but our men have fought gallantly and have not been defeated. We have inflicted much more than we have suffered and we have outmaneuvered the enemy at every turn."

General Maas laughed a short ironic laugh. "For more than five days now you are in full retreat. You have given up to the enemy how many positions? You have lost over half your men, and yet you say you have not been defeated? You have allowed an illiterate, undisciplined, untrained mob to take a fortified city from you and yet you speak of outmaneuvering them?"

Argumedo lost all caution. "I shall tell you one time, General," he said. "One time only shall I say this. That man out there is not what you think he is. He is not even an illiterate now, for he has learned to read and write these past months, even as he has learned to be a general. At this moment he knows how precariously he stands, and his attack of an hour ago was but to prevent us from attacking him, to lull us into believing he is as strong as he was at Torreón. His are not untrained troops, General, and as for discipline—I saw them near Juárez while they were yet untrained and they had discipline even then. I saw them in Chihuahua, and I have seen them now for more than fifteen days. With him, Villa has the General Felipe Ángeles, more noble than you or I, more able than any of our generals. You know him well, you have been his intimate in the past. General Ángeles had put together an army for Villa.

"We have not lost the battle for Torreón; we are yet fighting it. And we can win within a few hours. It may be that we can win the war with such a victory. That is all I have to tell you." His anger had subsided with his speech, but he was determined to maintain his dignity, and he added almost formally that which a moment ago he would have said in anger, "But I must respectfully inform you that if you insist on directing insults toward my General Velasco or me, I shall send my sponsor to make arrangements with your agents. Honor must needs be preserved."

General Maas looked at the younger man in astonishment. This insubordination was a capital crime. Maas had never fired a shot at a human being; in fact had very little experience in the field, having served don Porfirio for many years in administration and finance. But he was not a coward; yet there would be no duel. His disbelief was supplanted by anger and he stared at Argumedo, who looked unflinchingly in return.

Velasco spoke because he had developed a real affection for his companion and would now save him from court-martial and certain death. "General Maas," he said. "I hereby order you to prepare your troops for battle, or to turn your command over to me."

Maas sputtered, then in a loud voice he said, "You order *me?* You forget I am the ranking officer here!"

"That is nonsense," said Velasco, now calm and in full control of his demeanor. He had not made it an order earlier merely in respect to the older general. Now he was a military figure once again. "You were dispatched to reinforce my troops. You were not sent to take over my command."

"Your command was in Torreón!"

317

"We are fighting for Torreón!"

Joaquín Maas also spoke formally, now coldly. "As ranking officer here, I order you to have your men at ready to defend our position. I shall give you your military orders later."

Argumedo wrung his hands in disgust and frustration. And Velasco, aware of the impasse, said, "General Maas. If that is what you wish, to take my command, then I am agreeable. I shall place myself and my men at your disposal, only you must agree to attack Villa."

"I shall not be bribed," said Maas. "I have given you orders. See that they are carried out!"

Velasco looked at him for a moment and shook his head. "I am removing my troops to Saltillo, there to reinforce my army and to fortify the city, for Villa will not stop here. I am refusing your orders. I shall not fire one more shot in San Pedro."

"I say you remain here or face a court-martial!"

"We shall see about that later," said Velasco. "As for remaining here, you shall have to fight me to keep me. I will not jeopardize the government's chances to survive by catering to your pettiness and your incompetence." He spoke to Argumedo. "Get our people moving," he said. "Confiscate trains—there are more than enough here for five armies. Also alert our troops that we might yet do battle with our own people if they should attempt to stop us!"

Argumedo said, "Immediately, my General."

"I have spoken," said Velasco to the speechless Maas. "I leave you your city, General, and I wish you luck against the rabble."

Under the shade of a campaign tent in the hot desert sun, Villa spoke to General Natera. "They have not made up their minds to attack yet, Pánfilo. Surely they will before too long, they cannot be that stupid. We must discourage them yet one more time since they have doubts. Then we shall hold them here as long as possible while you get back to defend Torreón."

"Qué caray!" said General Natera, uttering the traditional mild expletive for a bad turn of fortune and which was almost like a sigh of resignation. "All over the landscape it seems we follow these people, and here, finally they are in our grasp or must evacuate and that Maas with his army had to be here. Qué caray!"

Villa laughed as he always did when least expected. He had pulled off his boots and ran his thick strong fingers between his toes, taking pleasure as he scratched and rubbed the dirt and sweat away. "Twice now on this battle the destiny has hit me in my balls, Pánfilo. First when that Goddamned sandstorm hid Velasco from me, and now when we have ended in this trap. And it had to be in the daytime—it could not happen at night so that we could walk the ten or twelve kilometers to where our trains are. As it is now, we must stay in the sun all day, for to begin a withdrawal out in plain sight would have them at us in a quick minute." He slowly put his socks and shoes back on and gave the word. But he heard a rumbling, a distant familiar sound and said, "Those seem like trains to you, General?"

"Surely they sound like trains," answered Natera.

They gazed at each other, unspeaking yet communicating that which they feared. And it must be, thought Villa. Who would have thought the Federals to be so smart or so lucky. Had they lured him out here to crush him? He called an aide.

"Bring me Heraclio Inés," he said. He stood chatting in the sun with Pánfilo Natera, waiting for the captain.

"Mi general," said Heraclio, walking up. "A good day to you, General Natera," he said, and saluted.

"Come, Heraclio," said Natera. "We are old friends," and he embraced the youth. "You have not been to see me—when we are out of this predicament we are in, come visit with me."

"Very well," said Heraclio.

"When you are finished with the family reunion I have a task for you, Captain," said Villa, but Heraclio discerned the humor in his eyes.

"Yes, my General," he was serious, straight-faced.

"And where did you get that uniform, my dandy?"

Heraclio permitted himself to smile. "I took it from one who needed it no more." He wore charro-type trousers and a blouse, and across his chest twin bandoleers, replete with shells. On his head was a huge hat, its string behind his neck. He wore his own sidearm.

Villa said as if annoyed, "And what was wrong with your uniform? You did not like it because I myself designed it?"

"It was soiled," said Heraclio, slow anger in his face because

319

he knew the General was aware of the need for different clothes.

"Soiled?" asked Villa, showing perplexity in his face. "How soiled? Did the brave Heraclio Inés empty his bowels in the fight?"

Always it was like this, thought Heraclio. Always this man teased him and made him lose his temper—why, he did not know. He said brusquely, "You know how I mean soiled, my General. I had all the blood of México upon my person!"

Villa laughed loudly. Natera did not laugh but looked upon them with a slight smile, and Heraclio stood rigidly before them both. "Ay, what a boy you are, Heraclio," said Villa. "Always you lose your control."

"Give me my orders," said Heraclio.

Villa said, still laughing, "Get you someone to go all the way around the town, to the other side, to see what is going on in those Goddamned freightyards. I do believe, and Pánfilo agrees, that more troops are coming in to help those people as if we did not have enough troubles already." And suddenly his humor broke through to Heraclio. He looked upon his general with open admiration, that he should stand here laughing in the face of such danger. Villa said, "I wonder what that idiot of a Pablo Gonzales is doing, allowing every Federal in eastern México to calmly go across his state?" He looked at Heraclio and said, "Well, why do you wait?"

"You were speaking," said Heraclio, and now he would not let the General anger him, yet he spoke seriously.

"I was speaking to the General Natera," said Villa. They both knew he was still teasing, yet neither smiled now. "Go give your orders and you had better send a half-dozen riders so that at least one will return."

"I shall myself go," said Heraclio, "and I shall take one other."

"You cannot serve me when dead," said Villa, but he was pleased.

"Then you should have left me in Chihuahua, there to administrate," said Heraclio.

It was almost evening by the time Villa had gathered all the ammunition available to distribute among the second of the two waves he would send, now that he knew his enemy was withdrawing toward the east. The first wave would be fodder. Those who survived were to fight hand to hand, with machetes and knives, while the second assault would carry the firepower. But the first wave did not need their weapons, such as they were, because Maas had followed Velasco out of San Pedro. The city was open, and the Federals were on the road to Saltillo. But Maas proved his incompetence by leaving eight million rounds of ammunition, some guns and fieldpieces, stores, and an intact railroad behind him. Furthermore, he left behind enough rolling stock to carry Villa's entire army to him.

The Division of the North followed that very night, to rest on the trains, and in the night bypassed Maas, who had disembarked his troops, sending his trains on to Saltillo, not wanting to join Velasco. Villa passed the Federals in the night, not knowing that Velasco, thinking perhaps that Joaquín Maas would not long hold San Pedro, abandoned Saltillo and was at that moment marching across Nuevo León, southeast, toward the state of Tamaulipas, there to entrain for México, which, he knew, must be defended before long. And Maas did not move into Saltillo at all, had moved his trains on a spur track to the village of Hipólito, planned to move in a wide circle to Monterrey, which was Federal, knowing that the General Pablo Gonzales, inept or not, was somewhere between him and that city.

Pablo Gonzales was nowhere to be seen. The rebels steamed into the now open Saltillo, and the citizens of that city came forward to join the ranks of the victorious army.

In the village of La Rosa, a shepherd coming home from a week in the prairie told a friend that he had seen trains—almost like a vision, he said—he had seen trains on a rusty, weed-hidden railroad. Replete with men, he said it was, but his fourscore-year-old eyes at times deceived him and perhaps he had not seen a train at all. But his friend, one Cipriano Azcarate, took his sarape, his mochila, and a lame buck mule and set off for Saltillo.

Villa knew that it could be only Maas who went north, and gave the order to pursue. And it was a simple thing to take Maas, because he had remained at Hipólito, and because Villa arrived in the night, the Federal general escaped. There was no battle as the conscripts, laughing joyously, joined the Division of the North. Now Villa's riders appeared with the news that Velasco rested at a hamlet south of Saltillo called Carneros.

Villa laughed at the fool Velasco, who should have escaped when he had the opportunity, and he said, "Eat him up, my little ones. Eat him up."

But Velasco, though never dreaming that Villa would follow him, fought at Carneros, and only until he knew he was defeated did he retire into the mountains of the Little Stench to a town called La Ventura, and there, because Villa refused to follow the lacerated army, he gathered his remaining troops and moved east to the railroad and Mexico City. Argumedo accompanied him, and when the older man embarked, they embraced and shed a tear, and the young, still-unvictorious Argumedo struck across the Central Plateau, in a direct line to Zacatecas, where General Barrón was building the last great Federal bulwark and where surely he would meet Villa once again.

VIII

In late April, Heraclio Inés, with two hundred men, returned to Zacatecas, there to operate from Río Grande. He was to gather corn and beans—food for Torreón; and cattle, horses, and mules—legal tender for the American munitions dealers.

Pancho Villa was equipping his army for the fight for Zacatecas, and the army grew daily, for from east and west, and from the state of Zacatecas, men who had held their peace for one reason or another—for family responsibility, for cynical reasons, for fear, or for irresponsibility—these neutrals now came forward to take part in the fight of the masses. This because in spite of the official status of the Carranza government in Sonora, the Revolution of the people was the strongest movement. And Villa was the people; and his army multiplied to twenty thousand and then thirty, to forty thousand organized and soon-to-be-equipped men.

In Juárez, Maclovio Herrera commanded the city, which was now a gigantic stockyard. No longer was it necessary for the rebels to meet in darkness with American agents along the Río Bravo, and there exchange cattle for money which would later be secretly exchanged for guns and shells. For although Washington had yet to recognize Carranza, neither had it recognized Huerta despite the efforts of Henry Lane Wilson, for Huerta foolishly refused to co-operate with the American interests and had begun trading with Germany and Japan. In retaliation, the United States forgot for a time that it had placed an embargo on arms.

In Saltillo, the compadre Urbina reigned as cacique with a strong force of five thousand men to protect the city from Pablo Gonzales as well as from the Federals. And being a Villista from the beginning, he had learned much, and in a few weeks the entire state of Nuevo León, where Carranza had once been governor, belonged to him.

Into eastern Zacatecas and San Luis Potosí went the General Rodolfo Fierro to harass small elements of the enemy where he might find it, and audaciously he crossed the railroad below the city of Aguascalientes and into Jalisco, sacking villages, leaving a wake of destruction among nonmilitary peasants. The General Natera was at Durango, and Celestino Gámez ruled Torreón.

In Chihuahua, his favorite city, Villa watched over the Carrancista governor, Manuel Chao, and one day ordered his execution. But Chao was rapidly becoming a Villista, though not a peasant, and was spared to help fight his master, Carranza. Dispersed throughout northern México, the rebel army now lacked food, and Villa opened granaries and warehouses but he knew that this would never do. He must urge the people to sell their products, but his soldiers could not buy, for they had no money. His own gold he did not see, because it went back into the United States, and so he printed his own currency. And only Villa money could be used to buy and sell. Government money could be exchanged at a fraction of its worth. Thus, the army which had existed for so long on pagarés was paid.

From Sonora, the appalled Carranza objected strongly, ordering Villa to recover immediately the bogus money. Villa answered simply, "Do not speak to me of economics. Only send me money to pay my men."

In Río Grande, Heraclio held his men under strict discipline, for he knew many people here and would not allow it to seem that the town was occupied. The Municipal President he knew well, and he explained to him why he was here. The citizenry would be respected; however, if a civilian in any way harmed a soldier, he would be summarily shot. The President was allowed to keep his home. The troops were sent to the embarcadero, there to live as in the field, but Heraclio established himself in the Municipal Palace. In the living quarters at the rear of the building he placed Xóchitl Salamanca. All this he did before he went home to see his wife.

Always, when he left Río Grande for la Flor, he followed the main road, circling east and then south to circumvent the huge mesas directly south of the town. On this day, however, for no reason other than an impulse, he rode straight out, climbing gradually, and although in no hurry moved faster than usual in a canter. His path became steeper, and soon he was between the mesas, up high, eventually having to climb atop one to get across. An old trail led down, and the railroad was ahead, not too far and down the tracks; a short distance away was the railroad stop for Tetillas, a small three-walled building with benches, its open end facing the tracks.

It was the middle of May, and he had been here now near his home for three weeks. He had been with his wife, Marcelina, and had seen his child, now at that age when a child is first alert to things outside itself. And oddly he felt no disappointment in that it was a girl and not a buck. She had named her Ofelia, Marcelina had, and already the creature, but a few months old, had a strength to her tiny hands and Heraclio thought, despite himself, of the Inés strength with a horse. And he smiled.

Although he had lived with Marcelina but a short while, his return was like that of a long-married man. He was a husband, and he cohabited with her, and it was not different from before because he had never—except rarely—displayed emotion. But she knew that something disturbed the fine, psychic balance of love, and she grieved silently.

Heraclio, knowing a happiness with Xóchitl in Río Grande, a happiness supported by the absence of responsibility, did yet retain the love he knew for his wife. He did not think at all about how his wife must feel; there was no need for that.

On a trip to la Flor, he stopped in—because he felt compelled to look after David—at the choza of María Contreras. He found her disheveled, her eyes discolored, and near her mouth there were yet traces of blood, crusted. And she seemed completely drained

324

of her strength, in mild shock. How she had been able to leave her couch to answer his knock he did not know.

He sat her down, fearful lest she should fall. Because he had been the instrument for her re-entry into the world of sensuality, he felt a guilt that she had contracted an alliance with a man, and had selected the wrong one.

But she said, "David!" The one word stopped him as he walked toward her with the water gourd and an earthen cup. "David?" he said, but this could not be. He thought her distracted, calling for her son, yet the inflection had not been such. "David did this to me," she said almost inaudibly. He thought this could not be, for it was if a man saw God and struck him, to do this to one's mother.

The water strengthened her and she said, "Because I would not put a curse on you—because I refused to help him kill you!" Her speech was in fragments, disconnected, and she did not tell him more, only that. She did not tell him that in the night, in the early hours of this very day, David had come to her, looking very unlike David, dirty and bearded, and he gave her money.

Other than his appearance, nothing seemed out of the ordinary, even his coming at this hour. They talked for a time as they always had, and she unaware that her son had changed so much. Although he was a quiet one, for the most part uncommunicative, he had always been able to speak out his wishes, his feelings, and had never depended on guile, nor had he resorted to dissimulation. Now as he spoke, he casually asked for news about Heraclio and her body felt as if drained of blood and she did not know why she felt fear, and answered instinctively although knowing that Heraclio was in Río Grande that there was no news of him but that his wife had given light a few months ago. There was a craftiness to him she could not understand. She waited, as if waiting for death, for the scene to continue.

"I tried to kill him once," he said without preamble.

She tried to match his calmness through her fear. "And why should you do that, my son? Him, whom you have loved, with whom you have lived almost as a brother? Why should you want to kill him?"

He said, cruelly, "My brother has cohabited with my mother.

325

He has cohabited first with my sister and then with my mother. Should there be more reason than that?"

She closed her eyes tightly, and she swayed, horrified that he should know of her lesser sin which was to have lain with Heraclio, shamed that he knew her greater sin from which he came. She was somehow able to speak. "At that time, when you say you attempted this—already had he done this other thing you say?"

Now it was he who was shocked. His pose and his composure were gone, for she had not denied, but had by her question admitted the fact. He sat as if unalive, and he finally spoke.

"It does not matter now that I did a wrong thing then, for in the end, had I succeeded all this would not have happened. You asked me why a moment ago and there was not reason enough then that I should kill him. You see, there was a man, an old man, whom I worshipped. I liked to think sometimes, perhaps in a mystic sense, for it almost seemed reasonable since you know magic, that it was he who put into your body the seed that became me. I wished it to be so; at times I could almost believe it.

"This old man—a very old man he was—died as he slept beside me in the prairie. And Heraclio did not remain to help me bury him. He let him lay out in the sun and went off to Villa to make himself an officer. That was the reason I tried to kill him. It was not because he had loved Carmen," he spoke now as if his relationship to the landowners had been shared knowledge all these years, "because somehow in a strange manner I approved of that. It was only because of the old man—because he would not mourn with me."

She felt now the love of a mother, for at this moment he was a child in deep grief. He was her baby for one of the few times in their lives and she did not know it would be the last time. He was borne of her and born to always suffer, and because she knew what he must do, her guilt was as if a weight upon her and she reached a hand to touch his face.

He looked up to her and said, not in anger, "Now he must die, for now there is real reason. He was my friend, my brother, as you said. Because he took you being that, he has deprived me of my manhood."

"I know," she said sadly. "I know that you must be a man again, my son."

326

He said, "Help me, my mother. Place a curse upon him that he should dry up slowly and when he is weak and ill, I shall come and carve his heart out."

"You know I cannot do that," she answered.

"Do you have love for him?"

"Of course. But it is not a lustful love. I know one of you must die and I grieve." She stopped a moment, near tears, and then she said, "It is that he does not believe, and to succeed in this thing of curses, the victim must believe I have the power. You must fear him greatly, David, to be grasping at straws."

"I fear no one," said David, and he came to his feet. He wanted Heraclio dead, and, true, he was not afraid. It was that he did not think he could succeed in killing him. This he did not understand; he simply knew that if he faced Heraclio he would die, and it was not death he feared but the knowledge that Heraclio would live. He wanted Heraclio to die, and he was embarrassed with himself, indeed, he had been grasping at straws, for he, himself, did not really believe in witchcraft.

And this admission to himself gave him strength, and because he was himself again, he said, "You refuse to do this for me?" he said this now, not really wanting her to do it, but wanting his mother to become his mother once again.

"I cannot," she said, and was about to add, because she accepted the fact that one must die, she wished that her son should survive, and she started to say that she would help him. That she would get Heraclio to come here, where unawares, David could kill him. She felt she owed her son that. And he would not be prosecuted nor maligned, in fact he would be respected, admired, and even envied that he had killed his best friend in his mother's bed.

But at that moment, David struck her in the face, and when she fell he picked her up and struck her again, and then again. He kicked her twice as she lay on the dirt floor sobbing, and did not say a word but went away.

And that very day, Heraclio sent a soldier for her. Taking but a few belongings, she was taken to Río Grande, there to serve as a house servant for Xóchitl. She feared for her life, and Heraclio could also not be certain what David might do next.

Now, as he approached the small railroad station, he saw a group

327

of men standing alongside a flat wagon, and looking across the plain toward the tetillas. It was obvious to him, even at a distance, that they were agitated, and he spurred his horse so that it galloped.

One of the men, the husband of a distant cousin from the people of his mother, walked a way to meet him, and said, "You know, Cousin, that your brother Concho lies dead out there on the prairie a half a league or so."

Heraclio said calmly, giving no indication of the sharp pain in his breast, "And why is it that you have not taken him up from there?"

The man looked to him, embarrassment on his face. "We have tried, Primo. But there is a man out there with a carbine—without a doubt the man who killed Concho—and from a knoll, perhaps a hundred meters distant, he fires at anyone who would approach the body."

Heraclio was angry, but only for a moment, for he knew these were not violent men. They were unarmed. He said, "We shall go see before the evil birds get him."

"They have already been at the corpse, for it is three hours that it has lain there. At least three hours. We saw him earlier as we were on our way to catch the train to Río Grande. He even rode with us for a time, but we moved too slowly to suit him and he went on ahead. One shot there was and only one. Concho lies out there with his gun still in its holster. We reached near enough to see that before we were driven away."

They moved to the place where Concho fell, and the unknown rifleman was no longer near. He had been shot on the side, near the back, and from a distance, for the bullet had not passed through the body. He had fallen or had turned his head so that it was partially protected by a chuckhole in the ground, but on the exposed side, the eye was gone, as was the flesh around his mouth and the neck and a part of his ear. And Heraclio picked the body up and pressed the mutilated, once handsome face to his chest, then kissed the lacerated mouth. He placed the body on the bed of the wagon, and covered with his jacket the raw face with its left side bare bone.

"Take him home for me, relative," he said to the man who had spoken to him. "As a favor, take him home."

328

He turned away and mounted, then moved toward the knoll where the gunman had watched for hours that no one disturb the vultures while they tore the flesh from his victim. There were discernible tracks, not many and not clear because the ground was hard here. But the sage had been disturbed only so the killer had left along the same trail he had followed here. There were, also, remnants of smoked cigarettes—manufactured cigarettes—and who here would carry things used only in the city? His thought was, of course, David, for he now traveled in the night, a bandit who, when peace came, would carry a price on his head. But this atrocity was done with much hatred, and David's hatred was for him, Heraclio. This man who did this, and it was one man, he knew from the marks on the landscape, must have been Concho's enemy and he knew what he was about. He had lain in wait for him, had killed him, and had made certain the vultures would get to him. This last, of course, was but a part of a revenge.

He followed the tracks, and he lost the trail, backtracked, and found it, followed again for a time, and then dismounted. It had been a long time since he had done this, and then he had never been especially good at it. If his brothers were here now, they could travel at twice the speed. But he did not want his brothers, for they would hack the man to pieces immediately. And he did not want that. He was the commander of this area, and he believed because he was in the fight and believed in the fight that the law should correct any wrongdoing, regardless of what it was. It would be impossible for him to fight for the idea of a sane México and think in terms of personal revenge, no matter how he hated the animal he now tracked. It was strange to him, because he wanted this man dead, but perhaps, because he knew the man would die if brought before a tribunal, he was willing and anxious that this thing be done in a legal manner. He thought suddenly of Maclovio Herrera because he was thinking of the military. Now he wished Maclovio could be here because Maclovio could follow the killer at a gallop.

He came to the railroad above Cañitas, and he crossed and followed for a time until he came to a place where there had been a gathering of men. He could not ascertain how many were in the group, but there were more than a few, and he turned and rode at a gallop toward the railway station at Cañitas, where there was a marconigraph operator. He would send for his troops—a hundred men would be enough, and he would find this band and execute them.

In la Flor, while waiting for his men, he said to Teodoro, "It is the wrong way, I tell you. There will be no place for banditry and wanton killing when the war ends, and in effect you are breaking the law by hunting down this man and breaking him."

"What is it with you?" said Teodoro. "Have you lost your courage? Did Concepción mean nothing to you?"

He would not be angry. "It is not that at all and you know it. We have authority here. I am that authority, and I guarantee the man will die."

Juan spoke, although it was Teodoro's place to do the talking.

"And what difference," he asked, "if you have him killed by a firing squad, or if we kill him? He will be dead, no?"

And because he himself would have asked such a question not too long ago, Heraclio was confused. "It is only that it should be done legally," he said. That was *all* he could say, and he wondered to himself why he was doing this. Was it because the other was so much a part of what was a pattern? He had come to Río Grande to perform a task for his general. He had, in fact, become a judge; although he did not hold court he made decisions upon civilian offenders. As such he had been lenient—far too lenient, he knew, —and he did not like the role. He had been very willing to fight Rodolfo Fierro, but that was a personal grievance, and it was at a moment when anger dominated him. This deliberate revenge was not a part of him, somehow. And all these months he had believed in the law; else why the thousands slain? Perhaps it was because he had seen the same Rodolfo Fierro kill, and because he knew from Antonio Rivera, who had witnessed it, that, in Torreón, Fierro had with a pistol killed four hundred Federal prisoners, firing all afternoon, killing one man at a time as his orderly reloaded fusiles for him until at the end his right hand had swelled so that he struggled to insert his finger into the trigger guard and his arm, inflamed sinews showing red, hung limp, and near the end it took three or four shots to down a man as he ran across a corral to escape the animal who shot at him. And Fierro, laughing at his own weakness because he could no longer raise his arm to

330

bear upon the doomed prisoner, held his gun with both hands to fire, and between his laughter screamed obscenities at his orderly, who could not load fast enough because he was nervous and also tired and terrified because he knew that this monster whom he served might suddenly on impulse turn and blow his brains out for a lark. At the very last, when the last man made his try for life and failed as he neared the far wall, Fierro, exhausted by his unnatural exercise, with his undergarments pleasurably damp, fell there to sleep among the strewn bodies, awakening only to dispatch with a curse his orderly to put the shot of grace into the skulls of one or two or three who had not yet died. Heraclio knew that he would be no different if he killed this man who murdered his brother. He did not know what else to say, except perhaps he would speak of vendettas, for he knew vendettas. All his life he knew of people who died violently because someone twenty, forty, sixty years ago had killed another. What need to speak of Fierro? Or, for that matter, of others with a disregard for human life?

"You are late with your justice," said Teodoro, "for we know who the dog is. Or is it that you will send your troop to hunt your brothers when we break the slimy beast?" His disgust was plain, and Heraclio, despite himself, felt a guilt and was ashamed.

"You know?" he asked. "You really know?" It seemed incredible, and yet, of course they would know, for if Concho had an enemy, they would surely be aware of it.

"Your good friend," said Teodoro, "David Contreras . . ."

"Not David!"

"One who rides with him," said Teodoro, "and for that reason the bastard shall die also. For certain we will get one or the other for this, perahaps both."

"But how?" asked Heraclio. "Why?"

"They came here sometime back," said Teodoro. "Three months or so ago it was, the bastard David Contreras and his friend, one called Lalo Solís. They visited with the witch for a few days. And they were quiet and remained near her hut. We would have taken no notice of the two pigs except that they rode magnificent stallions, obviously stolen from a breeder who knew animals, but they did not know what they had and treated them as one would treat a buck mule or an ox. I was about to ask them for the loan of their mounts to service our two mares now not in use. But then the Goddamn fool, that Solís person, dared look upon your brother's wife, Otilia. That is permissible, of course, to look upon a beauteous woman, and a compliment to the husband if the admiration is honest and pure, but the ugly pig followed her to the manantial where she was going for water, and there spoke to her. He would return for her, he said, because she with her beauty deserved a man, and Concho came, and there, before the women of la Flor, he horsewhipped the intruder but the cuckold would not provoke because he is a coward. And that is why Concepción died and that is not a good reason. We will go for this Solís sometime tonight and we would have you with us, for he travels with a good-size band which belongs to David Contreras. We shall go and we shall face them."

"They will kill you," said Heraclio, yet refusing to be included. "What good is that? Let me and my men run them down. There is good reason to hunt down these bandit groups aside from Concepción, for those who roam the hills outside the law violate and kill peaceful defenseless people every day. I promise you shall all be present when he dies, and die he will."

"Then there is no honor," said Teodoro. "Better you should go with us, which is your first duty. And if the destiny dictates that we should die, why we shall die well, like Ineses, like men."

And now Heraclio knew that which had eluded him a while ago. Destiny—that had been the magic word. That was his reason for his defense of laws, for he believed men should make their laws with reason, not through tradition. He meant to see Lalo Solís tried and shot. All his life he had believed without really knowing it that he had a right to shape and mold his own destiny. It was a sacrilege to think this way, true, because God meant that he should go against thirty or forty men and there die. He should not question this, for it was a strong law—but he objected, and he would not obey, and he felt joy that he should discover a thing about himself so valuable even at the moment when guilt was forcing him to follow Teodoro.

In the house, the people of la Flor gathered to help mourn, and the men stood in a group outside, away from the Inés men, for they were kinsmen, and their privacy was respected because they were discussing plans to avenge the death of a brother. From within, intermittent wails came in unison, almost as if the women deliberately gathered their strength for one long breathless howl, and then all was quiet as they gasped for air.

"What do you know of David's band?" asked Heraclio.

"Little except that he travels in an area of perhaps two hundred kilometers removed from the hacienda. We hear things, especially since his last visit when he beat the witch. He is changed, it is said, for whereas in the past he did not take part in the atrocities his men committed upon women, now he does. He has declared a war against all women, it is said, and has taken to violating even children of ten or twelve years. And a few have died. It is a beast that he has become, it is said."

They did not wait, and buried Concho then, for in his condition it was not fair that they should deny his right to rest and because Otilia mourned so intensely she might die from grief. His death she had been trained to expect from birth; his mutilation put her in a state of near shock. And so they buried the disfigured Concho a scant eight hours since he left that morning with a smile on his beautiful face. Behind the chapel, near his father, he was committed, and Heraclio left for Cañitas, there to meet his troop.

It was near dusk, and as he galloped to the south barely out of hearing, two men rode toward the house of Teodoro, leading a horse which had Lalo Solís tied to the saddle on its back. They stopped short of the first buildings of the settlement, and one remained there with the captive while the other rode on alone. Juan answered the knock on the door. Teodoro was at that moment speaking with Otilia. She had, remarkably, regained control of herself. After the funeral, she had stopped her visible mourning, had cut it off almost in mid-sob, and from that moment her grief would be within her. And with this, she regained her strength, and now, having no husband to prevent her, she spoke to Teodoro as a human being, not merely as a woman and therefore a chattel.

"I leave tomorrow for El Fuerte," she said, "there to be with my ancient father."

"It is your place," said Teodoro, "to remain with the family of your dead husband until you remarry."

"When I buried Concho, a part of my life ended," she said. "It was a wonderful thing to be the wife and a part of your brother. It has been, despite your tyranny, Teodoro, something special to be a part of the Inés pride, I must be honest about this. But now I am the Widow of Inés, only that. The time of your dominance over me has passed and never again will I be ordered by you. I leave tomorrow and you shall not detain me."

"Very well," said Teodoro, "if that is your wish, but the boy stays. He *is* an Inés and will be reared as an Inés. The blood is running out; there is a dearth of new males and too much Inés blood has seeped into the earth, too much Inés seed has been wasted or has been turned into women."

She faced him without fear, and for the first time in her life felt a sadness for him. She understood, and she also felt the tragedy of which he spoke. She, too, felt that family pride she had seen and had resisted for so many years. It was insidious, but she did not fear it, for she knew her strength. "My son," she said, "belongs to me and to no one else. He shall go where I go!" And Teodoro realized of a sudden that he was almost discussing this thing with her, a woman, who should not question his commands, and he ran his small, gnarled hand over his face. He spoke then with finality.

"We go this night, woman, in search of him who made of you a widow. You will be here when we return—without fail. If you dare leave, we shall follow you wherever you might go and reclaim our blood. The boy is an Inés!"

Juan said, moving from the doorway to strap on his gun, "God has favored us unexpectedly this night, Teodoro. Bring your weapon"—Elías was already armed—"and come outside." To Elías, he said, "Bring the beasts."

The horses had been saddled for their journey, and Elías led them through the kitchen and on out into the street. He closed the door behind him.

Outside, Teodoro said to the stranger, "And so where is he?"

"A short distance from here." They rode off, slowly, and the man said, "David Contreras, my chief, said I should tell you that he did not know Lalo planned to kill your brother. Had he known, he said to tell you, he would have prevented it. He would have had us execute Lalo immediately he knew, but he believes that is your right and would not deprive you of it."

"Perhaps he might be a man after all, this bastard David Contreras," said Teodoro.

And Lalo, now that he knew he was to die, was suddenly and

for the first time in his life brave. "Do not believe for a minute, muchachos, that David has done you a favor. It is you who are doing a service to him. He is a smart one, that David. Much more intelligent than what you people think. You see, he has no more need for me, in fact it is better for him that I should remove myself from his side, because I do not obey his every order the way these others do. And why should I, when we started in this thing together, he and I. And there was no talk of chiefs and leaders. But I am my own man and that is why I am here. So now, you perform an execution for him."

"You are not a man," said Teodoro. "You are a pig and you will in a minute or two die."

"And so I die. Why not today as well as tomorrow? David could have had my life just as easily, but he wanted to tease me by sending me here to you."

One of the men who had brought him said, "I have a message also for the one of you called Heraclio. Which one of you calls himself Heraclio?"

"He is not here," said Lalo. "At this moment he is out in the bush looking for me. He is not to be feared, for he kills quickly and surely. He is expert, an artist, and these people here are but amateurs and may very well do a messy job of it."

The man ignored him. "I am to tell this Heraclio, that David Contreras, although sorry his brother died, now considers himself Heraclio's father. He held no rancor toward Concepción, toward any of you, but he has a bitter hatred for Heraclio and will one day soon come to break him. He has made a vow—an official vow in a real temple in case there might really be a God—that he will kill Heraclio Inés and that he will do it in as painful a way as possible. He said I was to bring this message."

Juan had eased his horse around behind the two riders, and now, holding a gun on them, said, "These two, also, I think we should destroy. They are a part of this whole sickness, and, who knows, may live to someday help that maniac kill our brother."

"No," said Teodoro. "That kind of talk the bastard sends is personal man-to-man talk. A vow like that is not to be taken lightly, and he would break the vow if he does not attempt it by himself. Alone. Then, too, these boys have saved us days of riding, and they have come to us in good faith. Do not be an ingrate. They are almost as guests and it would be a discourtesy to harm them. Better, my brothers, to hold them so they may see how this one dies. Since the bastard David has seen fit to swear he will kill one of us, let him learn from two eyewitnesses what the Inés revenge can be. We have killed animals and know of many ways in which to do it."

Elías had untied Lalo and now pulled him to the ground. The man regained his footing, his hands still tied behind him, and laughed. "There is but one sad thing," he said. "And that is that I did not get to see her charms, nor she mine. Tell me, Ineses. Did one or all of you ever lay with the new widow, or are you loyal brothers who dream about the pleasure and imagine it but will not do it?" Teodoro was upon him in an instant and, catlike, struck him twice in the face with his quirt.

"You desecrate the dead, pig!"

"The thing," said Lalo, through his pain, "the thing I am most curious about is her hair. Like gold it is. I have seen gold. And I saw her and had to know—I absolutely had to know whether her hair was the same color between her legs as it is on her head. Golden hair!" He laughed.

Elías knocked him down with his fist. "You have talked too much, son of a bitch!"

Lalo rolled over and sat up. And he would speak again, but Elías asked:

"Have you decided, my brother, how the assassin shall expire?"

"I am thinking," said Teodoro, "that we should both take one of his ankles at the end of our reatas, paying out quite a bit of slack, of course, and then gallop away from one another." And Lalo, who had expected a sudden death because of his insults and because of the hatred which already possessed these three, hoping that anger would make them shoot him quickly, knew that they did not speak merely to frighten him, and now whimpered in terror.

"Get up and walk," said Teodoro. "Only a little way, to the arroyo where near the bank at one point there is soft ground and red ants. There we shall stake you out and sit with you for a few hours while you die."

Lalo Solís moved and stumbled and fell hard; Elías picked him up roughly and shoved him forward once again. He cried aloud now, like a child, pleading for the mercy of a bullet, and once again made friends with God.

They were there and Juan said, "First, make a gelding of him, or if you will, hold a gun on these two while I do it."

"No," said Teodoro, "it is not the fault of the gonads that they hang on the wrong man. There is a respect in me for balls. It is not the testes where the fault is but in the head and in the heart. Ah! There is an idea! Tie him to that alamo, Elías." And when Lalo Solís was secured to the tree, Teodoro asked, "You have your knife?"

Elías took from the sheath hid behind his chaparreras a hunting knife, double-edged. Lalo Solís now screamed in terror.

"Cut his heart out," said Teodoro.

And like an Aztec high priest who must have been his ancestor, Elías Inés opened the man, reached in, and pulled the throbbing organ free from the body.

In Cañitas, Heraclio awaited the dawn of the new day. His troops had not come from Río Grande, and it had taken him most of the night to find the marconigraph operator who no longer kept regular hours since trains along the line had been suspended for some time. Heraclio must remain until he knew why his people had not obeyed his orders, and he found the man in a private house, not a public brothel but a discreet establishment for outsiders like the marconigraph operator, who was from the city.

He received his message then, the answer which had come from one of his lieutenants. The search for David Contreras' outlaw band and the killer of Concepción would now have to wait. Orders had come from the General Villa. Heraclio was to return to Torreón with his people; Villa was ready to move upon Zacatecas. He was suddenly tired and did not want to ride in the night to Peñuelas, where Marcelina lived, and so he asked the lady of the house for a room.

"I have but three rooms," she said, "and there is a girl for each room."

"I shall pay you for the girl," said Heraclio, "only keep her away from me. I do not wish to be disturbed."

In the morning he walked to the restaurant—the only restaurant in the small town—near the railroad station he broke his fast and there saw a man from la Flor taking a café con leche.

"Buenos días, Manuel," he said.

"Buenos días, don Heraclio," answered the man. "I accompany you in your grief."

"Thank you," said Heraclio. "And why are you here at this hour?"

"I wait for the patrón with his cousins from Spain. They come on the diligence from Fresnillo now that there is no train."

"I did not know there existed a diligence these days."

"A special trip, only," said Manuel. "To bring don Domingo and his people from Fresnillo."

At that moment the stagecoach arrived across the street from the restaurant, and Manuel hurried over to meet his patrón. He remained there to transfer the luggage to his own coach and the travelers went into the restaurant. "We shall have a bit of nourishment," Domingo Arguiú was saying, "for we have a ways to go before we reach the Big House." Three men were with him, dressed in foreign attire and dusty and tired from the trip across the prairie. They took a table nearby, and Domingo saw Heraclio.

"Hola, Heraclio," he said.

"Qué tal, Domingo?" said Heraclio. Domingo Arguiú turned back to his companions.

And the sound was heard of the strong gallop of a horse, then a voice shouting, "Hide yourselves, hide your goods! Here come the Revolutionaries!" The people ran, justifiably frightened, for outlaw bands were called *Revolutionaries*. Throughout México, hundreds of groups roamed outside the law, taking advantage of the popular insurrection to label themselves rebels and willy-nilly attacked rich or poor, and killed, and raped, and then burned unprotected settlements.

In the restaurant, the Chinese proprietor took his meat chopper from the chopping block and, muttering unintelligibly, went toward the rear of the building and opened a trap door to a cellar. Domingo called to him, "Wait. We will come with you," as Heraclio moved toward the door to his horse.

"Do not be an idiot," said Heraclio. "If they come, this will be the first place they stop, and they know that every railroad town has a restaurant, and every railroad restrauant has a cellar for a

338

pantry. The Goddamned gringos, when they built this line, made every restaurant alike and even painted every one the same color. That unfortunate little Chinese man is dead."

"What can we do?" asked Domingo.

"Get on the coach with Manuel and pray that you are not seen, for you can never outrun them." He pushed the door open and they followed him out. Manuel moved down the street toward them, and it was obvious that it was too late to run, for firing was now heard from the other side of the town.

"Ride along with us, Heraclio," said Domingo as he and his companions climbed aboard the coach. "Perhaps you can hold them off long enough so that we can make our escape."

"And why should I do that, Domingo? Why should I invite twenty or thirty men to fire at me when I am in no danger?" It was true. He had but to ride away, and the attackers could never come near him. To resist here would mean nothing but his death, and so he had no desire to become involved in this. There would be a day, soon, when there would be peace in the land. Perhaps he could, from a vantage point, look for the leader and destroy him, but with these renegades, there was always one waiting to take the place of a fallen leader; in fact there were usually two or three.

Domingo said, "You will do it because you are from la Flor and I am yet your patrón."

Heraclio laughed and said, "Adiós, Domingo."

One of the Spaniards, speaking for the first time, said, "We have money and will pay you well."

"No, señor," said Heraclio, and then he thought of Carmen and of the peon, Manuel, who a few minutes ago offered to share his grief because of Concho, and he said, "Come, Manuel! Quickly follow me!" He rode hard down the street.

To the north of town, beyond the slaughterhouse and stockyards, not far from where the rail now lay, was an abandoned silo-like structure. It was called simply, by the people, the tower, and had been erected during an era of the traitor Santa Ana, before the time of don Porfirio, when Cañitas was a settlement of but three or four houses, and at a time when the Indians had declared a war to the death against the white men. Through the decades, children played at war in the tower, yet there was little damage to the formidable edifice. Perfectly round, its walls were three adobes thick. The door, of massive hard madrone on either side with adobe sandwiched in between, was also strong enough to survive. Inside, the room was fifty feet or so across, and there were seven peepholes at eye level. Six feet above the floor ran a circular scaffold, also very sturdy, and above that, again, were seven openings. There was a place for a fire, and a few pieces of wood, for this had been a larder as well as a miniature fortress, and at that time, in the far past, it had perhaps possessed an odor not unpleasant to the senses, but now the air was close, near foul, dank from urine and defecation.

To this tower, Heraclio led the peon, Manuel, at a gallop. The luggage was quickly unloaded and Heraclio sent his horse through the door, then yelled, "Cuaco!" and with his fist struck the near horse under the ribs along the belly, and the coach sped straight ahead onto the plain.

"And why did you do that?" asked Domingo angrily. He did not like it here, and already he sensed that they had done the wrong thing in coming to this place.

"The coach would be in our way," said Heraclio, "if those people come here. If they do not, why, it will not matter and we shall find it for you." He moved to the horse and took his carbine, then went to one of the openings in the wall and looked outside for a moment. "Perhaps we will be fortunate," he said. "There is no activity whatever." He returned to his horse and unsaddled it. To Manuel he said, "Look out there, to the left. If they come, they shall come from there."

"We are trapped in this place," said Domingo.

"Do not be a woman," said Heraclio. "There is no one out there —there may not be anyone out there at all." The other Spaniards were all looking through the firing holes. "One of you, if you please," he said to them, "go to the other side and look to the rear. If someone appears—anyone!—call me."

Domingo, agitated and persistently angry, said, "And why do you have your horse here?"

Heraclio looked at him for a minute. "I can leave now," he said, "if that is what you wish. If that is not your desire, stop this nonsense and understand that I but try to save your worthless life. The horse is to send Manuel for help if we are here past dark. In

340

the darkness it will be a simple matter for one man to escape from here. It may not be necessary, for even if they come, they would not stay here more than three or four hours. Yet one can never tell. They might feel obligated to remain and wait us out."

Domingo said nothing, but also moved now toward an opening in the wall. He was encouraged that he saw no one, and he turned to his companions and said, "Well, my friends, in a short while we will be on our way."

They, entirely foreign to this life, frightened by that which they did not know, only nodded.

Then one said to Heraclio, deliberately avoiding Domingo's glance, because he felt there had been a discourtesy to this boy who meant to protect them, "My name is Esteban Murillo, and I wish to tell you that I am grateful, and at the same time, I must speak for my friends also, because I believe they, too, are grateful for what you do." He looked to his friends defiantly, not expecting them to object to his declaration, yet almost daring them to say a word.

And it happened that the marauders knew that the Spaniards were here because they had a man in town; in fact he, too, had sat in the restaurant where Heraclio saw Domingo once again, and he had followed down the street when the party began its flight, and had watched while the baggage was unloaded at the tower.

A few of the bandits came into sight, not many, perhaps ten or twelve, and they rode directly to the tower at a slow pace, not cautious, almost as if they were riding for pleasure. Halfway to the tower they halted as Heraclio called out:

"Up to there only. You may now turn around and go back to where you were."

The leader of the group answered, "Who are you, amigo? And why do you take the side of the Spaniards?"

"I am one who will put a bullet through your head if you move closer," said Heraclio. He did not answer the second question.

The bandits hesitated. "He has a sidearm," said the man who had been spying. He had not seen the carbine in its scabbard.

The outlaw leader smiled. "Well, that is as nothing," he said. "A man cannot be accurate with a hand weapon at this range. Spread out and let us take them." And saying so, he moved his mount forward toward the tower, and uttered not a cry as

Heraclio's bullet caught him below the left eye. The others stopped, just as they had begun their movement, and for a moment seemed posed upon the open landscape between the houses of the town and the tower.

Inside the small fortress, Domingo said, "Now you have done it! Now they shall never let us off!" Heraclio did not speak, looking intently at the men outside who were now around the fallen man, and one detached himself and rode back in the direction from where they had come.

"He will come back with the others," Heraclio said to Esteban Murillo.

"I can fire the pistol," said the Spaniard. "If you will allow me, I can be of help."

Domingo said, "You should not have hit the man. You could have fired to frighten them."

Heraclio laughed as he handed his gun and holster to Esteban Murillo. "You should know these people do not frighten. And I would not waste a shell in that manner when I have but forty or fifty rounds." He was alongside his horse again, where he had dropped his saddle and mochila, and he unrolled the bedroll. He took his spare gun and a leather pouch in which he carried extra shells.

Esteban spoke to Domingo for the first time, looking somewhat incongruous in a business suit and holster, rimless glasses and benign expression. "It is futile to threaten people who come to threaten you, Domingo. And a gun is for hunting or for defending oneself. It is not for frightening people."

"You have been a soldier, perhaps?" asked Heraclio.

"I have been a hunter," answered Esteban.

The rest of the bandit force came into view, and it was not as bad as Heraclio had feared. Together there were perhaps twenty-five men and now one spoke but did not attempt to come closer.

"You, in there: You see there are many of us and it is futile for you to resist us. In the beginning we wanted your money and your fine suitcases. Now, in addition to that, we want the cuckold who killed our chief. Send him out with your belongings and your money, and you are all free men!"

Heraclio turned to the Spaniard, Esteban, who now had his gun, expressionless.

342

And Domingo cried, "Shoot him! Shoot him, Esteban, you great fool!"

Esteban looked at Heraclio and said, "I would sooner put a bullet through my own brain than do that." Then he shook his head almost sadly and said, "You must be very much accustomed to treachery."

"I am only much accustomed to protect myself. You are a man, don Esteban. In my country one can say no more than that. They will, of course, now surround us, so, if you will, go to the other side and let them know we are not blind here."

"One thing only I wish that you understand," said Esteban. "It is not because I know those out there are lying that I choose to stand with you."

"That is understood," said Heraclio. He turned to Domingo, and despite his disgust wished to give the big man hope. "They cannot remain here more than a few hours, and help should come before that. Two hours, I think, and that is all the time they have for us. And then they will spend an hour to sack the town, and flee. That is their manner, so try to relax."

The man outside called again, having waited for a time until a decision could be made inside the fort. "You!" he yelled. "Will you send him out, or do we come for all of you?"

Heraclio said to no one in particular, "I suppose it is time those people are again discouraged." He knew there was no need for talk. He would not wait for them to charge, and so, he shot one man, and then another, before they turned and fled to the safety of the first buildings.

They waited in the tower, and it was a long wait until finally, over to the right and near the tracks, they could be seen, coming around in single file, and Heraclio, when he knew that the greater part of the force would still come from the left, said to Esteban, "Wait as long as you possibly can. If you think you cannot hit the man, hit the horse."

They came then, from front and rear, but they had to ride two hundred meters, and as they neared the bandits rode low, so Heraclio killed three horses before he heard the report of his pistol in Esteban's hand. They were near enough so he could pick a man, calmly, making certain he fired. He gave the rifle to Manuel to load, and took his pistol from his waist, and fired more rapidly now that the men were almost upon them.

They turned and ran, leaving their dead behind them. Two yet crawled, and Heraclio took his rifle from Manuel and shot them again, for he would not know what they did when the next charge came, and they might yet crawl near enough at their leisure to kill him. Behind him, Esteban, too, reloaded, and along the wall, to his left, Domingo and the other Spaniards talked together.

One said, "They want our money, that is all they want. And our suitcases. Well, I say, let us give them those things which would be worthless if we die."

"They will kill you," said Esteban.

"They want also," said Domingo, "my friend Heraclio, and now perhaps Esteban there, who has betrayed us."

"We can explain that we could do nothing," said the first. "After all, they only want our money."

The third, the man who had not yet spoken, said, "And what will they do now, señor?"

"I do not know," Heraclio answered, "except that now there are only about fifteen of them remaining. One more attack and there will be half that many. We can hold them off, perhaps annihilate them—that is, if we can see them. But they are here much too long and might yet remain until dark. Then we will have trouble, for we will not be able to see them. Then again, help might already be on the way or they might decide they should leave. Who knows?"

Domingo and the other man had made their decision and gathered their luggage together.

"I always thought you a fool, Domingo," said Heraclio. "Even when you thought you were my tutor. I shall tell you one more time, do not go out there."

Domingo, for the first time, had color in his face. "I will not remain here until darkness and die for no reason. We can save ourselves and we will." He turned to Esteban and said, "Do you accompany us?"

And the clerklike Esteban, very unlike a clerk, said, "As you explained to Curro, they would not let me live," and he smiled, it seemed, in pleasure.

344

"We shall tell them that you are with us—that the peon, here, was firing," said Domingo.

"Thank you, Domingo, but no."

The third man was undecided. And he turned to Heraclio, but Heraclio was impassive. A man had the right to die if he wished to die, and a fool had the right to be a fool if it meant only his death and no one else's.

The three moved out, and Esteban said to Heraclio, "I do not know why Domingo has done this. I wish we could have stopped them."

"We would have had to shoot them," said Heraclio. "You are related with Domingo?"

"First cousins, we are."

Heraclio felt compassion for the man. "Here," he said, "a first cousin is as a brother. You must feel a great sadness."

"A little sadness," said Esteban, "for a human being. We Spanish, who taught you this kinship, have unfortunately forgotten it." He looked out, and Heraclio said kindly:

"There is no need that you should watch."

"I may someday have to relate how he died."

They all looked out to see Domingo and his companions now almost halfway to the buildings. Occasionally, they stopped for a moment, and set their luggage on the ground. They were resting thus when the marauders rode toward them firing and yelling as they came, and all three died before they reached them.

The bandits did not charge again.

Esteban Murillo and the peon, Manuel, took the bodies to la Flor in the night. And Heraclio went to Peñuelas, there to remain with Marcelina until morning when he left for Río Grande and then to Torreón, and from there to the Battle of Zacatecas.

The Third Book

Los Desgraciados

As the Federal survivors—those who escaped from Zacatecas before the rebels entered—fled toward Aguascalientes, tearing up great sections of track, Álvaro Obregón was at the approaches to Guadalajara and it was clear to Carranza that there was little resistance left to keep Villa from Mexico City. The great Constitutionalist victory at Zacatecas, which should have brought joy to the First Chief, was instead a blow and in his panic that the guerrilla would indeed move his hordes into the capital before his own General Obregón he labeled Villa a traitor for his insubordination.

Villa, who no longer considered himself as a subordinate, who with his decision to attack Zacatecas against the express orders of Carranza had severed completely his ties with the Constitutionalists, merely laughed at the old man's ineffectual harangue and made plans to move south. First, however, it was necessary to bring supplies from the north. His ammunition was depleted, his stores exhausted, and now that the embargo had been lifted by Woodrow Wilson, he had but to send his trains to Juárez.

Venustiano Carranza had ceased to be platitudinous toward Villa, and, astute man that he was, he reasoned that if the Division of the North lacked food and ammunition, it must also lack fuel and, since he controlled all the rebel coal, Villa must come to him. He gave the order that no coal be allotted to his ex-ally, openly designating Villa an enemy of the people. Villa was now incapable of moving in any direction; he realized his error in defying Carranza too early—even after Zacatecas he could have made his peace with the First Chief, but now it was too late. The Division of the North was immobilized and Álvaro Obregón was now within the city of Guadalajara.

Thus, as it had been early in the campaign, before Juárez, before Torreón and Zacatecas, riders roamed in every direction to bring food for the hungry city. Zacatecas was crowded, and the unsanitary conditions which the medical officer had feared did not diminish despite every effort. And before long, in different sections of the city, a child, an old man, or a woman complained of being ill. Nothing serious, a headache it was, and perhaps pains in back or in front down low. And a fever—but these were common ills among the poor, and no one wondered until the fever turned to chills and then convulsions. Three days later, small pimples appeared upon the exposed parts of the afflicted, and more people had the fever and chills. The small pimples became blisters and the blisters pustules. There was no denying now what the doctors had already told Villa, that the dreaded plague called variola had come to the Division of the North.

Villa was furious. Because the Indians in remote areas rarely knew this disease, he reasoned that it must have been the Spaniard who brought it here. The Aztec legions must have suffered this very thing. And that was his rage, the Spaniard always won in the end.

And now some of the sick began to hemorrhage and to die, and there were others whose mouths and throats filled with vesicles, who choked and also died, as did those who became delirious with the return of the fever, then comatose, who, being undernourished even before the epidemic, were too weak to resist death. In the mornings and then again in the afternoons, wagons rolled along the cobbled streets, and men whose pockmarked faces displayed their immunity collected the dead. There was no laughter now, no song or jest, for this was a mysterious death, without violence and therefore lacking honor. The people of the city began their own inoculations, with needles from the nopal, they took the pus from the eruptions, and pricked themselves, and when the lesion appeared on arm or thigh, they took from it and in the

348

same manner inoculated their children. But the fires burned again at the city's edge.

It seemed endless and continued until Villa ordered that the sick should be removed from the city. Two leagues into the western plain, a town built of tents and lean-tos became the place for death. Doctors and nurses were not allowed to go, for they were of more value within the city, and the exiled were beyond help now—they would die or survive, it was that simple. But those men and women who had sometime survived the disease went out to care for the doomed people. And no one could leave the area; even the healthy who had come to see their loved ones expire must remain there or be shot. Riflemen stationed around the area killed those who would return to the city.

To this strange settlement and the smell of death came Heraclio Inés to search for his woman. He had been away to the east, for a fortnight, and had not known of the pestilence until now. The house where he had placed her was devoid of life, and he turned to the next house, and then the next, and he felt sudden horror that the entire block was empty—in fact, the neighborhood was empty. He walked the streets, eerie in their quietness, until he saw a human hurrying into a building, and he followed the man, not bothering to be polite in his anxiety.

"Tell me," he said, "what has happened here!"

"They have been banished—like lepers, they have been sent out on the prairie to live or die as they will." He kept walking, reached a staircase, and began to climb.

Heraclio rushed and took him by the arm. "Stop a moment." The man attempted to wrest his arm free, and Heraclio said more harshly, "Stop!"

The man looked at him, suddenly patient, and there was fear in his face, but not for Heraclio.

"Now, tell me. What has happened here?"

"The variolas have attacked us," said the man.

"That I know," said Heraclio. "That there was illness here, I have been told. But the people of these houses, where are they? And what is this of banishment?"

"The General Villa has sent them away. My whole family is gone, how many are sick I know not, for the mother would never

349

break up the family. He has decreed, the General, that at the first indication of illness, the victim is taken from the city."

"And all the people from these empty houses," asked Heraclio, "everyone—is that where they are now?"

"They have all been banished like undesired animals."

There was a sound of gunfire, and Heraclio asked, "Do you know the meaning of that?"

"Executions—there are many who are looting, and Villa for once does not want his men to loot. When there is more than one shot, it is generally a firing squad. Isolated gunfire is for vultures—the other kind—which have now taken to coming in open windows to eat those who are not yet dead."

"You are going out there?" asked Heraclio.

"I but come for blankets. It is cold at night out in that desert, and I was not here when they were taken."

"We shall go together," said Heraclio.

And he found her, lying in a lean-to with the opening toward the southerly breeze. She slept, and a woman old as life squatted beside her, smoking. He sat on a box and waited, and after some time he said:

"How long has she been here, old woman?"

She did not answer, now rolling another cigarette, and he knew he must wait until she was ready, and turned once again to watch the face of Xóchitl. Sometime later the old woman said, "She came this morning, probably. I do not know. I have been here since before the midday, when my husband expired. She was alone, and I was right nearby, and so I came when Cleofas died. They would not allow me to return to the city and I might as well help her while she yet has life." She had been squatting all this time and did not change her position. She puffed on the cigarette once and continued, "After a while, her man came, and we, together, bathed her to alleviate the fever. He is gone now, to where they bring the food, but it will not matter greatly, for she is doomed."

Heraclio was angry. First, because the old crone had mentioned another man, then because she said Xóchitl would die.

"You talk much when you finally begin, old woman," he said gruffly. She shrugged her shoulders and looked in his face. He was amazed she seemed amused by all this—she seemed to be silently laughing at him. But he thought of the husband she had lost a few hours ago and was suddenly contrite and sad for her. "I am sorry you have lost your man," he said, not looking at her.

She said simply, without regret nor grief, "We were married eighty years."

They sat in silence, and Antonio Rivera walked behind them. "Heraclio, you have come," he said, and there was a weariness to him.

"I have come," said Heraclio, and in spite of himself he could not control a displeasure he could not explain.

Antonio said, "I am sorry, my brother, that I was forced to gaze upon your woman's body. But you were not here and she suffered."

He was ashamed, and said, "I am sorry, Antonio," but Antonio was already starting a fire and looked up, almost happy, and said:

"Perhaps she will take some broth when she wakes."

"I am awake now," said Xóchitl, "but I want no nourishment."

Heraclio went to her and placed his hands on her face. She seemed cool, but now he saw what he had refused to see: the beginnings of pimples along her hairline.

"At first I thought it was your son, Heraclio," she said.

"My son?"

She said, "When I awoke yesterday morning, I vomited and I laughed at myself because I believed I was pregnant. Xóchitl Salamanca, I said, you have blown yourself up with your own bomb—I think of bombs, you know because we are in the war. And although I have not wanted a child, I was gloriously happy that we were to have one. But then the fever came. And I was alone, and in the morning, today, I suppose—they came through the houses, for some people hide their sick, and they found me.

"I tried to fight them, the soldiers, for I wished to wait for you. I could not possibly win."

He stroked her hair. "You will get well, Xóchitl, and I shall take you from all this."

She chose to not hear him, and said, "I heard the old woman, Heraclio, and she is not to be blamed for thinking Antonio was my man. He has cared for me in the manner he would care for you."

"I know," he said, then, "You were awake all the while?"

"All the while," she said. "When you came, although I did not look, I knew you had come. And I wanted to rest—merely to relax and feel your presence for a time. For that reason I did not speak, will you forgive me?"

"Of course. But do not speak so much. You must rest so that you can be well again."

But she said, "I must speak while I can, for I will not live through this. I have always known that I do not have much time . . ."

He was angry. "Do not speak nonsense!"

She reached her hand to his own face, now. "Do not be angry and do not be sad, for it is true, my love. And I wish that you should know that I have lived a lifetime with you, that is only what I wish that you should know. Only that."

"Quiet," he said. "There is more, much more to be lived." But she had closed her eyes and shortly fell asleep. Heraclio walked outside to where Antonio boiled the beef. The old woman started to rhythmically fan the air before Xóchitl's face.

"The doctors," said Heraclio, "why could they not have treated her?"

"It was his wish," said Antonio, "that the doctors should not come out where they could do no good."

"She will live?"

"We cannot know before another three days."

Heraclio said, "I am finished here, Antonio. I am going home and I shall take her with me."

"And Marcelina?"

"This does not concern her."

Antonio did not argue. He could not, for he knew it could be done—that Heraclio could have a wife and family as well as a mistress. It was not unusual. But he said, "And the war? And your general?"

"The war must surely be over," said Heraclio. "If it is not, there is yet no reason I should remain, for with this unnecessary act my general has betrayed me. There is suddenly no cause left for me."

"I go with you," said Antonio, "because I never believed there was a cause, and I have felt the whip."

But Xóchitl refused to allow Heraclio to suffer long. She was to die, she knew—three days or four, perhaps, it would take, but she would die. And so she willed that she would die that night because a few hours more of life did not matter. And she lay immobile, conscious, listening, but the three who sat beside her held their vigil silently. And sometime in the night, she opened her eyes and looked into Heraclio's face but did not speak, and died. The three did not move toward her, nor did they attempt to help her now, for they knew death well, and yet there was no sound until Antonio said:

"This you must know, Heraclio. Because of my love for you, I must tell you that I loved her." Tears ran down his face.

Heraclio felt a loss he had never known existed. He grieved deeply, but could not cry, and he answered his friend, "Then she was loved by a man," and he put his arms around Antonio and cradled him.

The old woman, on her haunches, yet smoked and was silent, while almost at that very moment Álvaro Obregón entered Mexico City.

Two days later, even before he went to his own home, Heraclio Inés returned to the house of his brother, Teodoro. Even as he entered they knew he had changed. This not because he was quiet, for this was a family trait, but there was a change and they did not know what to expect until he spoke and said, "I am at your orders, Teodoro. I come to work for the hacienda and that of the Revolution is over for me."

Teodoro was overjoyed, but not so much that he was unaware of his young brother's unhappiness. He said, "I am happy, Heraclio, and your brothers are happy, for you belong here. Especially you belong here now that Concho is no longer with us."

Heraclio sat listlessly, and now, thinking of Concepción, he felt that it was then when disillusion began to work at him. It came to him how much he disliked war, and yet how much he had liked it when in battle, since almost every time things had gone well for him. But, too, he had at times fought against those with whom once he had battled side by side. This knowledge did not help. At times, he almost believed that someone was directing the whole thing—misdirecting would be the better word for it—and therefore it was a great futility and a useless war. He still believed the fight was for the people, especially when he thought of Villa, but

353

he now had an occasional doubt. His general, whom he knew to be cruel and callous as he was brave, had committed an inhuman act when he sent those people away from the city to die. They could have been isolated within the city, could have been attended by the doctors, perhaps many of them could have lived, but the war demanded that the healthy remain healthy. The war demanded that Villa remove the pestilence so that he could have the strength to fight. And somehow it was also the war which took Concho's life, and he had never been a part of the war. Xóchitl had been a part of it, but she had also been a woman and somehow that should make it a different thing. That day he found her in the prairie, he no longer knew whether the cause existed or not, and because he did not know, he must lay down his arms. When she died, his grief would not allow him to think, and now to leave, to get away, was a compulsion.

He said to Teodoro, because he was thinking of Concho yet, "And Otilia, she is here?"

"With her father in El Fuerte," said Teodoro. He seemed almost apologetic for a weakness, yet could not deny his weakness as Heraclio looked at him with disbelief. "Yes," he said. "I allowed her to go to her family. When Concho died and then we had our revenge, I believed that she should remain. Then two days later they brought the patrón's body home, I suddenly had no will to fight her. It all seemed to be falling apart, somehow—everything. Not a thing was as it has always been, and I was nearly happy that my father did not live to see the collapse of the order of things. So when Elías came to me and said, 'I will take Otilia and the boy to her people,' I had no spirit left. The boy will someday return, of course, for he is one of us."

Heraclio for the first time in his life felt compassion for Teodoro, knowing that what he had felt for a time was akin to his own confusion at the moment. He placed a hand upon Teodoro's shoulder and stood up.

Teodoro asked, "You will eat?"

"No," he answered. "I will go home. I have been a long time coming."

In Peñuelas, he took up the life he had never lived, and repressed every thought of the war, every thought of his general. He put his gun away, and he worked hard on the range. Teodoro sent peones to enlarge his house, and Heraclio played with his daughter, who was now learning to speak words, and he made love with his wife in the night, and behaved in every way as if now he was truly happy.

Marcelina was not fooled, however, and she passed her days in sadness that her man was mourning. She deceived him into believing that she suspected nothing. And thus the days passed.

When in la Flor, he visited with Antonio Rivera, who now took his regular turn on the range as long as he was never asked to break a horse. They talked, and occasionally they shared a bottle, but their reunions were tame for their youth and yet they were happy. Once, Antonio, who had never owned a gun until he went to war, said to him:

"It is pure folly that you do not wear a gun, Heraclio."

And he answered, "I do not like the gun, now, Antonio."

"Nevertheless, these are not really peaceful times although it seems peaceful enough here. Who knows how many are roaming up there," and Antonio pointed to the distant mountains, "and sometimes they might surprise you. Think only of what happened to your brother Concho."

"The gun did not help him," said Heraclio.

"With you it might be different."

"If it comes, it comes," said Heraclio, and he thought of what he said, knew that never in his life had he ever believed such a thing. "I do not like the gun," he said once more.

He went to the Big House after a time, to see Carmen, finally, because he felt he should and because he had long avoided this. She received him in the large salon, near the alcove where they had kissed so long ago. Her weeds enhanced her beauty, the severe cut of her dress accentuated her body. On her hair, she wore two plain combs above the chignon, pulling the golden tresses tight against her skull.

He enjoyed her beauty and did not speak. She took his hand and at her touch he felt desire, strong. But then he thought and, unlike the desire, the thought was sacrilegious and the mind conquered the body so she became once more an old friend.

"You have come, at last," she said. "I have waited long." Her face was unlined, there was no sadness there, but then she smiled

355

a small quick smile of pleasure that he was there, and then he knew a thing was lacking. There was no humor left in her.

They sat, and now he held both her hands as they partially faced each other. "I am happy that I finally came to see you. You look well," he said.

"I do?" she asked, and there was a small hint of the coquette remaining. "I have been alone here, now, and have no one to tell me this, I do not know."

Now Heraclio smiled. "You are beautiful and you are aware of it, Carmen." Then he grew serious. "I come to see you and to talk with you, but I come also to tell you how sorry I have been that you lost your husband."

"Thank you, my friend," she said. "But it is not unpleasant to the widowed." She sensed his disapproval and said, "Heraclio, you always tried to teach me candor—do not now be offended by my use of it. I am deeply sorry Domingo died. I am in mourning because he was my husband, and I would defend his name now and when he lived, as I honored him then, but I had no respect for him. He was not a man and ours was never a marriage—other than that I will say not another word because I would not further desecrate his name. I am sorry and yet I am not sorry. I tell you this because we have always spoken honestly, you and I, except that one time when you came to see me when Domingo yet lived. I was hateful that day."

His sorrow was that she was alone, and the quietness of the great house illustrated this fact. "If you wish, I shall describe his last hours," he said.

"There is no need. Esteban Murillo described the murders, and he also told me that you tried to save Domingo. I have not thanked you for that, and I do now. He also told me how Domingo behaved throughout it all, and I am sorry he acted in that way with you, for he had reason to be grateful—we both had reason to be grateful for what you have done for la Flor."

He did not speak, for he knew what she meant. In these last few months of war, the hacienda had been untouched. Horses, and mules, and cattle had been taken from the range, but the hacienda and its people had not been disturbed. And this was because of Heraclio. He wished to leave the subject and said, "And don Esteban, is he on his way back to Spain?"

356

"He is in México, but will return in another month to help me here. He is a good man."

"A man he is," said Heraclio.

"He wishes to marry me."

"And will you?"

She said, "It is much too soon for that—but no, I should not lie to you. I refused." She looked steadily into his face. "I told him I could never marry because I loved you. In time, perhaps, because a man is necessary here, I might again think of a marriage without love. At this time I cannot conceive of such a thing. I love you, Heraclio, I always have loved you and there is nothing that can change that."

He put an arm around her and held her head to his chest for a moment, then released her. Again he could not speak, and she said:

"I wish that sometime you would come and sit with me. When you are near here in your work and evening falls, come eat with me sometime."

"I will," he said. "I will come soon." It was not necessary to speak of Marcelina. They both knew she existed and that knowledge would always keep them platonic.

In this way, Heraclio Inés lived on, far removed from the war which was far from settled. As the months went by, in the city of Aguascalientes, revolutionary leaders from every point in the Republic squabbled endlessly to select an interim president who would serve until a constitutional election could be held. And it was clear that not everyone could be satisfied. Factions formed for another fight and the end was not in sight. Heraclio heard very little of this; only when he spoke to someone who had been to Río Grande or Cañitas did he learn news of the outside world. It was almost six months since Zacatecas, almost six months since Xóchitl's death, and he had not yet regained that part of himself he had lost when she died.

It was on the Good Night, so called because once long ago in a land far away a woman delivered on this day, that Marcelina told Heraclio that she thought herself pregnant.

"That is good," he said, but his voice was devoid of feeling. "It is time that my son be born."

She, having hoped that this announcement would so gladden

him that she could once again see the boyish, carefree look on his face, could not dissimulate her disappointment. Her mouth and chin quavered and she struggled and finally controlled her tears.

Heraclio watched her all the while, stuporlike in horror at his indifference. He had not realized he had changed that much. "I am sorry, Marcelina. So sorry." He took her to him, and held her as they stood, but she was rigid in his arms. He sat her down, very much in the manner he had done on their wedding day, upon the bed, half facing him.

"Forgive me," he said. "For the pain I have given you; for not realizing that you knew I have been different, forgive me. Yes, and for having changed, forgive me."

She looked down to her lap, seemingly fighting something within her. And then she faced him and took his head between her hands and kissed him. She spoke rapidly then, thinking that he might silence her, thinking how she had never done a thing like that in her life. "I have no right, I know, to speak to you in this way—to question you. But you are my life, and I must make things right again or I shall surely die. A thing has happened— what I do not know, except that it was strong enough to make you leave your general. I can think of one thing only . . . that she left you, and I cannot imagine why a woman should leave you. And I am afraid to think another woman meant so much to you."

"She died," said Heraclio. "And she did mean much to me, but that is not the reason for my state. It is that there seems to be no real cause for life. I suddenly have nothing in which to believe."

Marcelina was gladdened because he was not angry that she should talk of these things to him, and because it did not hurt her more to hear from him what she had known. "I waited," she said, "and waited, until I thought I should go insane before you came back to me. I even wished that you would take a woman, then I would know again that you were well. Always before, when you had someone else, I knew, and I felt pain, but when we were together I knew that you belonged to me. At this moment I do not know where you belong." He kissed her hands and she withdrew them. "I have always known," she said, "and now, when you have taken me, it is not as before. Now you use my body for a very short while, whereas before, I felt your love even as you emptied within me. We have conceived, and yet there was no feeling."

358

She did not speak of passion, he knew well. But there was nothing to be said except that perhaps with time things would be right again.

She said, "I have been thinking, that perhaps it is not wrong for a man's wife to also be his mistress, whatever it is that a mistress does for a man. It would seem that passion is the one thing a mistress is allowed, and I am thinking it would not be difficult for me to learn passion, if you would permit me."

He laughed and she felt a stab of pain that she should seem ludicrous to him. But his laugh had been so natural that she uttered a cry of joy. "You are an idiot," he said, and he was smiling. She took his hand and placed it under her shift to her bare breast. "Remember this?" she asked, and she trembled. And he remembered the first time he had touched her, and he asked, "How do you know so much?"

"Because I am Indian," she said. "From my great-grandfather, I am Indian, you know."

She startled him, and then he thought that must be it. They could have been sisters, he thought. He pushed her back and covered her body, and her eyes were open, wide, looking at him with a vague smile of pleasure, and for the first time she put her own arms around him, her fingers feeling his strong back, and she said, her great dark eyes perplexed, "You must tell me what to do, am I to move because I feel I want to move? I do not really know what I feel." He said, "Yes, yes, do whatever you feel you want to do," and again he said, "Yes," as she without thought or knowledge raked his back.

They were one now, as he had always known. For this reason he had chosen her to be his wife and he had forgot these past months. He left the bed, and naked walked through the house to the small shed alongside. The saddle he had used in Zacatecas was on a hook, the scabbard still attached. He took the short mauser from it, and from another hook took the bandoleers. He picked a chamois bag which held his clips and shells. He thought suddenly that he must have not been too certain he was finished, else why did he put everything away so carefully. And he laughed. The holster and revolver were also there, and he took that also.

She watched him as he cleaned the guns, and then as he worked on the gun belt. She said, and she attempted to hide her embarrassment, "I suppose I did not do badly—a while ago, I mean."

He looked up and saw how serious she was, how important all this was to her life. And he said, "I really think you will learn. You may practice again in a little bit."

She grinned that he should want her. "I am waxing sore, but of course I cannot deny my man."

"A mistress can," he said.

She sat up, and she had removed her garment and was bare to the waist. This also she had never done. "Then I shall remain a wife," she said. "With certain privileges, of course," and unaccountably she winked one eye.

In the morning early, he took her to Río Grande so she could hear High Mass. He left her at the church and went to a cantina where he broke his fast and had a few tequilas. And there he learned that David Contreras was again in the area. He had a fame now, it seemed, and he was one to be feared. And Heraclio thought he might take his family and leave the hacienda for a new place. He had regained his life, and he could not know when David might take it into his head to come for him.

But he did not remove himself from Peñuelas, thinking that in a few weeks he would build a house in la Flor near his brothers. It was unlikely that David would come there.

And now it was the month of February, and now, truly, Heraclio was enchanted by life. He had in the past been satisfied, and he had known happiness, but happiness unencumbered he had never known. Always there had been something disturbing the balance of things. Now he was a family man, and he was industrious. From deep in the bush, he had brought mavericks, one by one and because it was the law of the land they were his; he put his own mark upon them. And he had also cut off from a wild herd three mares, now tame, and soon to be serviced by one of the hacienda's great burros. He would have mules and one day, perhaps, a piece of land.

He did not brood about the war now, and had no doubts that there was a need for law and order and for justice, but he believed all this would come to pass. He had done his part, had played the role his destiny decreed.

360

Marcelina, too, was enchanted and knew contentment. Before the world, she was yet quiet, reserved, subservient, but in the privacy of their home, she became gay and vivacious, and they teased and played and loved—there was no reason to believe that they would not live forever.

When the time came that all this ceased to be, it happened quickly, suddenly, as David Contreras came riding down upon the isolated Peñuelas, whose men were on the range. Two or three ancient men were there, the others, women, and as David rode into the great corral which faced the houses, four men followed him into the enclosure. He was known here, for these people all at one time or another had lived in the main settlement; they had known his mother even before she bore him.

As the women scurried, attempting to hide, an old man basking in the sun seemed undisturbed and unafraid. He sat there peacefully, and David went to him and asked, "Where is the house of Heraclio?"

"Ask someone," answered the old man. "Anyone can tell you."

"Speak up, old one!" said David. "Or surely I shall put an end to your miserable life."

The old man spoke slowly; to him David was but a nuisance, and he said, "My life ended long ago, youngster. It ended on the day I could no longer stand up and destroy the likes of you; it ended the day I could not be bothered by such as you."

David whirled away from him in anger, then dismounted. He walked to the nearest house and there, cowering in a corner, he found a child. He dragged him out and shook him hard. "Where lives Heraclio Inés?"

The child stammered, his eyes wide with fear, and he pointed. David half dragged him from the house, and the boy led him across to the other side of the semicircle of buildings. David dropped him outside the door of the house and the boy scrambled and ran and climbed a stone fence, then lost himself in the prairie.

In the house, Marcelina placed her child, Ofelia, under the bed, the only hiding place she could think of in her fright, and as David entered, she fired at him with the small revolver Heraclio had given her so long ago, but he walked up and took the gun from her hand. He struck her then, and she lay on the floor, and at that moment, the child whimpered and crawled out, and David kicked her along the jaw so that she rolled back out of sight, and he picked up Marcelina, tearing her clothes as he did so, and then he ripped them off before he threw her on the bed. She struggled as he mounted her and his nails ripped her flesh as he spread her legs apart, and at the last moment before he entered her, he bit her on the shoulder so that blood ran on the white coverlet.

Not one word had been spoken, not one scream from Marcelina, and David left her there and walked out into the sun. And at that moment, from across the corral came Heraclio, and he stopped near a house and called out. There against a doorway he stopped and called to David, who had not seen him and had remounted.

He said, "You have come, finally, David. You have come for me."

"I have done that for which I came, Heraclio," said David. "I give you your life, for in that way you will suffer much more. Step into your house and see your woman."

"What have you done to her?"

"To her nothing, for she was but an instrument which I used to get to you." He laughed. "You wear the horns, Heraclio. A cuckold I have made of you."

"You have become the dog they always said you were."

"The little girl, also, you should see, for I believe she died. Yes, she must have died," said David, smiling, "because I have killed dogs with less force." He knew for the first time, had known from the moment Heraclio called to him, that Heraclio would die. Heraclio was armed, yet they were five and he would not be difficult.

Heraclio said, "An inhuman son of a bitch you are, David, and you lay with bitches."

David was casual, for it was not yet time and it was Heraclio who was becoming angry. He said calmly, "Then your wife must indeed be a female dog, Heraclio, for she has just this minute lain with me."

For Heraclio, the traditional vocal exchange was ended. He raised the short cavalry rifle and his shot hit David on the hip and knocked him from the saddle. He had not been able to raise his own gun. Heraclio fired again as the others spun their mounts, attempting to return his fire, and one more fell before Heraclio heard their guns. He leaned against the wall of the house and calmly aimed and fired another time. A third man dropped, and then Heraclio moved from the house as the remaining two turned and ran across the corral. The first of these died in a few yards, the second died nearly at the low stone fence. His horse jumped the fence easily and ran into the open plain.

The mauser was empty now, and Heraclio dropped it and drew his pistol. He walked to where David lay, now surrounded by women of Peñuelas. He was conscious and would live though he would never walk straight again, and a woman said, "Poor thing— unfortunate from the womb!" and crossed herself, uttering a silent prayer.

Heraclio said, "Stand aside." David lay on his good side, smiling up at him as if they were alone in the mountain with their sheep and he was merely resting. They were alone and they did not speak and Heraclio shot him three more times. He walked to his house, and a woman said, "They are both dead, Heraclio. Your woman and your child are both dead."

He found Marcelina atop the body of Ofelia. Somehow, she had been able to pull the child out from under the bed and into the center of the room. He saw at a glance the child's broken neck, but on Marcelina he could find no fatal wound. He turned to the women wailing behind him. "Go away," he said. "I shall bury my own dead."

II

In Río Grande, he remained in a drunken stupor for a week, and then, still drinking, he went to the house of his brother. No one disturbed him, leaving him to his sorrow, until Antonio Rivera came and said:

"Do you not think, Heraclio, that it is enough? To drink is no disgrace if it is for pleasure—but this is for pity."

"It is not for you to reprimand me, Antonio."

"I am the only one, Heraclio, for surely your brothers will not do it."

Heraclio would not argue, and he could never be surly, so he did not speak.

Antonio said, "I come to tell you that the patrona wishes to see you."

And Heraclio surprised him and said, "Well, let us go see her." At the door of the Big House, Antonio left him.

He did not knock, but walked straight in and to the cabinet in the far wall. He took a bottle of aguardiente and opened it. When he turned, she was standing a few feet away, watching him with a pained expression which she controlled as his eyes focused on her face.

"You wished to see me?" he asked.

She knew he expected disapproval, wanted disapproval so that he could have reason to defend himself. He was behaving badly deliberately, and she ignored this and said, "You came here not too long ago to tell me you were sorry my husband had died. I only wanted that—to offer my condolences, to tell you I, too, grieve that you have lost Marcelina. Aside that she was your wife, I mourn that she is dead because she was goodness. And I cannot forget that David was the son of my father. Foully conceived, he was, and he was foul."

He said, offering the bottle, "Take a drink with me—but it is not cognac."

She did not ask for a glass but took the bottle and brought it to her lips. She swallowed long. He seemed to be suddenly confused.

"Thank you," he said at last. "Thank you for showing me something about what courtesy is. I will not say I am sorry, for I have not been myself."

She took his arm, then, and said, "Sit. And we shall drink again but only one more time for me." This time she took his head to her, but he did not speak, yet she felt him relax against her. Then he moved away, and took the bottle once again. She took it from his hand and smiled sadly. Then she drank and returned it to him. But he did not drink now, and said:

"It has been a life, Carmen. For certain it has been a life I have had. There does not seem to be one more bad thing left that could happen to me."

"You have been thinking that?"

364

"I have been thinking that. Before, when I returned from the army, I was disgusted, I believed that there was nothing worth while remaining on this earth, and then I learned again the goodness of Marcelina—that goodness you spoke of—and I was alive once again. Now I feel that I am doomed to walk through life causing misery. Everything I place my hands on has somehow withered; I carry gloom wherever I tread; I carry death about me. I have fought the destiny so much for so long—and it has taken me all my life to learn that in the end the destiny rules. Everything that has happened to those I loved has been entirely out of my control, yet I have somehow been to blame. Of course I can say, as in the case of Marcelina's death, if I had turned around one half hour earlier—for I was on my way here when I had a premonition, I really did, and I shrugged it off, and then a while longer, I again had the feeling of an impending disaster, and I turned back, but I was too late. I can say that if I had turned back at once it would never have happened, but that is not true. I could say I should not have done those things I did to David, but again that is not true. Everything I love I somehow hurt. Even David, whom I once loved as a brother, I killed in the end. Even you, perhaps you I have injured the most."

She said, "Heraclio! Heraclio, my love! It is not you who have hurt me. It was but circumstance. And you were hurt as much as I."

"I do not know," he said. "I truly do not know. I feel almost that I must separate myself from my fellow man, else I contaminate everything. And yet I cannot quite believe that, because it is so necessary that there be a life form. I am going back to war, Carmen. That I do know. I will give the destiny every chance at me, and if I survive, then I will live again. Then I will know for certain that I can be my own master, that I can dictate my life. It is necessary for me to live again."

He drank now, and he did not offer the bottle to her. She said, "This I must say to you now, then, and I wish that you know it is not a sudden thought, for I have had it in my mind for days—and I have known a guilt for having such a thought so soon after Marcelina's death. I want that we should marry. I want you to be the lord of la Flor, to be the father of my children, to found a dynasty of strong men. I love you, and although I know you no longer have the same feeling for me, I do know you have affection and you have a love. Marry me and we shall do good things for our people. And you will be dictating your own life, as you say. I was not going to tell you this until later, but I have no choice now that you have decided to go away. I do not want you to go to war; I do not want you to die. I lost you once and I do not want to lose you again."

Heraclio now took her hands and pulled her toward him. His face close to hers, he said, "I remember well, Carmen, the love I had for you as I know now the love I feel. But, you see, I cannot do such a thing. Someday, perhaps, when I feel whole, I could do it. But now I think only that to marry you would be an injustice to you. I really do not think that I shall ever take a wife again." And then he jested for the last time, "But if I marry, I shall marry you."

She understood that the mystical explanation for all the tragedy in his life was at the moment a very real thing to him. She understood, and she was sad, but she said, "I shall hold you to it, Heraclio Inés. I will wait for you, only do not make it too long a wait."

He left the next day, Antonio Rivera with him, and they arrived in time to take part in the last great battle of the Mexican Revolution, for, in the first two weeks of April, in the cities of Celaya and León in Guanajuato, the forces of Alvaro Obregón slew or captured almost half of Villa's mighty army, then systematically hacked to pieces the great Division of the North as it fled in confusion toward the north.

III

THE LAST TRAIN TO THE NORTH left Irapuato on the fifteenth of April, two days after the second defeat at Celaya. Although it was not known to be the last train, there might not be another, and so civilian and military alike fled northward, for the hordes of Obregón and Benjamín Hill could not be contained now.

The train moved slowly, barely perceptibly at first, for it had but one engine and twenty coaches plus thirty boxcars. And these

366

were replete with humanity. Men and women with their children, entire families with all their earthly possessions; here and there a piglet, or a goat, perhaps a lamb was seen. All this and the statues of saints made the cargo overflow up onto the roofs of the cars. And up on top, in the stiff cold breeze, the children rode, fascinated by the experience of being high on a train, their young minds attaching no significance whatever to the fact that they had severed their ties with the earth, not knowing even that somewhere they would grow new roots. And their parents sat cold and impassively on the roof, patient like their forebears. They were going north, many not merely to the north of the Republic, but beyond, into another country.

Occasionally, a child bawled.

In the coaches, it was not much different, but in the boxcars rode those who were not strong enough to climb on top or to fight for a seat in the cars. And here was horror for young and old alike. Here, wounded soldiers moaned or screamed pitiably, and some died. Ill civilians, virulent or weakened by amoebic dysentery, barely breathed. There was no room whatever to move, and the coldness was relieved only by the heat generated by so many bodies jammed together. And this very proximity was sickening, for the refugees urinated and defecated where they lay. If a person moved, he lost his place immediately, or if a child changed his position, he might lose his entire family. The scant air was foul, and when a wounded soldier died, or when a civilian without family or friends died, he or she was thrown out onto the railroad to make room for the living. Only the civilians objected or attempted to stop this. They were Christians and would have a Christian burial. When a woman began to deliver prematurely and died with the creature still inside her, or a child, dehydrated by the intensity of dysentery or starved of nourishment, also died, the family tried to keep the body with them until there could be a proper burial. They attempted to hide the fact that one of theirs had expired, but in the end their wails revealed their secret.

But the soldiers were godless, having repressed the idea of God long ago, for to recognize Him would be to reject Him, since He had disclosed an imperfection in having created imperfect men. And they could not reject Him completely, which they would do if they began to blame Him, for they needed Him for later, when

367

peace came—when their problems and their suffering resumed a smallness which could be assuaged by faith or mere belief. But for now, this was not enough and so they learned that they did not need Him but only because they were forced to do so. They did not talk about this, they did not even deny Him, they but knew they were *los desgraciados,* a generation out of grace, and, more than that, a generation born out of grace, and then, of what use was it to seek divine solace in the face of such evidence to the contrary? So the respect which they knew only was a respect for the living, and, to make room for those of them who yet survived, they threw the dead out onto the plains.

And yet, amid all this it was possible under a sarape in a far dark corner of the boxcar, in the relative still of the late hours, for a soldier and his consort or a man and his woman, to come together. In the darkness, the male mounted the female, quickly, so quickly she was not ready for him, and hurting her, impaling her body so suddenly with his tumescence—a frenzy, a quiet spasm, and yet all done so quickly she hurt even as he withdrew. And at that instant, within the woman as in the world outside, a million living things swirled aimlessly until one found a place, a niche, and entered, clung tenaciously, and lived. A million perished and yet one lived, and here was the victory greater than Zacatecas, greater than Torreón. This was the answer from the animal, man. And regardless the number of treaties, conspiracies, and bargains, and the intellectual plans for the future by committees, from a moment of primitive copulation would come the man again and again. And the despot and the cacique could never deny the unalterable fact that even from the most horrendous rape springs life. And no amount of war, no amount of slaughter could stop this.

In the village of Symon, the easternmost point of the state of Durango, an old man, Glafiro García, father of Otilia de Inés, sat on his haunches at the railroad station waiting for trains from the south. He had been here for three days and two nights, ever since the first word of the defeat of the Division of the North had arrived, and this was the third night. He did not leave because no one knew when a train would arrive. He was not a familiar figure in the town, having come here but a few months ago from the

Hacienda del Fuerte after the death of his wife. His daughters were married and gone away; his sons too had departed, three of them to México to evade the war and to work in the factories there. Another was a sergeant in the infantry of Benjamín Hill, a Carrancista, and therefore a victor in the Battle of Celaya. The last son was also a civilian but in Gómez Palacio, twin city to Torreón, and the baby of the family, Otilia, now widowed, lived with the old man in an old house a few miles west of Symon.

He sat waiting for Heraclio Inés, a man he had never seen, and he did not know whether the soldier had got by him or not. But he did not despair because he believed in the destiny, and he was here because, if it was meant to be, he would find Heraclio Inés and it would be for a purpose. After a time, he walked into the station house where he had struck up a friendship or at least a speaking acquaintanceship with the stationmaster and the telegraphist and he curled upon the floor near the Franklin stove and went to sleep.

An hour later, the telegraphist, whose apparatus had been made inutile by fifty pounds of explosives two hundred kilometers away, woke him to say that a train would be in before too long. It was a rumor, of course, but somehow news traveled, and indeed at this time the last train from the south was but hours away.

It was four o'clock in the morning, and the old man took a piece of dried meat from his knapsack and chewed on it thoughtfully for a time, then went out to the end of the dock and waited there standing on one spot for an hour. Again he went to his haunches, almost enveloped by the huge sarape, occasionally lighting a cigarette.

He was still on his haunches two hours later, not having moved, not having thought one complete thought in that time, for that was a part of the patience, to not think, and he waited with the patience of a doomed man waiting for the shot of grace.

The train came in then, for an hour's stop to drop off the spare engine which had been picked up at Aguascalientes to get the train over the summit above the Bufa at Zacatecas. Glafiro García began his search. He did not seem to move fast, and yet he wasted little time. He asked a question here, another there, and it was in but a few minutes that he knew if he were to find Heraclio Inés it would not be in the boxcars or on the roofs, so he entered the first coach and painfully worked his way forward. He could not get through and so he went part way, fought his way back, and ran around to the other end, and came back through the coach a part of the way. In this manner he covered ten coaches, and it was in the eleventh that he found him.

Heraclio Inés sat quietly, not bothering to step out to stretch his legs, his hat down low over his forehead, unseeingly gazing out over the plains.

Glafiro, small, thin, red-faced, came to him and stood silently in the aisle until Heraclio was aware of his presence.

"They tell me you are the Señor Heraclio Inés; Villista and Dorado."

"Yes, old one. State your business and leave me alone. If you are selling food, I am not hungry," said Heraclio.

"I was told that you were gentle," said the old man with the slow, patient voice of one who has lived long. "They say that in spite of being a killer, you are a good boy, and a courteous boy, polite to old people. She told me that."

"You are annoying me, old one," said Heraclio. "You are more rude than I. Soon you will provoke me. I do not know you. I do not know what the hell you are talking about. I do not know what goes on in your senile mind."

"I told her she was deceived. That all you people who kill are insensate, and are arrogant because you can supplant God and take it upon yourselves to end a life whenever you desire to do so. I told her that, but she would not listen."

Heraclio spoke in a lifeless tone. "You are really demented, old one. Go away—I have no interest in your rantings." He turned toward the window and gazed to the distant mountains once again. The old man's voice was a murmur to him and he did not listen until a name penetrated into his thoughts.

"What is that you say?" he asked. "What was that name again?"

"Otilia de Inés, my daughter, your own brother's widow—she is the one who sent me here to watch for you. For over a week now, I have been here day and night whenever a train should arrive, and since the news of the defeat came, I have remained here and slept here. More and more people are fleeing north and it is a miracle that I found you in this crowd."

"Where is she?" asked Heraclio.

370

"Near here—out a few kilometers from town. We have a small house here."

At the mention of his dead brother's wife, Heraclio had shown life for a moment, but now his voice seemed disinterested once again. "What does she want of me? Money? I have some here which is of no use for me. Take it to her and tell her to go with God."

"She would see you," said the old man.

"I wish to see no one," said Heraclio. "Take the money to her in my brother's name."

"She would see you," repeated the old man. "And now there is another reason for you to get off this train. You cannot go into Torreón!"

Heraclio was now angry. "Cannot you say anything except that it must be in riddles? I tell you I have no desire to see Otilia. I am going to Torreón—I have been ordered to go there and join our people there. Now I have explained to you, take the money to her and say that one day, when all this is over, and when you are no more, or are unable to care for her, my family—what remains of it—will take her and the boy. Tell her she need not worry on that account."

Now it was the old man who was angry. "Do not believe that she searched you out because she seeks charity. Eh? Is that what you think, you young dolt? Well, I shall tell you that it is her concern for you, for your life, that made me lose my rest and my sleep to look for you. At first she wished to see you only. To talk to you, perhaps to offer you a glimpse of joy and even laughter to assuage your cynical heart. But now she will warn you so that you may save your worthless life. It is not safe to remain on this train, for Villa's people in Torreón are going over to the Constitutionalists and all Villistas of some rank or influence, civilian and military, are being taken off the trains and shot against the wall of the station."

"Why do you lie?" asked Heraclio. "You may have heard rumors —there are always such rumors, but this cannot be true." But even as he said the words, he felt the pain of grief and he had thought he could not ever feel such a thing again. And then he felt an anger, and this, too, he had not known since he killed David.

The old man did not argue. "Come with me," he said. "The train will be moving soon."

"If you do not wish to take the money," said Heraclio, "I cannot force you to do so. But go now, leave me be, for I have other business." And the people filled the train again, carrying their household goods—some with a chicken or two, another with a young pig, and the old man became excited and pulled on Heraclio's arm. "Hurry," he said. "Hurry! Or we will be unable to get off!"

Heraclio started to shake off the hands on his arm, then hesitated. What the old man had said was unbelievable. And yet, he had a feeling, and he had a doubt about the loyalty of Celestino Gámez. Urbina had betrayed the General. Why could not others do it? There was a doubt in his mind, and for him the smallest doubt must be investigated. He followed the old man, then helped him struggle through the crowded car until they reached the vestibule. Outside, the conductor called toward the engine, "Vámono-o-s," and the train began to move and Heraclio pushed the old man off and jumped after him. They sat on the road where they had fallen and watched the train disappear.

Later, when he had questioned a man who had come recently from Torreón, only the monstrosity of such a betrayal made him think the garrison was still faithful to Villa. He did not take the train that evening as he had planned; yet he must go there.

Alone with Otilia—her father had excused himself after dinner and gone off into the night—they talked of la Flor, and she told him that she would never return there.

"Never to Teodoro's home," she said. "When Concho was alive it was another thing, but now that he is gone, I cannot have my son around that man. He is ten years old now, Juan is, and I would sooner die than see Teodoro do to him what he did to you."

"He made a man of me," said Heraclio.

"You were always a man," she said. "He merely showed you that you were."

Heraclio marveled that she did not cry. She spoke of her dead husband and about her son almost matter-of-factly. She sensed his thoughts and said, "You think I am not mourning very much? Well, I am not. I have done with that, for I am young and will live long. You know how I loved your brother—I was almost mad when he was killed. You know I do not have to make a show of grief to prove that I have grieved. Right now my concern is for my son—

his father does not need me, but he does." She took glasses from the cupboard and brought a bottle of aguardiente. She poured drinks for both of them.

Again he was aware that life was different, that they had both changed. It seemed perfectly natural to him that they should drink together. "You are right," he said. "About Teodoro and the boy. A way of life has ended, you know, with the war. And with Concho's death, the idea of the Ineses as a family of great horsemen is also dead. Who will live the same when this is over? The hacendados will not return, and when we rise up again and retake the government, and land will be parceled out to every man with a family, there will be no need for great jinetes and the tradition will die out."

"And you may be sure that Teodoro will do everything to keep it alive, and to keep the idea of the great landowner alive, and glory in his fealty to the lord of the land." She poured him another drink but still sipped hers. "And if I come near him he will do this with my son."

"He *would* keep it alive. With your son and his son, and with any other male Inés. He may even include the bastards we have scattered . . . say a few Ave Marías and apologize to God for doing Him the insult of legitimizing bastards, and have a crew of Ineses to teach to ride in the family tradition, for he is a stupid man."

She laughed. Because she was safe and her boy was asleep in another part of the house and was also safe, she could laugh. And her laughter was infectious and he joined her, self-consciously because laughter was another thing he had forgotten.

"We are laughing at your family," she said. "I did not know such a thing was possible."

He said, "Pour me more drink, Otilia, and then tell me why you looked for me. What do you want of me?"

"You guessed I have something to say to you?" she asked as she poured.

He could not imagine what she would want. Not money, not safe-conduct back to Zacatecas; it could be a favor for someone else.

A sudden animation made her face light up, and her eyes became as if alive. She spoke rapidly, as if she were aware she should say it quickly before he could stop her from speaking out. "I want you to give it up, Heraclio! It has been five years and more—and for what? You have been very fortunate but good luck does not last forever."

"I cannot give it up, you know that," he said, but for a moment he slumped down in his chair as if he wished he could stop now, as if he wished the past had never happened.

"You *must* give it up. You did once, remember?"

"I did once—for how long? I was wrong then." He straightened as if to show that his feelings and his actions were in tune with his compulsion. "And it *is* for something, even if we are defeated again it is for something. Even now, if all these people are really defecting to Obregón, he is making concessions. He must compromise, and every compromise is a small victory. As long as the fight continues, even if we are defeated, even if I die or if my General Villa should die, there will be concessions and eventually there will be victory, do you not see?"

"I see, Heraclio! I see!" and she was excited although she went on in a calm voice. "But you have done your part. Other men have given far less than you. And I am speaking for myself as well as for you. And for my son."

"How is that?" he asked, and now he took the bottle and helped himself.

"You have done more than enough. I think it is for nothing although I understand what you mean. If you continue you will die! Do you not see? You have survived so long and it is time for someone else to take your place."

"I am not afraid to die," he said. "And what is this you say about yourself and your boy?"

She said, "It is because of that—because you are not afraid, because you are a man that I tell you this. I need a man, Heraclio, and you need a woman. I shock you, I know, but we have loved each other for many years, although not in the man-woman sense. Give it up, I ask you, and let us go away somewhere, you and I, and make a life." He did not speak. "In times like this," she continued, "it is for us who survive to make as much of life as we can, to renew life. We can build a happiness, and a family, and thus through happiness pay our debt to God that he gave us life."

He *was* shocked, yet something in him responded to her. It was a faint feeling, yet very real, and the only part unpleasant about it

374

was a sense of guilt. And as he drank, averting her face, he had a sudden vision of her lovely breast as he had seen it—how long ago? And the large, purple spot, and the nipple almost alive as it entered her son's gaping mouth. And he was suddenly aching for her, but it was because of the past and he was a small boy again for a moment and the moment was now past also and so the past was again a repugnance to him. He spoke and he said what his conscience should feel, his voice and his words censuring her for a moral lapse. "You are my brother's wife," he said. "What you suggest is abominable!"

She was angry. "Your brother's widow!" she shouted the words. "Concepción is dead and has been dead for some time. You know death, you who have killed, you who have seen death around you, who have been indifferent to it—can you not understand what Concho himself would understand?"

"No, I cannot."

"And also, I suggest nothing of what you are thinking. It is your own mind and your body telling you that you desire me and instead of seeing the good that can come of it, you become self-righteous like Teodoro. You are angry because you had a beautiful thought. You made it ugly."

He could not face her, so he walked behind her and paced the floor. She said more calmly:

"That is for later, Heraclio. Much later—as long as you feel you must wait. I have given it some thought because it was inevitable that I should think of it while coming to my decision. But I was not dismayed by the idea of physical love between us—I did not feel disloyal to your brother—I but realized that I do not know how I would be with you as a woman. I cannot tell how long it would take me to accept your body as a wife should, but I am prepared to do the act. Now—tonight if you wish it so. Even without the condition that you must stay with me, only with the condition that if you go away, when you return you come to me. And I am prepared to worry and to die every day you are away. I knew you would have to go, I suppose. I felt I might convince you that you have done your part, that you have done all you could for your country, for your people. I have forgotten all the arguments I had prepared. I only know that those people in the capital, those people who talk liberty and human rights and a free México, do not

375

know that a part of it is living. To live is an important part of freeing your country. And after all is done, and all the dead have died, and all the wounded have withered, there must be life to make the thing worth while. I have heard the talk of self-sacrifice and patriotism much too long. You have lost your family in the Revolution. I have lost my husband. That is enough! I do not know the complexities of life. I do not know the subtleties of how a nation is run. I care, but I do not know. But I am a woman—a healthy, young woman, and I have a desire to love and to be loved and to help fill the land with more life. And I feel that life is the most important victory of all.

"I did not want to talk about the physical side of a marriage between you and me. I did not even want to talk about marriage—just that we should live together until we could talk about such things. But you brought up the subject and now I am glad that you did."

He walked to the table, not speaking, not looking at her, and took the bottle. He drank from it and, still holding it in his hand, he resumed his pacing behind her. He stopped and stared out the small window.

"It is for later," she repeated, but now her voice seemed flat. "When we have learned to love each other in the only way—when you can learn that the past is merely that, *the past*. I say, let us go and build ourselves a new life, for unless we do that, we are dead. Let us go—and if you wish we'll marry and if you do not we can still be together."

Finally he spoke. "I repeat that I cannot stay. What you say could perhaps have been possible, but not now. I am already dead. I am walking around because of a sense of duty. If it were not for that duty, I would have gone on to Torreón openly and taken my chances with Celestino, for it really does not matter that much to me—to live. I now live for my General and my country but not for myself. I have no right to seek happiness at this late date when I am as dead as Concho and the others. I am tired. Sometimes I feel that all I want is to curl up into a ball, and remain in a corner of a dark, warm room, and not be bothered by anyone or anything. The vision comes to me and I know that it is my coffin I am looking for."

"No, Heraclio. It is not your coffin that you seek. Do not ask

376

how I know, except that being a woman tells me that you, too, seek life again. It is not for your general or for your country that you live. It is for yourself through them. Promise me only that when you are well again, you will return to me. Promise me that, Heraclio—but not as a favor."

"I do not know," he said. "I cannot make promises I may not keep." He stood behind her, not wanting to meet her gaze, and he dropped the bottle, then slowly, reluctantly, he placed his hands alongside her face. "I do not know, Otilia. I simply do not know!"

He lowered his hands to her shoulders and pulled her back against his middle. "Forgive me, my sister," he said. "I am incapable of feeling. I am incapable of acting, of making a decision. I only know that I must do what is expected of me, and that is to reach Celestino Gámez in Torreón and somehow get back to my General." She did not speak and he began again. "I did not speak all the truth. I *have* been incapable of feeling for some time now, but since I arrived here, I have begun to feel a great sorrow for Heraclio Inés. That may be why I did not wish to see you."

She reached up and took his hands and brought them down into the loose opening of her blouse and against her soft, warm breasts. She felt his calloused palms against her nipples, and then felt him with her nipples as they became erect, but the breasts remained soft, and suddenly she realized he cried above her. With joy and pain she removed his hands and half turned toward him as he came down to his knees, and then she undid her blouse, baring her bosom. She took his long, curly hair strongly, and yet tenderly, and pulled his face to her body. "Yes, Heraclio! Yes, my love," she could only utter as he cried against her breast, and her chest was wet with tears, and the wetness dribbled down her soft belly. She felt his arms around her strain as he tried to bury his face deeper into her flesh, and although she felt pain in her back, it was as nothing, for the wisdom of her sex told her that here was the coffin he sought, here was a moment of surcease. And she thought back to the day he became a horseman; remembered the weakened body covered with contusions and the welts across his face and back and thighs. She had anointed him with rancid suet then, but now his welts were not visible and all she could do was hold him while he cried.

Heraclio cried for the first time since that day, and he cried as he had never cried in his life. He was purged and slowly his sobs subsided until he merely gasped and occasionally whimpered. They remained as they were for a long time and the aftereffect was almost as if they had made love, each a little spent, neither of them completely relaxed.

When he stood up, Heraclio was not ashamed to look into her face and he saw such beauty as to seem somehow remote, somehow inviolable. "Thank you, Otilia," he said. "You have been my sister and now for a moment you have been the mother I have never had. Thank you."

"How like a mother's love is love I did not know," she said. "You have taught me something and I will yet speak out. You think me forward, perhaps bold, but these are not normal times and ours is not a normal relationship. I do not need to wait, Heraclio. I know now that I love you as a man, not as a brother. There is a physical strength about you that I realize now you had even as a child, for I had to see you again as a little boy to recognize it. I now yearn for you, and you will go away and I will die for you and be jealous, I know. But I will wait."

Because he did not speak, did not object as before, she knew the idea was not a shock to him now.

"You think about the past," she continued, "but what *is* the past? A happiness, truly, it was for me with your brother, and then a sudden death—but we exist and cannot live on the happiness and tragedy of yesterday. We are of the future, Heraclio my love, and we will take the past honestly, with our eyes open and merge it with the present to make a life for the years to come."

"Perhaps there may be something in that," he said. "I cannot say yes. But then, I cannot also say no, to what you suggest. Perhaps."

"That is enough," said Otilia, smiling now. "That must be enough for the time being."

She sat motionless, as she had sat while Heraclio cried, and she did not fasten her blouse until a discreet knock was heard at the door. Her father came into the room rapidly, speaking as he entered.

"Come, come," he said. "We must move quickly."

"You are at it again," said Heraclio. "How is it that you always say things that have no meaning?"

"We are leaving immediately, boy. You and I. I have horses outside." He walked through the kitchen to another room and returned immediately carrying a shotgun in his hands. "Otilia," he said, "make me a mochila, quickly. Then get the boy out of bed and pack a few things. A wagon is outside to take you to the train. It is due in an hour, so you have time enough for it will be late, of course."

Heraclio and Otilia looked at each other and then at the old man, who somehow made the kitchen seem crowded and in disorder as he bustled here and there.

Finally Otilia spoke in exasperation. "Papá, what is all this? This talk of horses and mochilas, and a wagon to take us to the train? And where are *you* going?"

"Why, I am off to the Revolution, my daughter. Finally, after all these years, I take up arms."

"And that relic," said Heraclio, "that piece you hold there which you call a gun—has it been fired in the last ten years?"

"But of course it has been fired. I have hunted the jackrabbit and the fat quail, and even a few dogs which have come to my house to shit."

Otilia giggled, and Heraclio had the sudden thought that both father and daughter were mad. He stared at the old gun in disbelief. "Sixteen gauge?" he said. "How many rounds do you have?"

"Rounds? Rounds?" asked don Glafiro. "Oh, I do not have ammunition."

"Now tell me, old man. What the hell good is a gun without shells? Are you to club someone with it? As it is you must practically be alongside anything you wish to hit with that thing. That is, of course, providing it does not blow up in your hands . . . but forget it. Forget I have asked you anything as I think I am insane too, actually believing that you are going off to fight."

The old man walked to the door and called out into the darkness. "Come in, boy, and help carry my daughter's things to the wagon." He returned to the center of the kitchen and said, "You think I am too old to fight?"

Heraclio thought he should placate him. "No, don Glafiro. Your pardon, please. I have seen men older than yourself in the campaign, who traveled with the young and strong, and distinguished themselves through their courage and stamina."

The old man looked at him for a moment, then turned again and said, "I shall get your son. Hurry, now, and do what I say, Otilia."

They were alone for a moment and Heraclio said, "Otilia, I do not mean to offend you, for I remember well how much you love your father. But believe me, please. He is in his dotage and if you can still communicate with him, find out just what the hell is going on. I must leave here. I cannot play games all night."

Otilia laughed. "Heraclio, my father is as sane as we are. He is just funny. True, he seems more strange since my mother died and the boys married and went away, but he always knows what he is doing—he has taken to insulting people lately, and that he has never done, but it is the only way he has changed."

A youth stood at the doorway. "Gather only your necessities, señora. You will not be allowed to take more than that on the train. People who have been stranded here on their way north are already congregating at the station."

The old man returned. "He is dressing," he said. "Now, here is the plan. You and Juanito take the train to Torreón, and when you arrive, walk to the market place, then take a hack to your brother's home in Gómez Palacio. Notify your brother that we will arrive. We come on horseback, in a roundabout way. It really would be simpler if we headed south and joined the General Villa, but Heraclio has his heart set on going to Torreón first. I do not know why he wishes to go there now, but if that is his wish, we shall go."

"Now, wait a moment," said Heraclio. "I go to Torreón because I must see for myself what has happened. I go alone—by train for a ways, and then I shall find other means of getting there."

"Which reminds me," said don Glafiro, as if he had not even heard Heraclio's words, "get the bundle, boy." The youth brought some clothing from the wagon. "Change into these, Heraclio, quickly. You cannot walk around with that uniform on."

Otilia saw that Heraclio would object and that he was now becoming angry. "Papá," she said, "tell us. You enjoy playing with us, but if you wish us to do anything at all, let alone quickly, you must tell us what you know."

Don Glafiro stopped in the center of the room and said, "You are quite right, forgive me. I should have told you immediately.

The hue and cry is on. In an hour or two at the most, some people will come looking for Heraclio."

"How do you know this?" asked Heraclio, and the old man was angry that they did not believe him. He was an old man, and he spoke the truth, and he expected others to know he was honest.

"How do I know? Why do you think I went into town tonight? Do you think it was to give you the opportunity to lay with my daughter, your brother's widow?"

"Papá!" said Otilia.

"Do not pacify me," said her father. "I have lived long and know of these things. It is not necessary to admit or deny a thing. I am going with Heraclio because I want to help him survive so that you can have him. That is what you want, is it not? To marry your brother-in-law? You have thought about it for some time, no? That you wish to marry this man? And I must be fair. I should not make it seem as if it is an unnatural thing. I approve because I like him, although he has no sense of humor. And because I love you so much and feel the responsibility of a father for the happiness of his daughter, I will now become that which I abhor—a killer of men. I go with Heraclio to help him, perhaps to take a bullet which would otherwise be meant for him." He moved toward them, and his anger was dissipated with his words, and he seemed to jest once again. "I approve of you two. It is the most natural thing in the world that you should take the place of an older brother, Heraclio. And if you should find a happiness, which I think you will eventually, it will be even more natural and good. I approve," he added to Otilia, "else I would have been out of my mind when I came in and found you with your tits hanging out, like a whore receiving clients. If you gave yourself to him, you had good cause, for I know you are not a dog."

The moment was awkward, and an excessive sense of sentiment filled the room. Otilia's boy entered and Heraclio could not utter the objection which was on his lips. Instead, looking at Juan for the first time in months, he suddenly recognized how much like Concepción was the son. The face, the head and hair, even the eyes belonged to his father, and remembering the young Concepción, riding hard, full of life and joy—remembering the ride of death that afternoon his own father died, through memory, Concho was beloved. And as the boy came forward to salute the uncle, and Heraclio felt his hand grasped by the firm small one of his nephew, and felt the warmth of the boy's breath as he brought his face down and felt the brush of his lips as he kissed the back of his hand, he suddenly picked him up and crushed him to his chest, and in that moment all the filial love, repressed in him so many years, was suddenly transferred to the boy, for Concho was slain and somehow here again was Concho. And he murmured deep within himself so that it was like a muffled growl that this was so.

He put the boy down then and said, "You shall never adore my hand again, Juan, for you are an Inés man, and an Inés kisses no man's hand."

"Yes, tío," the boy said. He had not been frightened by the sudden and furious show of affection. "Will you talk to me of the war?"

Heraclio would have taken time to talk to the boy, but don Glafiro said, "There is no time for talk now, son. Later your uncle will talk with you, but now we must depart."

"Very well," said Heraclio. "Now I must know all you have heard. We have spent too much time if what you say is true."

And don Glafiro finally decided to speak in a straightforward manner. "The same train which will take Otilia and Juan to Torreón is bringing a detachment of troops to hunt you down."

"The train is coming here and then returning? That is strange."

"No train goes farther south than Symon. The country south between here and Aguascalientes is enemy territory to the people who now own the trains. But they say it is not to be this way for long."

"Was it mentioned how many men are coming?"

"They say a company of cavalry. And there is someone, a great many someones, I fear, waiting at the station to point out this house when they arrive. And there are a few young bucks in town getting their courage up with tequila to make a try at you, for there may be gold for your killer. Now, I wonder what can make you so important?"

"I am not important," said Heraclio. "It is that Celestino knows I am loyal to my general. It is only that. I am believing that he did turn traitor, but he must truly fear my General Villa, although I always believed he feared no man."

382

Otilia and her son were in the wagon. "Thank your father for me," said don Glafiro to the young man. "I shall repay his goodness somehow." To Otilia he said, "You are not Otilia Inés, my daughter. You are García once again if anyone should question you. Coach the lad well. He must forget who he is for a few days. Go with God now, my child!"

Otilia felt tears roll down her face, but she made an effort and called out in a firm, clear voice. Heraclio came to her and kissed her cheek. "Do not forget," she said.

"I shall remember," he said, "but I still do not know. In time perhaps, but I cannot say at this moment."

"Go with God," she said.

"Luck be with you," he answered.

She was gone and he quickly changed his clothes while the old man scurried through the house, suddenly reluctant to leave his belongings. The change of clothing was cowboy dress, and a good fit. Heraclio buckled his gunbelt, then called to the old man to bring him a sarape. The only available one was poncholike, so he turned his holster forward so that it could be hidden. He had no hat and did not want to wear the military type narrow-brimmed Stetson, but the old man had a hat one of his boys had left behind, and he held it tenderly for a moment, drawn by the tendrils of affection he held for this last reminder of a lost son and a lost youth, before he handed it to Heraclio.

They burned the uniform and moved, but at the door, Heraclio took the shotgun from the old man and placed it in the house. "It will be more of a hindrance to you, old one. In a few days you will be back in your house and it will be here waiting for you. It will be safe for you and Otilia to come back here when I leave."

Don Glafiro did not insist on the gun, but as they rode away to the west, away from the railroad, he said:

"I am going with you, boy. I am committed so do not attempt to dissuade me."

"It is not necessary," said Heraclio. "And I do not even know where I will go. If everything is happening as you say, we may be in the mountains for a long time—as long as it takes to begin another offensive."

"I go with you," said don Glafiro stubbornly.

But Heraclio was not listening, for there would be time to

argue this out later, and he would have Otilia's help to break down the old man's arguments. It was a moonlit night, very light, and he suddenly seemed exposed in the barren plain. He did not really hear a horse, but he thought he might have, so he looked around and could see for quite a distance and they were alone. They had good mounts and he was reassured, and yet he could not rid himself of the feeling that he should be wary.

"You have a good eye for a beast, old one," he said.

"Did I not tell you we worked horses on the hacienda?"

"These town dandies you spoke of," he said almost casually, "how many of them were there, and what did they say?"

"Three, maybe four. And they did not say much, though they talked a great deal. They did not have a plan that I know of, but they said they were going to ride out to get you and others were daring them, and they were drinking. We need not worry about them, however, because they are most probably still talking."

Ahead were a few mesillas, and the first two were close together so that Heraclio and don Glafiro would have to pass in the shadow between them and there were a few trees already visible.

"Come," said Heraclio, "let us go around. It is time we headed north, and let us gallop a little."

"It is not necessary," said don Glafiro. "It is too early for the troops to have arrived here."

Heraclio was about to insist, then decided that he was being overly imaginative, and they continued toward the small mesas. They were almost in the shadows when the three men rode out slowly, impatient, and made bold by their advantage.

They appeared in the moonlight, very close, one slightly ahead of the others. He sat his horse looking very handsome, a rifle in his hands, and he called out, "Tell me, señores, which one of you is called Heraclio Inés, son of his fucked mother, for I, Ricardo Moreno, his father, have come to break him."

Heraclio shot him in the face.

One of the others fired once, and they both turned their horses and fled back into the shadows from where they had emerged, and don Glafiro was saying, "Have respect, men, for I am unarmed but I am unafraid," but he, too, was dead before he hit the ground.

Heraclio took don Glafiro's few possessions to give to his son and daughter, and that was all he could do. He left him there

384

knowing that later someone would come for the body of Ricardo Moreno and would take him back also. He took the other dead man's rifle and found shells on the body, then he retrieved the old man's horse, removed the saddle and bridle, and, mounting his own horse, went into the shadows leading the spare mount. He had no need to be cautious now, for the others had gone toward the town, riding hard.

On the fourth day at dawn he entered Gómez Palacio, going directly to the house of Benito García, whom he had visited many times during the war. The town was full of troops although it was in another state from the city of Torreón, five miles away. He kept his mount because it was more natural that he should seem to be a cowboy. His only fear at the moment was that he should meet up with someone who knew him, as these people had just recently been a part of his army.

He came to the house and the gate to the wall was unlocked. In the patio, troops slept on the ground, and he walked around to the kitchen entrance, for this was the hour of breaking fast, and some soldiers were washing themselves at a fountain. They were in his path and he must speak to them in order to go past. He did not hesitate, for he must be natural.

"With your permission, señores," he said, in the humble tone and attitude of the peon.

"Declare yourself," said a soldier who, having used his shirt for a towel, was now putting it on.

"I am Demetrio Chávez, come to visit my first cousin, Juan Chávez," said Heraclio. "Is there something wrong here, patrón?" The inflection of servility was heavy and unmistakable in his speech. The question was to forestall further questioning.

"Nothing is wrong here, why do you ask that?"

"The military is here, patrón. I do not understand."

"We are billeted here. Inside, in the spare rooms is my Coronel Guadalupe Morales and another officer because they rate better accommodations." The soldier was suddenly suspicious and said, "What do you do here?"

"I have told you señor, I have come to see my cousin because my sister is to arrive here from the south and I wish to know if she is here." Heraclio looked around to see what his chances were.

385

He should mount his horse and gallop straight out the still open gate, for there were too many, and in close quarters. Although he had never been close to Guadalupe Morales, they had been together many times since the first attack on Santa Rosalía.

He continued in the singsong voice, "I but come on my day off from my labors to see if she has arrived."

"He has a gun," said another soldier.

"It is for my work, patrón." The tone of humility became strained. "I work at the Rancho El Tecolote, some twelve leagues from here off the Durango road. I carry a gun to protect me from wild beasts. All the cowhands in my area carry a gun."

The first soldier said, "Let me have it."

Hesitating only the time any man would hesitate giving up his gun, not obeying too quickly, Heraclio gave him the gun. Again he casually glanced toward the gate, for he still held the reins to his horse and he had made up his mind that if they tried to take his mount he would bolt.

The soldier hefted the weapon, aimed it at an imaginary target and said, "A good iron. A Marlin, and a military weapon—far superior to my mauser. But tell me, what are you doing with a military weapon?"

"I bought it from a deserter two years ago."

Too much time was being wasted, and he must try to do something—but what? He would go to the door, perhaps dissimulate a conversation there with someone, and leave. At that moment, Benito García, Otilia's brother, came out the door, and Heraclio breathed deeply that it had not been the Colonel Guadalupe Morales. There was danger yet, however, if Benito should call out his name.

"What do you wish, señor?" asked Benito.

"I was looking for Juan Chávez. Is it that he has moved from here?"

"Juan Chávez has never lived here," said Benito. "I, Benito García, to serve you, own this house."

"Of course, I have been here but once, and that was in the dark of night," said Heraclio, aware that the soldier was watching him closely. "I swear this was the very place, on the Avenue of Diógenes, by the cross street of St. John of the Cross."

Benito García laughed lightly. "This is the Avenue of Diógenes, but the cross street you seek is two blocks to the south. Of course, all houses on this street look alike."

"That must be it," said Heraclio. "I remember now that the patio was not situated such as this one. Forgive my intrusion here, señor. It was not deliberate, I assure you."

Benito García's son chanced to come in from the street at this moment. He was twelve years old, and on Heraclio's visits to his house had developed an admiration which was near hero worship. Heraclio always managed to talk to him and thus made the boy happy, and so now, as he came through the gate, the boy saw his friend and broke into a run, his happiness showing in his enthusiasm.

"When did you come? When did you come?" he shouted with joy, and his father, Benito García, brought his arm around and hit the boy a backhand on the mouth which knocked him backward into the dust.

"Brute!" said Benito García. "You have forgotten your manners! Have I not taught you that you must not speak so familiarly to strangers?"

The boy lay on his back, fighting back tears, but he had spent a lifetime very close to violence. Twice in his short life he had been through a siege of Torreón, had seen men fight and die in the streets, and now, through dim eyes he saw in a glance what he should do. He jumped to his feet, and he dusted the seat of his pants. "A thousand pardons," he said, "a thousand pardons, señor. In the light of the sun you appeared to be my Uncle Pedro." He waited to see what came next.

"That is better," said Benito García. "He is but a boy," he explained to Heraclio, "or he would not be so rude."

"It was nothing," said Heraclio.

"He is looking for his first cousin called Juan Chávez, who lives down near San Juan de la Cruz."

"I know his son Aurelio," said the boy. "If you desire it, my father, I shall lead the señor there."

"Good," said Benito García, "there you are, señor," he said to Heraclio, "the boy will show you the way."

"Many, many thanks," said Heraclio. He turned to the soldier. "My gun, patrón. Please, I have need of my weapon."

The soldier laughed. "This stolen gun you claim?" he asked. "Are you going to insist and thus admit that you are the thief who has stolen it?"

"No, patrón," said Heraclio, and his sarcasm was measured. "I paid three months wages for the piece, but since you know it was stolen by the man who sold it to me, why then you keep it. I am certain that you will find its rightful owner and return it, since you seem to me to be a man of honor."

The soldier laughed once again. "Do not be concerned, peon," he said. "I will most assuredly deliver the lost gun," but Heraclio was already moving toward the gate, slowly, leading his horse, and the boy of Benito García walked also casually, a step before him and to the side.

He mounted the horse and walked it alongside the boy, silently, and at the corner they took another street and then turned into an alley.

He was off the horse again and he said, "Thank you, boy. You are a real man."

"It was nothing, don Heraclio," said the boy.

"I am but sorry you took such a blow for my sake," said Heraclio. He touched the boy's swollen lips lightly with his fingertips.

"It was for you, don Heraclio," said the boy, pleased that he had been of service, and he repeated, "so it was nothing."

Heraclio looked at the boy and felt for him. "It is now necessary that you again be much man," he said.

"What is it that you wish me to do?"

"First of all, you must not cry. You must carry a message to your father as if it were the most natural thing in the world. You must tell him that his sainted father was killed in the mountains two days ago. Did your Aunt Otilia arrive safely from the south?"

"She did not arrive," said the boy, and his face was impassive. "The train did not come, and it is said that it went south, all the way to the capital."

Heraclio had his mochila on the ground, unrolled, and he took a gun exactly like the one he had lost from within its folds. He took off his gunbelt then, first removing a handful of shells and dropping them in his jacket pocket, and rolled it in the bedroll. The gun he slipped under the waistband of his trousers under his shirt.

And so she was still in Symon, then—or in Zacatecas, or la Flor.

But then, if the train went all the way to México, it meant that the entire line had either defected to Obregón or was recognizing the Constitutionalists as the rightful government. That meant that even Pánfilo Natera had now gone over to Carranza and Obregón.

And where was the General Villa?

He thought quickly as he rearranged the mochila behind his saddle. Had the General Natera held Villa prisoner when he passed through Zacatecas? If he had been allowed to flee, he would be in Durango now, a few hundred miles away near Cerro Prieto in that place two thousand meters up in the sky which Villa, with a primitive awareness of possible treachery, had one day three years ago shown him as the place they would meet if he became a wanted man again. And yet, he must see Celestino to learn from him that he was a traitor. And, of course, if the General had defected, one of them must die, for he, Heraclio, would not be allowed to live. He had never killed a general, but to kill Celestino, whom he loved, would be to remain living.

He held a great respect for this man, Gámez. And he had a love for him, also, for he was a complete man. Once he had come upon him writing on a scrap of paper, and had asked what it was, being rude in his youthful curiosity. And Celestino had answered, "Why a poem it is that I am composing."

"A poem?" asked Heraclio, full of wonder.

"A poem," said Celestino, smiling at his innocence. "Do you know any poems?" he then had asked.

"Only the riddle kind," said Heraclio, "and one or two obscene ones."

"The riddle kind and one or two obscene ones," said Celestino in his rich peasant vernacular. Then he laughed. "But what a boy you are, Heraclio. What a boy!" Like Villa he always said that about him. Then Celestino had said, "Well, that is better than not knowing any poem at all, infant."

And also, although he had been a mountain bandit and a guerrilla most of his adult life, and although his Castilian seemed to be not as good as Heraclio's own, Celestino read books. This Heraclio knew because Celestino always managed to have a book or two in his mochila. And in the cities, after they had been secured, he sometimes dressed to look almost like the General Felipe

Angeles, although much larger, of course. He could drink tequila with anyone, yet in the large cities, he found always cognac, smelling the weed and then sipping it slowly in the manner of the gentlemen Heraclio had known in the Becerra Big House.

Once, Celestino had astonished even the General Angeles. It had happened in the sacking of a town or a villa that a soldier had discovered an elaborate hand-carved chess set. It was of no value to him, he did not even know what it was, but he reasoned that it must have some value, and so he carefully carried it with him for months, taking it out of his bedroll occasionally to gaze upon it and to rub the little figures. And it happened one day when he was polishing the set that another soldier came upon him, one who knew what the thing was, and he offered a bottle of sotol in exchange for it. The bargain was made, and each felt the other had been cheated. And the set became a gift to the General Angeles, who must surely—if anyone did—know how the instrument was operated.

Angeles was overwhelmed at the beauty of the set, and he uttered a cry as if in pain. "Oh," he said, "what I would give to simply sit and have a game with someone!" They had just secured a town and were in the great hall of the Municipal Palace, and of course there was no one there who could play with the General, for the gentry had all been shot. And Celestino Gámez said, "Why, with the General's permission, I shall gladly sit with you a game." He sat before Angeles, who had the board set out on an end table.

Obviously surprised, Angeles said, "You play, General? Now where did you ever learn the game of chess?" Immediately he apologized for his rudeness, but Celestino knew he was sincere and had meant no offense, and accepted the question as such and laughed.

"Why, I just learn things here and there, my General," he said. "Here and there. Shall we begin?" And they had sat all day and part of the night. Heraclio had watched for a time and then returned a few hours later to see the generals both staring at the board. How long they had been in that position he did not know, and then Celestino reached down to where he had a bottle on the floor, took a great drink of mezcal, and moved one of his figures. Then they both stared at the board again as if they expected it to fly away. A group of soldiers were around them, watching very quietly so as not to disturb the concentration of the stare, and Heraclio said:

"How rare!"

"It is much rarer," said the man beside him. "This same game they have been playing all day. It once took the General Ángeles one hour by the clock before he moved one of those little ponies there. I am certain there is no game in all the world slower than this, but it relaxes them, they said—although they surely will be blind with all the staring they do!"

All this was the General Celestino Gámez. And although Ángeles invariably won these games, he insisted, shaking his head in disbelief, that Celestino was the best adversary he had ever faced. And the General spoke of his "battles" with Gámez almost as if they were physical.

But to Heraclio, Celestino was much more because he was fearless and honorable and thus noble. And because he was a poet, he was also something special—why this, Heraclio did not know. He knew only, like his forebears had known, that those who made poems were as those who made songs and those who made music and those who made pictures, and were people who should be revered.

At this moment it was so clear for one time in his life what a man should do at a given moment. We must live, she had told him. We must live for ourselves and in that way we do for others, but he knew that he must also die for himself, and although that was beyond knowledge, dying could also be doing for others. And he somehow believed this—believed that there was yet a cause and that there still existed hope, for to change that belief now would be an admission that he had lived a lie all his life. He had seen so much, had seen more food for disillusion than for hope, but he knew himself, and he knew that he believed and was incorruptible. And Villa believed and was incorruptible, this he knew although he did not know this of any other man. And suddenly he saw the way clearly once again, for if Otilia was right, he also was right. To live was to win, but only because the ideal would also live and someday rekindle and take fire and one day also would be realized. And if he, Heraclio Inés, walked the earth with the idea, if only he of the millions committed to the struggle if against their will had this passion, then there was hope. And to die was as nothing, for from his very blood might spring a germ, to be picked up and nurtured, in a child, perhaps, like this boy here. About Otilia and the future he did not know, but of this very present he was satisfied.

He would now attempt what was the most intelligibly dangerous thing he had ever done and he had no idea it would be so simple.

The boy went home, with a message of thanks and condolences for his father. Like a peon, not even a cowhand, draped in the sarape, his hat low over his eyes, he turned his horse toward Torreón. Out in the open was the only way he could hide now, and although he appeared relaxed and half asleep as he allowed his horse to walk toward Torreón, he was wary and observed everything around him, his hand under the sarape on the gun butt, for there was one thing wrong about his disguise. He was riding too fine a horse for a peasant. On an errand for a don would be all he could say if challenged.

But he rode into the city without trouble, and once there he went to the market place and bought a hot meal, then went into a cantina and drank mezcal. After a bit, he struck up a conversation with another peon, and before long was seated at a table with field peones, as one of them, and with them he worked in one of the ranchos around Torreón. He drank as they did for over an hour, and then he began to hold onto his drink, gradually losing the slight edge he had developed. In another hour he was as sober as he had been when he walked in, but he appeared to be as drunk as the others. A fight or two flared in the cantina. A soldier shot a civilian in the thigh, but Heraclio, although he made as much noise as the others, always kept his back toward a wall, and was always in position to go through the kitchen if he had to do so. He knew the alley behind the building, and in his mind he knew exactly where he would go if he must flee.

But he had chosen his cantina well, a dingy, unkempt place, where only the lowly soldiers and civilians would frequent, and his wariness was because that was his life. And he must not drink too much, for that was foolhardiness not courage. For courage a man must have an awareness that it exists, it is experienced at the moment it is demonstrated.

There were women here, and along with the others, he made

awkward caresses to a breast, or squeezed a massive buttock, and once, when the servant stood near him exchanging risqué repartee with his companions, he reached an arm up between her legs and took hold for a moment until she screeched, and the men all laughed, even the soldiers around them, but it was as nothing although she wore no interior clothing, for he was not accustomed to this manner of receiving pleasure.

But he must survive the daylight hours, and he could not walk the streets for he knew people here, and he would not hide at a friend's house for he would mark anyone who would befriend him for death. And now he stopped being the buffoon, for people were talking about him, and he was drawing attention, so he put his head on the table and went to sleep. He was safe, for he was just a drunken peon, and if anyone touched him he would be wide awake. So he slept for the better part of an hour and it was nearing dark when he awoke and he bought a bottle for the table, and was kidded that he had passed out, and now there was music, for a mariachi had come in. He ate then, with the others, and drank again, then stumbled out to vomit, but as the doors swung back in place, he straightened and went to the stable where he had left his horse.

And this had been the most difficult part, existing through the afternoon and keeping his task in mind. To wait was second nature, but to wait with every sense acutely at ready was an exhausting thing. And he breathed deeply in the darkness. It was dark in the part of the stable where he talked to the hostler, and he said, "I am in the employ of don Francisco Dávila, who as you know is the renowned man of business affairs here, and I am to take another horse because he has house guests from México and he does not keep enough beasts here in the city. He said that he will keep it a fortnight, and settle with you at the end of the month as usual."

The hostler said, "The horse you have left here does not have the mark of don Francisco."

"Of course it does not," said Heraclio. And he could not remember the brand his horse carried. "There is a great celebration with the patrón because the war is finished. He has borrowed a few horses for the occasion, and yet he needs one more. His daughter, Ofelia, you know, is enjoying the visit of her fiancé, and as he is a city boy, and is obese as a hog to boot, they need a dispirited, very strong animal for him."

The mention of the girl's name and the exact description of the bridegroom-to-be satisfied the hostler's suspicions. "He is a fat slob, is he not?" he asked, and Heraclio, playing the part of the faithful house peon, said, "It is not your place to speak that way of my patrón's son-in-law-to-be. And it is not your concern that he is like a pig."

The hostler could not be certain just how Heraclio meant his words to be taken, but he was not in a position to follow this line of conversation. "I have just the horse for don Francisco," he said. "Big and yet gentle, and very strong. You must emphasize to your patrón how well I can serve him."

"I will. Now you have the horse ready, and I forgot to bring a reata, so get me one. We will not need a saddle, for we have that equipment. I will take advantage"—and he winked at the man— "to have another drink before I return to my duties."

The hostler laughed. "Do not have a care. The horse will be ready, or if you wish, I can have a boy take it to don Francisco's stables."

"No, no," said Heraclio. "Would you have me whipped."

"Have no fear," said the hostler. "The horse will be here."

"Just tie it up in back," said Heraclio. "That way I will not have to disturb you if you wish to sleep a little."

In the darkness again he rode slowly toward El Gran Faro, the biggest hotel in the city. He would begin here, for he had no way of knowing where the General kept his quarters, and as Celestino Gámez loved the game of chess, the hotel was as likely a place for him to find an opponent as any. If he did not find him here, he would listen and perhaps get an idea of the General's whereabouts from stray conversation.

In the patio of the hotel, he disappeared into the shadows, and then appeared at the steps to the entrance carrying an assortment of flowers. He walked into the lobby and then turned into a reception room where people in dress clothes or in uniform stood around in small groups, cocktails in their hands. He sold the flowers immediately for a peso, and could not leave fast enough, for across from him was the General Celestino Gámez, as unlike the guerrilla leader he knew so well as he could possibly be, holding a glass by the stem delicately, talking with a thin, enormous-breasted blonde, perhaps a North American. And as Heraclio left the room, he was forced to smile in spite of himself.

And now to wait again. He sat himself under a papaya tree and kept his hat low over his eyes, and his hands in his sarape, and now the gun was out and ready. He waited for hours, and by now a party was in full swing in the hotel and he knew he must go inside again. This time he entered and picked up a chair and took it into the salon, then picked up empty dishes and glasses and walked back out. Celestino was not there, and Heraclio walked to a maid and said in the peasant voice, "I have an urgent message for the General Gámez, a matter of discretion, you know. How can I find him?"

The girl grinned knowingly. "What is it, another woman?"

"If I could tell you," said Heraclio, "then it would not be a matter of discretion." But he gave the impression that she had guessed correctly, for he must make an ally of her or she would tell him nothing.

She shrugged. "It is the same with all these great officers. I have been changing linen here for three days now and the orgy is still going on—in a polite manner, of course." He allowed her to talk—to tell him what he wanted to know in her own way. And after she complained at length about the tribulations a decent girl must suffer around the vulgar, uncouth high command, finally she said, "Down the hallway, the last door on the right. The woman has just this minute left for her own room."

Heraclio thanked her and walked down the deserted hallway. Behind him was the salon, and a string ensemble played a waltz —there was speech and controlled laughter and activity, but on this side of the hotel, it was absolutely quiet.

The door opened easily to his touch, and now he was again extremely cautious, for everything had worked to perfection and it did not seem right that things could go so well for him. A gun and holster were on the back of a chair, a rifle stood in a corner against the wall, and he took a step and heard the General ask:

"Who walks?"

He moved forward rapidly, and stood at the open door of the cubicle, looking down at Celestino Gámez, who was rising from the commode, both hands pulling up on his trousers.

395

"Mi general," said Heraclio, and Celestino Gámez sat back down and his clothes fell to his ankles once again.

He chuckled. "But look at this," he said. "Who would have thought that you would catch me like this, in such an undignified way?"

"Not as undignified as the indignity of turning traitor, Celestino."

"You are yet young, Heraclio, my warrior. What I have done I have done for my country—a heroic act. We have finally triumphed, I believe this, so do not speak to me of treachery."

Heraclio leaned on the doorjamb. "And don Pancho?" he asked.

"My General Villa is now an enemy of the people," said Celestino. He sat calmly, not trying to rise, knowing that he might not live more than a few moments now.

"You wanted to see me," said Heraclio. "You sent men to bring me to you or to kill me?"

"To bring you here," said Celestino. "Come with us, Colonel. We are victorious, I assure you, and you have a great future in the forming of a new México."

"And don Pancho?" asked Heraclio once again.

"He will go the way of the rest," said Celestino. "He will be one of those who did not survive the great change, for he cannot be trusted."

"I was thinking for a minute that perhaps I would not kill you," said Heraclio. "I was thinking that you may yet be valuable to México and to the cause we fight, for in a short while you would realize that Carranza and Obregón are little different from Huerta and don Porfirio, but it is a futile wish, for you are a defector, and thus imperfect. And I think you already know that the new government will not be for the people, and that you had a price and were bought."

"What a boy," said the General, chuckling still. "What a boy, Heraclio Inés, killer of the tiger Celestino Gámez. Are we to exchange insults in the old tradition? You are calling me names and now I must call you names? No, muchacho. I think too much of you, for I know your courage well. And I do not blame you for taking me here when I am at such a disadvantage, for that is another measure of courage—to take your enemy in any way you can."

Heraclio drew his gun from under the sarape. "Commend yourself to your God, my General," he said.

"What God, Heraclio?" said Celestino, and he laughed. "From where you stand you can see my God hanging. And my other God you hold in your hand. All my life I have believed in my gun and in my balls. Should I change now? Because I have made a decision and acted does not mean that I have lost my courage. You have known me in the field, and you know I fear nothing. So shoot and send me to hell, for we are talking much too much."

"You were one of the biggest men I ever knew," said Heraclio as he squeezed the trigger. And as Celestino Gámez fell over sideways off the seat, he leaned down and shot him again behind the left ear.

He took the gun and holster from the chair, then took the rifle. He looked around for a moment and found the carrilleras hanging from the bedstead. All this took but a moment, and he opened the glass doors to the patio and stepped out into the night.

He picked up the spare horse and moved slowly through the streets. No one would stop him, for he looked exactly like the person he would claim to be should he be questioned. A peon leading a horse. He moved in an arc, toward Lerdo and the river. His first instinct had been to cut straight across through Gómez Palacio and on to Mapimí, there to cross the first mountains through the canyon. But there must be soldiers there, so he left the city heading southwest. After a time he knew he must move into the mountains to the west.

He felt safe and was able to think of what he must do. He remembered his first flight, how many years ago? Then all México had been a haven to him, but now the only safety for him was with his general in the mountains of western Chihuahua. But he would not go there. Those who had survived and were yet loyal to Villa would number only in hundreds. He was loyal, but he would not join his chief. For the proud Division of the North he had known would now be but a gang to pillage, and kill, and burn for no reason. Somehow the idea of a cause, small as it might be, could not be driven from his mind. And he could not deny that there was still hope. He believed in the Revolution as in the beginning, and because he believed, Celestino Gámez died.

And now he would remain well south of the area where he was to meet Villa. He had known long ago that he would never be an outlaw. He had seen what that life could do to human beings, not only David, but others. He would not allow himself to become dehumanized. And through the years of fighting, he had also learned a sense of order, a sense of logic to laws, and thus would not become lawless.

The great battles, won or lost, had been fought in honor and in glory for México. There might yet be another someday, and he could very well be a part of it, but for now he must flee. He had known all along that he must leave México, and he did not grieve because it would be a short while, one, perhaps two years.

He would go north, not to Texas, but to California. He would ride west over the mountains and valleys and more mountains. He was not known in Sonora, and would somehow reach the City of the Angels all refugees seemed to know.

He breathed deeply, shutting out the past. He was tired of the past, tired of killing his brothers. He knew suddenly that when he returned it was to help rebuild his beloved homeland, that he would never again take a part in its destruction.

In the near dawn he moved toward the mountains that would hide him in the daylight hours. He rode his horse in a gentle lope, then allowed it to canter for a bit, and then for a short while Heraclio let it gallop.

398

Ernestina N. Eger

Bibliography of Works
By and About
José Antonio Villarreal

A SLENDER STRING of literary works spanning 35 years makes the career of José Antonio Villarreal one of the longest in Chicano letters. His carefully crafted novels have appeared at decade intervals; evidence suggests that the time between served for their gestation and polishing (see items 8 and 175). Tracing the evolution of Villarreal's work within its historical, cultural, and biographical context offers a challenge to literary historians.

Pocho's watershed position—originally published for a mainstream readership, later reissued to fill Chicano Studies demands—is reflected in the pattern of its criticism: at least 28 majority reviews (and a single Mexican American notice, item 123) appeared in 1959-60, followed by a ten-year lapse; serious Chicano criticism did not begin until the dissertations of Alba Irene Moesser, Philip D. Ortego, and Sr. Helena Monahan in 1971-72 (items 68, 69, and 71). The late 1970s saw a consideration of *Pocho* in the context of Anglo-American literary tradition (e.g., items 37 and 52). Now, from the other pole of Chicano literature, don Luis Leal studies *The Fifth Horseman* as a novel of the Mexican Revolution. Critical approaches to Villarreal's work have included formalist (e.g., items 25, 27, 56), culturalist (items 23, 31, 36, 39, 40), historical-dialectical

399

ERNESTINA N. EGER

(item 41), biographical (item 30), linguistic (item 47), and post-structuralist methodologies (item 54). A critical balance has yet to be achieved.

This bibliography attempts exhaustive coverage of print materials concerning Villarreal. His works are subdivided by genre and alphabetized by title. References to *Pocho* in section B are to the Anchor (1970) edition. Works about Villarreal, subdivided by type, are alphabetized by author's name. Unseen or unverifiable items are indicated by an asterisk.

Les dedico este trabajito a Barb y Jo con mi cariño y sincero agradecimiento por todas sus gentilezas.

I. Works by Villarreal

A. Novels

1. *Clemente Chacón*. Binghamton, NY: Bilingual Press/Editorial Bilingüe, 1984.
2. *The Fifth Horseman*. Garden City, NY: Doubleday & Co., 1974.
Second edition. Binghamton, NY: Bilingual Press/Editorial Bilingüe, 1984. Introd. Luis Leal.
3. *Pocho*. Garden City, NY: Doubleday & Co., 1959.
Second edition. Garden City, NY: Anchor Books, 1970. Ramón Eduardo Ruíz, "On the Meaning of *Pocho*," pp. vii-xii.

B. Excerpts from Pocho

4. "From *Pocho*." In *Voices of Aztlán: Chicano Literature of Today*. Ed. Dorothy E. Harth and Lewis M. Baldwin. New York: New American Library/Mentor, 1974. Pp. 88-124.
Chapters 8, 9, and 10.
5. "The Odor of Pink Beans Boiling." *San Francisco Review*, 1, 2 (Spring 1959), 5-9.
From *Pocho*, pp. 37-40 and 42-45.
6. "Pocho." In *Literatura chicana: texto y contexto/Chicano Literature: Text and Context*. Ed. Antonia Castañeda Shular, Tomás Ybarra-Frausto, and Joseph Sommers. Englewood Cliffs, NJ: Prentice-Hall, 1972. Pp. 34-36.
From *Pocho*, pp. 106-08.
7. "Pocho." In *West Coast Fiction: Modern Writing from California, Oregon and Washington*. Ed. James D. Houston. New York: Bantam, 1979. Pp. 321-34.
From chapter 9, pp. 148-64.

8. "Some Turn to God." *The Reed* (San José [CA] State College), May 1948, pp. 3-4.

First-person version of *Pocho*, pp. 37-40.

9. "The World of Richard Rubio." In *Chicano Voices*. Ed. Carlota Cárdenas de Dwyer. Boston: Houghton Mifflin Co., 1975. Pp. 136-41.

Excerpted from *Pocho*, pp. 102-08.

C. Short Stories

10. "The Conscripts." *Puerto del Sol*, 12, 2 (March 1973), 51-72.

See also items 5 and 8.

D. Poetry

11. "Espanto." *Multi-Ethnicism in American Publishing: Southwest Regional Newsletter*, No. 1 (Spring 1973), p. 4.

12. "Life Is a Cookout." *Bilingual Review/Revista Bilingüe*, 3, 2 (May-Aug. 1976), 183-84.

E. Essays, journalism, and reviews

13. "California: The Mexicans." *Holiday*, 38, 4 (Oct. 1965).

Commissioned for "California without Clichés" issue, but published only regionally.

See item 125.

14. "Chicano Literature: Art and Politics from the Perspective of the Artist." In *The Identification and Analysis of Chicano Literature*. Ed. Francisco Jiménez. New York: Bilingual Press/Editorial Bilingüe, 1979. Pp. 161-68.

Paper presented at MLA, San Francisco, 29 Dec. 1975.

15. "The Fires of Revolution." *Holiday*, 32, 4 (Oct. 1962), pp. 82-83, 168-69, 171, 174-75.

16. "Mexican-Americans in Upheaval, Part I." *Los Angeles Times*, 18 Sept. 1966, "West Magazine," pp. 20-22, 24-26, 28-30.

Condensed version in *Readings on La Raza: The Twentieth Century*. Ed. Matt S. Meier and Feliciano Rivera. New York: Hill & Wang, 1974. Pp. 213-18.

17. "Mexican-Americans and the Leadership Crisis." *Los Angeles Times*, 25 Sept. 1966, "West Magazine," pp. 44-48, 50.

18. "Mexico's Big Novel—A Mixture of Styles." *San Francisco Chronicle*, 18 Dec. 1960, "This World," p. 21.

Review of *Where the Air Is Clear*, by Carlos Fuentes.

19. "The Olympics: Mexico's Affair of Honor." *Denver Post*, 19 May 1968, "Empire Magazine," pp. 52-55.

20. "A Tape Recorder Can't Write a Novel." *San Francisco Chronicle*, 28 Aug. 1961, Sec. 3, p. 39.

Review of *The Children of Sanchez*, by Oscar Lewis.

21. "Teatro Los Pobres Offers a Fine Evening of Entertainment." *El Paso Herald Post*, 8 Nov. 1972, Sec. D, p. 7.

Review of *La tercera palabra*, by Alejandro Casona.

22. "The valley was kind to us: Growing up in poverty and beauty in Santa Clara." *San José News*, 17 Oct. 1979, p. 11B.

II. Works about Villarreal

F. Critical articles and papers

23. Alarcón, Justo S. "Hacia la nada...O la religión en *Pocho*." *Minority Voices*, 1, 2 (Fall 1977), 17-26.

24. Bruce-Novoa, [Juan]. "México en la literatura chicana." *Revista de la Universidad de México*, 29, 5 (enero 1975), 13-18.

Rpt. in *Tejidos*, 3, 3 (otoño 1976), 31-42.

Rpt. in *Chicanos: Antología histórica y literaria*. Comp. Tino Villanueva. México: Fondo de Cultura Económica, 1980. Pp. 188-99.

25. _____. "*Pocho* as Literature." *Aztlán*, 7, 1 (Spring 1976), 65-77.

26. _____. "Portraits of the Chicano Artist as a Young Man. The Making of the 'Author' in Three Chicano Novels." *Festival Flor y Canto II*. Ed. Arnold C. Vento, Alurista, José Flores Peregrino et al. Albuquerque: Pajarito Pubs., [1979]. Pp. 150-61.

Paper presented at Floricanto II, Austin, TX, 12-16 March 1975.

27. Cantú, Roberto. "Estructura narrativa y sentido integrante de *Pocho*." Unpublished paper presented at MLA, San Francisco, Dec. 1975.

28. Cárdenas de Dwyer, Carlota. *Chicano Voices: Instructor's Guide*. Boston: Houghton Mifflin, 1975. Pp. 68-70.

Accompanies item 9.

29. Castro, Donald F. "The Chicano Novel: An Ethno-Generic Study." *La Luz*, 2, 1 (April 1973), 50-52.

Paper presented at CCCC, Boston, 1972.

30. Farkas, David. "Novelist José Antonio Villarreal." *Phantasm* (Chico, CA), 4, 6, (1979), [cover, pp. 3-7].

31. Grajeda, Rafael F. "José Antonio Villarreal and Richard Vásquez: The Novelist Against Himself." In *The Identification and Analysis of Chicano Literature*. Ed. Francisco Jiménez. New York: Bilingual Press/Editorial Bilingüe, 1979. Pp. 329-57.

31a. Hernández, Guillermo. "Del honor al remordimiento: Trayectoria del protagonista en la novelística chicana." Paper presented at MLA, New York, 29 Dec. 1983.

32. _____. "On the Theoretical Bases of Chicano Literature." *De Colores*, 5, 1-2 (1980), 5-18.

33. Hinojosa-Smith, Rolando R. "The Structure and Meaning of Chicano Literature." Paper presented at MLA, Chicago, 30 Dec. 1977.
On the Mexican Revolution in novels.
34. Landy, Lino, and Ricardo López Landy. "Literatura chicana." *Grito del Sol,* 1, 1 (Jan.-March 1976), 25-38.
Excerpted from Lino Landy. "Posibilidades de una literatura chicana." El Paso: Univ. of Texas at El Paso, 1973. Pp. 3-24.
35. Lewis, Marvin A. *Introduction to the Chicano Novel.* Institute Paper Series. Milwaukee: Univ. of Wisconsin-Milwaukee, College of Letters and Science, Spanish Speaking Outreach Institute, 1982. Pp. 6-13 et passim.
36. Lomelí, Francisco. "The Family Crisis in Three Chicano Novels: Disintegration vs. Continuity." In *Work, Family, Sex Roles, Language: The National Association for Chicano Studies, Selected Papers 1979.* Ed. Mario Barrera, Alberto Camarillo, and Francisco Hernández. Berkeley, CA: Tonatiuh-Quinto Sol International, 1980. Pp. 141-55.
Paper presented at NACS, Colorado Springs, 13 May 1979.
37. Luedtke, Luther S. "*Pocho* and The American Dream." *Minority Voices,* 1, 2 (Fall 1977), 1-16.
38. Lyon, Ted. "Loss of Innocence in Chicano Prose." In *The Identification and Analysis of Chicano Literature.* Ed. Francisco Jiménez. New York: Bilingual Press/Editorial Bilingüe, 1979. Pp. 254-62.
39. Madrid-Barela, Arturo. "In Search of the Authentic Pachuco: An Interpretive Essay." *Aztlán,* 4, 1 (Spring 1973), 31-60.
40. _____. "Pochos: The Different Mexicans. An Interpretive Essay, Part I." *Aztlán,* 7, 1 (Spring 1976), 51-64.
41. Marín, Mariana. "*Pocho* y *Peregrinos de Aztlán:* Contradicciones textuales e ideología." *Revista Chicano-Riqueña,* 6, 4 (otoño 1978), 59-62.
Paper presented at NACS, 1978.
42. Martínez, Eliud. "José Villarreal's *Pocho:* A Portrait of the Artist." Unpublished ms.
43. _____. "Villarreal's *Pocho* in Light of the Sixties." Paper presented at "The Ethnic Writer" symposium, Univ. of California/Riverside, Jan. 1978.
44. Melville, Margarita B. "Family Values as Reflected in Mexican American Literature." In *Understanding the Chicano Experience through Literature.* [Ed. Nicolás Kanellos.] Houston: Mexican American Studies, Univ. of Houston, 1981. Pp. 43-53.
45. Mickelson, Joel C. "The Chicano Novel Since World War II." *La Luz,* 6, 4 (April 1977), 22-29.
Presented as "The Chicano Novel in the Post-World War II Era" at American Studies Assn., San Antonio, Nov. 1975.
46. Moesser, Alba. "Notas sobre dos autores mejicoamericanos de California." Paper presented at AATSP, Chicago, 1971. ED 063 829.
47. Myers, Inma Concepción. "Language and Style in *Pocho.*" Paper presented at Midwest *foco* of NACS, Chicago, 4 Dec. 1982.

48. Paredes, Raymund A. "The Evolution of Chicano Literature." *MELUS,* 5, 2 (Summer 1978), 71-110.
Revised and expanded version in *Three American Literatures.* Ed. Houston A. Baker Jr. New York: Modern Language Assn. of America, 1982. Pp. 33-79.

49. _____. "Mexican American Authors and the American Dream." *MELUS,* 8, 4 (Winter 1981), 71-80.

50. Robinson, Cecil. "Chicano Literature." *Mexico and the Hispanic Southwest in American Literature.* Tuscon: Univ. of Arizona, 1977. Pp. 308-31.

51. Rocard, Marcienne. *Les Fils du Soleil: La minorité mexicaine à travers la littérature des Etats-Unis.* Paris: Maison-neuve et Larose, 1980. Pp. 272-90 et passim.

52. Rodríguez, Joe D. "The Chicano Novel and the North American Narrative of Survival." *Denver Quarterly,* 16, 3 (Fall 1981), 64-70.

53. _____. "God's Silence and the Shrill of Ethnicity in the Chicano Novel." *Explorations in Ethnic Studies,* 4, 2 (July 1981), 14-21. Critiques by Neil Nakadate and Gladys David Howell, pp. 22-25.
Paper presented at NAIES Conference on Minority Studies, La Crosse, WI, 4 May 1979.
Abstract in *Explorations in Ethnic Studies,* 2, 2 (July 1979), 58.

54. Saldívar, Ramón. "A Dialectic of Difference: Towards a Theory of the Chicano Novel." *MELUS,* 6, 3 (Fall 1979), 73-92.

55. Segade, Gustavo V. "Un Panorama Conceptual de la Novela Chicana." *Fomento Literario* (Congreso Nacional de Asuntos Colegiales), 1, 3 (invierno 1973), 5-18.

56. Shirley, Carl R. "*Pocho*: Bildungsroman of a Chicano." *Revista Chicano-Riqueña,* 7, 2 (primavera 1979), 63-68.

57. Tatum, Charles M. *Chicano Literature.* TUSAS 433. Boston: Twayne Publishers, 1982. Pp. 103-06.

58. _____. "Contemporary Chicano Prose Fiction: A Chronicle of Misery." *Latin American Literary Review,* 1, 2 (Spring 1973), 7-17.
Rpt. in *The Identification and Analysis of Chicano Literature.* Ed. Francisco Jiménez. New York: Bilingual Press/Editorial Bilingüe, 1979. Pp. 241-53.
Paper presented at Wisconsin Council of Latin Americanists, Milwaukee, WI, 14-15 April 1972.

59. Valdés Fallis, Guadalupe. "Metaphysical Anxiety and the Existence of God in Contemporary Chicano Fiction." *Revista Chicano-Riqueña,* 3, 2 (invierno 1975), 26-33.

60. Vargas, Margarita. "Disruption of Order in Chicano Prose." Paper presented at Popular Culture Assn., Pittsburgh, 26 April 1979.

61. Zamora, Carlos. "'El inconformismo' in José Antonio Villarreal's *Pocho.*" Paper presented at Popular Culture Assn., Pittsburgh, 27 April 1979.

G. *Theses and dissertations*

62. Brito, Aristeo, Jr. "Paraíso, caída y regeneración en tres novelas chicanas." *DAI*, 39, 4 (Oct. 1978), 2268A.

63. Cárdenas de Dwyer, Carlota. "Chicano Literature 1965-75: The Flowering of the Southwest." *DAI*, 37, 3 (Sept. 1976), 1582-83A.

64. Carrillo, Loretta. "The Search for Selfhood and Order in Contemporary Chicano Fiction.' *DAI*, 40, 7 (Jan. 1980), 4034A.

65. Gonzales, Lucy. "Conflict and Struggle: A Study of Themes in the Chicano Novel." Unpublished M.A. thesis. Univ. of Houston, 1974.

66. Grajeda, Rafael Francisco. "The Figure of the Pocho in Contemporary Chicano Fiction." *DAI*, 35, 8 (Feb. 1975), 5402-03A.

67. Jackson, E. Beatrice Hathorn. "Chicano Thought in Chicano Literature." Unpublished MA thesis. Midwestern Univ., Wichita Falls, TX, 1971.

68. Moesser, Alba Irene. "La literatura mejicoamericana del suroeste de los Estados Unidos." *DAI*, 32, 5 (Nov. 1971), 2648A.

69. Monahan, Sister Helena, C.C.V.I., "The Chicano Novel: Toward a Definition and Literary Criticism." *DAI*, 33, 3 (Sept. 1972), 1175A.

70. Morales, Alejandro Dennis. "Visión panorámica de la literatura mexicoamericana hasta el boom de 1966." *DAI*, 36, 10 (April 1976), 6731A.

71. Ortego, Philip Darraugh. "Backgrounds of Mexican American Literature." *DAI*, 32, 9 (March 1972), 5195A.

72. Padilla, Genaro Miguel. "The Progression from Individual to Social Consciousness in Two Chicano Novelists: José Antonio Villarreal and Oscar Zeta Acosta." *DAI*, 42, 12 (June 1982), 5123A.

73. Rainey, Marianne Pettersen. "Un estudio del anglo y del chicano en cinco novelas chicanas." Unpublished M.A. thesis. Southern Illinois Univ., 1976.

74. Somoza, Oscar Urquídez. "Visión axiológica en la narrativa chicana." *DAI*, 38, 7 (Jan. 1978), 4203A.

75. Thomas, George Aaron. "Tres etapas en el desarrollo de la novela chicana contemporánea." *DAI*, 43, 6 (Dec. 1982), 1987A.

76. Vowell, Faye Nell. "The Chicano Novel [in English]: A Study in Self-Definition." *DAI*, 40, 3 (Sept. 1979), 1473A.

77. Willey, Michael Lee. "The Debt to Minority Literature: Images of Change and Action in Recent White Literature." *DAI*, 34, 12 (June 1974), 7792-93A.

H. *Reviews*

78. Boulton, Joye R. "The Novel Scene: Mexican Revolution Utilized." *Fort Worth* (TX) *Star Telegram*, 22 Sept. 1974.*

79. Bright, John. "The Cut-off People." *Nation*, 190, 2 (9 Jan. 1960), 36-37.

80. Bruce-Novoa, Juan. "Into the Breach: José Antonio Villarreal and the Fifth Horseman." *La Luz*, 3, 10-11 (Jan.-Feb. 1975), 31.

81. _____. *"Pocho* and Assimilation?" *La Luz*, 4, 3 (June 1975), 29.

82. Brushwood, John S. "As It Was in Pancho's Day." *Kansas City* (MO) *Star*, 10 March 1974.*

83. Calbillo, Carlos. "Pocho or Vendido." *Papel Chicano* (Houston, TX), 1, 11 (3 Feb. 1971), 4.

84. Carnahan, Ken. "The Book Shelf—Ex-Berkeleyan Writes Impressive First Novel." *Berkeley Daily Gazette*, 28 Oct. 1959, p. 26.

85. Cinquemani, Frank L. Review of *Pocho. Library Journal*, 84 (15 Nov. 1959), 3587.

86. Dimicelli, Judith M. "A Chicano Twentieth-Century Book of Genesis." *Bilingual Review/Revista Bilingüe*, 3, 1 (Jan.-April 1976), 73-77.

87. Dooley, Eugene A. Review of *The Fifth Horseman. Best Sellers*, 34, 3 (1 May 1974), 63-64.

88. Review of *The Fifth Horseman. Kirkus Reviews*, 41, 24 (15 Dec. 1973), 1380.

89. Review of *The Fifth Horseman. Publishers' Weekly*, 204, 25 (17 Dec. 1973), 33.

90. Review of *The Fifth Horseman. San Francisco Examiner*, 27 Feb. 1974.*

91. Review of *The Fifth Horseman. Wichita Falls* (TX) *Times*, 18 Aug. 1974, magazine.

92. Gutiérrez, Carlos. Review of *Pocho. Sacramento* (CA) *Bee*, 15 Nov. 1959.*

93. Hogan, William. "An Impressive Novel of California Mexicans." *San Francisco Chronicle*, 9 Oct. 1959, p. 41.

94. _____. "Some Objections to Gamey Modern Prose." *San Francisco Chronicle*, 20 Oct. 1959, p. 39.

Response to letters about item 93.

95. _____. "World of Books: Mexican-American Dropping the Hyphen." *San Francisco Chronicle*, 29 Nov. 1974, p. 47.

96. Jones, George. Review of *Pocho. Peninsula Living* (Burlingame, CA), 1 Nov. 1959.*

97. Lawton, Harrry. "The Book Scout." *Riverside Press-Enterpise*, Nov. 1960.* Rpt. in *San Gabriel Valley* [Society of Technical Writers and Publishers] *Proofreader*, 1, 2 (7 Nov. 1960), 2.

98. Lewis, Marvin A. Review of *The Identification and Analysis of Chicano Literature*, ed. Francisco Jiménez. *MELUS*, 7, 1 (Spring 1980), 82-85.

99. "The Literary Grapevine." *Napa Register*, 24 Oct. 1959.*

100. Manges, Dayle. Review of *The Fifth Horseman. Library Journal*, 99, 4 (15 Feb. 1974), 504-05.

101. McDavid, Douglas. Review of *The Fifth Horseman. Library Journal*, 99, 8 (15 April 1974), 1236.

102. McLellan, Joseph. Review of *The Fifth Horseman. Book World*, 17 Feb. 1974, p. 4.

103. "Mexican Problem Novelized." *Salt Lake Tribune,* 6 Dec. 1959.*

104. Milligan, Joyce. "Villarreal Describes Mexican Revolution: Pancho Villa Flavor." *San José Mercury News,* 4 Aug. 1974, p. 8F.

105. Morales, Alejandro. Review of *The Fifth Horseman. Mester,* 5, 2 (abril 1975), 135-36.

106. Myers, Barbara. "Two Cultures Clash in a Sensitive Novel." *Columbus* (OH) *Dispatch,* 20 Dec. 1959.*

107. Narloch, Joanne. "Bow to Villarreal." *Los Angeles Times,* 23 Nov. 1980, "Book Review," p. 2.
Letter.

108. "The New American." *San José* (CA) *News,* 29 Oct. 1959.*

109. Nichols, Luther. "A Novel of Mexican Life in Modern California." *San Francisco Examiner,* 4 Oct. 1959, "Books."*

110. *Nightbeat.* Writ. and narr. Elmo Ellis. WSB radio, Atlanta, 21 Oct. 1959.

111. Review of *Pocho. Best Sellers,* 30, 23 (1 March 1971), 531.

112. Review of *Pocho. Booklist,* 56, 9 (1 Jan. 1960), 267.

113. Review of *Pocho. Brentwood* (CA) *Citizen,* 17 Dec. 1959.*

114. Review of *Pocho. Bulletin from Virginia Kirkus' Service* (now *Kirkus Reviews*), 27, 15 (1 Aug. 1959), 568.

115. Review of *Pocho. Publishers' Weekly,* 198, 20 (16 Nov. 1970), 78.

116. Review of *Pocho. San Dieguito* (CA) *Citizen,* 22 Oct. 1959.*

117. Review of *Pocho.* [*Valley*] *Sun* (San Fernando, CA), 24 Dec. 1959, p. 3A.

118. Pritchard, Alan. "A man must die well." *Sacramento* (CA) *Bee,* 7 April 1974, "Leisure," p. 9.

119. J.H.R. "Books: A Chronicle of Mexican Revolution." *Times* (CA, city unknown), 27 April 1974, p. 10A.

120. D.H.S. Review of *Pocho. Wilmington* (DE) *News,* ca. Jan. 1960.*

121. Schultz, Howard. "From the Fiction Shelf: Excellent First Novel." *Richmond* (VA) *Times Dispatch,* 20 Dec. 1959.*

122. Scott, N. "Good heart; poor book." *People's World* (Berkeley, CA), 12 March 1960.*

123. Sierra, Dave. "Villareal's [sic] *Pocho* outstanding book." *El Excéntrico* (San José, CA), 10, 16 (5 mayo 1960), [pp. 24-25].

124. Taylor, Coley. "New Novel of Mexican Expatriate Fails on Characterization Score." *Mexico City News,* 12 Dec. 1959.*

125. Trejo, Arnulfo D. "Mexican Manner." *Holiday,* 39, 1 (Jan. 1966), 6.
Letter about item 13.

126. "Wanderers." *Sacramento* (CA) *Union,* 11 Oct. 1959.*

127. Wood, Roberts S. "Mexico and her people in fact and fiction: The new books." *California Monthly* (Univ. of California/Berkeley), Dec. 1959, pp. 31-32.

128. "Young Man With an Old Mind." *Albany* (OR) *Democrat-Herald,* 16 Jan. 1960.*

I. Bibliographic annotations

129. Durán, Daniel Flores. *Latino Materials: A Multimedia Guide for Children and Young Adults.* Santa Barbara, CA: ABC-Clio, 1979. Pp. 126-27.

130. Lomelí, Francisco A., and Donaldo W. Urioste. *Chicano Perspectives in Literature: A Critical and Annotated Bibliography.* Albuquerque, NM: Pajarito Publications, 1976. Pp. 49, 74.

131. [Mann, Ralph.] In *The Mexican American: A Selected and Annotated Bibliography.* Ed. Luis G. Nogales. Revised and enlarged edition. Stanford, CA: Center for Latin American Studies, Stanford Univ., 1971 (1969). P. 128.

132. Melcon, Alice Kesone, comp. *California in Fiction.* Berkeley: California Library Assn., 1961. P. 52*

133. Orozco, Febe Portillo. "A Bibliography of Hispanic Literature." *English Journal,* 71, 7 (Nov. 1982), 61.

134. Sandoval, Ralph, and Alleen Pace Nilsen. "Multi-Ethnic Literature in America: The Mexican-American Experience." *English Journal,* 63, 1 (Jan. 1974), 61.

135. Tatum, Charles M. *A Selected and Annotated Bibliography of Chicano Studies.* Manhattan, KS: Kansas State Univ., Society of Spanish and Spanish-American Studies, 1976. P. 82.

Second edition. Lincoln, NE: Univ. of Nebraska, SSSAS, Modern Languages and Literatures, 1979. Pp. 93-94.

136. Zimmerman, Enid. "An Annotated Bibliography of Chicano Literature: Novels, Short Fiction, Poetry, and Drama, 1970-1980." *Bilingual Review/Revista Bilingüe,* 9, 3 (Sept-Dec. 1982), 248-49.

J. Interviews

137. Alurista. "Entrevista con José Antonio Villarreal." *Maize,* 5, 3-4 (Spring-Summer 1982), 7-16.

138. Bruce-Novoa, [Juan]. "Interview with José Antonio Villarreal." *Revista Chicano-Riqueña,* 4, 2 (primavera 1976), 40-48.

Revised and expanded as "José Antonio Villarreal." *Chicano Authors: Inquiry by Interview.* Austin & London: Univ. of Texas Press, 1980. Pp. 36-48.

139. Jiménez, Francisco. "An Interview with José Antonio Villarreal." *Bilingual Review/Revista Bilingüe,* 3, 1 (Jan.-April 1976), 66-72.

140. Reboredo, Aída. "Mi situación como escritor chicano es más de índole social que política: José A. Villarreal." *Uno Más Uno* (México DF), 23 julio 1980, p. 18.

K. News articles

141. "Author gives manuscripts to library." *Santa Clara Today* (Univ. of Santa Clara, CA), 17, 5 (Jan. 1975), 2.

142. "Author Honored at SCU." *Times* (San Mateo, CA), 20 Nov. 1974, p. 9.

143. "Author's Papers A Gift to SCU." *San José Mercury,* 30 Nov. 1974, p. 16.

144. "BBRC Employee is Author." *Ball Line* (Ball Brothers Research Corp., Boulder, CO), Jan.-Feb. 1971, "Lines about Ball Plants and People" [special in-house center section], n.p.

145. "Boulder Author Villarreal Will Speak at CU Tuesday." *Boulder* (CO) *Daily Camera,* 18 March 1971, p. 16.

146. "Boulderite's Book Tells of Mexican Migrant Life." *Boulder* (CO) *Daily Camera.* 7 Dec. 1970.*

147. Buchanan, Dan. "Villarreal explores 'Ethnic Novel' concept." *Highlander* (Univ. of California/Riverside), 26 Jan. 1978, p. 12.

148. "Cannery Worker Writes Novel About Mexican-Americans' Life." *San José* (CA) *Evening News,* 28 Oct. 1959, p. 12.*

149. "Chicano author to initiate Movement lecture program." *Colorado Daily* (Univ. of Colorado/Boulder), 19, 114 (22 March 1971), 3.

150. "Chicano Novelist to Talk." *San José* (CA) *Mercury,* 16 Nov. 1974, p. 37.

151. "Chicano Writer Speaks at Local College." *La Luz,* 3, 12/4, 1 (March-April 1975), 22.*

152. Costello, Eileen. "Author Returns to 'Wonderful Homecoming'." *Santa Clara* (Univ. of Santa Clara, CA), 53, 3 (17 Jan. 1975), pp. 1, 13.

153. "Distinguished faculty for new year." *Santa Clara Today* (Univ. of Santa Clara, CA), 17, 5 (Jan. 1975), 1.

154. Esquivel, Mary Ann. "He writes about what he knows, yet avoids title 'Chicano writer'." *Milwaukee* (WI) *Journal,* 5 Oct. 1980, "Accent," p. 10.

155. Gordon, Don. "Villareal [sic]: U.S. chicano struggle like that of 1910 Mexico." *Colorado Daily* (Univ. of Colorado/Boulder), 19, 116 (24 March 1971), 1.

156. [Kernahan, Galal.] "Las palabras también participan en la lucha." *Tiempo/Hispanoamericano,* 74, 1920 (19 feb. 1979), 50-54.

157. "Mexican author to give Regents' lecture tonight." *Enterprise* (Riverside, CA), 10 Jan. 1978, p. B-3.

158. "Mexican-American Writer: Author Stresses Artistic Values." *San José News,* 22 Nov. 1974, p. 27.

159. "Minority writer topic." *Kenosha* (WI) *News,* 2 Oct. 1980, p. 13.

160. "Novel by Villarreal Describes Migrants in California." *Newsletter, Ball Brothers Research Corporation* (Boulder, CO), 6, 7 (Feb. 1971), [4].

161. Peters, Steve. "Storytellers Gave Young Writer His Start." *El Paso Times,* 30 March 1973, p. 2-B.

162. "Pocho: Landmark in Chicano Lit, A Visit by the Author." *La Guardia* (Milwaukee, WI), Sept. 1980, p. 11.

163. "Professor's Second Novel Accepted For Publication." *El Paso Times,* 25 Feb. 1973, "Sundial," p. 26.

164. "Redlander writes article for October Holiday." *Redlands* (CA) *Daily Facts,* 8 Oct. 1962, p. 4.

165. Rodebaugh, Dale. "Chicano Writers Urged to Use More Art, Fewer Polemics." *San José Mercury,* 21 Nov. 1974, p. 57.

166. Sada, Kathy. "Villarreal to Speak on Chicano Literature." *Santa Clara* (Univ. of Santa Clara), 53, 9 (19 Nov. 1974), 1.

167. "Says Visiting Novelist: Art—Not Politics—Should be Emphasized."[*Sun-News*] (Las Cruces, NM), ca. Nov. 1972.*

168. Simmons, Joan. "Villarreal—the soul of a people." *Highlander* (Univ. of California/Riverside), 24, 21 (8 April 1976), 10.

169. "Storyteller to Novelist, Villarreal Evolves." *At UCR* (Univ. of California/Riverside), 3, 3 (March-April 1978), 12.

170. "Three Join SCU Faculty: Author, Scholar, Lawyer." *San José Mercury,* 6 Jan. 1975.*

171. "Villarreal, Hobart families saluted." *Star-Rocket* (Lockheed Propulsion Company), 6, 9 (Sept. 1967), 7.

172. Walker, Gail. "Author recalls Chicano culture." *Marquette Tribune* (Milwaukee, WI), 65, 13 (8 Oct. 1980), 6.

173. "Works of Novelist: SCU Adds Original Manuscripts." *San José News,* 2 Dec. 1974, p. 28.

L. Biographical listing

174. Martínez, Julio A., ed. *Chicano Scholars and Writers: A Bio-Bibliographical Directory.* Metuchen, NJ, & London: Scarecrow Press, 1979. Pp. 549-50.

III. Archive

175. José Antonio Villarreal Papers. Univ. of Santa Clara, Santa Clara, CA.
See MS 77-1196 in *National Union Catalog of Manuscript Collections, 1977 Catalog.* Washington: Library of Congress, 1978. P. 145.

CARTHAGE COLLEGE